T0370426

THE DEADLY HANDSHAKE

A Tale of Poisoned Politics

JOSEPH AMELLIO

authorHOUSE®

AuthorHouse™
1663 Liberty Drive
Bloomington, IN 47403
www.authorhouse.com
Phone: 833-262-8899

*This is a work of fiction. All of the characters, names, incidents, organizations, and dialogue
in this novel are either the products of the author's imagination or are used fictitiously.*

Published by AuthorHouse 05/29/2024

ISBN: 979-8-8230-2672-7 (sc)
ISBN: 979-8-8230-2673-4 (hc)
ISBN: 979-8-8230-2671-0 (e)

Library of Congress Control Number: 2024909952

Print information available on the last page.

This book is printed on acid-free paper.

DEDICATED TO PHYLLIS CHOCK

I am dedicating this, my second novel, to my beloved sister Phyllis Chock. She was truly a wonderful person, full of life and humor and a lover of animals extraordinaire. She was an inspiration to me and all who knew her. God rest her wonderful soul.

CONTENTS

CHARACTERS

John Meade, Assassin

Katherine Meade, Assassin's Wife

Aaron Roberts, United States National Socialist Party Senator

Betty Ryan, Senator Roberts' Campaign Staff Member

Annette Canter, Senator Roberts' Campaign Worker

Daniel, Exotic Creatures, Store Clerk

William Carlton, Secret Service Agent

Peter Jamison, Secret Service Agent

Nadine Waterman, United States Congresswoman

Nanette Pelovski, United States Senator

Jonathan Gauci, Attending Physician, Saint Mary's Hospital

Jim Levy, Campaign Volunteer

Lizzie Borden, Campaign Volunteer

Jeremy Long, Campaign Advisor for Candidate Collette

Michael Johnson, Attorney for Candidate Collette.

Sarah Foster Investigative Reporter – The Wall Street Daily

Jeanne Collette, American Patriot Party Candidate for the United States Senate

James Ellis, CEO of Filmore Aeronautics Corp

Bradley Newman, Computer Hacker

Marc Scarponi, Special Investigator- Florida State Special Crimes Unit

Raymond Gonzalez, Agent of the Federal Bureau of Investigation.

CHAPTER ONE

MURDERS DESIRE

A sinister idea of a deadly handshake took hold of the mind of a man who had become insanely absorbed with hatred for a particular politician. It was a time of heavy partisan politics throughout the government and vile vitriol sweeping across America, in all forms of communication, with half the nation leaning toward socialism and the other half toward a freer society with less government control. It was this climate of discontent that led John Meade to hatch a malevolent plot to eliminate the very politicians he saw as detrimental to the policies of his beloved American President.

It was late one evening, when John Meade was sitting back on his couch watching the news on television, when the CNC news anchor, Dirk Danvers, began speaking about what was happening with current political events and specifically what executive actions President David Tripp had taken that day. It was his vicious left-wing commentary that set John off, as he uncontrollably shouted, "You are so full of shit, you Socialist fuck. You partisan pile of shit. Tell the truth just once."

John's wife, Katherine in her usual calm tone, asked him quietly, "Why do you bother watching CNC if you don't like what Danvers says? You know he hates the President. He never has anything nice to say about him.

Even when we think that there can't be an argument, he always finds a way to conjure one up. The President can't win with him."

John replied, "I can't help it. I need to see these evil assholes in action. It reinforces my patriotic beliefs. Did you not just hear what he said about what the President said? That was an out and out lie. He left out the part where the president said he wanted immigration, but it had to be "legal immigration."

Just at that moment, Dirk invited National Socialist Party Senator Aaron Roberts on the air, and showed him on a split screen on the television. Dirk began his interview with, "Welcome Senator Roberts. What do you make of President Tripp's executive orders today? He shut down all immigration from several of the Muslim nations claiming it was in defense of America's safety."

Senator Roberts replied, "Well Dirk, it was a very prejudiced action on his part. There's no evidence of terrorist cells infiltrating our country and putting our citizens at risk. If he's concerned about terrorist cells, he should be more concerned domestically with FBI evidence of white extremists within."

Just as Senator Roberts finished his comment, John again shouted above the TV and said, "You don't hear any of them saying death to America, and that includes you, you jackoff."

Katherine quietly picked up the television remote and switched channels, causing John to ask, "What are you doing honey? I was watching that."

Katherine replied, "I don't want to see you have a heart attack. You get so angry your face gets red. There's nothing you can do about it. Let's watch Oak Island. I recorded the last episode. Did you watch it?"

"No, I didn't. I hope they discover something soon. They are drilling so many holes in the island, I think it will sink. I don't know why I keep watching that show. They've spent millions of dollars just to find a few trinkets and a few pieces of human bone the size of a thumb nail."

"John, it's because you're always curious enough to see if they'll find the treasure," she replied.

Katherine always knew how to get her husband off the political subject when he began to make threatening remarks like, "I would love to kneel all of those commie fucks down and shoot them all in the back of the head." She always responded to him after he made those horrible comments, by saying, "I don't like to hear you say those things." Even though she was right leaning in her political views, she had no malice in her heart towards anyone, regardless, if their political views differed from hers. Katherine felt his political fervor was starting to get too extreme, yet it never entered her mind that he would ever do anything to back up his words. He had always been a soft- hearted, fun-loving guy. His words, to her, even though being a little off the deep end at times would never amount to anything. He had even commented to her, "Honey, I like to fantasize. It relieves my stress. It makes me feel better."

She believed that was all it was. She truly felt her husband was harmless. She remembered him crying in front of the veterinarian when he asked her to put his pet dog Lobo to sleep as it suffered from cancer. Heck, she thought, he even cried at tear-jerker movies. She felt that he was just full of bluster and was harmless and would never hurt a soul.

As time went by, John agonized increasingly and began festering a deep hate for Senator Roberts. It seemed to him that this one Senator was going out of his way to spread what he considered hateful lies to undermine the President's freedom agenda. He felt that Senator Roberts was someone that needed to have his mouth shut. On a few occasions, when seeing him on television would say, "If I knew I was dying and had little time left to live, I would go and shoot that son of a bitch in his face." Katherine would always say, "Don't say that. That's evil."

John would always respond, "That man's extreme hate is evil. He needs to be put down like a rabid dog."

Anyone who knew John liked him, and found him to be a genuinely nice person. But something was happening to him little by little that was leaning him toward the dark side. No one outside of his home ever heard his outbursts. There was something about Senator Roberts that set John off more than any of the other Socialists that also railed against President Tripp.

Little did anyone know that John began to seriously think about killing the Senator. He never let on anything to anyone and the more serious he became about assassination the less he mentioned politics in a conversation, and even began to avoid it all together and when anyone else would venture into it, he would deftly say, "I don't want to talk about politics, it's too opinionated with no middle ground."

He thought about unusual ways to pull off his morbid scheme. Each time his mind mulled over the idea, he would consider every nuance, looking for pitfalls. Getting away with murder is difficult enough with today's highly evolved forensic sciences, and even more difficult when you are going to off a high-profile politician. Now you are bringing in the Federal Bureau of Investigation, and not just the local police, and he had no desire to be another John Wilkes Booth, jumping off a balcony onto a stage making a grand exit and gaining instant infamous notoriety.

He just wanted to get away with it and gloat, and if he did, he just might do it again to one of the other politicians he also despised. He wanted to send a message to Senator Roberts' other left-wing colleagues, hoping to strike fear into them. Thinking, they'll worry enough about their own asses that they might think twice about attacking his beloved President. He wanted the whole country to take note.

He made a list of things to be careful of and continued to avidly watch crime shows on TV, making mental notes of the things that might get him caught. He was in no hurry to pull off the crime of the century, so he thought, because he wanted it to be perfect with no evidence left behind. The real pleasure in his overly imaginative mind was not in just doing it, but walking away free, and with the ability to strike again. There were times in his deteriorating warped mind, that he thought of becoming a serial killer, profiling only Socialist politicians and left-wing phony news anchors who sold their lies to the sheepish public especially the lambs who were led to the slaughter.

Yet no matter how many times he plotted; he'd nix the idea. He began questioning himself; was he finding too many obstacles or was he really a Paper Tiger? You know, all talk and no action. Then he would answer his own query with, "Fuck you, John. How can you say that about yourself? Look at how many Taliban you killed in the Middle East. What's one more low life in the scheme of things and they were a matter of kill or be killed? Killing Roberts would be an absolute pleasure. It just had to be an ingenious plan that hadn't yet been tried; a way no one would suspect."

His main problem was how could he get close enough to the politician to pull off the crime while not being seen as an assailant during the commission of the crime or being stopped before he could execute his plan. He had to be able to murder the Senator while being under the watchful eye of the FBI. He ruled out using a sniper rifle because getting a good high advantage point would be difficult, let alone making a long-distance kill shot. He knew if he missed the first time, he wouldn't get a second chance. He broke down every detail of an action. He considered that if he purchased a weapon his face would not only be on the gun shop's surveillance camera, but the employee would also be able to identify him. His plot had to be like a Mossad hit job. Well planned, quiet, quick, clean with an unidentifiable assailant. He was not a criminal and had no connection to anyone selling unregistered firearms and didn't know who to ask about getting one.

Whenever he wrote his devious thoughts on paper it was never on top of another piece of paper. He wanted no imprints of what he wrote left behind. He knew extreme paranoia was his best friend. He never left any traces of his thoughts on his computer. He wanted to be sure that, if he ever became a suspect, he didn't want forensics to uncover anything that would be used against him. He thought about video cameras attached everywhere and how he could avoid any of those that mattered. He felt they were a major hurtle unless they were to his advantage. He thought about DNA and how to avoid leaving any at the scene of the crime or how it could become a non-issue. He considered fingerprints, footprints, different weapons, blood stains, blood spatters, and eyewitnesses. His list went on and next to each item he wrote down its pros and cons. He was in no rush. He wanted it to be the perfect murder.

John's mind was becoming more focused and methodical as he went about his everyday life. He was determined that no one, especially his wife, would ever know what he was plotting or what he did.

As time went by John watched political television with fervor. He tuned into his favorite conservative channels, always hoping to hear more of his own ideology. But even when he did that, he would get snippets of Senator Roberts attacking President Tripp with his outlandish lies and hatred for the man. He constantly urged new baseless investigations started against the President. Senator Roberts went out of his way to get his face in the news, and it was always by attacking Tripp. He would be coming up for re-election in another six months and was trying to stand out in his left-wing constituency. John began festering more and more, and hoped that Senator Roberts would be defeated, but he was realistic. He knew that Roberts came from a left-wing district and no American Patriot Party candidate had ever been elected from there in the last seventy years. That fact had been mentioned many times by political analysts.

John who had never used Twitter before, joined under the pseudonym, 'Demwithahammer.' He wanted to appear as a left winger and one who would be less likely to kill Senator Roberts to any agency investigating anyone who may have had access to the Senator. He made sure to challenge conservative posters and praise Senator Roberts whenever he could. He felt that by doing so he would seem least likely to do what he was planning. He purposefully made himself sound like a person with a far-left mentality.

He felt that it was going to be hard for any APP candidate to defeat the candidate going for his fourth term no matter who ran against him. All he kept thinking was Roberts needed to be stopped one way or another, and if no one else would, he would. But how, remained the question.

One day, while sitting back watching a movie on Netflix, the phone rang. John answered the call saying, "Hello." The party on the line responded with, "Hello, this is Betty Ryan with the Aaron Roberts campaign for his re-election to a fourth term in the Senate. Are you familiar with Senator Roberts and his progressive policies?" she asked.

At first John was going to blow her off, but an epiphany hit him at that very moment. He said "Yes, I'm familiar with his political platform, and I especially love how he tears apart the President and his agenda."

"Yes. Senator Roberts wants what's best for the American people," Betty, responded.

John thought to himself, "That's bullshit. The man is only interested in power. He's an America hating Socialist pile of shit."

John now finding the opening for the birth of his plot said, "I'd love to volunteer in his re-election campaign. Is that possible?" he asked.

"Oh yes sir, we are always looking for volunteers," she replied.

John asked, "How do I go about getting accepted and would I ever be able to say hello to Senator Roberts?" He then said, "He's, my idol. I love the way he uses President Tripp like a punching bag." John cringed at his own lying words.

Betty replied, "I believe you would get to meet him. He always comes to his campaign office and says hello to his volunteers and staff. I will send you out a volunteer questionnaire which you'll need to complete and send back as soon as possible."

"Please do, I'd like to become part of his efforts to seek re-election," John replied.

Betty asked, "Would you like to donate to his campaign?"

"Yes, I'd love to. Can you send me a donation envelope along with the application?" John asked.

Betty replied, "Yes, I can. Can I verify your address?"

"It's 1126 South Island Road, Fort Lauderdale, Florida, 33311," John answered.

"Ok. Thank you for confirming that," she replied.

"By the way, where's your campaign headquarters located?" John asked.

Betty replied, "We're located at 635 Cordova Road, Building A, Fort Lauderdale. Our office is about 30 minutes' drive time from you." She then asked, "Are you familiar with this area?"

John replied, "Yes. I've passed that way on a few occasions." He then asked, "Can I come to your office and fill out the application?"

"Yes, you can. We're here from 8am to 9pm. We make campaign calls up until closing," she answered.

John asked, "Can I stop over at any time?"

Betty replied, "Yes, but it's better to fill out the volunteer form before 5pm. That's quitting time for permanent staff."

"That's perfect. I'll be there within the next few days. Thank you, Betty," John said.

"It's my pleasure Mr. Meade. You can ask for me if you'd like."

John replied, "Okay, I'll do that."

CHAPTER TWO

BEST LAID PLANS

After the phone call ended, John felt elated, He was taking his first step in formulating his plot. Now he had to settle on his method of assassination. He knew that he needed to get the layout of the campaign office and learn the routines. He would also take the time to learn the Senator's agenda and when he would be visiting the campaign office and how often. He thought to himself, "Now I'm going to get you, you evil piece of shit. I don't know how yet, but I'm going to teach you, one way or another, not to fuck with my President."

After John hung up the phone, Katherine asked, "Who were you talking to?"

John ad-libbing a lie, replied, "Just a campaign staffer at American Patriot Party candidate Jeanne Collette's office looking for volunteers and donations to help with her campaign against Senator Roberts."

"So what did you say to her?" Katherine asked.

"I told her that I didn't have the time to work on a campaign, but I would donate. She's going to send me a donation envelope."

Katherine asked, "How much are you planning on giving?"

John responded, "I don't know. A few hundred bucks, I guess."

Katherine replied, "You know that once you donate, you'll be getting envelopes every week, for one cause or another."

"I know, but it's for a worthy cause. Beating that shithead, far left asshole Senator Roberts is worth it. Besides, I don't need to give to everyone for everything," John replied.

John purposely lied to Katherine about who he was talking to. He didn't want her to know anything or involve her in any way in his plot. He needed to protect her from his intentions.

John then went and sat on the couch next to Katherine to watch television and think about his next moves. Now that he took a definitive step, he needed to figure out how he was going to pull it off. He had confidence in himself that he could do it. One way or another he was determined to murder Senator Roberts. His personality change was like Yoda becoming Darth Vader. He was becoming a true psychological case study on how extreme politics can affect the human psyche and create a mental derangement, Political Stress Disorder.

After a few days, he told Katherine he had to get a few things at Home Depot's Garden Shop. But instead of going to Home Depot he headed off to Senator Roberts' campaign headquarters to meet Betty and complete his application for volunteer services. It took him about a half hour to reach his destination. When he arrived, he parked in front of the large three-story mustard colored, Spanish styled building with large windows, and barrel tiled roof.

John entered the lobby of the building and walked directly over to the reception desk and asked to speak to Betty, Senator Roberts' Campaign Manager and that he was there to sign up as a volunteer. The receptionist contacted Betty and after a few minutes she came to greet him. He watched her slowly walk off the elevator toward him and admired her beauty. He thought to himself, 'I bet the Senator is tapping her. He looks like a philandering fuck."

After their introductions, Betty took him up to the second floor to show him around the sprawling and remarkably busy office and to give him an application. As he glanced around, he could see several people on the phones he assumed were asking for campaign funds or taking polls. It really was not his thing, but he was willing to do whatever it took to rid the world of a person he considered a vile, lying evil power-hungry fuck. John never ceased in using profanity to describe the Senator. It seemed very apropos.

John was a very gregarious, handsome guy and easily ingratiated himself to people. There was an easy going very personable way about him, and he knew how to use it to his advantage. His outlandish sense of humor connected with people. He made people feel easy around him and willing to open- up without feeling suspicious.

After completing his application, he had to wait a few weeks for their vetting process to be conducted which was standard procedure for anyone working for the Senator. He was not concerned as he knew his background was squeaky clean, and his political conservative leaning would be void on the internet because he was never on any social sites like Twitter or Facebook. It was not his thing. He carefully gave them a few references that he knew would give him recommendations but didn't know his political ideology. He had to stay focused and methodical in his thinking. He could not afford to have any questions, no matter how slight, raised. He limited his stay as he didn't want to be gone from home too long.

After leaving Betty and the campaign office he made sure to back up his lie to Katherine by stopping at Home Depot to buy garden supplies. He didn't want to draw any suspicions from her although she rarely questioned him about how long it took him to go shopping.

After two weeks passed, he got a call from Betty. She informed him that his background had been cleared and welcomed him on board the Senator's campaign. She told him that he should come in so that she could get him started and to see what he was best suited for. John was happy to get the call, because now his plan would become activated. He knew his best shot at assassinating Senator Roberts would be during his re-election campaign. His opportunity to have a legitimate reason to get close to the man would only realistically develop through his volunteer work. He had only five and a half months to pull it off, but felt it was more than enough time. He knew that he'd have to murder the Senator just before Election Day. He didn't want to give Senator Roberts' party enough time to insert a replacement candidate allowing his opponent, Jeanne Collette, to run unopposed. That timing would assure her election, while guaranteeing President Tripp one more positive vote in the Senate. John knew that Tripp had already endorsed her, and wanted his beloved President to get his wish.

John timed his trip to the campaign office. He needed to consider every aspect of his plan that was now being set into motion. When he arrived, he met Betty. She introduced him to the staff and took him to a desk that he could use whenever he came in. She gave him cold call materials to help him secure donations and instruction materials for taking polls.

He just had to figure out how he could get out of his house so often and not have to explain his many absences to his wife. He knew if Katherine found out where he was going, she would become overly concerned about his intentions. She could only come to one conclusion; he intended to hurt the candidate and carry out his many idle threats. This was going to be his second critical obstacle. Thank God, that it was volunteer work, and he had no specific time to show up, but still it had to be often enough for him to be considered as a serious volunteer and ingratiate himself enough to be able to meet the Senator.

As he drove back home, he decided to take a different route. He wanted an alternate means of escape in the event he needed one.

He could not lie to his wife and tell her that he was a volunteer to the American Patriot Party candidate, because after he murdered the Senator, the FBI would more than likely question everyone who was near the Senator that day. If they should happen to question Katherine about him, they would without a doubt let her know he was volunteering for Senator Roberts, and when they did that, she would immediately assume he was the assassin. What else could she think? John was always spewing absolute hate for the NSP Senator and had expressed his wish to kill him, even if he said he did not mean it. If she lied to protect John, especially to the FBI, she would be putting herself in legal jeopardy. He could not chance that happening.

Whatever reason he gave her for being away during the coming weeks, would have to be aside from his normal routines. His volunteer work didn't have to be five days a week, but often enough for him to be an active volunteer in the eyes of the campaign office personnel.

He pondered the dilemma and decided that in the meantime he would play it by ear. He knew that he would have to produce something and soon. It was while watching TV that the answer came to him. A technical college advertised continuing education courses, which sounded the bell in his brain. Yes, perfect, he thought and one with a local campus. A legitimate way to get out of the house and provide him with the cover he needed to move his devious plan forward. He said to himself, after seeing the advertisement, "Yes, that's it. Perfect."

It really did not matter to him if he went or not, it was the unquestioned time away from home that he would now be able to legitimize to his wife without questions. He proceeded to request material from the local college so that he would validate his intention. Once he received the college brochures, he made sure to mention it to Katherine.

He told her that he was interested in Computer Programming. The course supplied exactly the cover he needed, both in class and in-home learning. The idea was perfect, he thought. It would let Katherine see him working on the course at home, so when he left to go to the campaign office, she would believe he was going to the in-class learning. John felt his scheme would shield Katherine and isolate her from being a co-conspirator. She would easily pass a lie detector test if asked to voluntarily take one. After all her answers would be honest. She would be able to confidently say she had no idea about his working at the campaign office, or plotting to murder the Senator.

What was ideal in his scheme, the timing worked out perfectly, because the computer course would be starting in two weeks. John began to feel a sense of urgency to murder Senator Roberts as the news reported that he wanted to start another baseless investigation against President Tripp. John felt sure that Roberts was behind several investigations being conducted by the Attorney Generals in a few of the National Socialist-controlled states.

John was convinced that if he ended Senator Roberts, a lot of the shit being thrown at the President would stop. He deemed Senator Roberts as the main provocateur of the continued attacks against Tripp. He believed in the adage "Cut the head off the snake and the body dies."

The first day of volunteer work came. He headed off to the campaign office to set his plot in motion. He was anxious to learn the office routine and get in with the Socialist scumbags he loathed because of their support for the Senator. John had a fanatical hate for the man and anyone who was associated with him. He truly reviled their political leaning. He even thought about blowing up everyone in the office, but knew that he would not do it. His one and only target was the Senator, besides, he had no idea on how to make a bomb and securing the necessary explosives would be far too risky. Who would he ask about getting the materials needed? He had no idea. Searching the internet for materials and do it yourself instructions would immediately alert the FBI and get him investigated. Any action he took would have to be off the grid. He needed to think about it hard. No matter how he decided to commit his act, it would have to be up close and personal.

When he got to the campaign office, he met Betty, and she got his day started by soliciting campaign donations. He told Betty that he could not volunteer full days. Betty had no problem with that as she was glad to get whatever help she could get for the Senator's campaign efforts. John spent four hours productively calling. He considered what he was doing as a noble cause in committing the ultimate evil, murder. After each hour of calling, he took a short break and introduced himself to the other volunteers. He slowly scoped out the ones he thought he could more readily pump for information about the Senator's habits, especially when he was at the campaign office.

He made a concerted effort to ingratiate himself to everyone around him, even though he had no need to, it was just getting their confidence to ask questions.

At the end of his first day, he walked out of the campaign office feeling elated. He said to himself, "Roberts! You evil piece of shit, your days are numbered." He reflected on seeing the Senator's photos hanging everywhere and thinking how they would make great dart boards with a bullseye being between the Senator's eyes.

When he got home, Katherine asked him, "What was your first day of class like?"

John replied, "It was good honey. It was mostly about the history of computers, programming, and the progressions it has made. The instructor laid out the different course material we'd be covering, like coding, systems analysis, and a working knowledge of industry elements. What I liked is that they start from scratch for neophytes like me. Honestly, my sweetness, I may be a little over my head. But I'll give it my best shot."

Katherine replied, "I have all the confidence in you. You'll do okay."

John said, "I hope so. You know that I'll be taking classes two to three times a week for six months?"

"That's fine with me. You're the one that'll have to do the work. If you get anything from it, you won't need Microsoft Tech Support anymore to fix your computer problems," Katherine replied.

John, laughingly replied, "Don't get carried away, honey. It would take me a lot more than six months of computer classes to do what they do."

John then thought to himself after his short conversation with his wife, 'This is going to work out perfectly. Step two completed. Now I need to figure out step three."

After a few weeks of volunteering, Senator Roberts came into the campaign office and waved to his staff and then after talking privately to Betty, his campaign manager, gave a short motivational speech to everyone. As John stood in the crowd facing him, and seeing him for the first time up close and deeply personal, he visualized himself killing the man. He had to hold himself back. His urge was almost uncontrollable. In his mind he could see himself rushing at the Senator and killing him. His urge was so powerful, that he hoped he did not show any outward emotions. He felt like he had an out of body experience, a mental orgasm. He thought, I need to figure out how to do him in. I hate that scumbag with passion. He then said, audibly only to himself, "You're mine, you fuckface."

After the Senator left the office, he could hear different people saying, "I hope he is re-elected" or "He's such a great Senator." But the one that had John blow steam from every orifice of his body was, when a female staffer said, "I hope he puts that racist, lying, Tripp in jail forever, along with his wife and kids."

John just found another target. He relished the idea and said to himself, 'I want to do something to that bitch. I'll have to figure out how." But being smart, he didn't want a small pleasure to detract him from the big one. "Maybe I'll take her out at the same time I do in the Senator, two fucking birds with one stone. I'll need to get to know her."

Before the Senator left the campaign office, John watched carefully how closely the Senator allowed himself to get with the campaign workers. He noticed that he readily shook the hands of those that approached him. He thought, "His Secret Service security and his familiarity with the general staff gave him no concern for his personal safety. Getting close to him does not look like it will be a major hurdle."

He told himself, "The next time he comes in I will approach him and look to greet him. I'll tell him how it's an honor to help him in his campaign and say something complimentary about his Senate accomplishments. I need him to feel comfortable with me and plant the first seed in gaining his confidence." He continued to be friendly and willing to do whatever they wanted him to do at the office. He had to work extra hard on the limited days he'd be there. He had to melt right in.

It became a routine for John to always say hello to Betty and ask her things like, "Is there anything special you need done?" or "Can I help anyone else?" He bent over backwards to weave his web. His goal was to build overwhelming trust. He also went out of his way to get to know the campaign worker that wanted President Tripp and his family in jail. When he saw his opportunity, he introduced himself to the woman he now considered a vile piece of shit.

He walked up to her in a small breakroom where they had a coffee machine. As he stood next to her, he noticed that she was putting a bunch of mocha flavored creamers in her coffee. He said to her, "I see you like your coffee in your creamer, instead of your creamer in your coffee."

She looked at John smiling, and with a little laugh replied, "You're right. I love my coffee really light, and I really enjoy the mocha flavor."

He then said, "My name is John, may I know yours?"

She extended her hand toward him and said, "My name is Annette Canter. It's nice to meet you."

"Likewise," he replied.

Annette then asked, "How long have you been volunteering for Senator Roberts?"

John replied, "Only a few weeks so far. He's a great guy. I hope he gets re-elected."

Annette said, "I have no doubt. He will beat that racist, right wing extremist Jeanne Collette. I don't like her NRA Second Amendment platform. Quite frankly, she's a gun toting anti abortionist bitch."

"Oh! He'll win his race with no problem. An American Patriot has never won in his district and they're not going to start now even if we have to print ballots," John jokingly replied.

Annette showing a wry smile and quite seriously said, "It wouldn't be the first time we printed ballots. We do what we must to win."

"I see you have as much enthusiasm about the Senator's race as I do. It's good to be on a winning team," John responded, while gritting his teeth and flashing a phony smile, knowing she admitted to stuffing ballot boxes with fraudulent ballots.

He had mental anguish and joy at the same time. He couldn't stand saying the things he was saying, but glad his mental anguish was for the good.

The opportunity with Annette worked out just as John planned. He felt sure that he'd connected with her. He thought at once about putting this insane woman, out of her fucking misery. He smirked when he thought about doing it. John's mental state permeated extreme hate, yet was cold and calculating. He mentally skipped with each little success he had. He just needed to find a way to pull off what he was now thinking as a two for the price of one, double hit job. He thought about secretly recording Annette after her jaw dropping comment about printing the ballots. He thought after she said it, "That was an admission of a federal crime and she volunteered it so easily, not even knowing me. I wonder just how much she knows and will say about the Senator?"

Whenever John was at home, he was careful to slowly quiet his hateful rhetoric toward his target. He stopped with his outbursts against Senator

Roberts, except for some casual asides. He wanted to become cool, calm, and collected. He needed to let Katherine be so far away from his scheme, that any thought of him hurting the Senator would not enter her mind.

Things continued to go his way in every aspect of his assassination plans, except for the method. He became a little perplexed by the fact he had not decided on how to do it. No method satisfied him. He ruled out knives and guns because they posed up close risks. He thought about the stupidity of facing the Senator's gun toting bodyguards and the difficulty he would face getting past the metal detecting security guards at the entrance to the campaign office.

One day while sitting back at home watching the Creatures of the Wild channel that the killing method presented itself. The show featured the most poisonous animals and insects in the world. When the show highlighted what they considered the most poisonous creature on the planet he sat up and watched with extreme interest. They ranked the Golden Dart Frog as the most toxic creature on Earth.

The program went into detail on how the indigenous Embera natives in the moist hilly forests along the Pacific Coast of northern Colombia used the sticky poison on the frog's skin to coat their arrows and blow darts to bring down their prey. The TV show mentioned that you could not pick up these frogs barehanded, as they would cause instant death or permanent paralysis. He began to listen intently and learned that the poison was still potent after one year. It mentioned its scientific name as Phyllobates terribilis, emphasizing the fact that its name contained the word "terrible" because its poison was one hundred percent fatal.

John had a really sick thought, "Man! I would love to rub that frog in Senator Roberts' face and watch his body stiffen in paralysis as he died." After the program was over, John did not think much more about the frog as he didn't think it possible to get one. It wasn't until a few days later when he was shopping on Amazon, that he segued over to Google and under search, typed in "Golden Dart Frog." He thought to himself, I need to learn everything about that frog. It costs me nothing, but just as he was about to hit enter on his computer keyboard, he stopped. He had almost screwed up. He said in a muffled voice, "Damn that was close. I almost left computer evidence. I need to be more mindful of my actions." He dropped his on-line search and decided to go to the public library to see what material they had on the frog.

He sat down at their computer catalog and found reference sources on the subject. In one book called, "Vertebrates of South America," he found facts about the Golden Dart Frog. He learned that the frog's skin becomes thickly coated in an alkaloid batrachotoxin which does not deteriorate and will not even do so when transferred from the frog to another surface. He thought, "Now that is an important piece of information." He wondered how long the poison once applied to a dart or arrow tip kept its potency. With each deadly fact he became more rapt by this tiny creature. He learned that the poison is absorbed through the pores of the skin causing immediate severe pain, and within minutes, seizures occur followed by paralysis and death. Better yet, he read that there is no antidote. They estimated that a human would die within five minutes. As he read about the potency of the poison, he said to himself, "Holy shit! It says that one little milligram of this stuff can kill up to twenty humans. I've got to get me some of this beautifully powerful shit. A full gram would wipe out all the NSP Congressmen and women and Senators in Washington D.C. or any other vile partisan fuck face, lying pieces of shit in the coverup media."

It took him little time to produce the information he needed about the creature. To his amazement he found out that he could buy one, but to his dismay, he learned that the frog lost its poisonous secretion when raised in captivity, because it was not fed what it consumed in the rainforest, which were poisonous ants, beetles, and spiders. After reading on he discovered that a wild caught poison frog would keep its poisonous alkaloids for years. This gave him hope because he felt he discovered his third step, a whole new clandestine method of executing the Senator. He just needed to figure out how to do it.

He was going to spend the next few weeks concentrating on the idea. He needed to figure out how to get the frog, or its poison and how he would be able to get it onto the Senator or anybody else he chose. John realized the beauty of the poison was that not only was it lethal as hell, but also needed such a miniscule amount to commit the crime. It could easily be transported without detection.

He knew that the clock was ticking. If he could not get possession of the frog or its poison the idea would be moot. He knew one thing. He would not rule it out until he exhausted all hope.

In the meantime he needed to figure out the delivery method while he was searching for a frog source. He knew he could not fly to Colombia to get one because that would automatically make him the main suspect once a toxicology report showed the cause of death, and the FBI determined the source of the frog. He knew that he could not deny being there because his passport would be stamped when entering Colombia.

The second thing he thought was that he had to figure out how to handle the frog without being poisoned himself. He knew that he couldn't stick the Senator with a poison laced needle or use a blow gun being amid so many people. It had to be something so sublime that when he got the poison on the Senator, no one would suspect anything, especially the Senator. Not even when it started to take affect minutes later. He would dwell on that until he figured something out. At times he thought the whole idea of using the poison from the frog was preposterous, but he knew it was so nefarious it could work. He thought being able to assassinate Senator Roberts in front of everyone without them realizing he was doing it would be exhilarating. No gunshots, no stabbing, no nothing that could be identified. Not even on surveillance video.

He needed to figure out the poison transfer method that could be used in front of so many people without them knowing it was being done. As crazy as it sounded, the only subliminal way was by shaking the Senator's hand, but that would entail applying the poison to his own hand first. He couldn't risk his own death and had already nixed the idea of wearing noticeable latex gloves laced with the poison. It wasn't just that people would be overly curious about him wearing them, the Senator would undoubtedly be apprehensive shaking his hand and he felt certain the Secret Service would stop any bodily contact while he was wearing them. Besides, after an autopsy revealed the poison, he'd be an immediate suspect because of the latex gloves.

He would continue to think about how to pull it off, but he thought first things, first. I need to figure out how to get that lovely little lethal frog or a small vile of its poison.

As days were quickly ticking away, John was becoming discouraged. He had not come across a way to get the frog. It became his only priority. Everything else was working out very smoothly. He was well accepted at the campaign office and had even been introduced to the Senator on one occasion by Betty, who touted him to the Senator as being a truly resolute volunteer and fan of his, and during that brief meeting had shaken his hand.

He knew that after that meeting the opportunity to again approach the Senator would be much easier, and getting to shake his hand again seemed more likely. He thought to himself, "Now that I've developed the opportunity to knock him off, his death sentence begins."

His home routine continued as normal. His wife Katherine suspected nothing. Why would she? He gave her not one scintilla of an idea about his devious plan.

He watched the news channels fervently. He didn't want to miss anything that was going on and especially wanted to keep up with everything that Senator Roberts was doing. One thing was for sure, Senator Roberts had become a media darling by all the left-wing news stations and appallingly received airtime by the so-called conservative channel Vox News. They were trying to appear fair and balanced in their news reporting. It was obvious to John that they weren't. He became increasingly annoyed as they hired too many left-wing commentators who received unchallenged commentary from the Vox News hosts on a conservative platform.

John's face would become red and the veins in his neck would protrude as he would become almost violent with anger whenever the hosts and the contributors discussed the politics of the day, and those discussions always included the one-sided left wing unchallenged comments that excoriated the President.

John would actually rise up off the couch and yell out, aiming his comments at the TV screen and the news channels host, "How in the hell did you not respond to the lying fuck? Fact check what Tripp actually said, and make that turd look like the liar he is. Why is he even a guest on a right-wing channel? You should be fired you worthless piece of shit. You're as bad as they are. Damn, that host is a APPer in name only."

CHAPTER THREE

THE GOLDEN DART FROGS AND THE DEADLY HANDSHAKE.

Some weeks went by when the method of delivery of the poison came about, and by sheer accident.

It was a trip to the drug store that the idea cropped its head. John went to buy an Ace bandage after spraining his wrist while working on his property. As he was searching along the shelves, he spotted something that piqued his interest. He reached up and took a liquid bandage product off the shelf and began reading how it worked. After a moment and feeling totally elated at his discovery, said, "This looks like it will work." He bought it with cash even though the product was an innocent purchase.

His thoughts moved very quickly as he envisioned covering the palm of his hand with the liquid then wiping the frog poison onto its solidified pliable gel-like surface and providing him with the clandestine delivery method he needed. It was perfect. It would give him insulation from the frog poison while not being detectible unless he turned his palm up. At that moment he gave birth to, "The Deadly Handshake."

He laughed and said without realizing he was not thinking the words to himself, but vocalizing them in a faint voice, "I got you now, Roberts."

Another piece of his plan had just fallen into place. There was only one remaining obstacle and that was getting the poison. After checking out of the store, he began singing, "Zip-a-dee doo dah, zip-a-dee yay, my oh my what a wonderful day, oh Senator Roberts, shit is coming your way, Zip-a-dee doo dah zip-a-dee yay."

With the Liquid Bandage in hand, he hurriedly headed back home to test it out. Even though he didn't have the frog poison, he wanted to see how well it worked at insulating the palm of his hand from moisture. He washed and dried his hands before applying the Liquid Bandage to his left palm. He waited until it was thoroughly dry. He then put some green food coloring into a small amount of water, applying it directly onto the Liquid Bandage with a small artist paint brush multiple times waiting a few minutes between applications. After being sure that he saturated the liquid bandage thoroughly, he sat down with his palm held up for a full half hour before slowly peeling it off. To his total joy, there was no green tinting of his skin. If there was, he knew his idea of using the liquid bandage as an insulation from the poison would not work. He then re-applied the bandage and this time put the food dye into a thicker cooking oil and followed the same steps as before. To his continued delight, the oil did not penetrate either. In his final test he would use honey. From what he read about the Golden Dart Frog poison it was a viscous sticky substance with little chance of penetrating the Liquid Bandage based upon his two prior tests. The honey did not penetrate either. He gloated, sat back on his couch, relaxed, turned on his TV and watched the news wearing a Cheshire cat grin. He was starting to feel more confident now that he had given himself two of the three things he needed, the opportunity and the poison delivery method.

It seemed like a sign, rather than sheer coincidence, that the first person shown on the news, as the TV came on was Senator Roberts. He was talking to the media outside the congressional building, spewing his same hateful rhetoric towards President Tripp while being amid his far-left colleagues. He thought to himself they look like the rogue's gallery. For one moment John forgot to contain his hateful rhetoric and spoke out to his wife Katherine and said, "That's one bunch of ugly evil fucks. I swear I hate those people." All she did was laugh and asked, "Honey, can't we watch the TV without your hateful side bars?"

John replied, "Sorry, I haven't said anything in a long time, you must admit."

Katherine laughed and said, "I'll give you that. You've been a good boy lately."

"Okay, I will not say another word about those evil fucks," John replied. After his last remark, John watched the news without making any more comments. Katherine picked up the TV remote and opened the channel guide. As she scrolled through the movies showing, she came across 'White House Down,' and asked John if he had seen it. He responded that he had not. With his acknowledgement Katherine put it on. All the while the movie was playing, John kept thinking about the success he had with the liquid bandage and how he needed to find a way to get the frog.

The next morning, John went to the Public Library to use their computers to research how he could obtain the frog. To his surprise, he found the Exotic Creatures pet store online. They specialized in pet frogs. They advertised exotic reptiles and amphibians and when he opened their website, they prominently displayed a photo of a Golden Dart Frog on their home page. He said to himself, "It can't be that easy." He immediately clicked on the picture of the frog, and it opened to a special page that gave many facts about it. Not only could you buy the frog and a forested terrarium for it, but they also sold all the nonpoisonous insects you needed to feed it, that is, if you were only going to keep it as a pet and not a weapon.

He read their terms of sale, and found that they guaranteed to ship any live creature overnight with feeding and care instructions. He continued doing more research and came across an article that said, "Golden Dart Frogs when raised in captivity lost their potency because they were not fed the poisonous insects, they ate in their Colombian habitat like fire ants, poisonous beetles, and spiders."

It also mentioned that the frogs, after digestion, metabolized the venom from these insects into a highly toxic sticky alkaloid poison that it secreted through its skin.

After reading about these insects, he learned that fire ants inject a toxin alkaloid called 'solenopsin' into its victims, and in humans it caused pustules and could cause severe allergic reactions including death. The beetle secreted a fluid called 'cantharidin' that caused swelling and blistering and is akin to cyanide and strychnine if ingested. The female Black Widow spider's venom contains 'alpha-latrotoxin' a strong neurotoxin, which can cause abdominal rigidity among other things, and death, and is reported to be fifteen times stronger than that of a rattle snake. It seems the frog, in its metabolic process of these digested insects, creates a poisonous cocktail that is un-matched by any creature on Earth.

He said to himself in a low tone, "I need to give them an untraceable call and ask a few questions. He wrote down the contact phone number and address. He noticed that they were a four to five-hour drive from where he lived. He thought that if they gave him the answers he was looking for, he would drive there and buy at least two of them along with a terrarium.

He considered everything he read and thought, if it's the venom from the fire ants, beetles and spiders that makes them poisonous, then I'll feed them what they need. He laughed to himself and said, "How easy is that? There are always fire ants on my front or back lawns. Hell they are on every property throughout the southern states. I'll have an endless cost-free untraceable supply."

He began to feel more enthusiastic about his devious plan. Now he had secured one part of the frog's diet, but he needed to find a supply of poisonous beetles and spiders. It did not take him long to find out about a striped blister beetle whose habitat is in the western part of the United States and is the most potent of the beetles. He again got excited at having determined that the diet necessary to re-invigorate the poison metabolic process in the frog was available to him domestically. Now all he needed to do was find a supply of them. He continued to search the internet looking for a live insect supplier. After going through a myriad of companies, and running into dead ends, he came across one that could give him as many as he wanted of both the beetle and black widow spiders. The last piece of his puzzle had fallen into place.

John considered all aspects of his murderous plan and wondered how much time it would take for the frog to re-generate its toxic coating after being fed its diet of the toxic insects. He felt confident about his theory, but knew that there were no guarantees his re-toxification idea would work. His dislike for Senator Roberts had become such an overly sick obsession that it manifested into an infestation of hate, permeating throughout his being. The slight uncertainty he had about the frog becoming his weapon made him consider putting together a plan B. He had no idea of what that plan would be as he had nixed so many other ideas. Right now, all he could concentrate on was getting his supplies, and as soon as possible, as time was of the essence.

Using a Spoof service and a throw away Sim Card to keep his call untraceable, he contacted the supplier to determine whether they would have available at least two of the Golden Dart Frogs and all the supplies needed to raise them in captivity, as he would go by and pick them up the next day. They gave him an affirmative answer to both his questions and estimated the total cost. That immediately prompted him to go out to his backyard workshop and make room for them. Still having time, he went to his bank to withdraw just enough cash to pay for them. He then went into several stores in a large strip mall buying small items using the largest denominations so that he could wash it locally, and in return use the cash change he received to pay for the frogs to avoid tracing any numbers on the money from the bank to the Exotic Creatures store. His thoughts to the smallest details was obvious and a little over kill.

He did not want to use a credit card or a check because both of those payments could trace back to him. He even coated his fingertips with the liquid bandage as he did not want to leave any fingerprints on the cash he withdrew even when paying for gas if he needed to, but felt with the gas he was taking with him he would not have to stop on his round trip. He was so overly cautious that he had filled up two five-gallon cans with gas and carried them in his car trunk. He did not want to stop at any gas stations where the FBI might identify him, should he ever become a suspect after his assassination of the Senator. He was sure that they would communicate with any pet supplier of Golden Dart frogs. He planned to wear dark glasses, and a baseball cap when he went into the store so that they would not be able to use facial recognition should the pet store have security cameras. He would be sure to keep the brim of his cap low and keep his head tilted toward the ground as much as possible and not wear any rings on his fingers, which might be identifiable on a photo enlargement taken from the security camera and then linked to him.

On the contrary he intended to place a quality decal tattoo on the back of his hand as a misleading means of identification. Certainly, the store clerk would notice it in such a prominent place and supply authorities with a verifiable tattoo that he would not have once he washed it off eliminating him as a suspect if authorities looked for that piece of identification on him.

When he returned from the bank, he went about harvesting fire ants on his property with a large jar baited with honey. He placed the jar right next to a mound where he would let it set overnight, hoping to have hundreds of those poisonous stinging sons of bitches by morning. He did not know how many of them the frogs would consume each day, but he wanted to be sure to have some ready for immediate consumption. He wanted the poison metabolic process to start upon their arrival. He figured he would be able to determine how much the frogs consumed each day from the Exotic Creatures pet store and then correlate that to the number of ants, beetles, and spiders they would need to eat.

The next day, he gassed up and took off to Georgia to make his purchase. He told his wife that he was putting in some extra volunteer work at the campaign office, after taking his computer course. Katherine readily accepted his absence as being normal to the routine he had established over the last few months. He figured it would take him about ten hours round trip. staying within the speed limits. He planned on being home by 4pm and early enough to be in time to have dinner with his wife and safe from any questions.

Before heading out, he checked his headlights, taillights and turn signals to be sure they were working properly. He did not want some stupid little thing to screw up his plans. He said to himself, "All I would need is to be pulled over by a cop for some avoidable traffic violation. It would not hinder my plan, but could hinder my freedom later. I've seen too many police shows on TV where an arrest is made because of the most stupid inane things. That's not going to happen to me, not if I can help it."

He had also considered his car being tracked by highway surveillance cameras, so he decided he would take as many rural sideroads as possible, popping onto the highways only when necessary. He intended on making it extremely hard to track him. In a worst-case scenario he wanted any evidence that pointed his way to be very circumstantial at best and impossible to prove beyond a reasonable doubt.

After making his trip to the Exotic Creatures pet store he felt excited about what he was about to purchase. He made sure that the brim of his baseball cap was down over his face and that he wore sunglasses. When he first stepped into the store, he scanned around looking for security cameras. He did not notice any, but knew that there just night be one he did not see. He went directly to the salesperson behind the counter and noticed the name tag on his shirt, and said, "Daniel, we spoke yesterday. I am the gentleman that called you wanting to buy two Golden Dart Frogs and whatever you recommended to raise them."

Daniel said, "Yes, you did speak to me and as requested, I placed two of the frogs into a terrarium for you. Come with me, they are over by the back wall. I have everything ready for you. I created a nice mossy habitat in it, that they should do well in. You'll need to keep it moist. I recommend using a mister. If you do not have one, we have them here," John responded, "Yes, add one to the purchase."

Once they reached the frogs, Daniel said, "All I need to do is get you a supply of food and some care instructions. They are ready to go. If you follow the instructions, they should do well. I highly recommend that you keep their environment between 60 to 80 degrees Fahrenheit. That is the temperature range of their natural habitat. I have placed a thermometer on the side of the tank so that you can monitor it. They are delicate little creatures."

John responded, "Thanks. Everything looks great and I will follow their care instructions faithfully."

Daniel then carefully reached into the tank and picked one up with his bare hand and said while doing so, "I would not do this in their natural habitat Their skin is normally highly toxic, and its toxin is quite deadly. When we breed them commercially, they are not toxic, because we do not feed them any poisonous insects like fire ants, and spiders. Just be sure that they never eat any, as they may become lethal again. We have placed a red warning label on the side of the terrarium.

John replied, "I can assure you that the only insects that it will eat are those that you will recommend to me. I am getting these frogs as a gift for my daughter. She likes creatures like this. She had beautiful saltwater fish, but soon found out that they required too much work, and it is an expensive hobby. John lied again; He had no daughter. He wanted it to seem an innocent purchase.

Daniel said," It is our policy when selling these frogs to mention the risk. I'm sure that your daughter will enjoy seeing them. Most people do. They have a beautiful vibrant color and are so ridiculously small and delicate looking. If we thought that they had a chance of re-metabolizing their poison when fed non-poisonous insects, we would not sell them period. We have been in business here for over twenty years and have sold thousands of these frogs and have never been confronted with an incident and based on that record are confident in the safety of this frog."

Hearing what Daniel said, John thought, "That information was nice to know. If someone investigated my purchase, they would soon learn that I am only one among thousands who bought the frog. Like the cops say in crime movies, 'We can't hold them on circumstantial evidence. It isn't proof enough.'"

He then asked Daniel, "I assume the care instructions tell me how much they need to eat every day?"

"Yes, it does. It varies with different frog species, but the Golden Dart Frog can eat up to thirteen mosquitoes a day or one to two non-poisonous spiders a day. After a week or so you will see what they have consumed daily and then feed them accordingly," Daniel replied.

"That sounds easy enough," John said.

Daniel then said, "Controlling the temperature in the terrarium is critical to their survival. Remember to keep the temperature between 60 to 80 degrees Fahrenheit. Their habitat may be in the tropical jungles of Colombia, but they live in the shade of a heavy canopy."

John responded, "I will be sure to keep an eye on the temperature. But I am not worried because we keep our home at 75 degrees all year round. Not hot, not cold, comfortable."

"Then you should have no problem with that aspect of caring for the creatures," Daniel responded.

John asked, "By the way, how long do these creatures live?"

Danial replied, "Three to five years in the wild, but can live up to ten years in captivity."

"That sounds about as long as the average dog," John said.

After paying for the frogs and supplies, John loaded them carefully onto the back seat of his car, then filled up his tank with the gas cans he had, and headed back home. "So far so good," he thought. That went smoothly and didn't take long at all. I should get back home even sooner than anticipated."

He relaxed at the wheel of his car, put on some music, and smiled as he drove. He had just put the last piece of his murder plot in place, the weapon. Now all he would have to do to make it work was re-toxify the frogs.

Once he arrived at his house, he went to greet his wife Katherine, but unexpectedly found her not at home. He figured she had gone out to do some shopping. Taking advantage of her absence he went immediately to his car and rushed the frogs out to his workshop and placed the empty gas cans back into his garage. "That went well," he thought.

John became excited like a little kid with a new toy. He then rushed to check his fire ant collection activity and found the jar with honey bait in it was virtually teeming with more than ants but other insects as well. He put latex gloves on before putting the lid back on it. He knew that the stinging ants would swarm onto his hands as soon as he gripped the jar. John had been stung on more than one occasion by them over the years while tending his property and did not want a re-occurrence of those itchy pustules they left all over him.

After capping the jar, he went out to his workshop to begin the frog's re-metabolic process. He removed the glass top off the terrarium, and then opened the ant filled jar. He then used a long-handled spoon to scoop up some honey along with some ants and then carefully placed the tip of the spoon on the dirt surface inside the terrarium and held it there while the ants crawled off. After he had gotten about fifty ants into the terrarium, he replaced the jar lid and terrarium top. He then watched to see what would happen. The ants moved throughout the bottom seeking their colony. He waited patiently, like an evil Mr. Hyde, watching the frogs to see if they would begin eating the ants. After several minutes some of the ants neared the frogs. The frogs seemed oblivious to the ants, they just sat motionless.

They made no immediate attempt to eat the ants. He even noticed one of the ants crawled onto one of the frogs. It did not move, nor did it seem bothered by it.

He became disappointed as he wanted instant satisfaction, like the frog immediately flicking its tongue and eating one after the other. He thought that he would come back later and check again, but as he started to move away, he noticed one of the frogs begin to move. He stepped back up to the terrarium to watch again and to his freaking absolute delight the frog ate an ant. His reaction was like having an orgasm, as he loudly said while looking up, "Thank you Lord. Yeah baby! It worked." Then looking down at the frog, said, "Eat all you want, my beauty, there's plenty more where that came from."

John, feeling euphoric, headed back into the house. Just as he entered the patio, he saw Katherine coming through the front door carrying some grocery bags. He spoke out to her and said, "Hi sweetness, how has your day been? Anything new and exciting happen?"

Katherine responded and said, "I just went to get some groceries. We were getting short on a few things. I bought some chicken breasts for dinner. Get the rest of the groceries out of the car."

"Okay," John responded.

After bringing the rest of the groceries back into the house, and while helping to put them away, John asked, "Are you going to make chicken cutlets?"

Katherine replied, "I'm not sure yet. I was thinking of making chicken parmigiana with some spaghetti."

John replied, "That sounds delicious."

Katherine then asked, "Well how did it go for you today?"

"Everything was good. Couldn't have been better," John replied.

The next day, he received his overnight delivery of the Black Widow spiders and the Blister beetles he ordered from the insect supplier. He was excited even more now, because he had obtained the remaining part of the frog's poisonous diet. It did not take him long to rush his package out to his workshop and open it. To his delight he could see the spiders crawling in their mesh covered jar along with another jar of poisonous beetles. He immediately went about placing a few of the spiders and beetles in with the frogs. Now it was waiting and seeing if his idea of the deadly handshake would become a reality.

He kept mental notes of the number of spiders and beetles he placed in with the frogs so that he could see how many were ingested each day. It was harder to do with the much smaller ants. He would add more when he saw only a few of them crawling about. It was easier with the spiders and beetles, because of their much larger size.

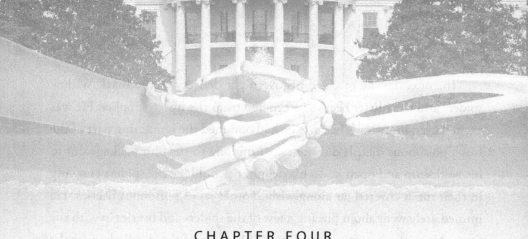

CHAPTER FOUR

THE METABOLIC POISON PROCESS BEGINS

As the weeks went by, John became increasingly confident that his plan was working. The frogs were eating all the insects and if what he had learned about the frogs was right, they would become the deadly creatures for which he was hoping. The one thing that he was still not sure of was how long it would take for the deadly alkaloid toxin to be re-metabolized by the frogs, if at all, and secreted through their skin. He had planned to buy a few mice and every few weeks rub their faces against the frog's skin to see what would happen.

After a full month of meticulously maintaining an ideal environment in the terrarium and monitoring the frog's eating habits, he went to a local pet store and purchased the few mice he needed to test his theory. After putting on latex gloves, he rubbed the face of one of the mice against the frog.

Based upon everything he read, the mouse should die instantly, or evidence some physical reaction, especially if only a few grams, as reported, could kill an elephant. Still holding the mouse, he watched carefully, but nothing was happening at first. After several minutes had passed, the mouse became lethargic, and then laid on its side, not moving. It was still alive but looked paralyzed.

With a jubilant shout, John yelled out, "It's fucking working, the metabolizing is beginning to take effect." He then took another mouse and rubbed it against the second frog. The same thing happened. He had determined that both frogs were going through the metabolic process equally. But he knew that the time it took to paralyze two small mice indicated to him, that it was going to take much longer for the poison to become more lethal. He would keep up with his same regimen until he had achieved instant death. After another two months he planned to try it on larger animals like cats or dogs, and if successful, would then try it on the ultimate test subject, a human. He had no idea who that unfortunate person would be, but whomever it was, he could care less.

John kept up with his daily routine and worked even harder at the campaign office to become even closer to everyone who worked there. He became remarkably close to Betty Ryan, so much so, that she began to confide in him about matters relating to the Senator. It was on one occasion, she mentioned to him that Senator Ryan was planning to create a false narrative against his opponent, Jeanne Collette. According to Betty, she heard him talking to a reporter from the New York Gazette. They were planning to come out with an uncorroborated story from an unidentified source, which was going to expose her for having sex with a few frat boys at some wild college party.

John listening intently said, "Wow, that's really a low blow if it's not true."

Betty replied, "All's fair in politics, especially when it will help give us a win. He wants to sully her goody two shoes image."

John responded with, "You know there'll be a complete denial and a request for retraction, followed by a lawsuit."

"Of course," Betty replied. "They expect that, but the damage would have been done, and any retraction won't be on the main page in the newspaper, and will be buried by the media. That's what he has done to President David Tripp on more than one occasion. Tripp doesn't stand a chance against Roberts. He's the party's dirty politics standard bearer."

John, fuming inside but maintaining his cool, said, "Politics is really nasty! It's too bad that campaigns are dishonest. The swamp in Washington does harbor some nasty political creatures to be sure."

At that moment, Annette Canter, who had finished a project she was on, approached them and asked Betty if she wanted her to start soliciting for campaign contributions or taking polls?

Betty replied and said, "Start soliciting. We need all the money we can get. The TV spots are exhausting funds, and we still have some months before election."

Annette then asked John, "What are you working on?"

John replied, "Sponging."

Betty and Annette looked at John with inquisitive looks, and simultaneously asked, "What's sponging?"

John laughed and replied, "I'm soliciting funds from the little people to pay for those costly hit job ads. To me it's sponging off the public."

Betty said, "I've never heard that sponging expression used in that context before."

John laughed and replied, "It's an old expression that fits."

Annette also laughing said, "I guess, in a way it is. But it's for a good social cause no matter what you call it."

John thought to himself, you mean the NSP cause, you communist bitch, while saying, "One thing is for sure, they only know what we tell them. But what are a few lies if it gets Roberts elected?"

Annette then asked, "Have you had lunch yet?"

John, replied, "No. Do you want to grab a bite to eat?"

Annette responded, "Yes! I didn't get to eat breakfast. All I had was a quick cup of coffee."

John turned to Betty and asked her, "Do you want to join us or have us bring something back?"

Betty replied, "No thanks. I've a ton of calls to make. If you don't mind, bring me back a mocha latte."

"Will do," John responded.

John and Annette then headed out for lunch at a nearby café. While on the way, John asked Annette if she knew when Senator Roberts would be coming back to the campaign office. Annette said, "Betty told me that he would be coming after the Senate Oversight Committee hearings about President Tripp's involvement with the Russians and his reported ownership in a Moscow Casino. The hearings start next week, so I suppose he will not be here for another two weeks at least. We expect that he'll be spending a lot of time here after that. He's expected to start actively stumping the state. Betty has been actively setting up his agenda, and arranging a Town Hall question and answer sometime next month."

John upon hearing her comments and wanting to subliminally defend the President, said, "President Tripp denied any involvement what-so-ever, and claimed it fabricated news."

"Fabricated news, who cares, if it damages that asshole that's all that counts. We need to get that jerk out of office by any means necessary," Annette responded.

John wanted to grab Annette by the throat and choke the shit out of her after her remarks about Tripp, but he maintained his facade. He continued with his Tripp hating act, and said, "I agree. He's an asshole and says some stupid things at times. Speaking of a Town Hall meeting, I watched Senator Roberts at the Town Hall Q and A he had in Tampa a few months back. Honestly, it all seemed contrived. The questions and answers did not seem spontaneous."

Annette immediately responded, in a questioning and defensive tone, said, "You can't be that naïve. They are pre-planned. We hand pick the audience and provide each of the expected participants with the questions we want asked, and provide the Senator with the answers. We cannot afford any fumbles and contradicting fact checks after the Town Hall meeting. It's all politics at its best."

John looking at Annette thought to himself, "I have just identified my first test subject. This bitch is going to die before I do in that scumbag Roberts."

After arriving at the café John and Annette sat and idly chatted about different things, but politics and Senator Roberts remained the main topic of discussion. John in a subtle way grilled Annette as much as he could about what she knew about the Senator. Any little tidbit of fact might be useful in his plan to assassinate him.

.. What he learned, and had no idea of, is that at his upcoming election eve celebration, a few other Senators and Congressmen were expected to attend. One of them was Congressman Andrew Shipp. Another scumbag in John's eyes. He hated Shipp about as much as Roberts. Wow, he thought to himself, "Two pieces of bird shit with one stone or should I say frog?" John as usual spewed profanity when it came to describing President Tripp's opponents. Katherine had chastised John on more than one occasion about using foul language to describe people. All John would say is, "That's how I see them. Evil scumbags."

Now his assassination idea became even more appealing. His efforts to revitalize the Golden Dart Frog's toxin output became even more appealing. Shipp was another Tripp bashing Capitol Hill Socialist. He could care less about the needs of the people or the truth. All he wanted to do was score political points and become a left-wing news media mainstay and someday one of their paid contributors. He also was heading up phony investigations of Tripp.

As time went by, he'd learned from Annette, that there in fact would be several other high profile law makers attending, including some well-known left wing media hacks. After hearing that, he became so elated that he said, "That's fantastic. I can't wait to meet them at his victory celebration. There will be many people that I'd love to shake hands with."

He then asked Annette, "Do you think I'll have the opportunity to do that?"

"Absolutely," Annette responded. "I know some of them from having worked on a few campaigns. I'll introduce you to whomever I know that shows up."

"That would be fantastic. I can't wait," John replied, and then said laughing, "I want to shake so many hands that my arm will become dead tired, and my hand completely numb."

As they were finishing their lunch John made sure to order a Mocha Latte for Betty. Brown nosing with the head of the Senator's campaign was going to become a steady ploy. His plan had to work. "Holy shit, it's going to be a smorgasbord of bodies," he thought with absolute glee.

While heading back to the campaign office, he began mulling his plan around in his head. He realized that if the poison worked too quickly, he might not have a chance to murder anyone other than the Senator. The commotion and circumstance would not lend itself to people being in a glad-handing mood. He would just have to see what happens.

Once they re-entered the campaign office, John brought Betty the Mocha Latte she wanted. She thanked him and then asked, "Where did you have lunch?"

John replied, "We ate at the Jump for Joy café. The food was good, but I don't know if I'd jump for joy, after eating it. I found it okay although the ambience was quite nice," John then added a little humor saying, "I would rate it three baby steps and a hop. It did not rate a jump for joy."

Betty laughed at his remark, and said, "You're too funny. That's one of your admirable traits, humor. You have a nice personality, John. It serves you well."

"That's nice of you to say. I appreciate that," John replied. He then continued and said, "That's the first time I've had a lengthy conversation with Annette. She's a highly intelligent woman and seems to have a lot of campaign experience. I enjoyed talking to her." John was sure to make his lunch with Annette seem like nothing more than business to Betty. He wanted to avoid having Betty think that he might be developing a relationship which she might frown upon. He had no idea if that would be the case. He was just using an abundance of caution.

Betty replied, "Yes, she is and yes, she does. We've worked on a few campaigns together over the years. I called her to come work with me as soon as Senator Roberts chose me to run his campaign office. She's made some valuable contacts and can be quite useful in working out some of the Senator's unexpected problems."

John asked, "Is there anything else I can do to help, if not, I will continue to solicit."

"No thanks John, just keep up your sponging," Betty said with a smile.

John replied to her humor, "I see you like my phrase."

"Yes. I found it funny," Betty replied and then continued, "You're doing great. You topped $50,000 the other day. That's fantastic numbers for someone cold calling. Your numbers have been steadily increasing as you become more adept at soliciting."

John said, "You know the adage, "practice makes perfect. We need to get the Senator re-elected."

"Yes, we do." Betty responded.

With that last remark, John went back to soliciting for campaign funds. Before returning to his cubicle he stopped to tell Annette that he really enjoyed lunch with her. She responded with a smile and said, "I enjoyed it as well."

John feeling confident after her upbeat response said, "We should do it again sometime."

"I'd like that," Annette replied.

John sensing he could take their relationship beyond a friendly lunch pushed the envelope and asked, "Would you be okay with dinner instead of lunch?"

She looked at him, and without hesitation said, "That sounds lovely. Do you have any place in mind?"

"Do you like seafood?" John asked.

"Yes, I do, very much," Annette replied.

"I know an Italian restaurant that makes incredible Cioppino, which, in case you don't know, is seafood on a bed of linguini. They have several seafood dinners. Their food is finger licking good. The owners are from Calabria," John said.

Annette, smiling said, "That sounds delightful, I love Italian food."

John, also smiling at Annette. thought to himself, "She must know that I'm coming on to her and that I'm married. I know I mentioned Katherine. Dinner is certainly beyond a friendly co-worker lunch. I'm going to see just how far I can get with a relationship. I may have to use her in some way to carry out my plan. I must admit she's quite attractive and making love to her, would get her closer and more trusting of me." Then thinking of his wife Katherine, considered the infidelity and in a callous way, said to himself, "Sorry honey, sacrifices must be made for the cause."

The rest of the day went by quickly and John headed home. He needed to check on the frogs to make sure they were thriving. As he was driving, he called Katherine and asked her if she wanted him to pick up anything on the way home. She asked him to pick up a pack of cigarettes. He hated doing that because he didn't want her smoking. He was a reformed smoker and hadn't smoked in fourteen years. He could no longer stand the smell of cigarettes, especially on her, and had pleaded with her many times to stop the nasty habit. It was a losing cause as far as John was concerned. Even though she developed COPD it didn't stop her. She was hooked, badly. He gave himself a questioning thought, thinking, "How can such an intelligent woman not see what those fucking cigarettes are doing to her health? She is committing suicide slowly." Then having an outlandish thought, wondered if he could Baker Act his wife for cigarette smoking. He considered it as a feasible way to force her off cigarettes. He thought a week or two in jail would force her to go cold turkey. He knew she wouldn't go voluntarily to a rehab facility. He then thought, "I should explore the feasibility of that. I know she will not get off cigarettes by herself. I wonder if my reasoning behind the request for a Baker Act, has even a modicum of feasibility?"

His mind moved away from his wife for that moment and began thinking of where he was in his scheme. He thought, "So far so good. I've gotten in with the mental retards and have developed a solid trust within their inner circle to move more freely within the campaign office. The metabolic process on the frogs is working so far and everything is a go. All I need to do now is keep feeding the poisonous insects to my little beauties, and test the hopefully increasing potency of the toxin on larger subjects. I will give it one more month before trying it on a larger animal. I need to see the mice die instantly before doing that. I must succeed the very first-time I try it on the Senator. There won't be a second chance. Thank God for technology, because that liquid bandage product works, on at least any liquids I've tried penetrating it with. The ultimate test will be when I rub the toxin on the palm of my hand once I've coated it with the Liquid Bandage. I'm going to be nervous as shit when I do it, but it needs to be done. If it doesn't work, I'm fucked. There is no anti-toxin for it."

John pulled up to his house and as he did, he could see Katherine sitting on the front porch, smoking a cigarette, and drinking a cup of coffee. He waved to her as he drove up the driveway. He thought, "How lucky we don't have to work for a living. Thank God for our Bitcoin and tech stock investments."

John walked up to his wife, gently lifted her chin toward his face and kissed her, saying "Luv ya babe."

Katherine replied, "Love you too." Then asked, "How was your day?"

"Everything was great. I think that I'm getting the hang of the computer programming part of the course. I don't expect to become a geek in just six months, but I'll be much more adept at using my PC," John replied with a smile.

"I'm making chicken cutlets, with buttered noodles and sauteed spinach for dinner," Katherine said.

"Sounds delicious. I'm actually pretty hungry," John responded.

As John and Katherine sat down for dinner, John turned on his favorite Vox News to see what was going on, while he enjoyed his meal. After about 15 minutes passed, he heard the news caster play a news clip of Senator Roberts holding another of his President Tripp hit job statements to the press. As John listened intently, he heard the Senator say that they were issuing subpoenas to acquire six years of the President's tax returns to see what crimes he may have committed through his corporations.

John stood up and said, "Katherine, did you hear that bullshit? Christ almighty! What kind of fucking shit is that? He has no crime to investigate, but wants to investigate to see if he can produce one. That man needs to die, he said in a moment of uncontrolled rage. How does he get away with it? I swear, I wish a 747 would fly into his home, killing him and his whole family. That is how much I hate that bastard."

Katherine said, "John, sit down. You go insane no matter what that man says. You can't do anything about it and besides, President Tripp always survives his attacks no matter whether they are warranted or not."

"That may be so, but look at the toll it's taking on his Presidency and his ability to do his job, not to mention what it's doing to his family. Look at those scumbags standing beside him. gloating at their evil. I swear, if I knew that I was dying with no hope, I would murder all those pieces of shit," John replied.

Katherine looked up at her husband and felt dismayed at his hatred for the Senator. She understood his feelings and how he doted over the President, but she saw something in his eyes that worried her. She would question his sanity at times. She, with her usual calm demeanor told him to sit down and finish eating, and to please let her enjoy her meal with him. She told him that she didn't want him watching the news anymore while they were having dinner.

John listened to Katherine and said, "I'm sorry, but I can't tolerate what Roberts does."

"Honey, I don't either, but I don't let the veins in my neck bulge with anger. You utterly lose it. Didn't you promise me that you would control your outbursts?" Katherine said.

John sat down again, looking at his wife and said, "Yes, I did. I just don't know how you can sit so quietly like a passive sheep at their shit."

Katherine responded, "I don't like how they treat President Tripp either, but since I can't do anything about what happens to him, I don't go crazy. All I can do is voice myself at the ballot box."

John replied to Katherine with sarcasm, saying, "Right! At the same ballot boxes that are stuffed with fake ballots against Tripp, silencing your voice."

"So would you not have me vote, because you think it would make no difference?" Katherine asked.

"No. I was just making a point that something more needs to be done besides casting a ballot," John replied.

"What do you suggest?" Katherine asked.

John having lost it, responded sarcastically, "I don't know. How about shooting the evil fuck dead in his face?"

Katherine, not liking Johns' response said in her own sarcastic tone, "Well since that's not going to happen, my vote will have to do."

John sat across from the table looking at his wife, and realizing he was blowing his cover, said, "I'm sorry honey. I just can't control myself at times."

"You have some serious issues. Politics are changing you. Ever since President Tripp won the election you've slowly become another person. It's like you have two personalities at times. I swear your eyes dilated when you were screaming at the TV." Katherine replied.

"Having outbursts every so often does not make me Jekyll and Hyde. It just shows how much I love our President," John said.

"Okay John lets quit this conversation and finish eating. Do you want some more chicken?" Katherine calmly asked.

"No. I'm good. Thanks honey."

As soon as John had the chance, after eating, he made his way out to his frogs. He checked the number of insects eaten and was happy to see that the frogs were settling in and consuming all of them. As he was adding more poisonous insects frog food, he noticed little baby spiders throughout the Terrarium. He thought, "Wow, I never noticed any egg sacs." He took a dowel and poked around the well forested terrarium and found an opened small grey colored egg sac under leaves hanging just above the ground. He could see more of the pinhead sized young still around it. He also noticed fire ants attacking and eating the baby spiders. Obviously, the Black Widow must have mated just before John received them. "What luck! More food for everyone," he thought.

He checked the temperature in the workshop and found it to be an ideal 70 degrees. The air conditioner was working well. He made sure to keep moisture in the terrarium and misted the leaves and moss. So far so good he thought. "Everything is still going well. I'll be assessing their toxin levels again by the end of next week on another test subject. I love animals, but screw it, I don't have a choice."

After being satisfied that everything was going as planned, he went back into his home, sat down at his computer, and played at doing computer class work. He had to keep Katherine unaware of his nefarious activity.

CHAPTER FIVE

TESTING THE TOXIN

A few weeks had passed since John had concerned himself about testing the frog toxin on a larger animal. He knew it was time to get one. He decided to go to a pet store and pick out the victim. He considered it the easiest way to get a test subject. He drove over to Pet World, walked around the store, and noticed a good-sized Ferret. When he inquired about its price, he was surprised to see that they were selling for $400.00 on average and soon realized that buying animals wasn't cheap. He decided to go to the ASPCA and adopt one. What was funny about his concern for the cost was that John had amassed many millions from his investments. Four hundred dollars was nothing to him.

After adopting an older cat for $35.00, he was content. As he was driving back to his house he looked down at the cat and said, sorry, but your life is for a worthy cause. He took the cat straight to his workshop where he immediately put on latex gloves, picked up a frog, and proceeded to wipe the frog against the cat's nose. He stepped back and watched how long it would take for the cat to die. He started counting off seconds 100, 101, 102, 103, 104, 105, 106 107, until he reached 120. The cat died at the end of his count. He did not know whether the toxin would work at the same speed for a 190-pound man. He had no way of knowing. Everything he was doing was speculation. He decided to go by a time and weight calculation, estimating that the poison would kill the Senator in a little over six minutes.

John felt that if he was right, the frog had become completely toxic again. Now he needed to try it on an even bigger subject to be sure. It had to be a human being. Who was it going to be was the question?

It had taken John four months to get to this point. He knew he had a little less than two months left before he would assassinate the Senator.

He had to be even more convinced that the toxin would kill a person and be sure about the speed in which it worked. He knew that he would need two minutes to get to the Men's Room to wash off the poison and Liquid Bandage after shaking the Senator's hand. It was the perfect place to do it. After all no one would question his proper hygiene habits. All the evidence would simply wash down the drain.

He was going to start picking out his victim. It had to be someone at random. Someone not connected to him or the campaign and someone that could be approached without being in view of some video camera. Someplace where he would not easily be identified. Where and when was his challenge.

John had originally thought of making Annette his first victim, but after giving it careful thought realized that doing her in would be too risky. She could be tied to him, and being in the campaign with the Senator and his dying from the same toxin later would tie both deaths together. He wanted nothing to throw a kink into his plans. He nixed the idea and decided to move on from her. He would off her when he offed the Senator.

As the days went by, he hadn't found a solution, at least not one that met his strict criteria. While sitting at his home watching television, a movie trailer advertised a new super comic book hero. As he watched it, he said to Katherine, "Let's see the movie. We haven't been to a theater in a long time." He asked her, knowing that she didn't like going out to the movies. He knew she preferred staying home watching Netflix, or any one of the movie streaming services. He was just laying the groundwork for his night out alone. It was the minute he saw the film advertised that he had an epiphany about the perfect place to try out the toxin on a test subject. A dark theater with lots of people. He just needed to figure out the best way to get the toxin on an unsuspecting person without them or anyone questioning his action.

The more he thought about it the better it seemed. He could immediately go into the Men's Room after committing the deed and wash off the evidence, just like he would at the campaign office, and no one would know how the individual died. He supposed that people would think they died of a heart attack. Why not? They would simply fall to the ground with no evidence of violence around them.

He became immediately cheerful knowing he had conjured up a full proof plan. He decided to do it on the weekend. His mind focused on his plan, and as he sorted through more thoughts, he realized that to murder someone in the movie, and to do it right and replicate the way he would knock off the Senator, he'd want to go full out, and put the toxin on the palm of his hand.

He said to himself, listening to his own quietly spoken words, "I know I can do this. The Liquid Bandage works and against less viscous liquids." As he listened to himself, he felt a reassurance and a confidence which overtook any semblance of sanity, as he said in a higher insane with hate tone, "You're dead meat, you mother fucker Roberts. I'm not just going to shake your hand; I'm going to squeeze it to death you Socialist pile of shit."

His thoughts became much more cunning and calculating as he started to relish his next move. Johns' personality was changing more by the day. It was reversing his mental state. He was now thinking more like Mr. Hyde instead of his more lucid and well-mannered Dr. Jekyll. It seems hard to believe that the divisive political climate which John was so deeply ensconced in, caused him to become a warped and unhinged cunning individual with an unwavering focus to accomplish his nefarious deed. John's mental collapse was because of too many political hate speeches and unwarranted investigations focused against his beloved President Tripp. The endless vile attacks were all conducted by his political enemies and by what John called the disgusting Hollywood elite. This constant negative bombardment against Tripp and to John's strong patriotic beliefs eroded his sanity. John no doubt was now suffering from Political Stress Disorder.

The weekend finally came with John totally focused on killing an unsuspecting stranger. He would be going to the 7:10 pm movie where he intended to fake a stumble going down the exit ramp in the dark believing that someone would stop to help him get up. He was relying upon the good Samaritan nature of most people and believed that if he extended his hand up from the ground seeking help, someone would take it and pull him up. He knew the grip would have to be tight to assist him up off the ground, and would create an ideal method of passing the sticky toxin from his palm to theirs.

After eating dinner with Katherine, he told her he was going to the movie to see the new superhero picture that was promoted on the television. Knowing Katherine would say no, John astutely asked her if she wanted to go. Katherine did not disappoint him, she said no as expected. After stepping outside his home, he went to his workshop, put on a latex glove, and placed one of the frogs into a large cookie jar which allowed him to reach in and place the frog on the wet moss-covered bottom. He placed a lid with small holes in it onto the jar. He also put a bottle of Liquid Bandage in his pocket. He placed the cookie jar on the front passenger seat of his car and drove off to the theater.

The clock began ticking off in his mind as he drove to the movie. He visualized the moment he was going to murder his test subject. He did not have any remorse at what he was about to do, no matter that the death of that innocent person would touch the lives of so many people. He took it as a necessary evil. Like collateral damage as they say in the movies. As he was driving, he said aloud, "If this shit works like I think it will, Senator, kiss your ass to God, because it's mine."

When he got to the multiplex movie theater, he went in and purchased his ticket and then went back to his car and covered the palm of his left hand with the Liquid Bandage, not once but a few times. He was about to chance his own death. He opened the cookie jar, looked down at the deadly little creature he created, and in a quick, fuck it moment, reached in and held the frog in the palm of his coated left hand. He then placed the frog back into the jar, replaced the lid, then sat, and waited to see if he had just killed himself. After two minutes had gone by, he had no reaction and thought to himself, so far so good.

He knew everything he was doing was risky speculation. He could not be sure if it would work at all, but everything he had done up to that point indicated it would. Another two minutes went by and still he felt okay. Finally after waiting a full seven minutes without any affect, he felt it was okay to head into the theater and do what he intended. He had just played Russian Roulette with a deadly frog and wasn't going to back down from his mission. There was only a thin ply of rubber skin like substance between him and death.

He walked into the movie house using only his right hand to open the door and to hand his ticket in. He was extremely careful to keep his left hand tightly at his side, not wanting to touch anything. even by accident. He went into the movie house and headed to the theater showing the film. He walked up the ramp to the seating area; scanned the auditorium and made sure to go into an aisle that was well above the rest, and one that most people would choose last. He wanted to avoid having anyone close to him, especially avoiding people trying to squeeze past him in and out of the aisle.

Once he became seated in a top row, the movie lights dimmed, the sound came on, and the picture began. He sat and watched the movie waiting for the moment he would execute his plan. Finally as the picture ended, he got up from his seat and moved quickly down the steps to be among the last of the crowd leaving. As he reached the bottom of the steps leading to the exit ramp, just ahead of the remaining movie goers, he made his stumble toward the ramp wall, cushioning his fall with his shoulder and right arm and then stayed down waiting for a few moments, feigning hurt, hoping one of the remaining people would stop to help him up.

Just as he expected, a man leaned over toward him said, "Are you okay?"

John replied, "Yes, I think so," and extended his deadly toxin coated left hand up and said, "Do you mind helping me?"

The good Samaritan stranger replied, "No not at all," as he gripped John's hand tightly, while pulling him up off the floor.

John felt his palm meshing with that of the stranger, and knew at that moment he had successfully transferred the deadly toxin. When John was standing, he said, "Thank you so much. I took a misstep and fell."

"Are you sure that you're alright?" the stranger asked.

John replied, "Yes. I wasn't dizzy or anything, I was just clumsy."

As the stranger turned to walk away, he said, with a smile, "Walk safely."

John replied after him, "I'll do that."

He kept looking at the man as he headed toward the Men's Room to wash the toxin off his hand, looking for any reaction. It only took John a minute to reach the nearby bathroom. He went directly to an automatic paper towel dispenser, grabbed a sheet, and vigorously washed his left palm after applying hand soap using an automatic dispenser above the sink. Even after seeing no evidence of anything remaining on his palm, he repeated the steps, out of absolute paranoia. Being a stickler for detail, he took the used paper towels with him, wrapped inside an unused one, which he intended to discard outside the theater.

As he exited the bathroom, he immediately looked across the lobby to see if the man had fallen from the effects of the toxin, but the almost empty lobby was quiet. He became a little disappointed at first, thinking the toxin did not work. He was sure that he had gotten an ample amount onto the stranger's hand. It wasn't until he had gotten outside the theater that he saw people, both standing and kneeling near someone lying on the ground in the parking lot. He had to see if it was the stranger, so he walked closer to determine if it was him. Once he got a glimpse, he smiled with a sick pleasure, saying to himself, "It worked like a charm."

He just kept on walking away toward where his vehicle was and without looking back or showing any emotion he got into his car and watched to see what would happen next. He needed to know if the man died. He thought that if they took the body away in an ambulance wearing an oxygen mask, he was still alive, at least for the time being. If they covered his face, then it would indicate he died.

He thought he'd better be dead. It was only a few more minutes when a police car showed up with the police officers moving the small crowd

57

of people away from the fallen stranger. He could see the officer put his fingers onto the man's carotid artery feeling for a pulse. After a moment, he looked up at his patrol partner, shaking his head side to side, as if indicating the person lying there was dead. The police officer stood up and spoke out to some of the on lookers, looking for anyone who might identify the stranger or knew what happened. John could only suppose that that was the case. He did not see them placing the usual yellow tape around the area of the body, which they did when considering it a crime scene. He made his suppositions based strictly upon what he had seen on television. He did not know their protocol in events like this. He supposed that without any evidence of violence, they would believe he died of a heart attack or stroke. They would not be able to determine the cause of death at the scene without an autopsy or evidence of obvious violence.

He saw a young woman carrying a cell phone in her hand, walk toward the police officer. He could see them talking for about five minutes. An ambulance showed up with EMT's moving towards the body quickly, carrying medical equipment. It took only two minutes for their examination and confirmation of death. By that time two more police vehicles showed up with one of them having a police lieutenant brought to the scene. The police had not recognized John watching them from his car and he did not want to be either. So he slowly drove away feeling content he'd tested the toxin, and knowing it worked. At least it was obvious to him by what he saw transpiring at the scene. He just didn't know if there would be an autopsy.

As he began heading home, he tried to figure out the amount of time it took for the toxin to work. He thought back to the moment the stranger had gripped his hand and then calculated the time it took him to get in and out of the bathroom, and then to reach the exit door. He saw that the toxin felled the man outside the theater and before he, himself reached the exit door. If he was right, the toxin took about six minutes to work. It was just like he guessed and the time he would need when he knocked off the Senator and at least Annette, who he planned to keep close.

During his drive home, he showed absolutely no remorse at the death of an innocent stranger. All he could do was congratulate himself on pulling it off and successfully re-invigorating the toxin metabolic process in the frogs. He simply got past what he had done by singing his favorite tune, "Zip-a-dee doo dah, zip-a-dee yay, my oh my what a wonderful day, oh Senator Roberts, shit is coming your way, Zip-a-dee doo dah zip-a-dee yay."

Something more had happened to John, after murdering a human being, besides not showing any outward remorse, he found a deep gratification, and knew that he could do it again without hesitation. There was no doubt that internally, he was no longer the person that Katherine remembered as a sweet, easy going, likable friendly man. When and if Katherine ever found out about what John had done, she would be hard pressed to believe it. Or maybe not, with his outburst's of hate against the Senator.

When John pulled up into the driveway of his home, he sat there for a few minutes, going over everything he had done and could not think of anything that could tie him to the man's death. He played the events that had transpired up to the moment of hand contact over in his mind. His thoughts followed his methodical process one step at a time. He spoke lowly to himself saying, "I faked my fall in a low-lit area, there were no security cameras, and I kept my face down away from passersby's. I'm sure that no one will be able to definitively identify me. I even looked down when I extended my hand upward toward the stranger, carefully not giving any of the few straggling onlookers a good look at me. The stranger and I were the only ones still on the exit ramp when I got to my feet. I did not leave with the man so I would not have been video recorded walking out of the movie with him, nor across the lobby by the obvious security cameras. I took the paper towels with me to not leave any trace of the Liquid Bandage, toxin, or my fingerprints, even if there was little possibility of that happening. Yeah, I did everything right."

After finishing mulling over his actions he looked up and said, with considerable excitement, "You did it, you genius mother fucker." He simply complimented himself.

He then left the car, went into the house, and walked over to Katherine, who was sitting on the couch watching TV, bent over and gave her a kiss, showing himself to be that loving husband.

Katherine asked him, "Did you like the movie?"

John replied, "It was really good. The superhero was Mystic. He had the ability to become like the invisible man with hearing like a bat, and with fighting skills like a hyped-up Jet Li. I had never heard of him before, but I haven't been into comic books since I was a kid. What made him super bad ass was that he could fight while he was invisible. No one would have beaten him even if they could see him, let alone fighting him while they couldn't. More than likely they'll make a sequel." He then asked Katherine, "What are you watching?"

"I'm watching the movie Battleship," Katherine replied.

"I love that movie. I've watched it several times," John replied and then said, "I 'm a little hungry, I think I'll have some soup."

Katherine said, "There are still some leftovers in the fridge. Just heat them up."

John then opened up about the man he had just murdered to Katherine and said, "I noticed a man lying in the parking lot of the movie theater as I was leaving. I could see people standing and kneeling around him. I don't know if he was all right. The police and ambulance showed up just as I was driving away. I don't know what happened to him."

Katherine in a concerned tone, said, "God, I hope he's alright."

"Me too," John replied, and then said, "Maybe it'll be covered on local news."

"It might be if he died. The news would cover that, before they'd cover someone who didn't die. They like something dramatic," Katherine said.

"You're right. If he died. they should have coverage on the 10 o'clock news," John said.

John went into the kitchen to get something to eat. He said to himself, "Everything went just as I planned, the Liquid Bandage worked like a charm. Not one smidgeon of the toxin got on me. The reaction time was just as I calculated. Now I'm ready for the Senator. I'll have to figure a better way to apply the toxin to my palm. I don't want to carry the frog in a jar. I'll have to find a way to harvest the toxin from the frogs, and not needing to keep one hand immobile for too long a time at the campaign office. Doing so might pose a problem."

As John noticed the time on the electric stove and saw that it was 9:55 pm, he called out to Katherine, "Honey, put the local news channel on. It's almost ten. I'm curious to know if they'll cover the incident at the movie."

John really could care less about the man. He just wanted to know if they would indicate anything more than what was evident to him at the scene, and that was death by natural causes as the immediate reason. He knew that only an autopsy would disclose the truth. He didn't know if they automatically requested one. There was nothing at the scene that suggested a homicide so the chances they wouldn't request one was in his favor. He just didn't know the legal protocol in situations like that. All he could do is continue and let it all play out.

As he was sitting down to eat on the couch in front of the TV, the local news came on. It didn't start with anything about his murder. It wasn't until the last minutes of the news hour that they mentioned the heart-breaking story about a man who, as reported at the scene, died from a heart attack in the parking lot of the Multiplex theater. The reporter who had responded to the scene interviewed the young woman who had witnessed his death and called 911. The reporter asked the woman who identified herself as Barbara Langston, if she could describe what she saw.

She said, "As I was coming out of the theater, the man who had died, was walking about ten feet ahead of me when I noticed his legs start to buckle and his hand go to his chest, just as he reached his car, where he collapsed as he was turning towards me. I saw a grimace on his face and heard a moan before his head fell to the side. I ran to him, and saw that he was not moving and that his eyes were wide open in a stare. He didn't appear to be breathing. I immediately called 911. At that moment, a man rushed over, placed his fingertips on the fallen man's artery feeling for a pulse. He told me he believed that the man died. Even after he said that he still tried giving him cardiopulmonary resuscitation, attempting to get him breathing, but to no avail. I told him It looked as if the man suffered a heart attack from the way he clutched at his chest grimacing in pain when he fell. He told me he witnessed the same thing. I don't see him here anymore."

The reporter thanked Barbara for her eyewitness account. She then turned and went to the police Lieutenant on the scene and asked him about what he thought was the cause of death. He responded to her question by saying, "Right now we are deeming it natural causes, but cannot rule anything out until we get a medical determination exacting the cause of death."

After watching the events that unfolded after he left the theater, and hearing the eyewitness account, John said to himself, in a self-convincing manner, "Nothing will lead back to me. I did everything right." He felt confident that he had just committed a perfect murder.

As the weeks went by, John heard no more about the incident. It was never aired again on the local news, nor was it mentioned anywhere online. He had no way of knowing if the assumed cause of death was upheld or if a police investigation was on going. All he knew is that no one came to his home inquiring. He felt comfortable to move ahead with the assassination of Senator Roberts. Time was drawing close to the day. The frogs were becoming more potent as he kept them on a steady diet of poisonous insects in their replicated cool moist jungle environment. He figured they were healthy and happy.

The biggest problem he had was keeping his fire ants from attacking the Black Widow spiders. They did not seem to fear any other insect. They simply swarmed their victims from every angle, stinging them to death. He was not worried about running out of the Black Widows, he just wanted to be sure that the frogs got what they needed.

His days at the campaign office ingratiated him to everyone. Betty Ryan and Annette liked and trusted him completely. Annette and he had become romantically close over the ensuing months because John purposely pursued her. His relationship with her was nothing more than a means to an end and that's how he thought about it. He found Annette's loose lips quite useful. Her political contacts provided her with inside dope on the Senator. John made notes of everything she told him in the heat of their moments. His successes had given him a cockiness and an overwhelming confidence in not only committing the deed but expanding his horizons beyond Senator Roberts. He even said to himself, "I'm going to hate wasting good sex, but I can't let her live. I'll take her out when I take out the Senator at the campaign office."

He found himself sitting back, and imagined how many assassinations he could commit within six minutes. If he were going to risk everything, he thought, he'd really make it worthwhile. He knew that there were going to be other political figures he had no love for at the campaign office on election day providing support for Senator Roberts. He thought about how many he could do in, in such a short window of opportunity. According to what he'd learned, just one of his little beauties would produce enough toxin on its skin to kill as many as ten humans and with two frogs he could knock off twenty of those, as he called them, Socialist left-wing scumbags.

John's mental state had changed him completely. He started to think that the only way to change the country was to eradicate those he thought were having a hand in destroying it. He felt like he was becoming the President's guardian angel. He started to swell with pride at being the one to eliminate President Tripp's detractors and clearly defined enemies. He thought his deeds could change the course of history. He even thought that if he got caught, he would be an inspiration to others.

CHAPTER SIX

ANOTHER ONE BITES THE DUST

As time was moving on, John went about his business in a methodical way. He never varied from his routines, and he quit thinking about the man he knocked off at the movie. No police ever showed up at his door. He felt that if they were going to, they would have shown up already. His mind was totally fixed now on the day of the assassination. He mulled over how he would be able to take the toxin with him without having to carry the frog in the same jar that he used at the movie theater. He decided to go back to the public library and do some more research on the creature. He tried to find a way to harvest the frog toxin other than rubbing its skin against his liquid bandage coated hand. After spending considerable time reading many articles, he couldn't find anything on that subject, but learned that the Colombian natives picked up the frogs with leaves, and then drew their darts or arrow heads along their skin, attaching the sticky poison to their weapon. It was no different than what he was doing now. His palm was the dart.

What John also found out, and something that excited him, was that the frog's toxin kept a person's nerves from transmitting impulses, causing their muscles to be in an inactive state of contraction, leading to heart failure. John, upon learning this vital piece of information said in a jubilant voice, "Perfuckingfecto." I bet the man I killed was diagnosed with a fatal heart attack. If all the signs were there, I must assume they didn't look for any other cause of death. It also falls in line with what Barbara Langston said to the reporter about the physical signs my victim indicated when he died in the Multiplex theater parking lot."

At that moment John thought more about his murder victim and decided that he would do some research on what was stated as his cause of death, which he assumed would be noted in his obituary. If it were declared a heart attack, he had a good chance that the Senator would indicate the same signs of death after he became toxified. He also thought that if he went on a campaign killing spree, they would know that the odds of several people dying from what would look like heart failure at the same time would be astronomical. An autopsy and toxicology report would undoubtedly be conducted almost immediately to find the real and common cause of death. The fact that he would be assassinating a high-profile political figure might cause them to do those procedures anyway, except that an autopsy might cause some consternation on Capitol Hill with objections to taking apart the Senator's body if his death were from natural causes. He had to weigh his odds. If he decided at the last minute to murder more than the Senator, he would have to not give a shit about what happened to himself, and in his mind, consider it his patriotic duty to kill as many of President Tripp's enemies as possible when he had the chance. One thing was for sure, he intended on weighing his odds, as he knew that that might be the only time he could knock off anyone of importance.

John went to a drug store and decided to buy a small plastic circular pill box for storing the toxin after having thought of an uncomplicated way to harvest it from the frogs. It would be the ideal container, exceedingly small, about as round as a quarter, with a screw on airtight cap. He did not want to take the slightest chance that anything would interfere with the toxicity and at the same time provide him with a very concealable container. As he was walking from the drugstore, he had an elating thought. "Wow! I don't need to cover my whole palm with the toxin any longer, which is very risky to me, all I need to do is cover my thumb tip with the liquid bandage. The pill box will work perfectly. Yep, just open it up and press my thumb into it for a fresh supply of toxin when I need it. Why I didn't think of this before after so much planning is beyond me. Fuck it. Better late than never as the old saying goes. It's going to work better and give me more freedom. I won't need to just shake hands, I can go up to someone and say, 'Excuse me, you have something on your face. Hold still, let me get it off,' and in a wiping motion with the tip of my toxin laden thumb tip take the piece of nothing off their cheek and kiss their ass goodbye."

After purchasing the pill box, he went back to his home and straight into the kitchen, got a plastic party knife and then headed out to the workshop to begin harvesting the toxin. He learned that the toxin had an incredible shelf life and maintained its potency for at least a year or longer. He could not be happier. He took each frog, one at a time using latex gloves, and proceeded to gently drag the plastic knife's dull edge along their bodies, beading up the toxin onto it, and then slowly transferred it into the plastic pill box. After doing the same to both frogs, he could see a small amount of the toxin had been successfully placed into the container.

John did not know how often the frogs produced the toxin, so he decided that he would do it once a week, thinking it would be enough time for them to recoat their skin. It'd be another thing about the creatures he'd have to research. He really had no concern because he knew that he'd get more than enough toxin to do the job with the scraping of just one frog, let alone two.

John went to the campaign office the next day and went to his desk to start sponging money, when Annette came up to him from behind, gently put her hand on his shoulder and said, "I was thinking about you last night."

He turned around in his swivel chair and asked, "What did you think about?"

Annette replied, "How nice it would be if we took a long lunch together at my place."

John immediately said, "I'd love that. I've been thinking about you as well."

Annette then said to John, "Guess what?"

"I don't know, tell me," he replied.

"Congresswoman Nadine Waterman will be coming to the campaign office. She'll be in town to meet with Senator Roberts to discuss an investigation that's looking into President Tripp's nonprofit corporation. She claims that he misused funds by avoiding taxes and violated campaign laws." Annette replied.

John went crazy in his mind as he listened to Annette's words, and envisioned himself stabbing the woman in her face. He hated her as much as Senator Roberts, without showing any facial expression. He responded to what Annette said, and asked, "How do you know that?"

Annette replied, "Betty told me she heard it from the Senator. He was giving her a heads up that the Congresswoman would be stopping by the campaign office next week with Senator Roberts."

John said, "I'd love to know what day. I'd really like to meet her."

Annette replied, "I'll let you know when Betty tells me."

John responded, "That's great. He then looked straight into Annette's eyes and said, "Let's take lunch now."

Annette smiled and said, "Give me a half hour. I must make a call to a reporter to give him a heads-up on Waterman's arrival. The Senator wants press coverage." Annette then said with a little laugh, "You must be really hungry?"

John, touched her hand, and said, "More than that."

Annette responded, "Me too."

Smiling, she turned and started walking away. She said as she was leaving, "I'll call you when to meet me outside."

John turned back around to his desk and said to himself in a mumbled voice, "I'd love to kill that bitch, Waterman. She's one vile, ugly, bigoted woman and one of President Tripp's main detractors. I need to think hard on how to get her ass. It would be an absolute enjoyment killing her. I need to weigh my options. If I knock her off now, it'll be well before I take out Roberts. She must be at least in her late seventies if not older. If it looked like she died of a heart attack, they might not request an autopsy. I wonder if she's on some blood pressure or heart related medication. That would help defer any suspicion. I need to learn as much about her as I can. I'll give Annette a special lunch with a blue pill appetizer. I'll use her to get more information on Waterman if she has that ability. I have only a small idea of how deep and personal her connections go. I will soon find out."

On the way to Annette's apartment, John began making idle conversation with her. He said, "So Waterman is coming to the campaign office. That's great. I never thought in my lifetime that I would meet so many high-profile politicians."

Annette replied, "You'll meet a lot more. The campaign office gets busier as we draw closer to election day. Many of the top NSP members will come to Florida and do some stumping for John."

"I know it's not nice to make fun of Waterman, but her sagging wrinkled face looks like a Shar-pei dog. How old is she? She must be in

69

her eighties. She's not ageing well," John said, in outward jokingly way, although he meant every word.

Annette laughed and said, "John that was cruel. A Shar-pei? That was descriptive to say the least. She's eighty-two."

John replied, "She should quit and give some young blood with more moderate ideas a chance. I remember a news channel showing her walking up the steps of the Capitol Building. I thought she was going to have a heart attack. I didn't think she had it in herself to make it all the way up."

Annette said, "I heard she's taking medication for blood pressure and something else. I can't recall what was told to me. I think it was calcium for bone loss. Neither one of those meds are unusual for her age."

When John heard Annette say blood pressure medication, an evil smile came over his face. He thought it would take the smallest dose of the toxin to put her out of her misery. "She's my next victim for sure," he uttered to himself.

John then repeated his previous comment and said, "I swear I thought she was going to have a heart attack when she struggled to go up those steps."

Annette responded, "She may look old and wrinkled, and be on some meds, but she's a wily strong woman with all of her faculties. I think she plans on being in office forever."

John saying to himself, "Not if I can help it."

John and Annette finally arrived at her apartment to have lunch, but really didn't take the time to eat. The only thing Annette was hungry for was sex and John was very accommodating. It took only minutes for them to be in bed. After their steamy interlude was over, they showered together, got refreshed, dressed, and headed back to the office. It was obvious to

John that Annette was becoming too emotional in her feelings for him. He would need to end it eventually.

To him she was no more than a useful tool. He could care less about her. He did at times wonder what would happen to her emotionally if he just ended their relationship. He was not ready to lose Katherine, at least not over another woman and one that was no more than a useful tool. He knew that he had to be careful. He concluded that he'd have to find a way to get rid of her permanently. He was beginning to think the toxin was not the answer. If he did use it, he would have to figure out a way to get it on her when he would not be anywhere near her and have an iron clad alibi. He thought that he would figure it out when the time came. Right now, he saw no immediate need. Although he had been incredibly careful in keeping their relationship a secret, and even though Annette said she was doing the same, he could not rely on her word. She had loose lips. That was evident to him.

When John got back to the campaign office, he went straight to his desk, where he found a memo placed on his phone. He picked it up and read it. Betty asked him to come to her office when he got back.

He immediately went to see her. When he arrived, she could see John through her windows and beckoned him in. As he opened her office door, he said in a jovial way, "I got your note to see you. Is there something you want me to do?" he asked.

Betty looked at him with a smile, and said, "The Senator is going to host an informal get together with his key staff here at the campaign office. Not everyone that works here will be attending. I have you on the list of attendees. I've told the Senator about your invaluable fund-raising efforts cold calling individuals on the phone. I don't know if you realize

71

how much money you have solicited from people, but you have set a record here. You have surpassed one million dollars and that is amazing. He wants to thank you personally."

John said, "That's really fantastic. It would be a real pleasure talking to him. You're right. I had no idea that I had sponged a million dollars already. I really thought that I'd struggle doing it as I had no experience at it."

Betty responded, "You took to it like a duck to water. You have an exceptional talent speaking to people. The Senator may want you to be more involved with him, but on a higher level. He's thinking of having you start soliciting corporate sponsors."

"Betty, speaking to people on the phone when you are not looking eye to eye is different than walking up to a corporate Chief Financial Officer and pleading for funds," John replied, "I have a lot of experience sitting face to face with corporate execs, but I know one thing, most of them are looking for is quid pro quo. I can't speak for the Senator. Only he can make those promises."

Betty responded, "John, you'll have the Senator's ears and an ability to call him about things like that. John, this is a fantastic opportunity for you to be amongst the Capitol elite. If it doesn't work out for you, you'll lose nothing. You will be as you are now. But if it does, you could be on the Senator's staff in Washington. Don't say no until you speak to the Senator."

John said, "Wow That's a lot to take in. Talk is cheap and you're right, what'll I have to lose?"

Betty replied, "I'm glad to hear you say that. I have every confidence that you will do well. I told Annette about your opportunity, and she was delighted to hear it. She thinks very highly of you."

John replied, "I think she's a highly intelligent and talented woman. Why wouldn't the Senator ask her."

"John, her talents lie elsewhere. She's a facilitator and handles many things that require quiet negotiations if you get my meaning. Things that are discussed outside the halls of the Capitol. She's well connected as is her family. I don't know if you're aware that her father is Randolph Canter, Chairman of the Board, and largest stockholder of Meridian Electronics Corporation," Betty said.

John asked, "Are you referring to the multibillion-dollar aerospace corporation? The same one that owns Micron Electronics, the largest chip manufacturer in the country?"

"Yes, and Yes," Betty replied.

John said with a surprised tone, "Wow! No I didn't know. That's money. I think she should pay for my lunch the next time we go out."

Betty laughed and said, "Maybe she'll buy the café and give you free lunch forever."

John then said, "If she's that loaded, why does she do campaign work?"

"Do you know how well her family is connected in D.C.? Her father has donated millions to a lot of campaigns. He's already donated money to Senator Roberts. Her father could get to meet with President Tripp, if he needed to, but he won't because he doesn't like the man personally," Betty replied.

John asked, "Why's that?"

"If you want to know that, ask Annette," Betty responded.

John replied, "I would, but I consider our conversation confidential, unless you have no objection to me telling her about it."

Betty responded as she sat further back in her seat, forming a smile on her face, with an admiring look and said, "John, that was extremely admirable of you. You certainly have confirmed to me that you're a man of good character. I'm pleased that you assumed our conversation was confidential, even though I never said it was. It's okay to tell Annette. We're close friends, and what I told you isn't exactly a secret on Capitol Hill."

John then thought, "I wonder if Betty knows about my intimacy with Annette? If Betty and she are that close, I'll need to assume, she knows. Regardless, I won't stop now. Fuck it, I'm on a mission."

"John! Congresswoman Waterman may be attending that get-together. It depends on her schedule. If she comes, I'll introduce you to her. She's someone you'll want to know," Betty said.

John responded, "Yes, I know. Annette mentioned the possibility. I'd really like to meet the Congresswoman. Do you know what day?"

Betty replied, "I believe it'll be next Wednesday. I'll know later today. I'm expecting a call from Senator Roberts. I'll let you and Annette know as soon as I've heard from him."

John replied, "That's great Betty. I'll let you know about the Senator's job offer. I 'll need to discuss it with my wife." John then asked, "Let me ask you, will the position require us moving to D.C?"

"John, I believe you'll be able to work from your home. But I can see you needing to meet me with the Senator in D.C. on occasion. That matter will need to be worked out with him. I'm not one hundred percent sure of what else he may want to put on your plate," Betty replied.

"If I'm going to get another million for the campaign, I better get back to my desk and get on the phones," John said, while wishing he were raising the money for APP candidate Jeanne Collette.

Betty said, "Sounds good. Speak to you later."

John went back to his desk and did exactly as he said, he got on the phone and solicited donations. But all the while he was calling, he became resolute in his plan to murder Waterman. He would do it at the first opportune moment. In between calls he'd sit back momentarily, and plan his move. He visualized many things, and after several run throughs in his head, he decided the best way to assassinate the Congresswoman was when she was leaving the campaign office, and not when she first arrived. He planned to shake both the Senator's and her hand upon their arrival where many people would have witnessed their formal but jovial hellos, without any aftermath.

He planned to be seen close to the Congresswoman, and would try to converse with her whenever she was receptive. He was carefully creating an image of innocence if they should be looking for a suspect later. John felt that Annette would be his perfect foil. Her apparent prominence and family name among the politicos would get him all the introductions and handshakes he needed. He expected that Congresswoman Waterman would be familiar with Annette and her magnanimous father and be willing to give us audience at the Senator's informal and lightly catered event. John thought the setting for the act was perfect. It'll be upbeat, informal, full of friendly people, with security being at ease in the lax environment.

He planned to go into the men's room, coat the tip of his thumb with liquid bandage and then toxin when the time for Waterman's departure drew near. He would, at the moment the Congresswoman began to make her exit, walk up to her with Annette and shake her hand in a goodbye, nice to have met you gesture, making sure to make good contact on the back of her hand with his thumb tip. He knew that it would take several minutes for her to keel over and after she left the campaign office. He was relying on the time being the same it took for the man at the theater to react to the effects of the toxin.

If her bodyguards reacted the way he expected, they would think she had had a heart attack. What could they or anyone else think, he thought? No gunshots, no nothing. Just an agonizing groan, and a grasp at her chest as she fell. There certainly would be a 911 call and some chaos after that.

He expected to clean off the tip of his thumb within minutes after applying the toxin to Waterman's hand and if possible, try to help with the fallen Congresswoman, again trying to be a least likely suspect if an investigation ensued. He expected that they would want to immediately carry her into the campaign office out of caution and lay her on the reception sofa to remove her body from public view. If they didn't, he would not approach where she laid. If there were reporters lingering outside, he'd stay in the campaign office. He couldn't afford to be recorded on camera and appear on television news. If Katherine or anyone that knew him saw him on the news, his cover could be blown. He wouldn't know how to explain being there. It would be awkward to say the least.

The entire scenario as he envisioned it would hopefully play out exactly as he planned. The day of the Senator's special campaign meeting arrived. John was ready and anxious to do his thing. He had the toxin filled pill box and the small bottle of liquid bandage in his pocket. He laughed to himself when he thought he had enough toxin to over kill.

As the day went by, John played it cool. He stayed at his desk and solicited funds. At noon time, Betty invited both he and Annette to join her for lunch. She wanted to confirm the expected arrival of Senator Roberts and Congresswoman Waterman, and to advise them that there would be news reporters showing up, although they would not be invited into the campaign office. The Senator and Congresswoman Waterman would meet with them in the lobby and do their political thing.

As the end of the day neared, the events played out as Betty had stated, the politicians held a joint press conference in the downstairs lobby that lasted for thirty minutes, after which they came up to the main operations area. Betty, Annette, and John were there to greet them as they exited the elevator with their security. The Senator immediately greeted

Betty, and Annette, before extending his hand to shake John's. He then introduced John to Congresswoman Waterman, saying that he was an invaluable fund raiser and volunteer. The Congresswoman extended her hand to John, which he eagerly took in a handshake, and with a smile said, "I am so honored to meet you. You are one of my favorite politicians." Congresswoman Waterman replied, "That's so very nice of you, I do my best up on the hill."

John said, "I love the way you handle the President. You've taken him down a few notches."

Nadine smiling responded, and said, "It doesn't take much to do that."

John thinking to himself after her remark, "It'll take even less to take you down, you dog faced looking hag."

After that brief greeting, John stepped aside and began walking with Annette alongside the Senator as Betty and he talked. Once they were in the operations center, both the Senator and Congresswoman Nadine Waterman greeted the invited staff, and guests. Betty handed the Senator a hand microphone as he started to speak to everyone. He spoke about what he expected of his staff and the approach they'd be taking in their upcoming ad blitz that would be tearing down his rival. The staff cheered "Aaron, Aaron," as he finished his pep talk. He then introduced Nadine and handed her the microphone. She proceeded to talk about the Senator and reiterated her support for him, touting his exemplary record in Washington D.C. After she was finished, everyone clapped and then went to get some drinks and hors d'oeuvres at the caterer's bar, as the mingling began.

Most of the staff ventured to Nadine Waterman to say hello and to have the once in a lifetime opportunity to meet this famous powerful longtime politician. She willingly shook their hands one after the other, and gave her autograph, which pleased John. The more the merrier, he thought. Everyone will be suspect if a criminal investigation were opened, and they are able to identify the toxin that killed the bitch. But he felt confident that she'd be deemed a heart attack victim. He also learned after doing extensive research that the results of a toxicology report could take a month or more, and that many of the labs are not set up to identify the toxin metabolized by the frog. He also learned that they are ordered when they deem the deceased is a victim of a crime, or dies for no glaring reason. The Congresswoman was old and taking blood pressure medications, which he considered underlying factors that could attribute to a heart attack. The groaning from pain and the clutching at the chest that would be witnessed by her bodyguards would tend to take away the "no glaring" reason. Any average person who heard the vocal sounds of pain emanating from her and the physical agony she'd display would have them shouting, "She's having a heart attack." Whether John was right or wrong, he felt confident that he'd pull off another murder and get away with it. He said, to himself, "I've gone this far, I'm not backing out now regardless of what happens later."

He also hated her and how she was grouped with those on Capitol Hill, who thought they were only elected to attack the President and not do their jobs representing the people who elected them.

Finally the time came. Nadine was starting to say her goodbyes and was preparing to leave. John was prepped and ready. He had already thickly coated his thumb tip with the Liquid Bandage. He reached into his jacket pocket, pulled out the pill box, unscrewed its cap and carefully pressed his thumb tip into the toxin. He quickly closed the pill box, placed it back into his pocket, and proceeded to walk toward the Congresswoman to say his goodbye, nice meeting you farewell. He walked to the exit door before she had reached it and said to her as she approached him, "Congresswoman, meeting you has been the highlight of my life."

She smiled at John, and said, "It was a pleasure meeting you as well. Keep up the excellent work for the Senator. I'll look to have you help me in two more years."

He extended his deadly hand and took hers in what would be her last moments of life. He, with absolute evil pleasure, pressed his thumb tip down onto the backside of her hand where it typically lands when shaking a hand, and made sure to have it drag back across as he pulled his hand away.

John said to her as she was now walking out the exit door toward the elevator, "Have a nice flight back to D.C."

Annette who was standing behind him as he turned around to immediately head towards the men's room to wash off his thumb asked, "What did you think of the Congresswoman?"

John replied, "She's a lovely, extremely bright, and articulate woman. Honey, I need to rush to the men's room. I'll be back in a few."

Annette replied, "I'll be with Betty. She's with the Senator in his office."

John responded, as he was quickly walking away backwards, "Okay I'll see you there."

John then turned forward in a hurried pace and went into the men's room and to his surprise, saw no one else in there. He expected a few men with as much drinking that had been going on. He immediately rid his thumb of all evidence using soap and water and a paper towel. Once he saw no evidence of the liquid bandage, he tore up the paper towel into little flushable pieces and sent them down the toilet. He stood in front of the mirror staring at his Mr. Hyde self and said, "You sly evil motherfucker, you did it. You just assassinated a Congresswoman without a soul knowing it was being done."

Even though John felt smug, his heart rate was up, his nerves were on edge as the gravity of what he'd just done truly began to sink in. As he looked in the mirror, he stepped back and said, "Okay, relax, be cool and get your composure. You have a few more to knock off."

John turned toward the exit door and left the men's room to meet with Annette and Aaron Roberts in his office, but expected that there would be people rushing about finding out the Congresswoman had just died. He calculated that at least eight minutes had passed since he applied the toxin to Nadine Waterman, and that she should've had just enough time to make it outside the building before the toxin took effect. Being that she was old and on blood pressure medication the toxin might have felled her in the main lobby.

As he exited the bathroom door, he was completely surprised to see Annette, Betty, and the Senator through the windows of his office talking and laughing. He immediately thought, "Damn it. The toxin didn't work. It should have killed her. It had to have worked. I tested it over and over. If she had died, the Senator, Betty or Annette would not be in his office laughing."

As John neared the Senator's office, Aaron beckoned with his hand for John to come in and join them. John said, "Great speech Senator Roberts. It had me even more motivated to do more to get you re-elected."

Senator Roberts replied, "Thanks John. I think that I've made enough speeches in my lifetime to get good at giving them. As for your motivation, I couldn't be more pleased. Betty told me that you solicited over one million dollars from my base of supporters. That's a phenomenal task from phone calling. Now that we're here together, I know that Betty mentioned to you, I'd like you to join my personal staff. I can use you. I know from Betty and Annette that you're very dependable, a resolute supporter of mine and genuinely concerned about confidentiality. My intentions are to run for the Presidency in another two years and I want people I can trust around me. You don't have to move to Washington. You can work out of this office. Betty told me about your conversation with her. It'll be a salaried position. Betty will discuss those details with you. You'll need to fly up to D.C. on occasion. The cost will be covered by my office."

John said, "Thanks for the offer. It certainly is something I never expected when I volunteered to help your campaign." John then looking at both Betty and Annette, continued to say," Thank you both for your friendship and support. I'm honored by your confidence."

Betty responded, and said, "John, you honestly deserve it. You shouldn't sell yourself short."

Annette added, "You outperformed the entire soliciting staff, and without any experience at it, and by a lot. Our large donations come from corporate supporters and from mass mailings and internet solicitation which reach millions of donors simultaneously. You unabashedly sat and cold called people in their homes, where they least like to be bothered. John, we're all amazed. You surpassed one million dollars, and the money is still coming in from your efforts."

John laughed and said, "Quit it, you're making me blush."

John then turned toward the Senator and said, "Thank you so much for the offer, I'd like to think about it. Working for you would be great, but I'm independently very well off and don't need employment. Tech stocks have been incredibly good to me, so much so, that I'll never have financial need. Volunteering for your campaign was something I enjoyed doing without a permanent commitment."

Senator Roberts responded and said, "John it's good to hear that you did well for yourself, and I can understand personal freedom, but selfishly, I believe that you can help me. Think it over and let me know. John, many wealthy people take jobs in DC and don't need the income. They do it for a multiple of reasons, and one is the influence peddling that permeates Washington." The Senator then said, "Just don't take long and don't say no." With a smile and slight hesitation said, "Just kidding."

All during the four-way conversation, John kept saying to himself, "What the fuck happened to the Congresswoman? The woman should be dead by now. Over thirty minutes have passed already. I'm sure I got ample toxin on my thumb and onto the Congresswoman."

Just as the Senator was finishing speaking, his phone rang. Betty reached over, picked it up and answered, saying, "Senator Roberts Campaign Office. Yes, hold on one moment." She then pressed the hold button, and said to the Senator, "Senator it's the Fort Lauderdale Chief of Police, Adam Devine calling. He needs to speak to you immediately."

Senator Roberts, looked at Betty with a questioning look, took the phone, released the hold button, and answered by saying, "Senator Roberts speaking."

As the Senator was talking, you could see his facial expression change to one of concern, as he immediately rattled off several questions to the Chief in response to what he was saying to the Senator. "Are you absolutely sure? How did it happen? Heart attack! You said in her limousine on her way to the airport."

John who was listening intently to the conversation, but only to the Senator's words, heard the Senator ask, "Where is she at this moment?" Then echoed the Chief's response, "The Fort Lauderdale Memorial Hospital?"

He then questioned the Chief by asking, "Are you sure about the cause of death?"

After hearing a response, the Senator said, "I see, the doctors who attended her confirmed it as a heart attack." Then reiterated what the Chief said, "You say they found strong blood pressure medications in her purse?"

He then asked the Chief as if questioning his statement, "Is that enough evidence to base a heart attack diagnosis on? Just finding blood pressure meds?"

The Chief had responded to Senator Roberts, who in turn, seemed more receptive when he said, "Oh! I see. All of her diagnosed symptoms were heart attack related. And you did say, they did a blood test at the hospital and the results verified her death resulted from a heart attack? They did. Okay. Thank you, Chief Devine. Please let me know when you'll be issuing your official cause of death."

The Chief then told the Senator that it was at the request of the medical staff that the Secret Service agents went through her purse to see what kind of medications she may have in it, if any.

"Okay, that makes sense," the Senator responded.

The Senator then asked the Chief, "If the Federal Agents are still there will you please have them call me. They have my number. Thank you, Chief Devine for informing me." With those last words, the Senator hung up.

From the conversation and the look of consternation on the Senator's face, John got the confirmation he was looking for. He gloated and said to himself, "The toxin worked. The hag died."

John's warped humor had him singing to himself, while looking at the Senator, "Another one's gone, another one's gone. Another one bites the dust, hey, hey, next it's you, next it's you, you're gonna bite the dust."

Betty spoke out before anyone and asked Senator Roberts, "Did I just hear you say that Congresswoman Waterman died of a heart attack?"

Senator Roberts answered and said, "You heard correctly, Congresswoman Waterman died of a heart attack in her limousine on the way to the airport. The Chief of Police told me the hospital confirmed the cause of death as a heart attack."

John said, "Oh! I'm so sorry to hear that. God, I just shook her hand before she left and wished her a safe flight."

Betty stood there with tears in her eyes, and said, "I can't believe it. She looked fine when she was here. I spoke to her a lot, and she evidenced no signs of being sick."

"Heart attacks, just happen out of nowhere. They say that blood pressure is the silent killer, and it will bring on heart attacks," John said.

The phone on the Senator's desk rang again. This time the Senator reached down and answered it himself. Everyone could hear him say, "Agent Carlton, Thanks for the quick call back. Tell me what happened on your watch?"

FBI Agent Carlton explained to the Senator that as they were driving Congresswoman Waterman to the airport, they heard her say that she was not feeling well, and that something was happening to her. The Agent said that as he had his head turned toward her in the back seat, asked her if she wanted them to pull over. He said they did without waiting for her acknowledgement when she began moaning loudly and evidenced severe pain on her face.

He said he had already unbuckled his seat belt and opened the car door as they were pulling alongside the road readying himself to aid the Congresswoman in the rear seat. He said that as he opened the back door, he saw her face evidence extreme agony, her hand clutched to her chest, and heard her last gasp of breath as she died. He said he climbed into the back seat and laid her prone across it, and began giving her artificial resuscitation. Agent Jamison called for medical assistance. Agent Carlton closed the back door, continued to administer resuscitation, and said to his partner to turn on their siren, and head to the hospital. He said he felt that they could get to the hospital before the EMT's could reach them. They called ahead to the hospital to be prepared for their arrival. He claimed he never stopped trying to revive Congresswoman Waterman even though she had no detectable pulse, or evidenced breathing. He continued resuscitating all the way to the hospital. He told the Senator that that they felt certain that she died of a heart attack, and have since gotten confirmation from her attending physician. He ended his conversation with, "As of now, that is the official diagnosis, and we have no other reason to think it was anything else."

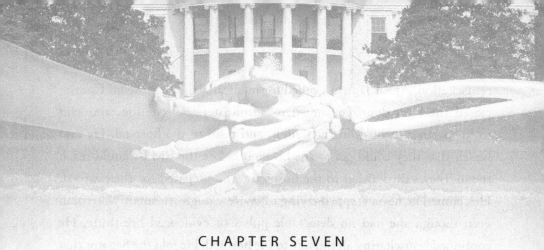

CHAPTER SEVEN

PLANNING THE NEXT FROG EVENT

When John got back home, he saw that Katherine left him a note attached to the refrigerator door with a small magnet. She wrote, "I tried calling you on your cell phone to tell you that I went to my sister's house. You didn't answer. I'll be back around 10 pm. Call me when you get in. Luv K."

John felt it was wise to call his wife back and provide her with some excuse. He dialed her sister Renee's number. Renee picked up the phone and answered by saying, "Hi John, hold on." John quickly replied, "You knew it was me from caller ID?"

Renee laughed and said, "You're so smart."

John laughing replied, "That I am."

Katherine, who had picked up the phone extension and was listening in asked, "Why didn't you answer your cell?"

"Sorry," John replied, "The battery was dead. I thought, I charged it overnight, but I didn't have it plugged into the outlet far enough, or something. I had no way to call you."

"Ok, I'll forgive you this once," Katherine replied.

John, making light of it, responded, "Just this once? Do you mean I'll no longer be forgiven by you no matter how small the transgression?"

Katherine replied, "Hmmm, I'll have to think about it. Ok, I won't make it forever. I'll keep it at ten years."

John, keeping up the humor said, "Ooh thank you. Ten years is so kind of you."

Katherine asked, "How was class today?"

John continuing his deception, replied, "It was good. It actually ran longer, because several of the students, including me, were needing more help with programming. The instructor was nice to continue class past the time allotted."

It was easy for John to deceive Katherine. He was living a second life and had no choice but to be good at it. The longer he lived his lie, the more he enjoyed it and the less he cared about deception or her, especially when he assassinated someone. His Mr. Hyde persona felt an elated perversion and nothing or anyone was going to stand in his way. His self-imposed mission was all that mattered.

John knew that when he killed the man in the movie theater, he had no ties what-so-ever to his victim. Linking him to a random act of murder would be difficult at best, but murdering the Congresswoman was going to be different. They could easily put him in her company if they should decide to start an investigation and question anyone who came into contact with her. But he had self-confident arrogance thinking his murder method was too perfect and he made himself appear to be the least likely suspect. Regardless of what would happen John was prepared to face his consequences, but not before he did in Senator Roberts. He would continue to move ahead with his plan, especially since he had conjured up a simpler way to use the Liquid Bandage and the toxin. Just coating his thumb tip, and harvesting the toxin worked better than expected. He intended to keep harvesting the toxin and storing it in the quarter size pill box. He originally had some concern about how much toxin the frog would produce, but learned that they continually produced toxin nonstop, just like humans produce saliva. The beautiful thing about the toxin was that it didn't need to be stored at a special temperature, while keeping its toxic strength beyond a year.

John turned on his television and went to the news channel to see if anything would be reported about the Senator. It was no surprise to see Anchorman Darren Dansk covering the "Breaking News" story about Congresswoman Waterman's death. Keeping it a secret for any length of time would have been impossible. Her admittance to the hospital was bound to be leaked. As he listened intently to the news coverage, Dansk mentioned that his sources confirmed Congresswoman Waterman died of a heart attack while being driven to the airport by her security escort.

What John enjoyed about his dastardly deed was Waterman's death would create a loss of a particularly important seat in Congress, and what was even more enjoyable to him was that with her death, her State Governor must arrange for a special election to fill her vacancy and there was far from a guaranteed win by another NSP candidate. Her district had turned from blue to purple. Redistricting had moved more Patriot Party residents into her area.

The more he thought about the effects of her death, the happier he became. He knew she would no longer be an antagonist to President Tripp, and the investigation she was heading up against him, would come to a halt or at least not driven with the same overly hateful fervor that Waterman had to bring him down.

After listening to the news and feeling satisfied that everything was going smoothly, he went to check on his frogs and found his little beauties thriving. John stood over the terrarium staring down, talking to his frogs. He said, "It's unbelievable that you tiny creatures, are so lethal. Christ! You pack one deadly punch."

After that brief moment of admiration, he took a few minutes to mist the terrarium foliage, add some water to the small pond in the center of it, and a few beetles which he saw lacking.

John genuinely believed he was a crusader for the cause of freedom. Instead of thinking micro murder he thought macro. He lost all sensibility when he decided to go to the library and compile a complete list of every NSP Senator and Congressperson and rate each one in the order of importance based upon his agenda. He would attempt to assassinate the NSP members of the Investigation Committee looking into President Tripp first, before going after anyone else on his hit list.

Realizing that the toxin caused heart failure, he decided to take age into consideration. He knew from reported statistics that the most probable cause of death with the aged was heart failure, so he decided that the oldest representatives would be his next victims, after Senator Roberts, unless an irresistible opportunity to take out a younger one presented itself.

He would begin murdering the sixty-five and older age group first. He knew that to draw less suspicion he'd have to space their deaths apart. Two heart attacks in the same place at the same time, wouldn't be considered coincidental.

He had no idea how he was going to execute such a grandiose killing spree, but it didn't matter. It fueled his sense of purpose. He looked at it as a lifelong endeavor. He would simply play it by ear. His fantasies were becoming more insane and riskier, but his insanity did not skew his lucid and cunning thought process.

His two murder successes played more and more into his psyche. To him, anyone on the left was fair game, especially those that attacked his President. Hollywood notables were being included in his ever-expanding lists of potential victims. John actually quit watching the movies of those movie stars who made vile comments about the President, especially those that actually wished Tripp harm with no repercussions from the Department of Justice, or as John called it, the Department of Injustice.

His patriotism was so radical that he lost all sense of reality. His hate for the left permeated throughout his very being as he became insanely focused on the President's political foes. If he had the opportunity to murder any Socialist along the way, he would. He felt the President was the true savior of the country and that the majority of the nation would embrace communism without his leadership. He convinced himself in his skewed mentality that he'd be the President's secret weapon, like an Angel carrying a sword for God, ridding the Earth of evil.

John felt certain that if he continued down his expanding road, the deaths would eventually be linked to the toxin. Even realizing that, he just didn't care. All he knew was that he was on a crusade to rid the world of the left-leaning lunatics and his life meant nothing compared to the good he would be doing. John laughed and said to himself, "I can only die once for committing one murder or a hundred, so I might as well enjoy myself, and kill them all." He found humor in the fact that he would never run out of ammunition.

John would step in and out of normalcy. He constantly talked to himself and no longer cared about Katherine in the same way or how his actions would affect her if she ever found out. He became oblivious to those thoughts because he convinced himself that he was too cunning and smart to be caught. He told himself that if Joseph De Angelo, the Golden

State Killer could get away with his rapes and murders for thirty years why couldn't he get away with his murders? He just needed to be smart and put all fear aside.

John watched the news constantly for any changes to Congresswoman Waterman's reason for death or anything that would have him prepare for an FBI visit, but nothing changed.

When it was announced that the Congresswoman would be laid in state at the Capitol Rotunda for two days, honoring her devoted years of public service and her achievements during her term in office, John said while brimming with an elated confidence, "I feel like a ninja with a stealth weapon knocking off these assholes. They're obviously satisfied with her cause of death, or just maybe the Department of Justice knows how she died and is keeping it secret. They might be more concerned about image than the truth because it would erode confidence in the Secret Service if everyone found out that a high-profile Congresswoman was knocked off while in their safekeeping. The repercussions would be irreparable."

Even though John thought that possibility, he felt confident that they just accepted the hospital's cause of death.

Who would be next on his list? That was his question. It had to be a Capitol Hill politician and one he could meet personally for his deadly handshake. He thought that he'd have a get together with Annette and subliminally pick her brain and try to produce his next candidate before his assassination of Roberts. He would love to take the job offered to him by Senator Roberts, knowing it was an ideal means to carry out his assassinations, but it made no difference at this point. He was going to kill the man before that would happen.

Right now he had Annette, and he would use her as much as he could. Her contacts were invaluable. He felt that one introduction would lead to another until he wrangled his way into the presence of his next victim. All he could do for the time being, is play it by ear and keep focused on doing in the Senator.

John decided to turn on the Vox News channel and watch one of his favorite segments The Capitol Hill Report, hosted by a staunch President Tripp supporter, John Flannity. He enjoyed watching this particular show, because he rarely brought on left wing commentators like Dick Feller or Rhonda Branille, and did not hesitate to call out the politicos. He felt it was one of the last bastions of good news reporting for conservative thinkers like himself.

As he sat back on his couch listening to Flannity's commentary, he became incensed at what he was saying. John said in response to what he heard "What the fuck! That is absolute bullshit." Flannity had just reiterated what was being falsely reported in the New York Reporter; that President Tripp was putting illegal aliens in chain link cages like animals while being forced to drink toilet water.

John responded further to Flannity's commentary and said, "Those pens were holding areas-built years ago, you lying dick wads, and well before Tripp became President and those toilets had water fountains in them. They didn't drink from the toilet bowls you ass holes. Those pens weren't built for comfort. I need to find out what fucking reporter made up that shit and shake their hand and watch as they take their last breath."

He listened to Flannity over the course of an hour and on more than one occasion let out outbursts of vulgarity at what he was hearing. He did not have to worry about letting out his hate-filled political commentary as Katherine was still out. He felt free to vent his anger and release his frustration at what he was witnessing in D.C. even if it was momentary.

He began to relive all of the events and again fantasized killing everyone. He drifted in and out of reality. The daily bombardment of left-wing politics, the intimidation of cancel culture and the insanity of the woke crowd affected him in such a way that his Political Stress Disorder, which was becoming increasingly worse, heightened his Mr. Hyde personality.

John then switched from Vox News to News Facts USA, after Flannity's hour was over. He had no desire to listen to the next host he considered an APP in name only. He felt that all she did was flank herself with her Socialist commentators. She never called them out on their lies. On more than one occasion he would shout at her as if she could hear him, saying "Why in the hell didn't you refute that lie." He finally decided he could no longer watch her cowardly self, and never would again.

John could hear the front door open and close and knew that Katherine had come home. His demeanor immediately became calm as he greeted her. "Hi sweety, how was your day?"

Katherine replied, "Everything was good. How was yours?" she asked.

"Everything was good," he replied and then asked, "How is your sister Renee doing?"

"She's doing fine. She's been busy painting her home and doing some remodeling," Katherine replied.

"What kind of remodeling is she doing?" John asked.

"She's upgrading her kitchen cabinets, and she changed her sliding glass patio doors to solid mahogany ones with designs in the glass. They are really nice. Her kitchen cabinets are mahogany as well. I think you'd like what she's done," Katherine replied.

John responded by saying, "If you liked it, then I'm sure I will. We have similar tastes."

Katherine looked toward the TV and asked, "Can we put on a movie or something? I really don't want to watch the news. It's depressing lately."

'It damn sure is," John replied in a somber tone. "I really can't stand the constant attacks against Tripp." He then responded to Katherine's request and asked, "Do you want me to put it on Netflix, or Prime? There's a ton of movies to choose from."

"That sounds good. Pick out some sci-fi movies. I'm in the mood for aliens and space travel," Katherine replied.

"There's another 'The Thing' movie out. I watched the preview the other day. The introduction read as a prequel to the original. I'm sure we haven't seen it," John said.

"Put it on. I'm going to make some coffee; do you want some?" Katherine asked.

"Sounds good," John replied.

All the while John and Katherine watched the movie, John's mind was on everything else. His thoughts raced from the things he had done to the things he was planning. Although he was anxious to murder Senator Roberts, he couldn't help but keep wondering if the Federal Bureau of Investigation was investigating Congresswoman Waterman's death. Yes, nothing had transpired in over a month to indicate they were, but that didn't mean they weren't. Congresswoman Waterman was laid to rest with no breaking news about her being assassinated. To be extra cautious, he decided to play it as if her death was being investigated. He would be even more careful moving on to Roberts, especially when he didn't want to stop there. He was now considering his assassination of Senator Roberts as his steppingstone into infamy. He had watched a documentary on the World at War which covered the roles of Prime Minister Winston Churchill, General Eisenhower, and General George Patton among others and focused on their world-changing achievements. He wanted to be remembered in the same way.

In his skewed patriotic way of thinking he thought, that as he rid the world of the National Socialist Party politicians, he would move the United States toward a more historical sense of country and personal freedom. He saw the collapse of his beloved nation under its present course, and he wanted to make his mark in history. He did not consider that he might be aligned with infamous serial killers, like John Wayne Gacy or Ted Bundy, because they didn't murder for a cause. He set himself apart from such infamous maniacs.

Over the course of the next few days John sat at his computer and worked on his online computer course. He needed to keep Katherine content with his efforts and to keep up his facade.

After those few at home days, John took a trip to the campaign office, and once arriving decided to ask Betty if she knew how Senator Roberts was taking the death of Waterman. He really didn't give a damn how anyone felt. He just wanted to see if she would let him in on anything that might be transpiring behind the scenes. If anyone would get inside information from the Senator it would be Betty, his most trusted confidant.

Without hesitation he walked up to her office, stood in the doorway, gently knocked to get her attention, and as she turned toward him, he said, "Good morning, Betty, do you have a second?"

Betty replied, "Yes, come in."

"I was wondering how the Senator was doing after the death of his close friend, Congresswoman Waterman," John asked.

"He's been saddened by her untimely death, but he has moved on. He's so busy that he does not have time to grieve," Betty replied.

"Her sudden death was a shock to everyone on the Hill. I still can't get over speaking to her, even for that one moment, just before she passed. She was such a wonderful person. I only wish that I had the opportunity to meet her again. Capitol Hill will miss her fiery spirit. I loved the way she tore into President Tripp," John said.

"Her death was a shock to me. I guess her age and very demanding stressful position was too much for her and suffering from high blood pressure didn't help. She was a nice person. I liked her," Betty replied.

Now that John had started the dialogue about the Congresswoman, he cunningly asked,

"I was curious. Do they do autopsies on high-ranking political figures, or is that a no, no?" John then said, "I would think that that would be frowned upon when dealing with such a notable person."

Betty replied, "From what I know, no autopsy was conducted, as they didn't see the need. The Secret Service Agents escorting her confirmed to the Senator that they accepted the medical diagnosis from the hospital. She passed away in her limousine while in their custody. There was no reason indicated that she died in any other way."

"I know they reported her death on the news as a heart attack. I was curious about whether they autopsied the bodies of Capitol Hill politicians. It's something that seems so gross and unnecessary to me," John said.

Betty replied, "An autopsy isn't a standard protocol to determine cause of death whether or not you are a politician. I think that they'd do it, no matter who you were, if the death seemed suspicious or was of violent nature, like President John Kennedy's was. They autopsied him after he was shot, and a bullet through his head is as obvious a cause of death as you can get. I don't know the laws covering autopsies, but I believe that someone's spouse or close relatives can either request or deny one from being done. I guess it depends on State Law."

John having heard the response he was looking for smiled, then smartly segued away from the conversation, and said, "Well, I think I'll start cranking on the phone and sponge up some more money for the Senator."

Betty smiled at John and said, "That sounds like the thing to do. Keep it rolling in. Congratulations on that $50,000 donation you solicited from the law firm of Justise, Collins and Worth. How'd you do that?" she asked.

"Wow! I wasn't sure that they'd even make the donation. I spoke to James Justise, one of the partners about helping the Senator out. He said he'd discuss the donation with his other partners and left it at that. That's terrific. I'm glad," John replied.

Betty asked, "How did you get to speak to a partner? They're a pretty good-sized law firm. They have at least one hundred attorneys on board."

"I was given a direct introduction by a dear old attorney friend of mine, after I called him to dig into his pockets and fork up a few bucks for the cause. He laughed and said to me that he was not interested in helping Senator Roberts as he was supporting Collette. But being my close friend, he recommended I call Mr. Justise. They graduated together from the same law school. William told me James evidenced a very liberal mentality in law school and to ask him to donate. He gave me Justise's number and told me to tell him that he said hello. What was funny about the whole thing is that as long as I've known William, I never knew he was a Patriot. I don't remember ever talking politics with him. Everyone has a right to their own thinking. As the old saying goes, 'That's what makes horse races. I believe that boosted my numbers this month," John replied.

"They're looking good. Your numbers already match last month and that was a record here for solicitations. Congratulations John," Betty said.

John then said, "Before I forget, Mr. Justise said that he'd like to meet the Senator one day and offer his legal services if ever the Senator wanted them. I told him I was only a volunteer, but I'd bring his request to the Campaign Manager."

Betty replied, "We may just want to take him up on that one day, but there are no guarantees as the Senator is well connected with law firms in D.C. That would be strictly up to the Senator. The donation certainly merits an introduction. What they discuss and agree to, is up to them."

John replied, "Thanks, I can't ask for more. Well let me get to my desk and see if I can top that."

CHAPTER EIGHT

THE DEADLY HANDSHAKE DRAWS NEAR

The days were rapidly dwindling, and the time was drawing ever so near when John would shake Senator Roberts' hand for the last time. He could hear himself saying to the Senator, "It has been a pleasure knowing you and a real pleasure shaking your hand. Good luck tomorrow on your bid for re-election," as he would firmly grasp his hand, with his thumb tip doubly coated with the frog toxin pressed against the Senator's hand.

John was now confident that he would be successful in his assassination. He saw no obstacles in his way and became insanely upbeat about what he was going to do. Every so often he could hear himself humming his favorite tune, "Another one's gone, another one's gone, another one bites the dust, hey, hey Roberts the next one's you. You're gonna bite the dust."

John was pleased at how well his deception was working on Katherine, and everyone at the campaign office, including Annette, who he held a deep hatred for, because he could not keep his politics out of the equation. Regardless of their occasional passion, she was no more than a useful pawn in his assassination plot. Speaking of Annette, John was going to be with her after his day at the campaign office. The last time he saw her, she enticed him to have dinner at her apartment and eat what he considered dessert.

John constantly would retrace his steps over and over in his mind, making sure of everything he had done and wondering if he could have executed his plan any better. But he found nothing he regretted.

The evening came when John reached Annette's home. With a bottle of wine in his hand, he rang her doorbell. After a moment she opened the door and let him in. As he stepped inside, he could see her dressed in a thin negligee. He stood away from her, taking in every inch of her slender body and said, "Forget dinner, let's get right to dessert. How do you expect me to sit and have dinner with you, dressed like that?" Annette laughed just before kissing him, then stepped back, and said, "I was hoping that we could start with dessert." With that said, she took the wine from John, placed it on the table, took him by the hand and led him directly into the bedroom.

Once they were inside there was no further conversation other than the sounds of passion. After making love, John looked down at Annette, with his body above hers and said, "Honey, I've worked up an appetite."

She reached her arm up around his neck, pulled him back down, kissed him along his ear and said, "Yes, you did."

John did not hesitate to get up and beckon Annette into the shower with him. He knew that he wanted to wash any scent of her off his body. He could not take the chance that Katherine would notice any hint of Anette clinging to him. Annette was becoming more romantic with John as their truly one-sided relationship developed. She was falling in love with him, while he was simply acting the part and using her. He intended on playing the lover role until he knocked off the Senator, and then, her as well. Besides never forgetting her vile comments against Tripp and his desire to murder her he didn't want to take a chance on her posing a risk to him in an investigation.

As John was eating dinner with Annette, their conversation, went from after sex banter to campaign politics when Annette said to John, "Betty told me that Congresswoman Nannette Pelovski would be coming to visit Senator Roberts sometime next week. She believes it'll be on Wednesday, but that date hasn't been confirmed."

John asked, "What do you think is the reason for her to come down off Capitol Hill to see the Senator? That woman rarely visits her own state district, let alone Florida."

Annette replied, "Betty told me that she's going to discuss the current investigation she's conducting against Tripp and wants to talk some strategy she's planning and wants his advice and support. Betty alluded to me that Pelovski is planning some devious moves against the President but wouldn't disclose what it was. She just laughed and said that Nannette was up to her usual conjured up accusations. She's always trying to distract Tripp from performing his duties as President."

While John was listening to Annette, his fist became clenched, his heart raced as an unbelievable anger swelled up in him. He fought against his emotions as he couldn't blow his fake persona by letting out Mr. Hyde and an outburst of rage. Annette would never to be able to comprehend such a display. She only knew him as a staunch left winger, and someone overly dedicated to their cause. He actually envisioned himself, not only killing Pelovski, but Annette and Betty on more than one occasion.

His mind raced back and forth, from one angry thought to another. Each one being eviler than the next. He lived instant fantasies of mass murder. He envisioned himself standing behind kneeling National Socialist Senators and Congresspeople with an automatic weapon, shooting them all, and saying as he pulled the trigger and blew their brains out, "Die you motherfuckers."

As Annette was talking, her voice became inaudible. All John could hear was his own inner angry voice. His thoughts became so real that he had an out of body experience. He became lost to all reality and surroundings. His eyes became glazed and fixed in a stare that blurred out the vision of Annette who sat right across the table in front of him.

After a moment, Annette's voice reached him like a repeating echo, "John, John, John, are you alright?"

With her echoing call, John snapped back into reality, bringing Annette into focus, and replied, "Yes. I'm sorry, my mind wandered for a second. I was deep in thought about us."

Annette asked, "You were? What were you thinking?"

Being quick on his feet, he said, "I was thinking that I would like another helping of dessert."

Annette, laughed, and said, "I think I'll have some more with you."

She then got up from her chair, walked around the table toward him, reached out her hand and said, "There's plenty more where that came from. Come let me give you another serving."

John, not really wanting to stay too late, considering Katherine, couldn't turn down another helping, and said with a smile, "I'll need a bib for this one."

When John got back home, he saw Katherine sitting in front of their home smoking a cigarette and talking to Delores their neighbor. He knew that he would need to get into the shower quickly. He remembered Annette's keen scent and realized he hadn't showered like he wanted to. There were times he thought Katherine suffered from Hyperosmia. Her heightened sense of smell was like that of a dog. She could pick up odors when he couldn't. It was weird, to say the least. He knew that he wouldn't be able to conjure up an excuse if she said something.

As he approached them, he said, "Hello Sweetness, Hello Delores. How are you?" Delores responded by saying, "I'm doing fine. Katherine was telling me that you are taking a computer course."

John answered, "Yes. I am. I felt a need to do something more with my time." Katherine then said, "You are later than usual."

"Yeah Honey," John replied, "I stopped by Home Depot to look at ceiling fans. The one in our bedroom needs to be replaced. I decided to look online at what Lowes carries before I buy anything."

Katherine responded, "I'm glad you remembered about that. It's starting to make an annoying hum."

John knowing his urgency to shower, said, "Delores, you'll need to excuse me, but I have an urgent matter to take care of, if you'll understand."

Delores, smiled, and said, "Yes I do."

John swiftly moved into the house and rushed to undress and shower. He made sure to put his underwear down under the clothes in the hamper. He did not want them lying on top, just in case. It was his overly cautious way of dealing with things.

John was incredibly adept at lying. He knew Home Depot was a perfect coverup and did not hesitate to use it as an excuse to account for his time. He wondered if he would be able to take a third serving of dessert with Katherine. John felt guilty that he had been neglecting her sexually, and needed to make sure he pleased her. The more he thought about it, the better the idea. Making love to Katherine, would keep her happy and unsuspecting.

When Katherine came in, John was standing in his bathrobe. He smiled at her, let it fall open, and displayed his toned nude body and a partial erection. She looked at him and asked, "What is all of that about?"

John replied, with a Cheshire cat grin, as he walked toward her and said," I was thinking about you all day and how much I love you and want you. I think you can see that."

Katherine walked up to John, wrapped her arms around him, pressing her body against his and kissed him. She then said in his ear with her cheek against his, "I love you too."

The next day, John kept thinking about what Annette told him, and considered killing Pelovski when she arrived. He had to carefully plan every move. He considered that if he knocked Pelovski off in the same way as Waterman, there was a high probability an investigation would ensue. Two deaths of high-profile powerful politicians in the same way at the same location would seem too coincidental for the Secret Service. He would weigh his options. He definitely did not want to miss the opportunity, but knew that his main target was Senator Roberts from the beginning.

John didn't know Pelovski's age, but felt certain she was a septuagenarian and a suitable candidate for his heart attack mimicking toxin. If he were going to execute his desire to kill her, she'd also have to die outside of the Senator's campaign office. Pulling that off would be extremely difficult knowing the reaction time of the toxin was about six minutes. That left him with a difficult window of opportunity.

As the day went by, his mind would wonder in and out of his dilemma. It was while having dinner with Katherine that an idea hit him. He realized that he did not have to kill her, all he had to do was render her incapable of carrying out the tasks of her office. He remembered reading that if the toxin didn't cause death, it would cause total paralysis and certainly paralysis would force her out of office. That 'Aha moment' gave him a momentary bit of excitement, until he realized he had no idea how to do it. He had no way of controlling the amount of toxin he applied to her hand. It was not the type of toxin that could be metered in doses, and if an amount no bigger than two grains of sugar could kill a person how could he even begin thinking of a way to apportion it in a non-lethal but debilitating amount and still be able to deliver it from his hand to hers? After mulling the idea around in his brain, he could not convince himself that he could pull it off. For the time being it would be a fully coated thumb tip as usual.

After continuing to ponder his dilemma, he decided to do some quick experimenting with the frog toxin. He went into his workshop where he decided to stir his toxin coated plastic party knife into a small paper cup full of water to see if the toxin lost any of its potency. He made sure to put on a pair of latex gloves during the dilution process. Once he completed the process, he placed the cup in a safe place. He then went to the pet store and bought a few white mice for his test subjects. Once he had them, he went back home to test the effects of the diluted toxin. He placed one of the mice in a small cage and firmly gripped the other in his hand while he dipped a Q-tip into the poisoned water, then carefully wiping it across the mouse's nose. He proceeded to place it into the cage for a wait and see. As he watched the mouse move around, he heard Katherine calling him. He could see her standing across the lawn waiting for him. As he neared her, she said, "John, here is your cell phone. You had a missed call; I couldn't get to it in time to answer it for you."

John rarely got any calls on his cell phone, and made sure that both Annette and Betty knew only to contact him by text using WhatsApp, which Katherine had no idea about, so he felt it wasn't them.

John replied, "Honey, it's some spam bullshit. I rarely get calls on my cell. The only one that usually calls me is you." When John reached

Katherine, she handed him his cell. He looked down at the number that called and said, "I don't recognize the number. I'll call it later. I'm straightening out my workshop. I always mean to clean it up, but never get to it."

After his comment to Katherine, he put his cell in his back pocket, and headed back to the workshop. John, said to himself, "Why in the fuck did Annette call me? She knows better." He recognized the number the minute he looked at it. He became incensed at her for doing what she did. Putting his phone immediately into his back pocket was John's subliminal way of indicating to Katherine that the call had no importance.

As soon as John went back inside the workshop, he aimed his anger at Annette by saying," Damn you. I told you not to call me on my cell." He then focused on the mice. He could immediately see the toxin infected mouse was lying on its side, with no sign of movement. He reached into the cage and picked it up. He looked at it really close and carefully touched it to see if it still had life. At first it appeared dead, but he then detected it was still alive. He could see its eyes open, but showed no sign of other physical movements.

He couldn't ascertain whether or not it was paralyzed other than the fact it wasn't moving. He knew that the diluted toxin had some affect, but wasn't sure, to what extent. He couldn't tell whether or not it was permanently paralyzed or in a coma. He placed the motionless mouse back into the cage and would check it again later in the day. He hoped it would still be alive when he came back. If it remained alive and motionless, he would assume that the dilution idea for limiting the toxin to paralysis worked. But just getting lucky with a mouse was far different than getting the same results with Pelovski. He needed to mull the idea around some more. He had to be absolutely certain about the outcome.

John didn't forget the phone call from Annette even when he was toying with the mouse. He remained irate and needed to speak to her at his first opportunity away from Katherine. He locked the workshop and left. He went back into his home, but before doing so, erased all of his "Recent calls." He had memorized Annette's number and had no need to store it.

He paced around his house fuming. The more he thought about Annette's call, the angrier he got. John's mental state was no longer stable after killing two people, let alone suffering from Political Stress Disorder, which continued to get worse. Being among his socialist enemies and hearing their constant attacks and plots against President Tripp was an even greater catalyst that fueled his need to kill.

John needed to call Annette. He was becoming beside himself. Seeking a reason to leave, he asked Katherine, "Do you need anything from the store?"

Katherine replied, "I think we need some milk. Check and see if we have enough bread. What store will you go to because Winn Dixie is having a sale on Chicken breasts? They are buy one, get one free."

"I'll go to whichever store you want. Winn Dixie, Publix, Fresh Market, it makes no difference to me, they're all clustered together," John replied.

Katherine then asked, "Would you get me some cigarettes?"

"I guess. I wish you'd quit those nasty things," John replied.

John left immediately and drove away from the house. As he got a few streets away, he pulled over to the side of the road and immediately called Annette.

As soon as the phone rang, Annette answered, as if she were anticipating his call. John said in a somber tone, "You called me while I was at my home. My wife tried to answer the phone for me as I left it in the house. Thank God she couldn't get to it in time. What would you have said to her if she asked who you were? Why didn't you just send me a text on WhatsApp? I told you that I don't have sound alerts on my phone for incoming messages, but I check them constantly. If she knew about us my life would become a living hell and I'm quite honestly, not ready to deal with a scene like that."

Annette, being insecure because of her emotional ties to John, replied, "John, I'm sorry. I know what you told me, but I had to let you know that something urgent has come up at the campaign office."

John after listening to Annette, simmered down, but not letting her off the hook said, "You still could have sent me a written message."

John then softened his tone saying, "I'm sorry that I was so abrupt with you. I should have reasoned that you would not have called me the way you did unless there was something important. It was the way I found out that got me crazy."

Annette replied, "It's okay John. I would have reacted the same way if I were in your shoes. I'm sure it was awkward."

"Annette, my love, it's okay. I'm past that now. What earth shattering thing happened at the campaign office?" John asked.

"We got a visit from the Secret Service about Congresswoman Waterman's death," Annette replied.

When John heard Annette's words, he got immediately queasy, but maintained his composure, and asked calmly as if unaffected by what she said, "What were they asking?"

Annette replied, "They said, that they were just doing a follow up inquiry about her death as a matter of routine, because of her position in the government. They just needed to complete their report because the Congresswoman died while in their protection, and it needed to include interviews with those that were in her company just before her death."

John asked, "What's so urgent about that? It sounds like they're just dotting their i's and crossing their t's to cover an embarrassment."

"What I wondered about, is why they questioned her behavior and asked if I noticed anything strange about her physical movements when she was at the campaign office. They asked if she seemed sick at any time. I told them that I didn't notice anything unusual at all. I didn't see any signs of a pending heart attack if that was what they were asking," Annette replied.

"What did they say to that?" John asked.

"They asked me if I knew the signs of a heart attack and I said from what I understood, people experienced sweating, shortness of breath, crushing pain in the chest, and shooting pain in the arms and neck," Annette replied.

"Why do you consider what seems like a routine visit to complete a report so urgent?" John asked, then said, "They were concerned that their agents should have been more observant of her physical condition and were trying to find out if they missed the signs. The woman died of a heart attack, and they can happen instantly without warning."

Annette replied, "John, they seemed interested in you. They went down a list of the personnel that work at the campaign office and then asked about you. I told them that you were a valued volunteer for Senator Roberts. They wanted to know if I knew when you would be here again. I told them the days you volunteered and that you always showed up like clockwork. They told me that they would be back to speak with you and a few of the others that were not at the office when they were there. I just wanted to give you a heads up."

John said, "Thanks. I'll talk to them. I have no problem with that. I don't know anything more than you. I'm not a medical professional to render a medical observation about someone who is going to die of a heart attack. She seemed chipper whenever I talked to her, but you know that. We were usually together when we talked to Waterman. I expect that they'll be there tomorrow when I arrive."

"Will I see you tomorrow after work? I'd like your company," Annette asked.

"I think so. Right now I would say yes unless something else stands in my way. See you at work. I need to go," John replied.

After John ended his conversation with Annette, he thought about what she told him and said to himself, "I don't trust those sneaky fucks. I will act completely calm and just answer their questions and not elaborate. They're not stupid and would love to have someone say something that they shouldn't, just like what happened to General Wynn. He felt comfortable talking to them and ended up in jail even though he was innocent. That shit won't work with me."

He continued on to the supermarket. When John got back from the store, he made a quick dash to check on the condition of the mouse, and found it still alive, but still not moving. He could only assume that it was paralyzed, and his dilution idea worked. Even with that apparent success, he still didn't know if the same dilution amount would have the same effect on Pelovski. He had no way of measuring it.

The next day, John headed out to the campaign office with an air of confidence. He kept reassuring himself that the Secret Service did not do an autopsy, and held firm in his mind, that they knew nothing other than what was reported in the news.

When John entered the building, he noticed two men dressed in business suits standing at the reception desk. He immediately assumed that they were Secret Service. He just walked past them and headed to the elevator. As he pushed the up button, the men started walking his way. John acted nonchalant and paid them no mind. As the elevator doors opened, he stepped into the car, with both men right behind him. He pushed the third-floor button and turned his back toward the side of the car as he faced them. They looked at each other and John smiled, and nodded his head as a greeting. They did not say anything, nor did they acknowledge his hello. As he stepped out of the elevator and began walking away, he could see them walking toward Betty's office. He was now certain that they were the Feds.

He stayed calm, went toward his desk, and sat down. He picked up a few memos and began reading them without glancing towards Betty's office. He acted completely aloof at their presence and did not want them to even think he knew who they were. If they wanted to talk to him, Betty would call him on his desk phone and ask him to come to her office.

After reading the messages John decided to go to the break room and get a cup of coffee. As he was pouring a cup, Betty came up to him and told him that there were two Secret Service Agents that wanted to talk to him. With that announcement she said, "John, there is nothing at all to worry about. They are just asking anyone that spoke to Congresswoman Waterman if they noticed anything unusual in her behavior before she left here."

John looked at Betty and simply said, "I didn't see anything wrong with her. She seemed fine to me. It's no problem, Betty, I'll talk to them, although I can't say anything more to them than what I just said to you. I assume they're in your office?"

Betty replied, "No John, I placed them in the conference room. There are a few others that they will talk to after you."

John walked away from Betty and headed to the conference room. As he entered, he walked up to the conference table where they were sitting across from him. He set his cup of coffee down, extended his hand and said, "Hello gentlemen, I'm John Meade." Both agents stood up and reached across the table, each shaking his hand while introducing themselves. "John, nice meeting you, I'm agent William Carlton and this is Agent Peter Jamison." Agent Jamison said, "Nice meeting you. Please have a seat."

John sat down at the agents beckoning and when doing so said, "Betty briefed me as to why you wanted to talk to me. Like I told her, I didn't notice anything odd about Congresswoman Waterman's behavior. She seemed perfectly fine to me. She was an overly sweet person, and it was an honor meeting her. That's all I can say."

John was now in a zone. He acted as any normal unsuspecting innocent person would. He was calm and jovial. As he picked up his coffee asked, "Gentlemen would you like a cup of coffee?"

Agent Jamison responded and said, "No thank you John. Betty already offered us one." He then asked, "Do you know how Congresswoman Waterman died?"

John replied, "From what I heard on the news and what Betty told me, it was a heart attack." John then asked, "When and where did it happen? It wasn't when she was here."

Agent Carlton replied, "She had a heart attack in our government vehicle on the way to the airport. We tried to revive her on the way to the hospital, but we weren't able to, nor could the hospital personnel. They confirmed her cause of death as a heart attack."

John said, "Wow! That must have been a bummer on you. I'm sorry to hear that you were put into such a situation. Having a Congresswoman die in your custody must suck."

Agent Jamison replied, "Yes it does. It requires a thorough report and that's what brings us here to talk to you and the rest of the volunteer staff that was in the Congresswoman's presence that day."

"I really don't know what else I can say, except what I told you," John replied.

"To be sure, you saw nothing in her physical condition that would make you think she was experiencing discomfort?" Agent Carlton asked.

John replied, "Like I said, I saw absolutely nothing." John then slyly reversed roles when he asked the Agents, "Let me ask you gentlemen, did you notice anything yourselves? You were close to her for the whole evening. I spoke to the Congresswoman only a few times."

They were caught off guard with his query. Agent Jamison, not liking being questioned, responded abruptly, saying, "No! we didn't. Our focus is on the activities of everyone around the Congresswoman. Preventing someone from harming her is our job and we wouldn't be doing that if we only focused on her. That's why we are asking those who had their eyes on her if they noticed something."

John could tell from the tone in the agents voice, that he didn't like being questioned and responded by saying, "From the sound of your voice, you took my honest question as an affront to how you handled your job, but in all honesty, I meant nothing by it. I'm sorry you took it the wrong way. I can see what you're saying. I didn't think about it that way. What you said makes sense. I apologize for my ignorance."

Agent Jamison replied by saying, "It's fine John. If you remember anything at all call me or Agent Carlton. Here's our business cards."

"If I do recall something I will. But at this moment I don't. I need to get to making calls on behalf of Senator Roberts. Will you need me anymore?" John asked.

Agent Carlton replied, "No John. You can go."

John, then stood up and said, "Nice to have met you gentlemen."

He turned and walked out of the room, saying to himself, "They don't know a thing. They were just fishing." As, he came to his desk, he picked up a note from Annette saying, "Call me when you can."

He sat down, with a wry smile, thinking that all is a go with Pelovski and Roberts. He just wasn't sure which one he would do next.

CHAPTER NINE

PELOVSKI BITES THE DUST

John picked up his phone, called Annette, and started his conversation with, "Hi my love. I got your note."

Annette asked, "How did it go with the Secret Service Agents?"

"It was fine. The meeting didn't last long. They asked me if I noticed anything wrong with Waterman, and I told them no. What else could I say? You were with me when we talked to her, and you didn't notice anything either. I'm sure if you had you would have said something to me or asked Waterman if she was all right," John replied.

"You're right John. I didn't notice anything either," Annette said.

John replied, "It still seems odd to me that they would ask everyone that question. They must be looking for something else. It seems like a fishing expedition to me. The woman died of a heart attack, and the hospital confirmed it. What difference would it make if you noticed a bead of sweat on her forehead, or I noticed a hand tremor, or Betty noticed an uneven step, or her grasping at her arm, the woman died naturally. What else is there?"

"John, I don't think they are looking for anything else. I think they need to cover themselves. I'm sure they were asked, and they said that they had not noticed anything wrong with Waterman either, or, twenty other people saying the same thing, closes the matter," Annette replied.

"I guess you're right. I think I watch too many spy movies and don't trust the Feds. There's always a rogue agent in them. Plus, I remember hearing on the news that they lured General Wynn into a meeting without an attorney and brought him up on charges of lying to them. That was entrapment, I believe," John replied.

Annette said, "Honey, I think you're reading way too much into it. It's nothing. Let's talk about better things like lunch."

John replied, "That sounds good to me. I feel like some tempura today. Is that okay with you?"

"Yes. You know I love Japanese food," Annette replied.

"Okay meet me outside at noon," John said.

As John was waiting for Annette, he noticed the two Federal Agents he had the meeting with come out of the building. He smiled at them, and they acknowledged him as they walked toward their car. He then noticed agent Jamison, using his cell phone to take pictures of the parking lot and the campaign office building. John wondered about the reason behind his actions, but gave it no concern. He felt if they had anything at all on him their line of questioning would have been much different, or he would have been arrested.

John then turned toward Annette as she approached him. He smiled at her, and when she reached him, he took her hand and gently squeezed it, and said, "You look beautiful. I love that color lipstick on you. I've not seen you wear it before?"

Annette replied, "Thank you John, that was sweet of you to say. No, I haven't worn this color before. It's new. I just bought it. It's called Cardinal Red. I was hoping you'd like it. Do you think its's too red?"

"I don't think it's too red at all. It highlights your lips beautifully," John replied.

Annette responded, "Thanks my sweetness."

As John and Annette ate lunch, he asked Annette if she knew anything more about whether or not Nannette Pelovski was still coming to the campaign office. Annette responded, "As far as I know, she is."

John said, "I'd love to meet her. She's a heroine of mine. Her many years of battle against the APP is admirable, and the way she goes after President Tripp is enjoyable to say the least. She's one relentless attack dog. His body is covered with scars from her attacks against him."

Annette replied, "You will definitely get to meet her. She'll be at the campaign office preparing to stump for Aaron. Betty and I will be making a few stops with Senator Roberts. I believe I can arrange for you to tag along with us if you'd like."

John replied, "Annette, I wish I could, but I can't. You know that I don't have that much leeway with Katherine. Look, to be completely honest. She doesn't know I am working at the campaign office supporting Senator Roberts. Katherine is an avid Conservative and strong Tripp supporter. She knows I can't stand the man, but we maintain a harmonious relationship, because we avoid politics. If she knew that I was here she would freak out and insist that I stop. You have no idea how much she hates NSP members. She thinks we're all insane."

Annette sat back in astonishment and said, "John! You're joking right?" Then out of curiosity asked, "How are you able to come and work at the campaign office without her knowing?"

John replied, "I joined a computer school that has local classes three days a week. She thinks that I'm attending classes when I'm at the campaign office. When Senator Roberts' campaign is over, I'll tell her that my computer class has finished. Please, keep this between us."

Annette looked at John, reached across the table, squeezed his hand, and said, "I'm so sorry that you need to live like that. Why should it make any difference to her if you and she share different political opinions?"

John deftly continued to fabricate his line of bullshit to Annette, and said, "Really Annette? We are the worst purveyors of hate towards anyone who thinks differently than us. We started the Wokeness and Cancel culture against anyone that does not uphold our ideology. You can't deny it. I've heard you make several comments along that thinking. I've done it myself. I know how we are and so does she. It bothers me to tell you, but I don't want to keep excusing why I can't do certain things, especially with you." John then wanting to seal her lips said, "I care about you very much and was hoping you felt the same."

Annette reached for his hand again, held it, and said, "John, yes, I do. Very much so. Don't worry. Your secret is safe with me."

John would not have broken his silence to Annette under any circumstances, especially when he considered her loose lipped. But he was shrewdly spinning a tighter web around her. He played on her emotions and took advantage of her love for him. Besides, he was intending on sealing her lips permanently when the time was right. He knew that by exposing his secret, he was going to be able to get around Annette without needing to tip toe with constant excuses and that she would be more willing to help him pull off his murder plot without even realizing what was happening. He had just layered another level of trust on her.

John had gone well beyond the point of no return in everything he had done and became totally jaded to the taking of human life and became methodical in his plan execution.

After their noon tryst was over, they headed back to the office. Their sex that afternoon took on a special meaning. It created a tighter bond between them. Annette felt that John bared his soul to her. At least that's the way John intended it.

A few weeks had passed, and John found himself facing his next victim, Nanette Pelovski. The time had arrived when she'd be heading to the campaign office to meet with Senator Roberts and to do some stumping for his campaign around the state. John was fixated and determined to do something about her. He just didn't know whether he would give her a full dose of the toxin and assure her death, or give her the diluted version and hope for the best. His test on the mouse caused paralysis as far as he could determine. He was not a veterinarian. The mouse eventually died as it lay immobile for several days without being able to eat or drink. He was not comfortable with the diluted method. He really didn't have a formula.

All he knew was that her mouth had to be shut one way or another. He kept weighing which method to use, knowing that this might be his only chance to get close to her. John knew that any move on Pelovski might kill his chances of taking out his main target Roberts and would certainly start an investigation, which he did not want. He had bigger and more grandiose plans in mind and according to his target list there were many left-wing Socialists that needed eradication.

He sat back on his couch trying to get past his dilemma. The uncertainty of using the diluted toxin was his stumbling block. After mulling it around in his mind, he sat up and said to himself, "Why not." He realized that he didn't have to transfer the diluted toxin from his hand to hers but put a few drops of it in her drink. Certainly, she would want a cocktail, cup of coffee, drink of water or some beverage while she was at the campaign office. All he needed to do was put a few drops of the toxin in her drink, if given the opportunity. How he would manage that, he would play by ear. He thought, it should work. It might be even more effective when ingested. He liked the idea and said to himself, "Fuck it. If I can't pull it off, I'll just have to look forward to Roberts. He'll get a full dose."

After sitting there for a few more moments, he got up, went to his medicine cabinet, took out his eye drops and emptied the contents from the small bottle into the sink. He rinsed out both the bottle and dropper several times not wanting to chance that anything in them would counter the effects of the toxin. He went to his workshop and proceeded to harvest some of the toxin. He used his usual plastic knife to scrape off the frogs back and then stirred it into a small paper cup of water. He then proceeded to use the dropper to fill up the empty bottle, being sure not to get any on the sides of it. He twisted the top tightly. Once he finished, he held it up with admiration and said, "You've done it again."

John then looked down at his other mouse, and decided to test his liquefied toxin on it. Only this time he would not rub it on the mouse, he would put a few drops of it into the small empty water dish he had in its cage. He looked at the mouse and said, "I'm sorry I forgot to give you water, but here, try this." He proceeded to empty the remaining water from the paper cup into the dish. He then placed the small bottle into a snack sized plastic bag and sealed the top in an abundance of caution and then placed it inside a small toolbox. As he left the workshop, he made sure to lock it. Adding a lock was something he decided to do a few months back, as he did not want his wife or anyone else finding his poisonous beauties when he was not at home. He didn't want to leave anything to chance.

John was now in a more upbeat frame of mind. He got past his dilemma and just needed the right moment at the campaign office to slip her his specially made Mickey Finn. As he left the workshop, he spoke to himself and said, "I'll check the mouse tomorrow. I hope the hell it works." As he continued to walk across his back lawn, he laughed and said, "Shit. I can knock off a lot of the campaign staff by adding toxin to the coffee water and that's easy. There's plenty of opportunity to do that. Ooh! I like the idea." He started to sing his favorite song, "Zip a dee doodah zip a dee yay, many of these assholes are going away."

The next morning after having breakfast with Katherine, he decided to go out to his workshop and check on the mouse. He was really anxious to find out if the toxified water worked. He went into his workshop, turned on the light, and immediately looked down into the mouse cage. The mouse was dead, and he didn't need to be a veterinarian to know that. He assumed that there was far too much toxin in the water, but felt that it would be much more diluted when he dispensed only a drop of it into Pelovski's beverage. He did not want to kill her because he wanted to avoid another death tied to the campaign office. He was hoping for paralysis which they would attribute to a stroke. John had become a really mentally warped individual because he genuinely wanted her to suffer mental anguish every day of her life the way she made his beloved President Tripp suffer.

John educated himself about toxicology and knew that the toxin was not likely to be discovered by the hospital, as they didn't perform the same type of in-depth tests on a living person as those conducted by a forensic pathologist on a cadaver, which went well beyond, taking samples of blood and urine. His execution of Congresswoman Waterman proved that.

The medical doctors would assuredly not be looking for a toxin that's rare and not readily identifiable. He also learned that if the patient were taking prescription drugs, many tests could be compromised. John learned from Annette that Pelovski was taking meds for some time, but was not sure exactly what they were, except that some were for hypertension.

John's research indicated that a hospital would need the patient's consent to conduct very invasive medical procedures on them such as an extraction of vitreous humor from the eyes, or collect samples of the liver, kidneys, or hair, tests that would be well out of the norm on a living person, and tests that are usually only performed by a forensic pathologist when doing a postmortem examination on a cadaver.

John knew the chances of learning the real cause of the paralysis inflicted on Pelovski by the hospital would be slim. Even forensic pathologists investigating a homicide still take weeks to determine the exact cause of death and John had no intention of killing her. Knowing that, he felt his chances of getting away with his deed were excellent if she didn't die.

The day finally came when Senator Pelovski would be visiting the campaign office. John was all wound up. Excitement rushed through him. He couldn't wait to Mickey Finn her drink and incapacitate her for life. He wanted the woman permanently on a breathing apparatus, or with tubes down her throat. He could care less so long as she suffered the rest of her Socialist nasty life, staring at the ceiling wondering what she did to deserve such a fate.

John went into the campaign office, and met up with Annette, and acted all excited about getting to meet the immensely powerful Senator. He said to Annette, "I can't believe how lucky I am to meet all of these Congresspeople and Senators. I consider myself extremely fortunate to be here working on Senator Roberts' campaign, and to have the opportunity to meet Senator Pelovski."

Annette replied, "I'm so happy that you have the opportunity. Just think that we would not have met if you didn't volunteer and at a risk of ruining your marriage. Telling me about your secret meant everything to me. I love you even more for it, because now I totally understand why you've acted the way you did with me at times."

"I needed to get it off my chest. I didn't want secrets between us. It made me need to lie to you when it wasn't what I wanted," John said.

Annette, showing affection, gently squeezed John's hand, and said, "We're past secrets and I truly understand your reasons."

John then changing the course of the conversation asked, "I don't remember if you told me, but have you met Senator Pelovski before?"

Annette replied, "Yes, I have, but not near as many times as I've met Congresswoman Waterman."

John smirking to himself said, "I hope that she's healthy and doesn't experience any medical problems while she's here. I would hate for her to have the same fate as Waterman. I believe she's older than Waterman and I remember you telling me that she suffers from hypertension and takes meds." John then showing some dark humor with an inner knowledge of coming events, continued, "Can you imagine the odds in something like that happening?"

Annette replied, "God forbid. John don't even think that. It would be devastating. Everyone would think Senator Roberts was jinxed."

John said, "Sorry. I don't wish evil on anyone. I was just thinking of the similarity of both women. Both of them are about the same age and have similar medical conditions. I have no idea why I would even think about it. It's just a thought that came over me."

Annette replied, "I can see why. I think Waterman's death touched you, and now you're worried about Pelovski."

"I think you're right. Her death did bother me, especially when I was the last person to say goodbye to her just before she left here," John responded.

Annette said, "John, I remember it well. I was with you. We should keep an eye on her condition. You never can tell. Stranger things have happened."

John, now trying a little levity and luring Annette into his plot said, "We can do the Secret Service's job for them. I remember what they said to me about needing to pay more attention to those surrounding Waterman, than the Congresswoman herself."

Annette replied, "I remember you telling me that. We should, if we notice something, alert them right away."

John started laughing and said, "What a crazy conversation we're having. "He then asked, "Are we going to start worrying about every elderly politician that visits this office?"

Annette laughed and replied, "I doubt it. I think that we got a little morbid."

John laughing, and with foresight knowing Pelovski would be stricken said, "I wouldn't say morbid, just a little off color."

John had just spun his web, like a spider trapping a fly. He was going to have Annette give Pelovski something to drink at the right moment. One with the toxin in it. He would watch for an opening, and play it by ear. It would be a momentous occasion for him if he could get Annette to unknowingly cripple the Senator. He considered such an event poetic justice.

John looked around the operations center and noticed caterers setting up the cocktail bar. He then asked Annette, "Is it usual for Senators and Congresspeople to drink at campaign offices whenever someone from on the Hill shows up?"

Annette laughed and said, "John really! Politicians will use any reason to sip cocktails. It's their favorite pastime when not working in the Capitol. Senator Roberts always likes to treat his peers well. God knows, I've seen him soused on a few occasions."

John then asked, "Do you know when Pelovski will arrive?"

Annette replied, "I believe she's expected at about 2 pm. We can check with Betty to see if she has confirmation. Senator Roberts should be here any time now. I know he'll have his usual meeting with Betty before Pelovski arrives."

John then said, "I think I'll get a cup of coffee. Do you want one?"

"No thank you. You go. I'll head back to my desk and get a few things done in the meantime," Annette replied.

John headed away, and after getting his coffee, went to his workstation, sat back, and just scanned the room. He reached into his pants pocket, felt the small bottle filled with the toxified water, and said to himself, "Let's do this shit. I hope the mix is right and it does what I expect; just please don't kill her, make her a zombie for life."

John took a deep breath, exhaled, and relaxed. He picked up the phone and called Annette.

As Annette answered John asked, "Did you confirm the time that Pelovski would be here?"

Annette replied, "Yes. She'll arrive at 2 pm as expected. Senator Roberts just went into his office. I can see him from my desk. I expect that once he settles in, he'll be meeting with Betty."

"Sounds good. Just wanted to say that you have one sexy walk. You most definitely excite me," John whispered.

"John, are you putting the make on me? Shame on you," Annette said, laughing and then added, "I like your sexy walk as well."

"I guess we have a mutual butt admiration. Yours is firm and beautifully shaped. I'm so glad that you work out. Every part of you is toned. The only part of Katherine that's toned is her right arm from lifting her cigarettes up and down, ten times a day," John said.

Annette said, "John, not everybody is the same. Certainly, there are good things about her that you admire."

John was taken back by Annette's candor. He didn't expect her to come to Katherine's defense. For that one moment, he found his hate for

Annette put aside, and admired her, especially knowing that she loved him. He expected her to go along with his ridicule of Katherine. Something at that moment came over him. He wondered if he was falling for her. Then in a sobering flash, thought, "No way."

John replied, "There are many things I like about her. She's a gentle loving woman with impeccable taste, and like you, dresses to the nines. I do love the way you dress very much. You look absolutely stunning with an air of sophistication. You remind me of Audrey Hepburn. Annette, I am getting turned on. Oh my lord, you can't imagine how much I want you right now."

Annette said, "John I hope nobody can hear what you're saying."

"No one can. There's nobody near me," John replied.

"The wanting part will have to wait until after work. Go take a walk and cool off big boy," Annette said laughing, then added, "Thank you for those wonderful compliments."

"John! Hold on a moment. I have a call coming in on my other line." After a few moments passed, Annette came back on and said, "John, I'll talk to you later, Betty wants me in her office." With that said Annette hung up.

John decided to get up and head back to the break room because he knew that he would be able to see both Betty's and the Senator's offices better from there. He wanted to observe their goings on. He wished that he could install a listening device in their offices. He actually thought about it on a few occasions but never moved forward with the idea. But as things were starting to heat up, he started to think that it was time. Staying ahead of everyone was becoming the utmost importance, especially if an investigation ever started. Knowing what everyone was thinking and saying would give him an advantage and know when to disappear. John was all set to go into hiding at the drop of a hat. He had his updated passport and a sufficient amount of cash to last him for a few years stored in a small metal box, with a combination lock, hidden in his attic. It was a place that Katherine would never go.

As John watched all three of them for a few minutes, he could see Senator Roberts walk into Betty's office where he proceeded to sit down next to Annette on the office sofa. He could see some laughter break out among them and wished he knew what they were saying. He then turned away and headed back to his desk, knowing he would find out from Annette. The one thing that stuck in his mind was the bug that he needed to plant in their offices. He now considered it a serious requirement. He would begin researching what he needed and where to get it. He did not care about the cost, it had to be like what the Central Intelligence Agency would use when they spied on people. He now considered it a priority and decided that he was going to plant a bug in Senator Roberts' and Betty's offices.

John sat at his desk and began soliciting funds for the campaign. He just needed to bide his time until Pelovski arrived. He knew today was the day that all shit would break loose, and he would be the purveyor. Every so often while sitting at his desk, he would check his bottle of toxin, as if it could disappear from his pocket. It was not like it had legs and could run away, or someone could reach in and take it. It just gave him an overwhelming feeling of invincibility. An indescribable feeling of patriotism. A feeling that he was the sword of justice. Sadly, he was none of those things. He was nothing more than a mentally disturbed, cunning thinker with a murderous agenda.

As two o'clock came around, the office staff started milling about in excitement waiting for Senator Pelovski to arrive. John decided to walk over to Annette's desk and to be with her when Pelovski came into the building. He knew that she'd be part of the welcoming party, and he wanted to be part of it too. It would be the beginning of the end for the Senator, and he intended to see to that. The anticipation of watching her sip her toxic drink was overwhelming John with a sick excitement.

As he walked up to Annette, she looked at him and to his utmost surprise, she had fixed her hair in a French twist, just the way Audrey Hepburn wore it in the movie, Breakfast at Tiffany's. He stood back away from her desk and said, "You did your hair like Audrey. It looks amazing and so do you. She smiled and said, I wanted to live your compliment."

John replied, "You certainly did that. You look amazing. When did you do it?"

"I went to my salon at noon. I wanted to surprise you. Do I look like Audrey Hepburn now?" Annette asked with a smile brimming across her face.

John thought at that moment, she was telling him, "I love you," because for her to do her hair that way after his earlier Audrey Hepburn compliment, was her way of pleasing him. He then said to himself, "I'm going to hate killing her. God what a shame, but it needs to be done. I can't go soft now. I've come too far with too much to risk. She'll be a liability to me. Fuck! I wish she weren't such a venomous Socialist, who wants to put Tripp and his whole family behind bars. If she weren't, I would enjoy keeping her around. Oh well, c'est la guerre."

Annette got up from her desk and walked over to John. She said, "Let's go down to the lobby and wait for Senator Pelovski, so we can greet her upon her arrival."

John replied, "Sounds good."

When they reached the elevator, Annette and John stood looking at each other and he said, "You look absolutely ravishing."

Annette smiled and said, "Ravishing! That's a wonderful compliment."

John smiling said, "It describes you well."

At that moment, the elevator opened. They entered and took it down to the lobby. As they stepped out onto the main lobby floor, they could see several reporters milling about outside waiting for Senator Pelovski to arrive. It was only a few minutes later that both Betty and Senator Roberts came down to the lobby. Annette and John waved to them and slowly walked in their direction. When they met, John extended his hand and said," It's nice seeing you again Senator."

Senator Roberts replied, "Thank you John, it's nice seeing you again. I hear that you're still cranking out substantial numbers for my campaign."

"I do my best Senator, especially when it's in support of someone, I have profound respect for," John said.

"John, that was a genuinely nice compliment. I appreciate it. I try my best for the people," Senator Roberts replied.

John's mind was full of hate for the man and playing the role of his supporter was eating him alive. He looked at the Senator and said to himself, 'You lying piece of shit. You haven't done a thing for the people. The only thing you're good at is attacking a man that loves this country and is doing something for the people. I'm especially going to enjoy shaking your hand and when I do it'll be the last time, you'll shake it with anyone."

Just as John was finished expressing his hate for the Senator to himself, Senator Pelovski's staff car pulled up in front of the building.

Senator Roberts said, "Excuse me John. I need to greet Senator Pelovski."

The Senator walked outside of the building and met with Senator Pelovski as she approached the building. News reporters and cameramen swarmed around the two politicians with shouts of questions and cameras clicking away. As they stepped into the main lobby, they went to where they had two microphones waiting for their news conferences. As both the Senators stood behind the microphones, Senator Roberts addressed all of the media. He mentioned how honored he was to have his esteemed colleague Senator Pelovski come and campaign with him around the state. He mentioned that he was leading in the polls against his rival Jeanne Collette by a full ten percentage points and that no APP candidate had won in his district for seventy-five years.

One of the reporters shouted out, that his opponent had shaved seven points off his lead over the last month after being down by seventeen and that President Tripp was going to come and campaign with her in the following weeks. Senator Pelovski stepped in and said to the media, "The people will not support her gun toting, anti-abortion, racist rhetoric. Senator Roberts has nothing to worry about. He's working on a lot of legislation that will help the workers and create jobs."

As the news conference continued, John listened, and only became more resolute in executing both of the left leaning politicians. He could not bear to listen to what he considered absolute bullshit and lies. He said, under his breath, while clenching his fist, "They don't give a damn about the people. They only care about enriching themselves. Roberts has done nothing but sold the same packaged shit year after year but with different ribbons. This man is an absolute phony and Pelovski, that old hag, has no idea about what's happening in her own ravaged district. The homeless are piling up along every avenue of her city. There are drug needles by the thousands strewn everywhere along the streets. She has ignored the desperation of thousands. What a fucking waste she is. I'm going to finish her political career today. I will see to it one way or another. Say goodbye to everyone, cause it's going to be your last uttered words. The only way you'll communicate is by blinking your eyes. One for yes, and two for no."

John watched as the news conference ended when both Senators turned from the microphones and walked into the lobby. Even after their departure from the press, they were still pursued, with reporters still shouting questions, but with no further response from either Pelovski or Roberts. The one question John heard aimed at Senator Roberts that excited an enthusiastic "Yes" from him was a challenge to the Senator's empty promises when a reporter shouted, "Senator Roberts! These are the same campaign promises you made at your last election. When are you going to deliver on what you say?"

John couldn't tell what news station the reporter was from, but based on the exposing question, knew it had to be from one of the right leaning conservatives. It was his one moment of joy, but the question itself only invigorated John's determination to assassinate the Senator. John thought at that moment, "You can't answer that you lying shit."

Annette looked at John and asked, "What did you think of the news conference?"

John said, "I thought most of the questions posed were, in all honesty, soft ball. I noticed he avoided answering a few of the ones that challenged his promises. I don't blame him, but it could cost him down the road when he debates Collette."

Annette smiled and said, "John, that's politics. Why confront adversity when you don't have to. He'll do simply fine against Collette. He's running in a NSP stronghold, and second amendment issues and anti-abortion stances don't fly with left wingers."

"I've listened to Collette. She's no push over. She's an intelligent woman and has a strong platform. Senator Roberts shouldn't take her too lightly. The stronghold you're talking about has turned purple and is no longer going to be a cakewalk. If he beats her, it'll be by a slim margin. The latest polls show that this state now has more registered Patriot Party voters than

Socialists. Is that why Roberts is having some of the heavy weights from D.C. stumping with him? If winning were such a slam dunk, he wouldn't need help. I'm just concerned," John said.

Annette replied, "John, if it gets down to the wire, we have enough votes ready to do a late-night dump, if needed. But we're sure that he'll win. Admittedly he took his win over Collette as a fait accompli. Don't worry love, we have it under control."

"So the things they say about stolen elections is true. Damn, I heard about it, but refused to believe it. I'm happy he'll win one way or another. We don't want that gun toting bitch Collette winning under any circumstances," John replied.

It took every ounce of restraint for John not to grab Annette by the throat and choke her to death. Her comments angered him so much that both his fists clenched momentarily. He said to himself in a restrained rage, "You fucking cunt. You just erased any feelings I had for you. You're now permanently on my hit list. I'll make it another day. Today I need you to poison Pelovski."

John said to Annette, "That's what I love about you, your resilience to get things done. It seems to me you do the Senator's dirty work for him. He must be overly glad to have you. Just be careful and don't get caught. People end up dead when they know too much. I don't put it past any politician to order a hit job to save their political careers. I worry about you."

Annette replied, "It's sweet of you to care, but Aaron isn't that kind of man. He'd step down before he would consider such a thing."

"You're right. I just worry. You've become very dear to me," John replied.

As they got on the elevator John thought that he must begin recording all the conversations he could. He couldn't believe how brazen Annette had become with him. Was she that much into him that she trusted him explicitly. He thought he had played the perfect spider and caught her in his web. Now he'd finish the job.

As they exited the elevator, he could see the Senators surrounded by the campaign staff, with many holding their phone cameras up videoing them. A few even asked for selfies, which Pelovski gladly obliged. The atmosphere in the office had become one of revelry. Everyone was at ease and their guards were down. He knew he had to strike. He was ready.

Betty and the Senators convened in the conference room behind closed doors. They talked at length for some time. John thought, 'I need to put a bug in there. I would love to know what they're saying. I bet I could get to learn a lot of under handed shit that's going on. These are some really scummy people. I bet Collette would like to know some of what I've learned, especially about the vote dump if it were to happen. Catching those scummy people in the act would be fantastic." Then he realized that he wouldn't need to worry about the election fraud if he knocked off the Senator as planned."

As John and Annette walked through the Operations Center, John noticed Betty looking through the conference room window beckoning him in. He stood there a little surprised, wondering what she wanted.

He turned to Annette, squeezed her hand gently and said, "Wait for me a moment. Betty wants me in the conference room."

John then turned away from Annette, walked to the room, and opened the door when Betty asked, "John, would you be so kind to do the Senators a favor and bring them something to drink. Senator Pelovski wants a Mai

Tai and Senator Roberts would like a Gin and Tonic. Nothing for me at the moment. I'll start enjoying the merriment when our meeting is over. Senator Pelovski, this is John our top campaign solicitor of the working folk. He has surpassed well over a million dollars cold calling, or sponging as he likes to call it."

Senator Pelovski extended her hand and said, "Nice to meet you. Senator Roberts must certainly be glad to have you on board."

John replied, "It's an honor to meet you, Senator. I have watched you many times on the news. You're one of my Washington favorites. You and Senator Roberts work well together, especially when bringing the President down a notch or two."

"John, what a wonderful thing to say," Senator Pelovski replied.

"Let me get your drinks. Are you sure you don't want anything Betty?" John asked.

Betty replied, "No thank you John."

With that said, John turned and walked out of the room and headed to get their drinks and thought, "How fucking convenient is that? I couldn't have asked for anything better. Now I just have to put a drop of the toxin in her drink without anyone noticing. I'll figure it out on the fly."

As he was walking toward the bar, he beckoned Annette to go with him. When Annette came up to him, he said to her, "Betty asked me to get the Senators' drinks from the bar."

Annette said, "I bet Aaron wants a Gin and Tonic. It's what he always drinks. He loves Monkey 47. Hopefully, the caterer was able to get it for him."

When they reached the bar, John put his drink request in, and then said to Annette, "Wait for me, I need to go to the men's room for a few seconds."

John turned and moved quickly away and went inside where he immediately took out the bottle of toxin inside a stall. He placed it on top of the toilet paper dispenser, uncapped it quickly, then filled the eye dropper by drawing the fluid up into it. He laid the eye dropper on its side and then put the recapped bottle back in his pocket. He picked the dropper up, cupping it in his hand and quickly went to Annette at the bar. He kept his hand close to his side as he walked up to her. She stood there holding both drinks in her hand, smiling at him."

When John reached her, he said, "Thanks my dear. I'll take them."

Annette replied, "No need, just open the conference room door for me."

John needed to act quickly, as they moved away from the bar and while Annette was walking slowly, he stopped her for a moment, then asked, "Who is that tall man standing over by the copy center?" He hoped that she would turn away from him and look toward the copy room. She didn't disappoint. John quickly extended his hand over Senator Pelovski's drink in a pointing gesture. As he did so, he quickly released the toxin into her drink while shielding the dropper in his cupped hand. He immediately placed the emptied dropper into his pocket.

He knew that only time would tell if he was successful in his intended outcome. He prayed that the Senator would not be able to taste it in her drink. He had no way of determining that before committing the deed.

Annette asked, "John, are you talking about that tall gentleman in the charcoal grey suit?"

John said, "Yes. I've not seen him before."

Annette replied, "His name is Thomas Canter. He's the accountant for the campaign. He has been here a few times; it's just that it may have been on the days you were not here."

Just as they were approaching the conference room, he said, "Annette, let me take those drinks from you. I would feel better since they asked me to get them. Just open the door for me please Audrey."

Annette smiled, and said, "Now I'm Audrey Hepburn to you?"

John said, "You're as beautiful as she is."

Annette replied, "I love you; do you know that?"

John replied, "I got an inkling that you do."

At that moment John reached the conference room door, and entered while Annette held it open. John said, "Here's your Mai Tai Senator Pelovski, and here is your Gin and Tonic Senator Roberts. It's made with your favorite Gin, Monkey 47. Annette told me that it was your favorite."

Senator Roberts replied, "Been drinking that same Gin for years."

John replied, "Well enjoy them. I'll go about my business while you conduct yours."

Betty said, "Thank you John."

"It was my pleasure," John replied, as he turned and walked out of the room with Annette.

As they stepped outside of the room, Annette said, "I'm going to go check my phone for messages. I'm expecting an important call back. I'll see you when they get out of the conference room and the staff gathers and celebrates Senator Pelovski's visit."

"Okay, see you later," John replied.

The minute Annette turned her back to John he began walking around the campaign office killing time. He was nervous, excited, and unsure all at the same time. He was nervous because, he was concerned that the dose he gave might be too much and kill her before she left the premises. He wanted the toxin to work slowly in its highly diluted state and put her into a preferred paralysis after she left the premises. He knew when he put the toxin in her drink, it was before the time he would like. But the unplanned opportunity was too much to pass up. John simply played it by ear and went for it. All he could do was wait and hope for the best. So far, she seemed in good spirits from what he could see of her through the conference room windows. Several minutes had already passed since she received the toxin without any noted reaction. He began to wonder if the dose was too diluted, or became ineffective in alcohol or just worked much slower when ingested. This would be a learning experience.

Another hour had passed when finally Betty and the Senators came out of the conference room. He could only assume that the toxin was too diluted to be effective. He still had some left in the bottle and could try again if given the chance. He was glad that the Secret Service accompanying Senator Pelovski had been stationed in the lobby in front of the elevator. It would have been more difficult trying to spike her drink with them watching everyone's movements.

As the evening wore on, John was unable to make a second attempt at toxifying her drink. He realized that the method he was using was awkward. He was lucky on his first attempt, but was not afforded another unrehearsed chance. It was not long after that Senator Pelovski left to go to her hotel. John observed the Senator constantly hoping to notice some sign of physical distress, but he observed nothing. Annette, who had mingled among other less notable guests, finally returned to John's side. She asked, "Do you want to go to my place for a while?"

John was super tempted, but declined her advance. He said, "You have no idea how much I'd like to, but I need to get home. I promised Katherine to take her to dinner. You know I'm starting to want to be with you now more than her. It's a real tug of war on me emotionally."

"I hate to see you leave, It's not always easy for me either. But I knew what I was getting into the first time you went home with me, and we made love," Annette replied.

John said, "I'd like us to spend a weekend together sometime. I just will have to figure out how to do it." John then changing the subject of them, said, "You know what is funny? I found myself watching Pelovski for any physical abnormalities, remembering our conversation about Waterman."

"She seemed fine to me, but honestly, I really wasn't paying attention. I forgot about watching for signs of illness. The only thing I heard her say just before she was getting ready to leave was that she was feeling a little queasy and felt a little chilly. She blamed it on the drink and the air conditioning," Annette said.

When John heard Annette mention the symptoms that the Senator was having, he hoped that it was the toxin starting to work. Other than that small ray of light in his attempt to paralyze the Senator, he was disgusted at what he felt was a botched attempt. He thought, "Score one for the bad guys."

John asked, "Are you leaving now? I want to walk you to your car."

Annette smiled and said, "No John. Since you're not going to go home with me, I think I'll stay a little longer."

John said, "Walk with me to the lobby."

As they stepped onto the empty elevator car, and watched the doors close, John reached over and hit the stop button, halting the elevator momentarily between floors. He turned to Annette, pulled her close, and kissed her. Annette responded with considerable passion.

John said, "I couldn't resist. You have no idea how much I'd like to go home with you." Then looking into her eyes, he kissed her again. He stood looking at her while holding her hand and pushed the down button with his other reactivating the elevators decent. Annette looked into John's eyes and said, "I feel the same."

John stepped off the elevator, turned to Annette and said, "Go take care of your things. I'll see you next week." He reached into the elevator and pushed the up button, sending Annette back up.

CHAPTER TEN

THE WAITING GAME

John went home to Katherine. As John was driving, he thought to himself, "What the fuck is the matter with me?" Out of frustration, to his own weakness, he yelled out, "Stop the shit. Quit letting your little head do your thinking. Stay the course. You're on a mission and she's only a means to an end." His mind raced with so many thoughts.

John's noticeable mental lapse behind the wheel could be seen by other drivers. He looked crazy as he shouted inside his car and wildly waved his hand around. It was obvious, from the spectacle he was creating, that he was not in control of his faculties.

As John walked through the door of his home, he saw Katherine, watching television. He walked up to her and said, "I missed you. He leaned over and kissed her. Then continuing his lie said, "There's not too many weeks left for me to complete the computer course, then I'll be home all of the time."

Katherine said, "Time goes by quickly and I don't mind. It's not as if you're gone all day. If you were working, it would be no different. Believe me I keep myself occupied."

John replied, "Thanks sweety for being so understanding." He then asked, "Where would you like to go for dinner? I promised to take you. Let's go enjoy the evening together. We'll drink a lot of wine, get tipsy and make love for the rest of the evening."

Katherine replied, "Sounds good. Let me go put some makeup on."

John was overly romantic with Katherine all evening, as he psychologically felt the need to mend a marriage that had no need for mending. His paranoia was without merit. At one minute he didn't care about Katherine's feelings and the next he felt guilty. Katherine was happy and had no idea about John's extra marital affair. She was happy and was glad to see John doing something with his life taking the computer course. John created a blurred line between his assassination plans and using Annette as a foil, and developing unexpected feelings for her. There were times he lusted for her without giving thought to the very reason he started romancing her to start with. When John railed at himself in his drive home to take Katherine to dinner, he was angry at himself for even thinking he was falling for Annette and losing sight of his mission.

His ranting at himself was his way of conducting self-flagellation, and bringing himself back into reality, and to regain the unemotional selfish meaning to it without regard to anyone's feelings. He needed that more than anything and would be more guarded moving forward.

After coming home from dinner and making love to Katherine, they stayed in bed, propped up their pillows and turned on the television they had in the bedroom. John purposely went to the news. He could not help it. He needed to see if anything had been reported about Pelovski. To his consternation, there was nothing. All he had to say to himself was, "Damn it. I blew my chance. I'll have to just focus on Roberts."

It was around noon the next day that John came in from checking on his thriving frogs to watch the news. Even though he believed he failed in his Pelovski mission, he still kept a glimmer of hope that he hadn't. After watching some local news about a drive by shooting outside a convenience store, the news station displayed a breaking news flash across the bottom of the screen, saying that Senator Pelovski had fallen ill while stumping with Senator Roberts on his campaign trail and had been taken to a local hospital for treatment. As John was reading the banner, the station broke in with a reporter who was with Senator Roberts, covering the story.

The reporter asked the Senator, "Can you tell us what has happened to Senator Pelovski?"

Senator Roberts replied, "I'm not sure. The Senator told me earlier that she had been feeling a little sick since last night but felt she could still take the stage and give her endorsement to me. She said, if she began to feel any worse, she'd let me know. When she showed up at my rally, I assumed that she was okay. It was just after giving me her endorsement on stage that she told me she felt a weakness in her arms and legs and felt wobbly. I immediately had the Secret Service take her to Saint Mary's Hospital, which was only a few miles away. I asked them to please keep me informed regarding her condition. As they were helping her to their staff car, she lost mobility in her limbs and collapsed into the arms of her security. A 911 call was put out and an ambulance took her to Saint Mary's, which I understand has an excellent emergency staff. We are all praying for her. The last report I received from her security detail was that she was alive, but given oxygen to help her breathing. If you'll excuse me, I'm heading to the hospital now. I'll be canceling my next campaign stop, until after I see the Senator."

The reporter said, "Senator, your colleagues don't have a lot of luck endorsing you. Didn't Congresswoman Waterman pass away after visiting your office?"

Senator Roberts became irate and said, "For God's sake. How can you say such a thing? I cannot help what happened. It's an awful coincidence and nothing more."

With those last words, Senator Roberts, being really angered, pushed her microphone away from the front of his face and moved with his security to his staff car where he left heading to the hospital.

The reporter turned toward the camera, facing her TV audience, and ended her reporting with, "It looks like Senator Roberts has run into some bad luck with Congresswoman Waterman dying of heart failure shortly after leaving his office and now Senator Pelovski has fallen ill after taking Senator Roberts' campaign stage. For those of you who are not aware of the two unfortunate circumstances, Congresswoman Waterman passed away from heart failure shortly after visiting Senator Roberts' office and now Senator Pelovski has fallen ill the day after visiting the Senator's office. These are unfortunate incidents. We'll follow the story as we go to Saint Mary's Hospital to learn more about Senator Pelovski's condition. This is Chanel Brian signing off for WACC News."

After that brief news coverage about Senator Pelovski, John changed the channel. He thought, "It looks like the diluted toxin is having a delayed reaction. I hope it was enough to paralyze her permanently. I want that bitch staring at the ceiling the rest of her miserable life."

He turned to Katherine and said, "I don't want to sound morbid, but I hope she doesn't recover from whatever she has. It'll silence her mouth against Tripp. I wanted to throw my shoe at the TV whenever she came on and babbled her bullshit against him. Hopefully, it'll end her constant investigations of the man."

Katherine said, "Honestly honey. I wish you wouldn't wish harm against her. Not agreeing with her politics, shouldn't warrant such hatred from you."

"I can't help it. I hate that dried up old bag of shit," John replied.

"John! Enough, please," Katherine said.

John, not saying another word, started channel surfing, trying to find a good movie to watch. As the channels slipped by, Katherine said, "John, please go back up to the Discovery Channel. I believe they're doing coverage on the Indigenous people in the Brazilian rain forest. I would like to watch that."

John did as she requested, and watched the show with her. He stayed quiet, although his mind wasn't. His thoughts raced from one thing to another. He just watched the TV blindly. He couldn't concentrate on it. John said to himself, "She needs to live so no FBI autopsy is performed. If she dies, they just might deem her death to be too coincidental and want to investigate." If she lives, he felt the hospital would do its usual blood testing and if what he learned about their limited capacity to detect rare toxins holds true, they won't detect the alkaloid. He also considered the limited trace amount of toxin that she ingested would make it even harder to detect. The one thing he knew for sure, was that little frog produced some incredibly powerful stuff.

John and Katherine watched TV for a few hours when Katherine got up and asked John if he would like a snack or something to drink. John replied and said, "No thanks hon."

While Katherine was in the kitchen, John flipped back to the news channel to see if he could get an update on Senator Pelovski's condition.

As soon as he turned on that station, the coverage was about the Senator. He expected as much. The Senator was an immensely powerful and quite prominent person, and their ongoing coverage of her condition would be continuous. After watching it for a while, he turned it off. The coverage offered nothing new on the status. It just covered her years in the Senate, playing old film clips. He thought, "Who the fuck cares what she did then. It's what she's doing now that I care about."

It wasn't until the next day, that the Attending Physician held a news conference to bring everyone up to date on their prognosis of the Senator. As soon as the Physician introduced himself as Jonathan Gauci, news cameras began recording and microphones were extended his way.

He said, "We would like to inform you that, although Senator Pelovski is in control of all her faculties, she's unable to move her limbs at this time. We have not as of yet been able to identify the source of her quadriplegia. We are conducting extensive tests and are hoping to identify what has caused her condition. We can tell you there are no signs of spinal cord damage, nor does she appear to have suffered a stroke. We have conducted a full body scan, an Electromyogram test, and a spinal tap. So far, we have not been able to pinpoint the reason for her condition. It's our strong belief that she's suffering from an, as of yet, undefined neurological disorder as the two most prominent reasons for paralysis have been eliminated. Because she has no identifiable spinal cord damage, we are optimistic that the Senator will eventually regain mobility. As of the moment she's not getting brain signals to the nervous system in her limbs. The Senator will be going through another battery of neurological tests today including a brain scan using contrast. We will not let any stone go unturned in seeking a cause for her affliction. We will inform the public of any changes in her prognosis. We are also conferring with top paralysis specialists at Massachusetts General Hospital and Mayo Clinic Neurology. We've also been in contact with the Center for Disease Control."

As soon as the doctor finished speaking, he told the news people that the hospital would not be answering any questions and was not at liberty to disclose anything more than what was stated. He turned and walked away back into the hospital. An unidentified reporter ran up to the doctor as he was leaving and asked, "Is the Senator on a ventilator?"

The doctor responded, "No, her lung function doesn't require mechanical ventilation, but we have her on a nasal cannula providing a few liters of oxygen therapy."

John became startled when he heard they eliminated a stroke as the source of the Senator's paralysis. A stroke diagnosis is what he expected. The frog toxin was supposed to mimic strokes and heart attacks. It did just that when he knocked off Congresswoman Waterman. He became concerned that they would begin searching for a nefarious reason. He knew that they might consider the possible use of paralyzing toxins like curare or tetraodontid. If they did, it would lead to a federal investigation assuming they could isolate the rare Golden Dart Frog toxin in their lab blood work. He had to consider his options going forward if they did. Regardless of different possibilities John stood resolute and decided to wait it out before jumping the gun.

John sat back on the couch, took a deep breath, exhaled slowly, and considered everything he had done and everything he learned from his research about the frog's toxin. He knew that it would either kill or completely paralyze a person requiring ventilators for survival. But in the Senator's case, the doctor denied the use of a ventilator, although he indicated that a nasal cannula was inserted. That last comment indicated to John, that Pelovski was breathing on her own without mechanical assistance.

John remembered from his research, that the frogs alkaloid toxin structurally mimicked neurotransmitters that interfered with their receptors and signal transduction, leaving him to reason that it caused the nerve impulses to somehow isolate heart and lung function from the rest of the paralyzed body. He could only guess. He was not a doctor. He really didn't know if such a thing was possible. If he was by sheer coincidence right, the frog toxin was acting contradictory to its effects and those of other deadly toxins. If it was, then it would more than likely steer the doctors away from considering toxin as a cause for the Senator's illness. He wondered if his dilution using water combined with the alcohol in the Senator's drink, caused the toxin's effect to become less potent while changing it molecularly? He just didn't know. He also considered that it was ingested into stomach acid instead of being introduced to the blood stream through the skin, or injected into the blood using a dart. John then nixed that thought thinking that many poisons are swallowed, and the stomach acids don't seem to affect them. In the end, and after his self-analysis and anguish, he said to himself, "I have no clue about what is really going on."

After coming to an uncertain conclusion, he considered that just maybe, the doctor lied about the Senator's real condition and did so under the insistence of the FBI.

After several days had passed, the day came when John would be going back to the campaign office. He made up his mind about Annette, and was not going to let his emotions become confused again. He would still knock her off when the time came to sever ties with her.

John couldn't wait to find out from Betty what she knew about Senator Pelovski's condition and if her sudden illness was affecting Senator Roberts emotionally and what his updated polling numbers showed. According to the Vox News Network, Collette's numbers had climbed again and now was only 5% down. Her rise was rapid. She was pulling within the 3% margin of error of the polling numbers.

He knew that when he heard the latest numbers, Senator Roberts could not be happy with Betty as his campaign manager. He felt that she should've known the trend and what was causing it and taken counter action to slow down Collette's likability. All John knew is that Betty and Annette were there to have the Senator's back and to assure his re-election. He started to think about whether or not he would need to apply his deadly handshake to the Senator. If Collette overtook him in the polls over the next month, Roberts could lose his re-election bid, and if he did, he would no longer be in D.C. to hamper President Tripp. John knew that election polls can be wrong, and he didn't trust what Annette and Betty might do to manufacture ballots to steal the election.

John was going to be ready for anything. The one thing he wanted badly was to learn whether or not Annette planned to dump fraudulent ballots into the count. Knowing when, where and how would put her behind bars and stop the steal. John knew that if he found out those details, he'd contact Collette immediately, and leave it to her to contact the Federal Bureau of Investigation.

John arrived at the campaign office knowing that the election would be taking place in just another thirty days. His planned assassination of Roberts was getting close. Everything he had done over the past five months he considered monumental. He learned firsthand about running a campaign and what nefarious activities went on behind the scenes. The things he heard and witnessed disgusted him. John didn't regret the murders he committed. Everything he did in his hate filled mind, was for a higher cause. He had to speak to Betty first. He had not gotten anything else different from the news on Pelovski's condition. He was sure that

Senator Roberts would've been receiving periodic updates and keeping Betty informed.

As he entered the Operations Room he headed straight for his desk. He picked up his phone and called Annette. He let it ring several times but there was no answer. He had no idea if she was at the office or away from her desk. He decided to walk to the break room and get himself a cup of coffee. He knew that he'd be able to see Betty's office and Annette's desk from where it was located. As he approached the door of the break room, he could see both Annette and Betty and a well-dressed gentleman in there as well. He immediately wondered if it was an FBI agent. He felt sure that they would make a visit after what happened to Senator Pelovski. He stood watching them for a minute before stepping into the break room.

As he was pouring coffee, he felt a hand touch his arm. He turned and saw that Annette had joined him. She smiled at him and said," I missed you."

John said, "I missed you too. How was your weekend?"

"It was fine," Annette replied.

"Have you heard anything more about Senator Pelovski's condition?" John asked.

Annette replied, "Betty told me that the Senator's condition was holding steady, although she experienced a slowing heart rate. The doctors are medicating that condition and appear to have it under control. Her breathing had also become a little more labored, but was still on a nasal cannula. Jonathan Gauci, her attending physician, spoke to Senator Roberts and told him that they had not been able to identify the reason for her condition. He admitted to the Senator that he was a little perplexed but hopeful they would identify what triggered her paralysis. He told Senator Roberts that they were now of the opinion it was neurological. They will be doing nerve conductivity tests to see if they could isolate the reason that brain signals were not being sent to her extremities. He said that because she was able to breath on her own and her heart was functioning, they ruled out toxins as a cause of her condition. He said that they were confident that they would find the answer."

John was elated at what he heard. He said to himself, "Yeah Baby! It worked better than I expected. It camouflaged itself as neurotransmitters. God! I love those frogs. Zip-a-dee doo dah, zip-a-dee yay, my oh my what a wonderful day, oh Senator Roberts, shit is coming your way, Zip-a-dee doo dah zip-a-dee yay."

John said, "Annette, I'm so glad that she's not getting any worse. She has a really good doctor. I'm sure he'll find out why she suddenly became paralyzed. There can only be so many ways that something like that happens. Hopefully when they do, they'll find a way to cure her."

Annette replied, "I hope so. Capitol Hill will miss her outspoken voice."

John said, "Well time is getting close to the election, and I see from the polls that Collette has really narrowed the gap to within the three-point margin of error. What is Betty planning to reverse that trend? She better pull something out of her hat soon. The race was a runaway for Roberts only a few months back, and now he's neck and neck with his opponent. It's now a real dog race."

"Betty has been on the phone with Roberts constantly regarding the situation and is trying to do damage control. The death of Waterman and the illness of Pelovski after visiting here is being played hard by Collette's camp. They're taking two unfortunate circumstances and making them seem like Roberts is the kiss of death. Collette is an evil bitch. I won't let her win if I have to print those ballots myself," Annette replied.

John replied, "Don't say that too loudly. That's a federal crime. I just don't want you to get caught planning that. When you're ready to do it, let me know so I can help."

John had no intention of doing it. He just wanted Annette to think so, so that he could be in on her scheme and fuck her over with the Feds when she was making her move.

Annette squeezed John's hand and said, "You would do that?"

John said, "Only with you," as he squeezed her hand back and then said, "You need to start filling me in on how and when, so that I'm comfortable we can get away with it. I'm not looking to do time."

"Let's leave a little earlier today and go to my place. I missed you lying next to me. I will also take you through how we inflate the votes and get past an audit. I think you'll find it quite efficient. We've got it down to science. We've been doing it for years," Annette said.

John replied, "You've got my interest. It must be a trip knowing what you do secures a nomination."

Annette said, "It does give me a high when I know that what I've done has helped shape America's political landscape."

"I assume the candidate knows what you've done for them. It seems to me that you have some favors owed to you," John intimated.

"I have a few and I wouldn't hesitate to use them at the right time," Annette responded.

John said, "You can tell me all the details later." Then asked, "When do you want to leave?"

Annette replied, "How about one o'clock?"

"Sound's good," John replied.

After their brief conversation, John and Annette went about their business at the campaign office. John couldn't help but get excited over his conversation with Annette. He was about to get the details of her criminal activity conducting voter fraud. He decided to use his phone to record their conversation. He knew that it was illegal to do so without both parties consenting in the State, but it would allow him to play it for Collette. It would give his story the credibility it needed so that a sting operation would catch Betty, Annette, and everyone involved in the act. If it all happened, it would surely hit the news and put a political hurt on the National Socialist Party and cause considerable fighting in Washington over voter laws.

The day went by quickly for John as he kept himself busy soliciting for the campaign. John, over the past five months, became extremely adept at conjuring money out of people and while doing so, got many introductions directly to corporate money. John had one thing that put him above other campaign solicitors, and that was his silken tongue. He had a way of convincing people about anything, no matter how absurd. He had a very gregarious personality, was highly intelligent and people found him quite likable almost immediately. When you take all of his positive traits and combine them with his Political Stress Disorder, you would be dealing with a Hannibal Lecter type individual, who was smooth talking, and methodically focused, only John would never subscribe to cannibalism. But like Hannibal, he had no remorse about his victims. He actually enjoyed knocking off anyone who fit within his hateful political profile.

CHAPTER ELEVEN

PLANTING THE BUGS

John and Annette left the campaign office at one o'clock as planned and headed over to Annette's place where they immediately stripped and went to bed to enjoy an afternoon of sex. John went out of his way to make Annette feel totally fulfilled, as he wanted to spin his web even tighter around her by making her love him even more. He had his mind focused on one thing, and that was fucking over all of them. He made sure that he no longer let sex with Annette cloud his purpose or real feelings, like he had briefly experienced before.

As they lay next to each other relaxed, John asked, "So are you going to fill me in on your covert operation? I'm really interested in learning everything. I want to help my sexy lady pull off an election victory for Roberts. I'm beginning to believe he'll need our help."

Annette asked, "Are you really sure you want to get involved? It's not a game John."

John replied, "I don't say things lightly and I'm well aware of the seriousness of committing election fraud. I'm not afraid of getting involved. I want to be involved. I want to make sure that that gun toting bitch, as you've called her, does not win and it's beginning to look like she might pull off an upset."

Annette said, "Okay, I'll explain what we do and how you can help. We've been reviewing voting trends in the state by district for years and have studied every detail of the process. In order to pull off stealing an election by inserting votes during the count, you have to know where and when to deliver the ballots and to whom. Because it will take thousands of ballots to swing the election, we need to disburse them throughout the system so there are no large single dumps at anyone polling station. To our benefit there are a little over 4,600 of them scattered throughout sixty-seven counties. Florida only uses the paper ballot system."

"If the race is close, we know that there will be a re-count with all the ballots processed through mechanical tabulators which favors us because the machines only read the blackened circles next to the candidates' names and counts the vote. It does not check voter information."

"Betty and I already started the process. Although neither one of us mentioned our true feelings about the outcome of the election, we both felt the race would go down to the wire. The outcome for Roberts, we felt, was too dubious not to take preliminary action. It's our job to stay upbeat and not dash the hopes of all our volunteers by telling them that Roberts could lose what was supposed to be a no contest race."

John asked, "Why do you and Betty feel Senator Roberts might lose?"

Annette replied, "We both thought that his attacks against President Tripp, and his family, went a little too far when he went after the President's business dealings that occurred six years before he even decided to run for office. They were not legitimate attacks, and we started to see the bulk of Independents taking umbrage to what Aaron did. We need the Independents. I personally hate Tripp and his whole fucking family and clapped at the attacks, but that was personal. Politically it's bad politics when you go too far below the belt. If you're far left, you condone it. If you're a centrist Independent, which the majority are, you don't."

After Annette explained their reasoning, she continued on about the illegal ballot operation and said, "Irregardless, right now we have door to door seven days a week canvasing going on in every district with thousands of volunteers collecting usable ballot information for us in and out of public records, which includes all of the recently deceased. We have even paid informants in the Immigration Offices providing the names and addresses of legal and illegal aliens. Hell John, we even have some Post Office employees providing us with all the out-of-state changes to addresses weekly. We take all of those names and addresses and put them on ballots."

John said, "That is one considerable effort in collecting usable voter names."

Annette replied, "Yes, it is. It took us two years to put the entire operation together. Getting the right people on board took the most time. We had to be sure of where their heads were. They had to know the risks and be completely on board."

Annette then continued from where she left off before I commented, saying, "Each time we compile several thousand names, we print that batch and ready them for their destination. Many of them become early voting by mail. I cannot mention to you how it's done, but we have access to the tabulation machines. If you know what they do, then you can surmise that we alter their count in our favor. John, we even use the exact same paper so that there is no distinction between the sanctioned ones and ours. And so that the ballots are not questioned in any way, we even fill in the down ballot races in favor off all National Socialist Party candidates."

John interjected, "Now that's smart. Very few people will vote for just one candidate. They will typically vote party line and fill in the entire ballot."

"Exactly John. An audit earmarking questionable ballots would yank those first," Annette replied, and then continued the details of their fraudulent activity, when she said, "We know the number of registered voters by county and district and how many of our printed ballots can be inserted into the count in each of those areas without raising eyebrows. We try to stay within an accepted swing. We only need to increase the vote count of each of the sixty-seven counties by about 3,800 votes in our favor. That amount is not significant enough to raise an eyebrow in anyone of them, but when you add all sixty-seven counties together you've inserted at least 250,000 votes statewide and that should be enough to take the election. We're giving Senator Roberts a significant handicap."

John listened intently to everything Annette was saying. She kept telling him more and more nonstop. He never interrupted her flow of information again, as everything she was saying was being recorded on his phone. He had deftly placed it on the night table next to his side of the bed. He had it hidden in plain sight. He sat back smiling, thinking he was going to rat her and Betty out and take down the whole campaign operation and the Senator too. It's when he thought of the Senator, he said to Annette, "My lovely sweet little devious sexy lady, pause for a moment, I want a kiss."

Annette stopped speaking, smiled, and did what John asked, she kissed him. As they pulled their mouths away from each other, John looked at her and said, "Okay now you can continue. I just couldn't resist."

There was one thing about John, he could play a scene to the hilt. He had Annette so off guard that she fell willingly into his trap and felt comfortable telling it all.

John then smartly asked, "The Senator must be happy with how you're so stealthily ensuring his re-election. I must assume he knows and has given his blessing?"

After asking Annette to implicate the Senator without her realizing her words were being recorded, justified his intimation by needing to know for his own sake he said, "I wouldn't want to be involved if he didn't know. Because if we were to get caught, he would be able to deny all culpability and we'd be without his support and left hanging out to dry."

Annette replied, "John, believe me he knows. We have secret meetings with him, and get his okay on this and other things we do for him. Which is something again."

John said, "I'm glad you said that; that makes me feel a lot more comfortable. It certainly sounds like you've got it well in hand."

Annette said, "My love, It's not my first rodeo. I helped him in his last election. Aaron pulled me away from Congressman Burns in Virginia. I worked with Burns for three years before coming down to Florida. I set up a similar operation for him. He ended up being an ungrateful son of a bitch. After I risked my ass and pulled off his election, he felt like he didn't need me anymore. It was Waterman that introduced me to Aaron. He treats me with the utmost respect. I like him and his wife a lot."

John said, "I didn't hear you tell me where you get the ballots printed. Are they done out of state?"

Annette replied, "John, no. That would be adding another layer of risk. We have a print operation set up in a small private warehouse right here in Broward County. When we drop off our voter list on a special disc it's uploaded onto a computer which is programmed to run the printer. The printer is high speed and can handle the workload. We can modify the list at any time. The print production is set up to run batches by county and district. We load our delivery vehicles by destination, and put the boxes going to the furthest polling places in the back of the van and the ones going to the closest places up front. Our drivers have preset routes and when they arrive at the drop off, it takes only minutes to unload. They make calls ahead of their arrival to someone that is waiting to help unload and get them into the count. It's a smooth transition. Everyone that's onboard with the operation is on their game. John, we've had test runs to work out any glitches. Once all of the ballots are delivered and mingled, the phones used to communicate are thrown away. We sever any evidence of communication between the drivers and the polling stations."

As John listened to Annette, he thought to himself, "Holy shit, this voter fraud operation is one shrewd woman running one well-oiled machine. The whole operation is like what you would see in a spy movie."

John said, "Wow! You're too much lady! As I was listening to you, I felt like I was living a spy movie. Now I can see why you took a few years to set it all up. The amount of reliable, same thinking people working as one cohesive team, pulling all of it off only once on election day is remarkable. Shit, babe! You deserve an Oscar for your winning production. You've got me all excited about being a part of it. Just tell me when and how I can help."

Annette replied, "Don't worry my love. I'll find something for you to do."

John said, "Annette, I hate to say this, but I need to leave."

Annette looking at him, smiled then moved closer to him, placing her hand under the sheet, and touched John between his legs and asked, "Can you spare a few more minutes?"

As her hand movement aroused John, he said, more than willingly, "I guess I can stay a little longer."

Annette moving her body over John, said, "Yes, I noticed."

After having sex again, John made sure to shower quickly. He made it a habit. He was always worried about carrying the scent of Annette home with him because of Katherine's ability to smell scents like a dog. There was no way he was going to put himself in the same position as the last time. Soon after showering John left. While he was driving, he felt an excitement of overwhelming accomplishment. He had every reason to feel that way. He crippled Senator Pelovski and had just recorded Annette indicting herself, Senator Roberts, and Betty, along with her minion volunteers in committing election fraud. It emphasized his need to record everything that went on at the campaign office. It was now imperative for him to find a way to do it.

After getting home John made sure to heap attention on Katherine. He did that every time he came home, especially after leaving Annette. It reinforced the reason for his actions. His affair with Annette had to be nothing more than business as usual. He made sure of it. He did not want to relive his prior angst.

As soon as he walked through the door of his home, he said to Katherine, "Hello sweetheart. Anything new happen today?"

Katherine replied, "Nothing happened. How was your day at school?"

John said, "It was good. I'm finished with it after this month. Speaking of school. I have to complete a computer assignment. Let's go to dinner at Longhorn's before I abandon you for the rest of the night. The course work will take me a few hours at least."

Katherine replied, "Okay. You should take another course with the school. You've taken me out to dinner an awful lot since you've been going to it. I enjoy not having to cook so often."

John replied, "Maybe I will take another course. I really enjoy it."

Katherine's comment opened another window of opportunity for John. It would enable him to use the school excuse to continue his charade after he knocked off Roberts.

After John and Katherine went to dinner, he went online and researched surveillance recording devices with external microphones, and found one that enabled him to plant a ridiculously small microphone in Betty's office, while being able to put the recorder in his desk drawer. The device had a seventy-five-foot recording range which was more than ample distance for his needs. Betty's office was no more than forty feet away from him. He was delighted to learn that the recorder was a small slim device that could be put in his pocket and not be noticed. John laughed when reading its specifications and said, "I love technology. This is James Bond shit." When adding the item to his online shopping cart, he ordered two. He intended to bug the Senator's office as well. He would just have to figure out how and where to plant them without being found.

When the recording devices arrived, John went berserk with joy. He became like a little kid with a new toy. The first thing he did was test them out to be sure they worked. He put one microphone in his car, turned on the radio, lowering the volume, and walked sixty feet away to record. After a minute, he put the recorder on playback and listened to absolute clarity. John said to himself, "Okay, now let's see how much more dirt I can get on these left-wing scumbags."

It took a week for John to receive the bugging devices, and right after they were in his possession, he drove to the campaign office to clandestinely plant them. He couldn't wait to get dirt on the Senator and Betty. He already had enough on Annette to put her ass away. But just having Annette implicating the others would not be enough legally. He had to have them all implicating themselves. One of the things John hoped would happen was that Betty and Annette would speak to Senator Roberts about the ballots before election day. He wanted the Senator to implicate himself. If he did, John wouldn't have to shake his hand. If it didn't, he would simply carry out his plan. He became jaded about taking life and cared less, but knew that getting him to admit to plotting a federal crime was cleaner. He would have to be patient. There was still another twenty days until election day.

When John arrived, he immediately passed by Betty's and the Senator's offices. He saw that the Senator's was unoccupied, and that Betty was at her desk. He had to find a way to get into his office and plant the microphone. The Senator kept it locked while he was away, but John knew that Betty kept a key. He recalled seeing her open the Senator's door when he was on Capitol Hill. It made sense to John at that time because he knew that Betty was more than his campaign manager, she was his trusted confidant. John was not worried about getting the microphone planted. He had three weeks to find a way, and he knew that the Senator would become a daily fixture in the next few days, as he would go all out on the campaign trail in these last weeks before election day.

As for Betty's office, John could easily walk in to see her for some reason, sit down in front of her desk, and while sitting there, simply reach under the overhang and stick the microphone on it. He could also fake dropping something, and while bending down to pick it up, stick the microphone under the bottom of the desk. He would do that sometime during the day.

When John arrived at his desk, he found a note from Annette. She said, "I loved the other evening. It was heavenly. I'm excited about doing what we discussed together. Call me when you get in. A."

John, said to himself, "I got you now my sweet." John sat down at his computer, and searched the web to get information on Collette. He needed to determine where her campaign office was located, and get contact information. He planned to get Collette involved in the next few weeks. He felt that giving the information to her was the better way to go knowing that if she contacted the Feds, they would have to act. If he did it, they might bury everything, take his recorder, and then conveniently lose it. He had a hate for the Feds and felt the Department of Justice was a left-leaning government agency. They certainly didn't comply with President Tripp's request for the release of unredacted documents to the APP controlled

Oversight Committee. They always stone walled using the usual excuse that it would violate security secrets, or some horse shit like that. And when they did release the classified documents, they were so redacted that there was almost nothing disclosed. He knew, from reports that they issued illegal warrants to spy on American citizens, when the warrants were only to be used against foreign nationals. There was no way he would approach them. He also knew that Collette had a battery of attorneys to review the legal aspects of his recordings, knowing that Annette and the other's were taped without their knowledge, in a State where it required consent of both parties to do so. Besides all of that, he wanted to stay anonymous if at all possible.

He had other ambitions and did not want to hamper his ability to go down his list of names, and continue to do damage to whom he considered, the vilest Socialists.

John decided to get his call to Annette over with, because if he didn't, he knew that she'd walk over to see him, and he wasn't ready for her yet.

Annette picked up her phone and said, "Good morning. Did you just get in?"

"Yes, only a few minutes ago. I was about to get some coffee. Meet me in the break room," John replied.

"Okay," Annette said.

John reached the break room just ahead of Annette. He could see her walking toward him and could not help but look at her from head to toe, and said to himself, "I shouldn't say this, but she looks fine. I need to take stock of myself with her. I don't know why I get these fucking lapses where I want to take her off and sex the hell out of her. I must admit she's one beautiful woman. I remember when she did her hair like Audrey

Hepburn just to please me. Why does she have to be such a vile Tripp hating Socialist with a penchant to commit federal crimes, especially for two ultra-left Senators."

As he watched her walk, he could see the silhouette of her legs through her silky skirt as the sun gleamed through the large windows behind her and made a hmmm, hmmm, sound, displaying pleasure at the sight.

Annette saw John standing there looking at her with his eyes looking up and down over her body and smiled. As she came up to him, she asked, "Like what you see?"

"Love it. What can I say. You look absolutely lovely," John replied.

Annette said, "I'm glad you like it. You're pretty hot yourself."

Annette gently touched the back of John's arm as they turned into the break room. They made their cups of coffee and joked for a few minutes about nonsensical things as a few other personnel walked in while they were there.

As they walked out of the break room, John said, "Let's walk over to Betty's office and see what's going on with the Senator Roberts and if she has any more news on Senator Pelovski."

As they came up to Betty's office door, John said, as he stepped across the thresh hold, "Good morning, Betty. I thought I'd ask if you had anymore word on Senator Pelovski. I hope that she's recovering."

Betty looked up at John from her desk, and said, "She's still holding on, and I understand has shown some improvement in her breathing. They have her on a strong cocktail of medications, but she still shows no signs of regaining control of her limbs. Senator Roberts told me that the hospital is perplexed about the cause of her paralysis. They believe it to be some form of neurological disorder involving neurons. They'll be putting her on a new experimental drug that's in phase three human trials. The hospital contacted the FDA, got past the red tape, and received their approval to administer it to the Senator. They hope it will help her gain movement by stimulating nerve conduction. Senator Pelovski has agreed to take the drug under the Right to Try legislation."

John replied, "That's good to hear. At least there's hope that she'll be able to recover."

Annette asked Betty, "Have you sent flowers to the Senator?"

"Yes, I sent them a few days ago on behalf of Senator Roberts," Betty replied.

John, after hearing Betty relate what she knew about the Senator's condition, had an elation about what he had done. As wild a stab as it was using the untested diluted toxin, and the one lucky moment he had in dosing the Senator's drink, it all came to a result that gave him exactly what he was looking for. The beauty of it all was that they still did not discover the cause of her paralysis and he was at liberty to try it again. Only the next time, he had to find a more clandestine way of dosing his victims. He thought, I need to be smarter the next time."

John didn't see the opportunity while standing with Annette in Betty's office to plant the microphone he had in his pocket. After he had asked Betty about the Senator, John turned and walked back toward his desk, and said to both Annette and Betty as he turned away, "Excuse me ladies, duty calls."

All throughout the day, John kept an eye out for an opportunity to plant the bug, but Betty did not afford him any, as she stayed in her office the entire day. John resigned himself that he would have to stay vigilant for his chance.

The opportunity came when John received a phone call from a corporation he had been trying to solicit for campaign funds. The President of Blackwell Electronics, James Joyce, contacted him and told John that he would contribute $100,000 dollars to the Senator's campaign.

John knew that he would be able to go into Betty's office with the perfect excuse, that is telling her about the large donation. As soon as he thanked Mr. Joyce, he hung up and headed straight to Betty's office, knocked on her door and said, "Do you have a minute. I have some great news for you?"

Betty replied, "For great news I'll give you more than a minute." John walked over and sat down in front of her desk and said close your eyes and stick your hand out."

Betty said, "Why?"

John said, "Please humor me, Betty."

Betty said, "No tricks John."

"I promise. No tricks," John replied.

Betty then closed her eyes and stuck out her palm. As soon as she did that John reached into his pocket, took the bug, and stuck it under the overhang on the front of her desk, with his right hand while he reached across her desk and placed a folded piece of paper into the palm of her outstretched hand. Once John had done that, he said, "Okay Betty open your eyes."

Betty looked at the folded paper and asked, "What's this?"

John, showing a big grin said, "Read it."

Betty opened the paper and read what John had written on it before leaving his desk. After looking at it said, "John, is this real?"

"Betty, yes, it is. I just gave wire instructions to Mr. Joyce. I asked him if he could get it to the Senator's fund as soon as possible as we had only a few weeks left before election day and were in the process of releasing an ad blitz against his opponent Collette and could use all the financial help we could get. I thanked him immensely. He said it would be wired tomorrow. Betty, that's $100,000 dollars."

"John this is wonderful. I'm so amazed at how you do it. The Senator will be incredibly thankful. I'll tell him what you did when he comes in tomorrow. He should be arriving about ten in the morning."

"Betty, I couldn't help the dramatics. It was just that I was excited. I wasn't sure that they were going to donate anything. But they came through with flying colors," John replied.

"That was okay. It was funny the way you told me," Betty replied, and then asked, "How were you able to solicit this company?"

"Do you remember James Justise the attorney that donated $50,000 dollars to the campaign about four months ago, and asked to be able to speak to Senator Roberts?" John asked.

"Yes, I do," Betty said.

"It was through one of the referrals he gave me. One door opens another," John replied and then said, "You owe me a lunch for that one."

Betty laughed and said, "John, you got it. Keep up the excellent work."

John, grinning, said, "Well let me see if I can top that before this campaign ends. I'm looking for a free dinner."

John thought about the bull shit note and the close your eyes ruse to plant the bug, gloated at how fast he did it all. He was pleased with himself. Now that he had planted the bug in her office, the Senator was next.

John went to his desk and turned the recorder on immediately. He needed to test it to be sure it was receiving the audio. It didn't take long to find out because Betty was constantly on the phone. After a few minutes he played the recorder and could hear everything she said loud and clear. John gloated because he knew the game was on. Every so often he would listen to what Betty had been saying in her office hoping to get dirt on her.

As the day drew to an end, John noticed Betty leaving earlier than usual. He also noticed that the cleaning crew was already going about their business and that's when it dawned on him that they had keys to the offices and opened them to clean inside. He realized that he may just have gotten a window of opportunity to plant the bug in the Senator's office. He decided to go to the break room and observe the Senator's office from there. It took about fifteen minutes for the opportunity to break his way. A woman from the cleaning crew opened the Senator's office, walked inside, turned on the light and then came back out and started walking back towards Betty's office. He assumed she was going to retrieve her vacuum cleaner or something. He took that brief opportunity and rushed toward the Senator's office hoping he could get in and out before she returned, when he noticed Annette heading toward him.

He said to himself, "Damn it. This woman has some sense of timing. I thought she left to meet someone. What the fuck is she doing here?" He had no choice but to give up any attempt at planting the bug. John played it cool and smiled at Annette, and when she was close enough to him, he asked, "What are you doing here? I thought you had to meet someone?"

Annette replied, "My friend Lisa called me on my cell when I was in the parking lot and canceled because something came up at her home. I came back in to finish some work for Betty."

Annette asked, "Why are you still here?"

"I just finished a Corporate Donors solicitation report on how much in pledges I realistically expect to receive by end of the month. I've not had to do that before. I guess since I've been doing good numbers in that sector, Betty wants to know. I think it's because Collette isn't sinking in the polls, and she wants an all-out ad blitz," John said.

Annette replied," No matter what the polls say, I'm getting two hundred and fifty thousand ballots run. We don't have a lot of days left and we can't afford any delays. They all need to be printed, signed, and sorted by districts, and boxed for delivery before election day. Some of the places will receive the boxes the night before, where we have an inside Poll worker that will receive them. I'm lucky that I was able to get back most of my delivery people who know the routine and are supporters of our cause. That's not always easy after six years and especially when a crime is being committed. It requires a special type of person willing to lay it all on the line. Some will do it for the cause, Some will do it for money."

Annette than added, "It was easier on his last election because we could bulk more to any one location. Overall security was ridiculously lax. This year we expect conscientious watchers, that's why we're spreading out the ballots to as many districts and polling places as possible."

"It seems like you have it all under control. I don't see how I can help," John said.

"I'll need your help at the printing warehouse. You can box and label. I can use some extra hands there.

John replied, "Not a problem. Tell me when."

John looking past Annette saw the cleaning woman finishing the Senator's office, took a wild stab at planting the listening bug while no one else but Annette was around, asked her, "Do you think it would be all right to go into the Senator's office? I wanted to look at the photo gallery he has on the wall. I could not see all of the famous people he has been photographed with. His life impresses me?"

Annette looked toward the Senator's office, and said, "Sure why not? He wouldn't mind."

With her assurance, they walked over to his office, and when entering told the cleaning woman that they would only be a minute, and that they were just going to look at the Senator's photo gallery. There were at least twenty photographs artfully arranged along his back wall behind his desk. John let Annette walk ahead of him. He reached into his pocket, put the bug into his hand, and readied himself to plant it at the right moment. That moment came when the cleaning woman went to pull the electric vacuum cleaner cord from the wall socket. He knelt down quickly shielding his action with the side of the desk while the woman and Annette were looking away from him. He quickly stuck it onto the bottom inside rim of the desk.

Once he did that, he quickly grabbed his shoelaces. Annette looked back to John, and saw him kneeling on one knee, asked, "Are you alright?"

John replied, "My shoelace came loose."

John then rose to his feet and went to look at all of the Senator's photo's.

As John pretended to look at the pictures he thought, "Damn, I did it. Now that's done."

Annette looking at the same photo's she had seen many times before said, "They're impressive."

John replied, "Yes, they are. I see he has some taken with former President Carter and the French President Macron. Wow! Here's one with Brenda Streiban. I love her voice, not only when she sings, but when she gets very vocal against President Tripp."

"Yes, she has. Brenda and the Senator are good friends. She's helped him with the Hollywood crowd fund raising," Annette said.

After a few minutes, John said, "Now I'm really impressed with the Senator. You know for as long as I've been here, I never got to see the photo's up close. Even when I was in this office with you and Betty some months ago," John said.

Annette replied, "You just should've asked the Senator. He would've been happy to let you see them."

John replied, "I guess you're right, but the few times that he's been here, he's always been extremely busy, and when he hasn't, his office was always closed, and I honestly forgot about wanting to see them until now.

I only remembered when I watched the cleaning woman go into his office and again noticed the photo display.

John was an excellent bullshitter. He made up his crap on the fly. He was damn good at it.

Once they left the office, John said, "I need to head home. Katherine will wonder why I'm late. If you hadn't made plans, we may have been together this evening. You know I always figure things out," John said.

Annette replied, "I know. We'll see each other tomorrow."

John, seeing that even the cleaning woman was gone, took Annette in his arms and kissed her. He said, "Since I can't see you tonight, I wanted to take that kiss with me."

Annette just smiled, took him by the hand and walked toward the elevator, where they kissed again and, on the way down inside the elevator.

CHAPTER TWELVE

THE SET UP

As John walked toward his car, he spoke lowly to himself saying, "I needed to show her love. I can't let her think anything has changed, especially now that she's going to take me inside her operation. I need to get another mike. I have to record our conversation at the warehouse when she takes me there. I need it to have my accusations backed up, even if I'm recording her illegally. I want to put them all in jail, the cheating scumbags and that includes Annette."

As John drove home, he called Katherine. When she answered she asked, "Where are you?"

John replied, "I'm in the car heading home. I'm about fifteen minutes away." He then asked, "Are you dressed?"

Katherine replied, "Yes. Why?"

John answered, "Because I want to take you out for dinner, get you buzzed on wine and then carry you into the bedroom."

"Oh you think so. What makes you think I'll go along with your nefarious plan?" Katherine jokingly asked.

John replied, "Honey, how can it be nefarious when I told you what I was going to do?"

Katherine answered, "Because you told me you wanted to get me high on wine so I would be submissive. That's why." Laughing, she continued to ask, "You don't consider that underhanded?"

"Not really. Seriously my love. You would have let me carry you into the bedroom anyway."

"Oh, you're that sure of yourself," Katherine replied.

John trying to sound like Clark Gable, said, "Quite frankly, my dear, yes."

Katherine started to laugh and asked, "Who were you trying to be?"

John asked, "Geez, you didn't recognize Clark Gable?"

Katherine replied, "No. You didn't sound anything like him. You sounded like your ridiculous self, trying to sound like him." She then asked, "How close are you to the house?"

John answered, "I'll be there in about twelve minutes. Wait outside. Love you baby."

John was continuing to keep Katherine happy and unaware of his fabricated double life. So far, he has played everything like a virtuoso violinist. His marriage continued to be even better than before because he went out of his way to please Katherine, and Annette at the same time. Thank God, Annette was okay with the arrangement they had. They shared mutual interests, so she thought, and they had a steady love thing going on. John's feelings for Katherine were really no longer the same. He went out of his way to make her happy only so that she didn't upset his apple cart. John was now a different man in heart and mind. He did not want Katherine to be hurt, but if he had to leave her, he no longer cared. His mission was all that really mattered. He was now playing his wife, the way he played Annette and he had gone too far to turn back.

John pulled up to the house and saw Katherine waiting for him. When she entered the car, he leaned toward her and kissed her. Katherine said, "I don't know what has come over you, but I like it. You've become your old self. The man that I married. You are attentive, loving, and romantic. You weren't that for some time."

John replied, "I think that I was in a little bit of a funk for a while, staying in the house and just futzing with the garden. I needed something else going for myself. The computer school has made me feel better about everything."

Katherine replied, "I see that. Keep it up. I like the change it's made in you. So you're going to get me high on wine and take advantage of me. That's your plan?"

"You've got it my dear. That's exactly what I'm planning. That's my nefarious plan," John answered.

"Katherine, laughing said, "Okay. Let's stick with the plan."

"I almost want to forget dinner, go home, and take a bottle of wine to bed with us. I love you very much Katherine. I desire you as much as the day we met. Nothing about you has changed for me. It's as if you've been frozen in time. Your lovely brown hair, blue eyes and gorgeous slim body still suck me right in," John replied.

"Wow! Don't stop. I'm enjoying this," Katherine said laughing.

John said whatever needed to be said. He just wanted nothing, including Katherine, to mess up his plans. He was becoming cruel, and hurtful in his intentions, with little regret.

The rest of the night went as planned. John knew that Annette could never replace Katherine in his life. Annette was exactly as he wanted, a means to an end. What she gave to him he considered no more than icing on a clandestine cake. Katherine was certainly much more to John, and regardless of his words to her, she was becoming expendable.

The day came when John took Annette to the warehouse where she was having all of the printing done. When he met her, she was wearing skintight jeans, sneakers and a T-shirt that had a slogan on the front that said, "Let's do it." When John saw her, he said laughing, "Did you wear that shirt for me?"

Annette, smiled and said, "Maybe."

"I'll take that as a yes," John replied.

After arriving at the warehouse, Annette punched in a code to open the door. John tried to see the numbers but was only able to see the first one. It was five. He was not certain, but he thought she pushed seven next. He made a mental note, hoping it would help him recognize a connection later. When she opened the metal door, and walked in, John followed right behind her. As soon as he entered, he could see a few people working inside. He could hear the computerized press running and the steady kacheeuur, kacheeuur, beat of ballots shooting out. As he approached the operation, he realized that he recognized the man working at the press. It was Jim Levy, another volunteer at the campaign office. He also noticed a young woman, who he recognized as a real zealot and left-wing radical, who also worked there. He considered her the type that would wear a mask and run with Antifa. He was convinced that she had been radicalized at the college she went to and even by her parents. He had no evidence of his feelings. He just got that impression from what she said and how she acted at the office. Annette had introduced him to both of them when he first started his volunteer work.

He said to Annette, "I recognize Jim Levy and that young woman standing at the long table. I can't remember her name. I know I should know it by now, but she works on the other side of the campaign office, and I rarely speak to her."

Annette replied, "Her name is, and don't laugh, Lizzie Borden."

"No shit. I remember when I was a kid saying, 'Lizzie Borden took an axe and gave her mother forty whacks.' I'm sure she must have had some ragging about her name. What were her parents thinking when they gave her the name of a murderess?"

Annette said, "I'm sure she's had some joking about her name growing up."

As John walked closer to Jim and Lizzie, he smiled and waved. They returned their recognition and waved back. When he reached the press, he extended his hand to Jim, and said," "Nice to see you here."

Jim shook John's hand and said, "Nice to see you join the team. We're going to need the help."

Annette asked Jim, "How far have you gotten so far?"

"The printer counter shows 7,000 so far," Jim replied.

Annette asked, "Did you get the delivery of blank ballots?"

Jim replied, "Yes. We received another 10,000. It's enough to last until tomorrow night. You need to order more ink. We're running 10,000 a day. Based on that, we should finish all 250,000 with enough time to finish our deliveries. We need more help in sorting, signing, and boxing. If we don't catch up, we could run into a time problem. The only one so far that has been doing it is Lizzie. She's been working nonstop since yesterday. You can ask her what she's done with the districts. Your insistence on less ballots to each polling center could create a problem. That's a lot more deliveries and manual labor. I understand your reasoning, but without more help and delivery vehicles we might not be able to get all these ballots added to the count."

Annette said, "I've got it covered. I have commitments from three more drivers. I'm going to start drop offs the day after tomorrow to the districts that I have arranged to accept them. I believe we will do it with time to spare."

"Are we running those districts? You didn't tell me which districts to run first," Jim replied.

"Let me see what Lizzie has done and then we'll go from there," Annette said.

After Annette spoke to Jim, we walked over to Lizzie. Annette asked, "How are you doing Lizzie?"

"Okay, but I need help on the district sorting. We need to get the programming to print by zip code. That would speed up the sorting," Lizzie replied.

Annette said, "I'm more concerned that the zip codes fall in the right Congressional District as opposed to polling places. Just so long as we don't do more than 9,300 in any one of the twenty-seven districts. That'll speed up the sorting. Our delivery vans will not have to do more than three districts each. We can even get away with seven vans. I'm not concerned. I believe we've got it covered. Senator Roberts is going to be re-elected, one way or another."

Annette then said, "Excuse me Lizzie, sorry John. Lizzie, you know John from the office, I assume?"

Lizzie replied, "Yes, I've seen John many times. We've never really spoken to each other because we work on opposite ends of the floor." After answering Annette, Lizzie turned to John and said, "Nice to see you here. I'm surprised. You don't look like a radical because what we're doing is some radical shit."

John replied with a little sarcasm, "What does a radical look like? Is there a certain look? You don't need a scruffy beard and bandana to have the same political ideology and find for the same cause."

Lizzie responded, "John, you just surprised me. That's all. I guess you can't tell a book by its cover."

John moving away from a slight confrontation with Lizzie, asked, "What can I do to help?"

Lizzie replied, "You can start signing the printed ballots. Don't be fussy with the signatures. Just make them all look different. We're not expecting comparisons. The way we do these ballots will not be questioned. They're being separated into different districts for delivery and shuffled with the other volunteer signatures. Annette has this shit down to a science."

"I assume I just sign the voter's name that appears on the ballot?" John asked.

Lizzie responded, "You got it. There's a box full of pens at the end of the table. There will be several more volunteers coming any minute now to help you with signing. Unfortunately, they can't be printed on."

Annette said, "I'll leave you two together. I'm going to call my programmer and see how fast he can re-write the program to instruct the printer to print by zip codes located in each district. If I can get him to do that by tomorrow, our sorting time will be cut in half. I can see that the way we are doing it is too cumbersome and time consuming. I didn't have to worry about this before because we just did a couple ballot dumps at a few of the districts and didn't care about zip codes, or controlled amounts because the political climate was different. We didn't have to worry about poll watchers and audits like today. We need to avoid as many raised eyebrows as possible. Once we get the ballots into each district, we have volunteer poll workers that'll break them down further by polling offices. Lizzie was extremely helpful in lining up very willing volunteers throughout the state through her organization called Young Citizens for Socialist Principles.

As John was listening to Annette, he was smiling because everything being said was recorded and also videotaped by his new belt buckle spy camera that he purchased at a security equipment outlet he located in Jacksonville. He had both the audio and video receivers in the trunk of his car parked just outside the warehouse entrance. Both receivers were well within range.

John made sure to turn it in all directions to do a 360-degree scan of the warehouse. He already had enough on them, in the first ten minutes, to have them all investigated by the Feds. John hoped to get a few more names and addresses out of Annette by the end of the day.

John managed to get the contact number for candidate Collette and planned to communicate with her the coming week. He hoped that he could get the names of the poll workers that were in on the steal before meeting her. He would play it by ear, day to day. He also knew that the Senator would be at the campaign office full time up until election day and expected that he would be able to get many hours of conversation recorded. He knew that the phones would be busy over the next few weeks.

Regardless, he wanted to approach Collette and strategize how to handle the information.

The thing that was set in back of his mind was being able to yank the mikes out of the offices if he needed to do it quickly. He wanted to be sure that any information he turned over to Collette would not be leaked. He knew that if anything like that happened Senator Roberts would immediately be concerned about a leak in his campaign office. He had seen many movies where they did electronic sweeps to locate bugs and the Secret Service could do that. If they should find it, he knew that they could track the device back to him. It was a real concern, but he felt if he were careful in working with Collette, he could avoid that concern.

After Annette spent time talking to her programmer, she came back to us and said, "Okay, Lizzie, point me to a stack of ballots. I'm ready to help. I spoke to Brad about what we needed, and he said he could do it for us easily by tomorrow. He said it was just a matter of writing in some simple codes. All the information he needed was already on the hard drive.

I also gave him what we already printed so that he would not have us doing double work."

"Lizzie responded and said, "Wow! That's quick! We'll speed up the process tremendously. We should easily be able to box the 10,000 a day that Jim is running.

Annette said, "That's my goal. I will have drivers here tomorrow to load up and begin the drop offs. I want them there ahead of time, so I know that they'll be counted."

When John heard Annette say that he said to himself, "Damn, I'd love to know the drop off points and who was in on it at the other end. This woman is like a one-man band, she has everything covered. I need to work fast and get with Collette. I only hope that she can do the things I think she can."

John said, "Annette, you're amazing. You're giving Senator Roberts a 250,000-vote lead before the first vote is cast. That's a pretty tough handicap for Collette to overcome."

Annette replied, "That's the whole idea. We need a guaranteed win."

John said, "I'm beginning to think Senator Roberts might lose without them. The polls that I heard on the news yesterday are claiming Collette is now tied with just a two-point difference and that to me is a dead heat, when you know the margin of error is three percent."

Annette replied, "John, I'm well aware of it. That's why I'm doing what I'm doing. In the last election there was about 8,200,000 votes in total cast. Roberts won by 120,000 votes. That was about a three percent margin. I'm guessing he's ahead by a slim one percent now and that's only 40,000 votes more or less."

John replied, "From the way it looks, he'll need every vote you're giving him. It's all going to depend on turn out and from what I see happening,

Collette's ground game is really strong. Her door to door get out the vote push is massive."

Annette said, "I know John. Betty, the Senator, and I discussed it in detail. He's a little disappointed in Betty for not doing better in that area. She told him she actually had more feet on the ground then Collette, but the state is turning redder each year, especially since the voters elected an American Patriot Governor who admittedly is doing an excellent job and that's influencing voter opinion, especially when they see what is happening in the National Socialist led states and cities. We can use our old racism excuse for so long. It begins to get stale."

John said, "We have to re-examine the issues more closely. Steal the American Patriot Party play book and seal the borders. That's what we National Socialists wanted for years anyway. It wasn't until our leaders thought they could expand our voting base with the illegal Hispanics pouring across our borders that our closed borders philosophy changed. American Patriots picked up our mantel and started selling immigration as part of their political platform and it's resonating with the voters. That's what I think. Regardless I'm a party loyalist and I go with the flow."

Lizzie who was listening to our conversation said, "John, how can you want sealed borders? There should no longer be borders anywhere in the world. We're all citizens of the planet Earth, and we were not meant to be segregated or our movements controlled. One world order and one world government is what we the people of Earth need."

As John listened to Lizzie, his eyes rolled up, then down toward Lizzie thinking, this woman is fucking bonkers. He then said, "Lizzie! I hear what you're saying, but it's not practical today in so many ways. Think about the United Nations, they're representative of a world governing body. They have not been able to get together on anything. Besides, I would hate to see the cultures of so many nations be lost. It used to be wonderful to go to France and enjoy their way of life. Go there now and it no longer has that gay Paree feeling. So much of that city has become like the Middle East, recognizing Sharia law, and not the laws of the French."

Annette said, "Okay, let's not get into a political debate. We need to get these ballots ready to go."

Just as she finished saying that Jim Levy came over pushing a cart with a few thousand more ballots on it. As he approached, he said, "Annette, here are 2,300 more. I have 3,000 to go and all of Districts twenty-five through to twenty-seven will be completed. I can stay late today and continue on, but I'll be using the original thumb drive. I think waiting until you get us the revised one from Brad makes more sense. I gain on the printing, but the sorting will take even longer. In the end, we'll lose time. What do you think boss lady?"

Annette said, "I agree. We'll wait. I'll be able to get it from Brad by late today or tomorrow early, knowing Brad." She then asked, "How long will it take you to run the last batch?"

Jim replied, "An hour and a half at the most. We'll need more ink for tomorrow if we're going to print another 10,000 to 15,000. I can work all day tomorrow into the wee hours printing and knock out at least 25,000 more. That will cover another three districts."

Annette responded and said, "Yes, please by all means. We'll still have another twenty-one to go. That's another nine days of around the clock. I'll need more volunteers to sign and box it all up and shipped. I need to make some phone calls and see who I can get."

Lizzie spoke out and said, "I can get volunteers from my Young Citizens Group that would love to be a part of this. Do you want me to call Annette?"

Annette replied, "If you're absolutely sure they are trustworthy. I don't want any of us going to jail. What we're doing is no joke."

"Don't worry Annette, they're that and more. I can even get members of Antifa here if you want guarding the door with automatic weapons," Lizzie replied with a braggadocious tone attempting to elevate her importance to Annette.

John hearing her say that, said to himself, "This little terrorist bitch needs to be arrested. Keep talking. I love it. Everything is on tape."

Annette said, "Okay Lizzie. I'm counting on you because the wrong people will put you in jail as well. When can you have them come and how many do you think you can get by tomorrow and would be willing to work over the next week?"

Lizzie replied, "I'm sure that I can get three on a minutes notice, and at least ten over the next few days. I have to reach those with flexibility in their daily schedules. I'll start calling tonight when I get home."

Annette said, "That'll be great. If you can't do it for any reason, please call me."

"No problem, Annette. I will," Lizzie replied.

John kept smiling at it all. The conversations he recorded were more than he could hope for. He only wished it were legal.

After working eight hours, John went over to Annette and said, "Sweetness, you know I can't stay any longer, but I'll be able to help for the next two days. I'll just come here in the morning and pick up where we've left off. Will you be here early tomorrow?"

"I should be, but if I'm later than you, you know what to do. Lizzie will be here. She'll be able to get you started," Annette replied.

"Damn, I just realized we came together in my car," John said.

Annette asked Lizzie, "Can you drop me off at my home later. John needs to go, and I came in his car."

Lizzie replied, "Absolutely. That's not a problem."

John then said to Annette, "Take a moment and walk me to my car."

Annette looked at John with a smile, then put her hand on the back of his arm, and turned with him toward the exit door. After they stepped outside the warehouse, John took Annette into his arms, and kissed her. He then said, "You look so hot in those skintight jeans. Every time you bent over putting the ballots in the boxes you turned me on. You have a beautiful tush."

"John. You're such a cad. I bent over an awful lot of times. You must be the horny boy by now."

"That's putting it mildly," John replied.

"Well, we can't resolve your problem now, so you'll have to take it out on Katherine. She'll get to appreciate the fruits of my labor," Annette said.

"Annette, you didn't have to say that. Really!" John said.

Annette then touched John lightly on his cheek, leaned forward and kissed him, then said in his ear, "You're right. But I do get jealous at times, even though I know there are no guarantees about our relationship. Go home. I'll see you tomorrow."

John turned and walked away. As he was getting into his car, he couldn't wait to pull off someplace and listen to his recordings and watch his video to be sure that everything was being recorded. After driving for fifteen minutes, he pulled into the back end of a Publix Supermarket parking lot where he was isolated. He hopped out of his car, opened the trunk, and played what he had recorded. He became excited about the clarity of his recordings. The voices were clear, and the videos were more than he could have hoped for. He had Annette, Lizzie and Jim and the entire warehouse, and close ups of the ballots, which he had smartly held up in his hands facing his belt buckle camera.

After seeing that everything was going well with his plan, John sat back in his car, and began hitting his steering wheel with open palms saying, "Yes! You mother fuckers. I got you!"

John then proceeded home to Katherine.

When John arrived at the house, he went to Katherine and gave her his usual kiss. This time he didn't stop with one, he kissed her several times, and said, "God. I love you." As he held her close, she said to him, "I love you too. Is there something special going on with you that makes you so loving?"

"You're what's so special," he said as he reached down, put his arms around Katherine's legs and picked her up, carried her into the bedroom, and laid her on the bed. She started to laugh and just watched him undress quickly. It didn't take her long to notice how aroused he was. With that she pulled off her panties and welcomed him to her.

As John was making love to Katherine, he knew that Annette was the one that had gotten him into his sexual frenzy. He thought of her as he made love to Katherine, and hated Annette for getting into his mind. He thought he had the thought of her under control, but realized he was still fighting a battle within himself. As John climaxed, he said, to Katherine, "God, you're wonderful. I'm sorry honey, I just couldn't hold out. You were unbelievable."

Katherine said, "It's okay. I'm happy that you're happy."

John looking into Katherine's eyes said, "I want to renew our vows."

Katherine just smiled and looked up at John's face, with a tear welling up in her eyes, said, "Do you really mean that?"

"Yes, Baby. I do. Do you want to?" John asked.

Katherine said, "John, Yes, I do. But it's not necessary, because I gave you my heart all over again when you asked me."

With her words John moved to her side and pulled Katherine close to him where he held her and kissed her gently several times on her face.

John made love to Katherine again that night making sure that she reached her climax the second time. John was becoming a sick soul. He didn't need to say those things to Katherine, and he knew it. Just building her up for a big letdown later was uncalled for, should something happen to him, or he needed to flee out of the country. How far was he going to take it. He had become a merciless murderer that enjoyed the mission he put himself on.

The next morning John got up and after having breakfast, went to his workshop, and checked on his frogs. He was meticulous in their care. He kept the temperature controlled, their environment moist, and fed them as needed. He couldn't be more pleased. They were as toxic as they could be. He could even see the glistening toxin on their bodies. The one thing he made sure of was that he never put his hands inside the tank without wearing rubber gloves or keeping his arms covered. He had seen the frogs on the side of the tank a few times, and realized that they were leaving toxin trails on the glass. He always made sure to wipe off the inside glass for no more than his own safety.

CHAPTER THIRTEEN

THE PLAN PLAYS OUT

Once he had checked on his frogs, he left to go to the warehouse. Along the way, he stopped at a Krispy Kreme, and picked up a few dozen donuts to bring to the warehouse and a cup of coffee. He went back out to his car, opened his coffee, picked up his cell phone and dialed Candidate Jeanne Collette's phone number.

The call was answered by a receptionist who asked, "How may I place your call?"

John answered, "Please connect me with Senatorial Candidate Jeanne Collette."

"May I ask whose calling?" the receptionist asked.

John replied, "Please tell Candidate Collette that John is calling and urgently needs to talk to her. That I have some extremely valuable information for her eyes only."

"May I have your last name?" The receptionist asked.

John replied, "Just tell her John. She doesn't know me. I'll disclose who I am when I meet her."

"Let me ask you, are the Candidates' phone conversations recorded?" John asked.

The receptionist replied, "No sir. They're not. It's not legal in this State without two party consent. Please hold a moment."

After a few minutes passed, the receptionist said, "I'll put you through to Candidate Collette."

"This is Jeanne Collette. May I ask who you are and who you represent?" Collette asked.

"My name is John. My last name is confidential for the moment. What I need to discuss with you and show you must be held in absolute confidentiality. I will only do it in person. It's about your opponent Senator Roberts. I have very damning information. That's all I'm willing to say on the phone. Are you available for me on Friday, at your office?"

"How do I know who you are or if this isn't some kind of ruse?" Collette asked.

John replied, "I can assure you I'm legitimate and one hundred percent behind your candidacy. I will meet you with your attorney, or anyone else you feel comfortable with, but I must insist that you vouch for them and their ability not to divulge what I'm willing to give you. I'm sure you'll seek consultation on what I have. I'll tell you that the information is very explosive, and I expect the Senator will drop out of the race the minute it gets out. Either say yes or no. I will not say any more than that over the phone."

Collette replied, "John, hold a moment, I want to confirm if I can get my campaign adviser here. What time on Friday?" Collette asked.

John replied, "I can be there by 10.30 in the morning."

"That sounds okay with me. I'll juggle my schedule and make the time. I must admit you have me quite intrigued. But hold on for a moment, I need to make a call on my cell," Collette replied.

John waited for five minutes and was beginning to get a little nervous about the long hold time, when Collette came back to the phone. "I'm sorry for the long wait, but my campaign adviser didn't answer right away, so I sent him a text. Ten thirty Friday morning is okay."

"I was getting a little nervous and was going to hang up. I must be overly cautious. When we meet and I disclose what I have, you'll understand why. I'll see you then," John said.

After making his call, John headed to the warehouse to work on the ballots. As he drove, he weighed what he had just done, and felt excited about the evolving sting operation on the Senator's illegal voting operations and taking him and his minions down. Many things went through his mind, and one was wondering how Senator Pelovski was holding up. He had not inquired over the past week. The last thing he heard from Betty was that she was going to be moved to her home where she would continue to receive the same type of care she was receiving at the hospital. The news mentioned that her Senate Seat would be vacated and that it would be filled with a temporary replacement selected by the Governor of her State.

The joy in his evil deed was that the APP Governor did not have to replace National Socialist Pelovski with another party member. He could choose an American Patriot to temporarily replace her, if he did as John expected, he'd increase their majority in the Senate, boosting President Tripp's power. He was overly anxious to see who the Governor would select.

He knew that the replacement process for a Seat in the Lower House could only be done with a special election in Nadine Waterman's State. Congresswoman Waterman's Congressional district was no longer solid Socialist. It was now considered purple, so the chances of her being replaced by an American Patriot Party member were good. Her election was being held in the coming week and both parties were ad blitzing her District. All he could do was keep his fingers crossed. He thought, "God please make it so. If it turns out as I'd like, I would have affected the balance of power in the government with my little Golden Frogs."

John reached the warehouse, carrying the Krispy Kreme's with a smile on his face. He said, as he approached everyone, "I hope you like donuts. Is there any fresh coffee?"

Lizzie said, "Yes and yes. I love Krispy Kreme's, especially their blueberry flavored ones and I made the coffee about twenty minutes ago."

John replied, "Lizzie, you're in luck. I love blueberries myself, so I bought a half dozen of those. Come and have one with me."

"I see that we have more hands today," John said as he noticed three additional people sorting and signing ballots. He continued, "I would have bought another dozen if I had known that."

Lizzie replied, "Yes. They are friends of mine. We all belong to the Young Citizens for Socialist Principles. We're a progressive leaning organization. There'll be a few more tomorrow. I'm hoping to have ten people helping over the next few days."

John said, "That's terrific. We'll need all the hands we can get."

Annette looked at John with a smile, and watched him talk to Lizzie as they all walked toward the coffee machine.

Annette moved over to him at the coffee table and said, "Now I know why I got here ahead of you."

John replied, "I couldn't resist. I was in the mood for a Krispy Kreme. Have one. I have jelly, lemon, blueberry, and Boston Creams. What's your flavor?"

"I think I'll have a Boston Cream. They look delicious," Annette said.

John turned and waved at Lizzie's friends, beckoning them to have some donuts. It took only minutes before they were all having donuts and coffee.

John asked Annette, "Did you get the revised thumb drive from Brad?"

"Yes, I did. It's going to make an enormous difference in time. I knew he would come through," Annette replied.

"Sounds good and with the additional help we should be able to knock out the entire lot and have everything ready for delivery, I'm guessing that each person should be able to sign between thirty and forty ballots a minute, If I'm right that'll give us at least 1,800 per person per hour, We should easily knock out 25,000 by the time they need to be delivered," John said.

After several minutes, everyone went about signing, sorting, packing, and labeling all the cartons in different stacks on the floor. Each separate pile was earmarked for different districts and would be loaded onto the vans, with the closest polling place being put on the trucks last.

John had his spy equipment operating and continued where he left off the night before. So far everything was going along smoothly. There was little conversation taking place except for the occasional question posed by Annette. John and Annette would throw glances at each other. He just couldn't help himself. He was attracted to her in a perverse way. He thought about his call to Jeanne Collette and knew that he was preparing to sell Annette out to the Feds and enjoyed the thought. Yet, at the same time felt a twinge of guilt for doing it. Even though he wrestled with his conflicting feelings, he convinced himself that under her sweet persona she was an evil criminal socialist bitch and needed to pay the piper.

He was too far gone mentally to rationalize anything different. All he could see was evil people in an evil party, doing evil things and she was as evil as they get. She was changing the results of elections and denied the will of the people. John didn't see himself as evil, he saw himself as a warrior and patriot doing good for the nation. Even when coming to the same conclusions, time after time, after struggling with his thoughts over her, she could still get hm physically aroused.

As the day was coming to an end for John, he enticed Annette to go with him to the small supply room where they kept blank ballots, and all the supplies they needed. As they entered the room and stepped to the side out of sight of everyone, he took her in his arms and kissed her passionately. He pressed his body next to hers in a wanting fashion.

Annette said, "John, stop. Not here."

John looked at her in surprise, as Annette had never told him to stop before. He responded by asking, "Did I do something wrong? Are you upset with me?"

Annette replied, "John, no you didn't do anything wrong. I can't do this with you anymore. I know that our relationship will not go the way I'd want it to go, and I knew when I started with you, it wouldn't, and I didn't care then, but I've fallen in love with you, and it hurts when I see you leave to go home to Katherine. I've been denying my true feelings for you to myself, but I can't any longer. It's best for both of us to end it the way it is. We can still be friends and work together. I don't want to be the one to come between you and Katherine. It's obvious you're in love with her. With you it's lust. With me it's so much more."

John stood there speechless at first. He knew that what she was asking was for the best John, looked at her, touched his hand gently to her cheek, kissed her lightly, and said, "I'll see you tomorrow. I understand."

He then walked out of the supply room and headed home without looking back. He was torn between feeling rejected and relief that it was over. He got what he wanted from her and did not think he would need to worry about their relationship. He felt that her feelings for him would not just disappear and that if he needed something from her, she would still oblige him. He got in his car and headed home. Just like all the times before, whenever he drove anywhere, he would have conversations with himself. The cabin of the car was his think tank.

He would openly talk aloud and found himself doing the same, as he said, "I didn't expect that from Annette. I was caught off guard. But hey, fuck it. I'm glad she did, now when I put her away, I really won't give a fuck."

It was easy for John to switch his emotions back and forth. He was two people wrapped in one brain. His Jekyll and Hyde persona was always present. He switched from one to the other many times without realizing any difference in himself.

In a sudden outburst he slammed the palm of his free hand against the steering wheel a few times yelling out, "God damn you!" and then took a restful moment after his outburst to gather his emotions. He said, "I know what she did was for the best and I can't find fault in her actions, but I know that I'm one twisted individual. I hate her for what she represents and passionately, but I so deeply love the good side of her. How fucked up is that? John, John, John, get a hold of yourself. You're misconstruing good sex for love. That's exactly what it is. Man! Can she fuck."

After that John's mind stayed blank as he drove down the street towards his house, when he noticed a Collette campaign sign in the front yard. He smiled and said, "Don't worry lady, I got you covered."

John relaxed the rest of the day with Katherine, keeping his mind off of Annette and everything that was going on behind Katherine's back. He just relaxed on his recliner couch with Katherine next to him. He held her hand and thought, how in the hell did he allow himself to do all the things he did. It was becoming normal for John to debate himself. The winner was always Mr. Hyde. Then in a nano second concluded that what he was doing was for the good of the nation and his beloved President Tripp and anyone that affected it had to go.

The next day came around and John headed off to the warehouse to continue helping on the election steal with Annette. When he got there, he saw three vans parked outside being loaded with the ballot stuffed cartons. He knew that they were the delivery vans that were going to take the ballots to the drop off places, before being illegally inserted into the voting count on election day.

When he came up to them, he purposely walked to the rear of each one taking pictures of the license plate numbers with his belt buckle camera. As he walked past the open vans he looked inside, and recorded the stacked cartons and everyone involved in loading them.

The first person he saw was Jim Levy. John said, "Hey Jim, loading already?"

Jim replied, "Yes, we need to get them out and gone."

John said, "I'll go help."

"John, we only have one dolly, and these boxes are heavy," Jim said.

"I'll stack the dolly and drop the boxes off here. I'll keep going back and forth while you load. They look a little heavy for Annette and Lizzie," John said.

Jim replied, "They are, and they get heavier as you keep lifting them. Lizzie has a few friends helping. It shouldn't take long to load everything. I need to keep printing. You can pick up what I'm doing so I can get the printer working."

"It sounds like a plan," John responded.

When John stepped into the warehouse, he saw Lizzie and another woman he had not seen before, labeling, and sealing the cartons. He noticed Annette and two more volunteers at the sorting tables.

As he reached Annette, he said, "Good morning." Then he became all business and asked, "Do you want me to load boxes?"

Annette looked at John, and politely said, "That would be nice." The tone in her voice seemed timid. It was as if she regretted telling John what she did. John sensed an apologetic tone. He did not react to her in a manner that would show Annette that she was all he wanted. He stayed calm and businesslike. If anything changed between them, it would have to be Annette's move. John resigned himself to why bother any longer. He was going to have her arrested at some time, once the FBI got involved in what she was doing.

"How many did Jim get printed?" John asked.

"He worked really late into the night. He doubled his output. He told me the counter showed 22,452 for the day," Annette replied.

John amazed said, "That's fantastic. So that's over 30,000 in a little over two days?" He then asked, "Am I right?"

Annette replied, "32,652 to be exact. He wants to do another 15,000 more today. It will give us twenty percent of the total with thirteen days left until the election. We can easily do 10,000 a day guaranteed. I expect to have a three-day window of opportunity to make sure everything has been delivered and ready to be seamlessly filtered into the ongoing count."

John said, "I'm sure you'll get it done, and when Roberts wins, no one will be the wiser. The numbers added should not jump out in any one of the county's with the way you blended the increases. We should be celebrating with the Senator election night."

"That's what this is all about," Annette replied.

John said, "Well let me get the cartons onto the vans before I start signing again."

As the day passed, Annette told some of Lizzie's volunteers to go home. All the boxes had been signed, sorted, and loaded and there was far less to do, except wait for Jim to run more ballots. Annette's idea, as simple as it was, made processing the ballots a cake walk.

They came out of the printer already sorted by county zip codes just needing to be signed and placed into cartons for delivery to the district polling places. The arduous time-consuming work of separating all the zip codes had been eliminated.

The three delivery trucks that we had loaded earlier in the day had left. John figured they had all reached their destinations and were on their way back for another run.

When there was a lull in the workload, John decided to have another cup of coffee and another donut, if any were left. He and Annette had hardly spoken to each other throughout the day. John had no problem in talking to Annette, but he could not find anything to say, other than, "Are there any more labels printed?" Annette did not look toward John very often. John was well aware of it because he kept looking her way throughout the day. She was constantly working with her back towards him. He felt she was doing it on purpose. He shrugged it off, and told himself, "Screw it. She's finished with me anyway." But what he said and how he felt despite everything he did, and was going to do, still had a fatal attraction for her.

As he was standing at the coffee table pouring a cup of coffee, he looked into the donut box and saw that there were two remaining. He said to himself, "That's luck. I thought they'd all be gone by now."

He took a bite of his donut, sipped his coffee and was enjoying that moment when he felt a hand touch his arm and heard Annette's voice ask, "Is there another donut for me?"

John replied, "You're in luck, there's a Boston Cream left."

The touch of her hand on his arm sent a warm feeling through him. He looked at her and she looked at him. They just stood that way for a moment speechless. John smiled and said "You've accomplished what you set out to do so far. It looks like you'll make it with a few days to spare if Jim can average 20,000 a day from here on out."

Annette replied, "He can do it now because the change in the program allows us to keep up with him. We lost valuable time in the first few days because of the unnecessary sorting. We should've had more counties delivered initially, but no matter we'll still get it done. Even if I only have one day before election day, the longest drive to drop off ballots in the few remaining southern counties by then will be no more than one - or two - hours tops. Delivery will be quick enough for ballot insertion well before voting begins."

John asked, "Do you just open boxes in the polling place and dump them on a table? That would raise some eyebrows, wouldn't it?"

Annette laughed and said, "John, we're not crazy. The boxes are already in the polling places the night before, opened and dropped into the ballot boxes which we then open later in the day when votes are counted. All day long walk in voters keep dropping their ballots in the same boxes commingling ours with theirs. We will also insert them into the postal deliveries. It is a seamless operation. I can assure you no eyebrows will be raised. This election will be handled much more covertly then before."

John replied and said, "That's good to know. I'd hate to see a voting fraud scandal break against the Senator, especially when there'll be more poll watchers this year."

Annette said, "There will be, but we'll keep them at a distance. All they'll be able to see are ballot boxes being opened and dumped on the tables for counting."

John with a smile thought, "Now that was a good bit of recording. She keeps digging herself deeper in a hole. That was about as incriminating as you can get."

Annette then said, "I'm sorry about what I said to you in the supply room. I know that I want more from our relationship, as impossible as it seems. But I don't want to lose any chance that things will change or those wonderful moments we have together."

John replied, "Annette, you don't have to apologize. I totally understand where you're coming from. I find no fault in your thinking. I thought about what you've said, and I realized how selfish it is of me to seek your love, when I know I won't divorce Katherine. I think that we should just stay friends and have casual sex once in a while."

"John, you are without a doubt, an asshole, but a lovable one," Annette replied.

With those words, she turned and walked away. John smiled after her. He took the "Lovable one" comment to mean she was open to casual sex.

The time came when John needed to leave. He wanted to go home and put his recorded conversations on disks and get ready for his meeting with Candidate Collette. He was anxious and yet apprehensive. He didn't know for sure about being exposed to the FBI. He needed assurances from Collette and her campaign advisor.

Friday came around with John getting ready to go to Collette's office with the downloaded disks in hand. He had still an hour to kill before needing to leave, so he put on the news. After watching it for twenty minutes, a segment came on about a news reporter that refused to give up her sources, when she published some scathing information about a Congressman who got paid for political favors by Ukrainian mobsters. His ears perked up when he heard them say the part about the reporter's refusal to relinquish the name of her confidential informant and claimed privilege under her First Amendment Rights. As soon as John heard that, he said, I should've thought about that." He went to his computer and posed the question in google and produced the information he needed. He read that many states and federal courts subscribe to such a privilege and that over fifty percent of the states uphold a shield law protecting the privilege as a constitutional right. He immediately checked on the State of Florida and was pleased to see that the State upheld that law as well.

He now had a decision to make. Should he give up his information to Candidate Collette or to a reporter of some notoriety. The more he weighed his options the more he leaned toward the reporter. Regardless of his new alternative he decided to keep his appointment with Jeanne Collette to see how things played out.

CHAPTER FOURTEEN

THE TRUTH BE TOLD

When John arrived promptly at Candidate Jeanne Collette's office building, he took an elevator up to the seventh floor and when the elevator doors opened, he stepped into a lobby with a security guard sitting on a stool behind a high narrow desk. Behind the guard were double glass doors with a receptionist desk behind them.

The guard asked John who he wanted to see and to show his identification. John said, "I don't want to show my identification, but Candidate Collette is expecting me. I have an 11.30 appointment with her. Please let her know that John is here."

He picked up the phone and dialed her, telling her that, "There is a man in the lobby who refused to show his ID, but identified himself as John and claims to have an appointment with you."

John heard him say, "Please wait sir, Candidate Collette's Campaign Advisor, Jeremy Long will be coming out to get you." After saying that he came from around his desk and scanned John. John lifted his arms without saying anything. When the scanner made a warning sound, John knew that the only thing he had on him that was metal were his car keys. He took them out of his pocket and laid then in a small basket on the guards desk. He raised his arms a second time and let the guard rescan him.

John stood and waited several minutes before Mr. Long came out to get him. As he walked up to John, he extended his hand and introduced himself. He said to John as they began walking towards Collette's office, "So I understand from Candidate Collette that you have some damning evidence against Senator Roberts."

John replied, "Yes. Very damning."

Jeremy said, "Well you've certainly peaked our curiosity." Then said, "This is Candidate Collette's office." He opened the door allowing John to enter first. John walked toward Jeanne as she came from around her desk to him. Collette was a thin short woman who dressed casually. She had blond hair and light blue eyes, that he could not look away from. He thought, "They are really captivating." They shook hands and greeted each other. Collette beckoned John to sit down in a lounge area inside her office.

She said, "Well tell us John what you have on the Senator."

John replied, "I know that when I disclose what I have, you'll want the FBI to get involved. You'll have no other choice. But before I give you that wow moment, I need to tell you that I have video and voice recordings that I got without the consent of the other parties. That being the case, I'm not sure how you'll be able to use it. You can say that I acted like Project Veritas in how I obtained it. The other thing I want is total confidentiality. I under no circumstances want my name disclosed. Can you figure a way to use it and protect my identity? Give me an answer to that, and you can have what I have, which are video's and voice recordings of the Senator's staff plotting to guarantee his election. I can tell you it is continuing to be well orchestrated, by a very articulate person."

Jeremy said, "Before we go to our legal counsel, we would like to hear some of what you have so that we know it is as damning as you claim, and it is real. You must understand that."

John replied, "I do. But I will need you to take a chance on me. It will cost you nothing to discuss the matter with your attorney's. All you need to tell them is you have someone that illegally obtained video's and voice recordings without the consent of the parties being recorded and what I claim them to be and that I want confidentiality. It seems to me that they should be able to advise you. That is it in a nutshell. I'm certain in their attempt to steal the election they have in fact guaranteed yours. I have the where, how and who is involved incriminating themselves, but without their knowledge. If you can't guarantee me those few things, then I'll have to decide what to do next. If you can't, I can go to a News Reporter and get protected under The Shield Law. It's a First Amendment issue and is protected under the Constitution and upheld under Florida law. Which way I go is up to you. Let me know by tomorrow."

Candidate Collette said, "John, okay. What you ask is reasonable under the circumstances. We'll call you between today and tomorrow with an answer."

John replied, "That's fine with me." Then having an epiphany said, "What if I became a client of your attorney and you paid his fee. I could disclose what I've got, and he wouldn't have to disclose what we discussed under attorney client privileges."

Jeremy said, "John, that's a thought. Let us call you back. We'll contact our law firm and get the answers you seek. But what you said sounds like the easiest way to do it, and because Candidate Collette is his client as well, she can be in on that meeting and be protected under the same laws." He then asked, "What's your real purpose in doing this?"

"I can't stand the Senator. He's a National Socialist, excuse me Candidate Collette, a scumbag and I hate Socialists and anyone who attacks President Tripp on trumped up bullshit. I'm an American Patriot for a better America."

Candidate Collette said, laughing, "I've actually called Senator Roberts that myself."

John replied, "Get the meeting with your attorney set up. I'll be there. I'll have a video and audio disk with me."

John stood up and extended his hand to Jeremy and said, "Nice meeting you. You represent a great candidate." John then turned to Jeanne and extended his hand to her and said, "Nice meeting you as well Senator Collette. That title suits you better. I'm truly on your side and available when you become Senator."

"I'll make no promises John, but I will definitely keep you in mind," Collette replied.

John then turned and walked out of her office and headed out of the building, pleased that he met with Collette and her advisor. His next move was going to do some research on investigative reporters and determine which one would best suit his needs and one with a ballsy editor that would back up their refusal to disclose their information to the FBI.

Some of those things he was concerned about would have to be guaranteed by the reporter.

John headed home to do some google searches. Getting the right reporter was his next priority. While he was driving an unbelievable urge swept through his body. He had the thought of killing somebody else. His Mr. Hyde personality came out of nowhere. At that moment he needed to do it again. He said with wry humor, "If I feel like a frog I'll leap. I don't know if it should be someone from the campaign office again or not.

Those are the only National Socialist Party members I know. But I would be pushing the envelope too far."

His thoughts switched to his frogs. "I have to check on my little beauties. I can't afford to neglect my little friends and I need to harvest some more toxin." Then with an uncontrolled outburst he said, "Ooh the feeling of rubbing death onto someone is exhilarating. I must admit I got perverse pleasure in doing it. I need that rush. Fuck it. I'll randomly fuck somebody up this coming week." He then started to sing, "I'm going to knock somebody off, do dah do dah, I'm going to knock some asshole off, oh do dah day."

John arrived home and found that Katherine was not there. He really didn't care at that moment as he headed out to his workshop to check on his frogs. He found them in good health. The temperature inside was at a comfortable seventy-five degrees, and his poisonous insects were thriving and providing sustenance to his little friends.

He scraped the toxin from the frogs and put it into his plastic pill box. After carefully harvesting the toxin, he went back into his home and straight to his computer where he started to research investigative reporters. His first thought was Vox News. He felt that they'd give him the confidential protection he needed and would certainly reach a huge audience. He felt comfortable that that conservative leaning media channel would not bury his story like the left-wing media, or leak the information to Senator Roberts before the information was released. He also considered the Wall Street Daily. He knew that they were strong President Tripp supporters and felt sure that they would give him the confidentiality he needed and protect his anonymity. He remembered that a reporter from the Newspaper refused to give the Department of Justice her source and was willing to go to jail before disclosing it. She had defied a government subpoena, and even with the threat of imprisonment still refused to comply.

John researched the incident and found her name. He decided after reading the article about Sarah Foster, that she was the one he would call. He thought, "If she did that once for someone, she'd do it again. Hell, she was tried and tested." He figured that once the worldwide circulated paper released the story, Vox News would pick it up and air it anyway.

The first chance John got, he called her up, but was unable to reach her. He did confirm that she still worked for the paper and was now considered their Lead Investigative Reporter. He left a contact number for a burner phone and a message for her that said, "If you're still willing to stand up for a confidential source, and want a political story that will light up the airways, then call me. I must hear from you soon, or I'll reach out to another news outlet."

John was becoming more adept at the spy game he was playing. He used his Bitcoin account to buy several burner phones. He would use them for as long as he needed to. John was one of those Bitcoin believers when they first came out even though they were not backed by any standard. He was worth millions with Bitcoin alone. His stocks and bonds portfolio added several million more. He could rub elbows with the rich, but he chose to downplay his wealth. John personally thought that most of those people were all full of shit.

He remembered his humble beginnings and his hardworking blue-collar father and mother and would never forget the times that he had to wear worn out shoes, and get his clothes from Goodwill. But he also remembered that there was no disfunction in his family. Everyone loved each other, and showed it. John was now the last of the siblings, both his older sister and brother passed away well before their time. John was quite content living his middle-class lifestyle. Katherine did not demand more, because she lacked for nothing. They had a beautifully decorated 3500 square foot home, which they felt was more than enough for two people. It was nestled in a beautiful older community with tree lined streets. John enjoyed his home and his simpler lifestyle because he knew it was what he wanted, and not what he could afford.

Two hours had past when John got his call from Sarah Foster. He knew who it was when the phone rang. She was the only one that had the number to his burner phone. John answered and said, "I assume that I'm talking to Sarah Foster."

Sarah replied, "Yes this is she."

"I appreciate your call. I need to ask you up front, if I give you damning information about a Senator and his re-election bid on both audio and video recordings exposing criminal activity that you will protect me as a confidential source," John asked.

Sarah replied, "Yes, I will. But you need to tell me how you obtained the recordings?"

"I made them myself without the parties involved knowing they were being caught on camera and audio. You may liken my activity to that of Project Veritas, although I'm freelancing. I did what I did because I don't like what they're doing. They think I'm on their side. I'm far from it," John said.

Sarah asked, "Exactly what are these people doing?"

John replied, "They're in the process of stealing an election, and if you want to do some undercover investigative work, you'll need to move quickly, because I expect that they'll close their clandestine operation down the day before election day and all traces of their operation will be gone. Knowing the ringleader, she'll leave the place immaculate. The video captures the entire operation in progress and the audio has them indicting themselves for the Commission of Federal Crimes. Sarah, I'm giving you and your paper a gift. I'm not looking for money. Believe me, I don't need it. I'm doing it because I'm a patriot and I love my President."

Sarah replied, "I'll come to meet you and I will bring you a guarantee of anonymity. You'll need to give me one day to get the guarantee drawn up and to book a flight." She then asked, "Where am I heading?"

John replied, "The day after tomorrow is fine and you need to book a flight to Ft. Lauderdale. I can pick you up at the airport. We can go directly from there to see what I was telling you and watch the video on your laptop while I'm driving. Hopefully, you have an internal optical drive."

Sarah replied, "Yes, mine has one. I use it often in my line of work."

John said, "I can understand that. While you're watching the video, I'll also let you listen to the audio recording. Some of the planned election fraud has already been completed and delivered in place but they'll need until the day before election to complete the steal. I need you to come. This will be a major breaking news headline in your paper. I'll take you to the warehouse operation while the election steal is in progress and when all the people involved will be there.

I think a sitting Senator cheating in his re-election efforts should cause quite a stir in DC, and have the Socialists running for cover. where they won other questionable heavily contested elections. Think about the impact you'll have on this hotly debated fair elections issue. The outcry and demand for same day voting with paper ballots will be deafening. This will be a story as big as Watergate. Who knows, you could be nominated for a Pulitzer Prize."

Sarah replied, "John, I'm well aware of the implications a story like that will have. I will be there with your agreement in hand."

John then continued to say, "You can ask me all the questions you want, and I'll answer them. I strongly suggest that you stay a few days, so you can tail a van to one of its secret destinations. I won't be able to do that part of the investigative work for you. I'll continue to get more audio and video, but that's as far as I can go. I'll be working on their operation up until election day continuing to gather more incriminating evidence and turn it over to you as I get it. I'll act as your inside confidential source."

Sarah said, "I'll call you back with the flight info and meet you at the Ft. Lauderdale airport." She then asked, "How will I know you?"

John replied, "I'll hold up a sign with your first name on it. I imagine all you'll need is carry-on luggage. If that's right, you'll see me as soon as you disembark in the terminal."

Sarah answered, and said, "I will only have a carry-on. If for any reason we should miss each other, take my cell phone number down. Can I use the same number I'm talking to you on to reach you?"

John replied, "Yes, you can. I wanted to say, you are one ballsy lady. Standing up for your confidential source and giving the finger to the Department of Justice was beautiful. That's why I picked you."

John then went on to say, "My life would be hell with the insane left if my name got out there. I don't want to have to worry about Antifa spray painting my home or even trying to bomb my house or some other insane shit. My wife has no idea about what I've been doing. If she did, she'd be overly concerned, and I don't want her to be stressed over it. I'll explain everything to you when we meet. I'll wait for your call and look forward to meeting you."

John felt like he was on a roll carrying out his animus against the people he despised, and the more he did the more elated he felt. He envisioned himself wearing a red cape with the letter P emboldened on his chest, signifying Patriot. He began to think of himself as the hero of the people. He was riding the country of vermin.

The next day, John got a call from Jeanne Collette. "John, this is Jeanne Collette. My attorney agreed to your request and assured me you would be protected under attorney client privilege. Don't worry, I'll cover his legal fees."

John replied, "No, I've changed my mind. I'll pay the legal fee. I don't want any legal loopholes to pop up. I'm not sure there is one with you paying the fee, it's just that I know that there's no doubt about who hired him. Someone might throw up a legal argument that you'd be the only one protected. There's nothing in the law that says we can't have the same attorney represent both."

"John, that's certainly okay with me. I have to say I didn't think of that. What you've said makes sense," Jeanne replied and then asked, "What day and time are good for you? My attorney Michael Johnson said he would make room for us on his calendar whenever we needed."

"How about tomorrow morning at nine?" John asked.

Jeanne replied, "That's okay with me. Let's make it nine. Come to my campaign office. I'll ask Michael Johnson to be there."

John answered, "That's fine with me. I'll see you then."

With the call the stage was set for the wheels to turn by both Jeanne Collette and Sarah Foster. He decided to use both of them for his devious plan. He had no intention of telling them what he had done because he wanted two investigations going at the same time independently. One by a well-known and reputable investigative reporter and the other by the Federal Bureau of Investigation, who he assumed that Jeanne Collette would contact. John was doing so because he didn't have full faith in the integrity of the FBI. He felt that they showed political bias on too many occasions, and were a left leaning part of the deep state. Sarah was his ace in the hole to keep them honest. They couldn't bury the story or cover up for the Senator and would not be able to squelch a story that would be put out by the prestigious Wall Street Daily. He wanted jail time for all of them.

John thought long and hard about his plot and was getting overly anxious to see the outcome played out. But his plan originally was to assassinate Senator Roberts, and deep down that was his real desire. Regardless of the investigations and the Senator's eventual indictment if all went as planned, he still wanted the man dead. He paced back and forth thinking about what was rapidly unfolding, and decided to still execute the Senator. He said to himself, "Jail time is not enough for that criminal politician."

The more he talked it over with himself, like Dr. Jekyll talking to Mr. Hyde, the more he worried about the Senator denying any culpability saying he had no idea about what his overzealous volunteers were doing behind his back. John could almost hear him say, "I would never do such a thing. Why would I have to? No National Socialist has ever lost an election in my district."

John thought back through all of his taped conversations and couldn't find anything that would guarantee the Senator's indictment. He had no recordings of the Senator that had him admitting to knowing anything about the election stealing being carried out by Annette and Betty. The Senator was powerful enough in D.C to escape prosecution. The DOJ would see to it. The only thing that could indict him was accusatory and corroborating testimony by Betty and Annette. That would leave the DOJ hard pressed to ignore. But if Betty, the Senator's close confidante, denied the Senator's involvement that would counter Annette's accusation if she made one, or vice versa. It might even be possible they both refused to implicate the Senator's involvement completely. Anyone of those scenarios was possible.

John weighed the chances of the Senator getting off, and he didn't like the way he was thinking. He spoke out to himself and said, "I need to assassinate that fuck. He's not going to get away with unamerican activity against my President, or committing election fraud. I know he has to know what's going on. I'm convinced of it."

John resigned himself to do what he started out to do. Assassinate Senator Roberts.

CHAPTER FIFTEEN

THE INVESTIGATION GROWS

John grabbed his cell phone as soon as it started ringing. He looked at the incoming number and knew that it was Candidate Collette calling. He hit accept and said, "Hello."

Candidate Colette said, "John, we'll need to meet tomorrow at Michael Johnson's office at 10 am. instead of here at the campaign office. Does that work with you?"

"That's fine with me," John replied, then said, "Can you text me his address?"

"Yes, I'll do that. We're quite anxious to see what you have. So is Michael Johnson to say the least. I hope it's everything you claim it to be," Collette said.

John replied, "I can assure you it is. You will not be disappointed. I'll see you tomorrow."

"I texted the address. Let me know if you got it," Collette said.

"Hold a second. Yes, I got it. I see his office is not too far from yours," John said.

Collette replied, "He's ten minutes from here. See you then John. I have to take a call."

After he hung up with Jeanne Collette, he felt really excited about what was about to happen. He only needed Sarah to call him with flight information and with her on board, the game was on. He couldn't wait to meet with her. All he wanted at that moment was to pass the baton on to her. He had no doubt that she had the ability to pull whatever resources she needed to take on the investigation of Annette's operation.

John hoped that her flight arrival would not conflict with the meeting he had with Collette.

He thought about bringing Sarah Foster to the meeting. Everyone would be on the same page. Collette could actually use Sarah for the breaking story. He had to feel everyone out about the idea. It seemed good to him.

Another half hour had passed when Sarah called. "Hello John, it's Sarah. I have my flight info."

John replied, "Are you coming in tomorrow?"

"Yes. I'll be arriving at two in the afternoon on American Airlines, Gate C." Sarah replied.

"I'll be there waiting. I'll be holding a sign with your name on it. I'm quite anxious to meet you. You won't regret the trip. I promise you that," John said.

Sarah said, "I hope not. I had to do some quick juggling of my itinerary to make the flight."

"How will I know you?" John asked.

"I'm five feet five with auburn hair and light hazel eyes. I'll be wearing blue jeans, sneakers, and a white top. I like casual when I'm doing undercover investigative work," Sarah replied.

"That sounds good to me. I'll see you there," John said.

John was pleased that Sarah's flight would not conflict with his meeting with Collette. He would watch the time and make it known to Collette that he had to leave by no later than one o'clock. That would give him ample time to make the airport and walk to the gate to meet Sarah.

He was going to have a busy day. In the meanwhile he would spend more time at the campaign office trying to get audio on Betty and Senator Roberts who had arrived. He needed to get his recorder within range of their offices again. He had enough on the ballot printing operation. Annette had everything under control and with Lizzie's help, had enough volunteers to get the work done. He did not need to be there. John called Annette just to say hello and to tell her he had been thinking about her, and asked her how everything was going.

During his conversation, he asked Annette, "How are you doing on the ballots?"

Annette replied, "I'm ahead of schedule. We reached 150,000 yesterday. Jim has been a bulldog getting them out. He has pushed himself, working late nights."

John said, "He's a good man. Dedicated to the cause." He then asked, "Have you delivered them yet?"

"They will be delivered tomorrow evening," Annette replied.

"What time will they be going North?" John slyly asked, thinking he could get Sarah to tail one of the vans to their destination and get some video of the ballot handoff.

Annette replied, "About 6 pm."

John said, "Annette, I saw on TV that Florida has a new scanning system to count the votes and it'll be used to audit should the need arise." He then asked, "You have no concerns about that?"

Annette replied, "John not at all. It scans the ballots looking for votes indicated on the ballot that were not clearly marked in the oval circles. It will kick out any that it picks up outside those designated spaces, like someone drawing a circle around the name of a candidate. Our ballots are computerized and believe me, I considered everything. The computer is set up to vote for Senator Roberts on every ballot, but it will vary on the down ballots. We did not want every one of them to be exactly the same. That's what would stand out in an audit. We 're not concerned about them."

Annette set off a light in John's head when he realized that he didn't know Brad's last name. He had programmed the entire election steal. He needed to have it and his address. He wanted to be sure that the FBI broke his fucking door down and got him and all the computer evidence before he could pull out his hard drive. He knew he had to find a way to get it out of Annette without her being suspicious. He made that need a priority. John, who we know by now was a quick thinker, spontaneously said, "Annette, do you think I could talk to Brad? I need him to do some hacking for me. I want him to break into the computer school's computer system."

Annette replied, "John, I would need to ask him about that before giving you, his information. He understandably wants to remain underground. I thought you were volunteering at the campaign office instead of going to the school?"

John hearing the caution in Annette's response, replied, "Annette, yes that's right, but the course is also taught online, and I've had to play that part at home. I told you Katherine thinks I'm going to class, which obviously I'm not. I need to try and get a certificate of completion or have Brad hack one for me. She'll wonder why I didn't get something. But that's okay. I can certainly understand why he wants to stay anonymous. Forget that I asked, but honestly, I'm in this with you and can be indicted along with everyone if anyone finds out about what is being perpetrated at the warehouse. Do you think that I would say anything about Brad?"

John smartly put Annette on the spot. He said, "You trust me to abet in a federal crime, but you don't trust me with Brad's name."

Annette replied, "John I didn't mean to have you think I didn't trust you. It's just that Brad is overly cautious, and I would need his permission to give you his contact information. That's something he made clear to me when I was introduced to him."

John decided to twist his knife a little deeper. He was going to play hard on her feelings for him. He told Annette firmly, "Annette, I said that I could understand his position, it was you questioning me about me being at the campaign office instead of school, so why was I needing to worry about getting some help. Look, I have to go. I'll speak to you later."

John hung up abruptly on Annette, he hoped that her love for him would weaken her resolve and drop her guard.

John headed to the campaign office to see what conversation he could pick up from the Senator and Betty for the rest of the day. John was near the campaign office when Annette called him. John answered her call and said, "Annette we don't need to discuss the matter any longer. I'll deal with my own problem."

Annette said, "John. I'm sorry I questioned you. I really had no reason to with everything you've done for the campaign, your honesty with you and Katherine, and our close relationship. Can you come over to my place later? I can leave here early. Let me apologize to you in my way."

John knowing that softening his position at that moment was his best move, said, "Sweetness, that's very enticing, believe me, but you don't need to apologize."

Annette's voice sounded like she was going to cry. He could hear it in her voice when she said, "John, it's not just that, it's because, I'm sorry I turned you away at the warehouse. I know that I'm willing to be with you anyway I can, even though I know you'll leave me at the end of the day

213

and go home to Katherine, instead of waking up with me in the morning. That's something that has never happened between us. I put in a call to Brad, but he didn't answer. I left him a message. I'm sure he'll call me back. I'll tell him that I want to introduce you to him and assure him of your involvement and that he can trust you. I'm sure he'll call me by the time you meet me if you will."

"Annette, my dear, I'll be there after putting a few hours in at the campaign office. I have landed a few big donor introductions and want to see if I can pull in some money for the Senator quickly. Candidate Collette is breathing down his neck in the polls. I'm sure that he'll need the cushion you are delivering for him. I certainly hope he shows his appreciation for what you're doing and risking."

John finally heard what he wanted to hear from Annette. An absolute confirmation that Senator Roberts was aware of what she was doing, although he wisely stayed arm's length from any part of the operation, when she responded to John by saying, "Believe me he's incredibly grateful. He was satisfied with the added vote count that I was injecting into the ballot boxes. After he wins, I intend to be on his staff in D.C. I miss that power selling on the hill. John we could be a power couple there if you wanted to be with me."

John replied, "It's certainly enticing. I'll give it serious thought. I'll come over to your place at three. Is that okay?"

"Yes, that's good. I'll see you there," Annette replied.

As soon as John got to the campaign office, he listened to his recorder to see if he had captured any incriminating conversations by Senator Roberts. He found all but one of the conversations held on the phone to be useless. Not knowing what the other party was saying made what was said by Senator Roberts to be no more than hearsay evidence, The one thing he heard the Senator say that was a sit up in the seat moment was, "I know what the polls show, but believe me, I have it covered. My sources are telling me that I'll have at least a 250,000, vote margin of victory."

When John heard that 250,000 figure mentioned, it perked him right up. He said to himself, "That just can't be coincidental. He has to know what Betty and Annette are doing. I'd bet on it. I just wish I knew who he was talking to." After listening to twenty minutes of recordings, his ears perked up, when he heard Betty speaking to the Senator.

He heard Betty say, "Aaron, I spoke to Annette, and she said that everything would be in place the day before election. She confirmed the 250 number she guaranteed will be inserted."

Senator Roberts asked, "She's taken everything into consideration, I hope. There cannot be one slip up. Everything is going to be watched that much more closely this time around."

Betty said, "Don't worry, Annette's the best. This time instead of one or two large drops, she's doing a separate drop in each of the twenty-seven counties. That guarantees a seamless insertion into the total across the board. Brad rewrote the program he used the last time under Annette's guidance. I was impressed with what it does. She's thought of everything. I need to tell you that John Meade knows about everything. She's been having a thing with him. She assures me that he's behind the whole operation and was at the warehouse volunteering. I told her it was a bad idea to get anyone outside our tight circle involved. It was very risky."

When John's name was mentioned, he listened even more intently to what was being said. He smiled and said to himself in a low murmur, "And as the spider ate the fly. Now I have the dope I need on him and Betty. The only word missing in the conversation was ballots. It would have been nice to hear that word used after the number 250,000."

John did get one unmistakable clarification from the things Betty mentioned, and that was she knew about his relationship with Annette.

Joseph Amellio

Betty continued to say, "Annette used Lizzie and a few of her radical friends to assist her with boxing and shipping the ballots. She told me her old crew was no longer available except Jim Levy. Senator, I call her Looney Lizzie. She's an extremist with a far-left mentality and hates Tripp with passion. I think she'd be in heaven as a Bolshevik. Annette made it clear that she had to use them, or she wouldn't have been able to accomplish the number you needed. She also told me she made it clear to Lizzie and her comrades, that if they spoke one word about what was going on, and it was leaked, that everyone was doing federal jail time."

John said to himself, "Yes thank Betty, telling about federal jail time is an admission that everyone is involved in the commission of a federal crime and that crime is 'Election Fraud.' What is even sweeter dumb ass, is that you named everyone except Brad's last name. But I'll get it today and that'll complete everything I need, for Sarah and Jeanne, tomorrow."

Betty still talking with Senator Roberts said, "Lizzie told Annette that she would never say a word, nor would any of her friends. She said they needed you to get Tripp out of the office with your investigations. Annette's comment about John was one of praise. You know that he's now the single highest campaign solicitor we've ever had. He works hard at it and has never had anything but praise for you. After thinking about everything he's done, I would agree with her decision about him."

Senator Roberts replied, "There's nothing we can do about it now except go along with her decision. I'll talk to John and Lizzie myself and feel them out. I'll ask him to come in after you leave. I need to re-assure myself."

John said to himself as he leaned back in his chair, "You do that Senator."

At that moment John's phone rang. He picked it up and heard a voice ask, "Is this John Meade?"

John replied, "Yes, it is."

"John this is James Ellis. I'm Chief Executive Officer of Filmore Aeronautics Corp. I understand you spoke to Anthony Ricci, our Chief Financial Officer seeking a donation for the re-election of Senator Roberts."

John responded with, "That's correct. I was hoping that you would assist the Senator financially in defeating Candidate Jeanne Collette. We're at the wire and could use a little bit of a boost. Our coffers are taking a little bit more of a beating than we anticipated, because of the extra heavy ad campaign we've launched. We have one last blitz before the election. We have effectively halted her climb in the polls. The Senator, according to our very thorough internal polls, is now ahead by two percentage points. External polls had her in a dead heat."

James Ellis said, "John, Anthony Ricci told me that we needed a large write-off for tax purposes, and we'd rather help the Senator than the Internal Revenue Service and we like what he is doing in D.C. We'll be donating $300,000 dollars. I can Federal Express our corporate check overnight."

"Mr. Ellis, that's very generous of you. We cannot thank you enough for your support. I'll tell the Senator immediately. I'm sure that he'll call you personally and thank you," John replied.

Mr. Ellis said, "I'll ask my Executive Assistant to take the mailing information from you. She'll handle getting the overnight check to you by Federal Express."

John said, "Let me thank you again. I'm not the one that makes the invite list, nor am I high enough in the ranks here to invite you, but I will ask if they can put you on the Senator's campaign and election win celebration party here at the campaign office."

Mr. Ellis responded, "Thank you for that John, but don't bother. I'll be flying to Japan on business. I won't be here in the States on election day. Tell the senator I wish him luck."

John replied, "You wished him more than luck, you've assisted in his success."

"You're welcome. Here's my Executive Assistant Janice. Be well John. You represent the Senator very professionally," James said.

After John provided the information, he got up from his desk, and headed straight for the Senator's office. He thought what better way to have the Senator feel self-assured about him then to lay that bit of information on him. It was like laying down honey to feed a fly. He knew that he would now have gained the utmost confidence in the Senator to reach out and shake his hand anytime he needed to. John no longer cared about his own life and safety. He just wanted the Senator to die. Everything he heard and saw put John on his final mission and past the point of no return mentally.

As lucid as John seemed outwardly, little bits of his sanity was being lost on an almost daily basis. John walked up to the Senator's door just as he was hanging up his phone. He gave a courtesy knock and said, "Senator, do you have a minute?"

Senator Roberts said, "John you have a good sense of timing. I just tried calling you. Now I know why you didn't answer. I would like to talk to you about some very confidential matters. Please close the door."

John said, "May I tell you some good news before we get into whatever you want to talk to me about?"

"Sure," Roberts replied.

"I just pulled in $300,000 dollars from Filmore Aeronautics Corp. They are FedExing a check overnight. You'll have it tomorrow," John said.

"John, are you serious? That's one hell of a donation. Wow! Splendid work. You absolutely amaze me. Betty has constantly told me you're the best campaign funds solicitor we've ever had by a long shot. How much have you pulled in so far?"

John replied, "Close to $3,000,000 dollars with this donation."

At that moment, the Senator stood up, reached across his desk, and gave John a handshake.

While John was shaking his hand, he smiled like the Cheshire cat and thought, "I've got you now. You're dead meat. I no longer need to figure out how I can gain your confidence to get close enough to you to shake your hand. Bye, bye fuck face."

John then sat down to hear what the Senator was going to talk to him about, like he didn't know.

He asked the Senator, "What is it that you wanted to talk to me about?"

The Senator said, "John, I just found out that you've been helping Annette at the warehouse. That's what this is all about."

John replied, "Senator, there's no need to get into the phony ballot operation. I know everything and it doesn't bother me in the least. That's why I volunteered to help Annette. I know it's election fraud. But I say beat Collette anyway we can. We need to keep power in the Senate. I'm one hundred percent behind your re-election. We need you in D.C. I personally hate Tripp and want you to keep turning the screws into that waste of a man. You can bet your life on it. I will never leak out anything about the steal. I'm not crazy and could never hurt anyone especially Annette, for whom I hold a fond affection. Put your mind at rest Senator. We're all good."

"John, thank you for making it easy on me. I really don't need to say anything more. John, I hope you don't mind me having FBI Agent Martin check you for a wire. It's not a matter of distrust, it's a matter of caution."

John smiled with self-assurance, and said, "No problem, Senator, You're doing the right thing. I have no objection whatsoever. But if you have no objection, I don't want to be frisked in your office, especially with the large windows you have all the way around. I'll let him check me in the men's room."

John was quick minded again. He didn't know if the agent would use a scanner. If he did, in the office, John thought it might notice the bug he placed under the Senator's desk. He didn't know the range of the scanner and wasn't about to take any chances.

The Senator summoned his Secret Service bodyguard and asked him to check John for wires in the men's room.

John simply turned to the Agent and said, "Let's go."

After several minutes they both walked back to the Senator's office. The Agent said to Senator Roberts, "He's clean Senator."

Senator Roberts said, "Thanks Agent Ryan and thank you John for your understanding. I really meant no distrust of you personally. But I would throw caution to the wind if I didn't check out everyone involved if you understand."

John played it cool. He acted nonchalant about the pat down, especially knowing he had the bug under the Senator's desk and incriminated the Senator in their conversation.

John replied, "Senator, I take no offense. Under the circumstances I would do the same." John then asked, "Senator, do you still need to talk to me?"

"John, no. You answered any concerns I had, and I'm satisfied. Thank you again for getting the donation. It'll help my campaign for sure. You've been great," the Senator replied.

John smiled and then extended his hand toward the Senator, seeking another handshake. The Senator willingly accommodated John. John said, "No worries, Senator. I'm cool with everything. You're a good man. I subscribe to your politics."

John actually didn't need to shake the Senator's hand again. He was just getting into practice for the kill. His gesture was to bring the Senator mentally closer to him, building even more trust between them. John knew that his handshakes were instilling a subliminal acceptance ritual between them. He was simply setting the Senator up for the final toxic handshake.

John turned and walked out of the Senator's office. He looked down at his watch and saw that he had to meet Annette. It was one meeting that he looked forward to. He needed to get Brad's info and enjoy some apologetic sex that Annette alluded to.

When John arrived at Annette's home, she was already undressed under her robe. When he saw her like that, he simply walked up to her, opened her robe, and gently moved his hand over her breast while he kissed her. She reached down and touched him between his legs. Without speaking she led John to the bedroom where they continued their foreplay working themselves up into an uncontrollable passion. As John placed himself on top of Annette, she went to speak, but John put his finger on her lips before she could say anything. He moved his finger away as he brought his face down to hers, kissing her passionately and began making love to her.

John was adept at using psychology and mind fucking people. His move putting his finger on Annette's lips was a simple but affective move. He made Annette feel that there was nothing more that he wanted except to make love to her and that nothing was more important to him than her.

After finishing intercourse, John smiled down at Annette, kissed her again gently, then rose up slightly above her body, looked down at her smiling and said, "Now what did you want to say?"

Annette, who was still emotionally high, said, "John you erased my memory. I can't think of what it was at this moment. Just lie next to me. When I remember what it was, I'll tell you."

When John laid next to Annette, she placed her head onto his chest and her arm over him, cuddling up close, while saying, "It's moments like this that I cherish with you."

John replied, "I feel the same way, but we can only have moments like this. I can't promise you more."

Annette said, "I spoke to Brad, and he agreed to help you. He said it was okay to give you his phone number."

John said, "That's great. I'll call him."

"Just tell him what you need him to do. I didn't tell him anything, except that you were trustworthy, or I would not have asked him to help you. That's all I can do. He's a very guarded person," Annette said.

John replied, "You did good my love." Then asked, "What's his last name?"

Annette replied, "John you need to ask him. Whatever he's willing to tell you about himself is strictly up to him and how important it is for you to know. John, please don't ask me to tell you anymore about him. I gave him my word; I would give you nothing more than his phone number."

John, knowing that not getting Brad's last name was not critical anymore, having his phone number. He knew that it could be traced back to its owner. He felt certain that Sarah, Candidate Collette, or Michael Johnson, her attorney, could get it through their many connections. He knew it could be traced.

John thanked Annette for the phone number and said, "You did good, and I appreciate just being able to talk to him." He kissed Annette, thanked her, and soon after headed home.

When John arrived at his house, he gave his usual kiss to Katherine, then made sure to wash off any scent of Annette before having a relaxing evening with his wife. The only thing he made sure to do was check on his frogs. He harvested more toxin, misted their environment, and added more water to their pond. He threw in a few more beetles and shook some more fire ants from his honey jar into the terrarium. John was meticulous in caring for his murder weapons. Just before he left the workshop, he looked down at the frogs and said, "I have one more important job for you."

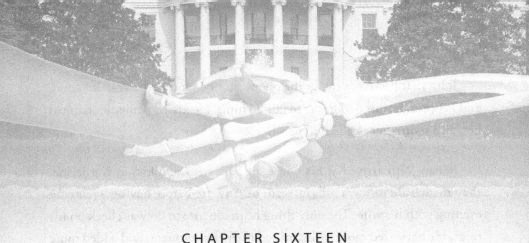

CHAPTER SIXTEEN

THE AMERICAN PATRIOT PARTY CANDIDATE

The next day, John headed to the campaign office early so that he could listen to the recorder through his synced earpiece before he headed out to Attorney Michael Johnson's office. He listened to his conversation with the Senator and was pleased that he had him incriminating himself. He inserted a thumb drive and copied the conversation. Even though John knew that what he had would put the Senator in jail, he wasn't going to dissuade himself from killing the man. John tried him, found him guilty and sentenced him to death. John was the judge, jury, and executioner in his own court of law.

When John arrived at the attorney's office, he was immediately told by the receptionist to go right in, that Michael Johnson, Candidate Collette, and her campaign Advisor were waiting for him.

As John stepped into his office, he could see Candidate Collette, Jeremy Long her Campaign Advisor and Michael Johnson all sitting in a separate conference area adjacent to his office. Michael Johnson got up and greeted him. He said, "Nice to meet you, John. I believe you know these fine people."

John replied, "Yes, I do," then turned toward Candidate Collette and said, "Hello again." He greeted Jeremy Long with a handshake then sat down. John smiled and said, "I bet you are all really curious about what I have to show you, which I will do once Michael here becomes my attorney. So let's get that put aside first."

Michael Johnson said, "I'm ready with my disclosure which you need to sign. It covers my Retainer Fee for legal services which Candidate Collette said you insisted on paying. Once you do that, Attorney Client Privilege will protect your conversation."

John replied, "Sounds good, hand me a pen."

After John signed the Legal Agreement, he took out a check which he knew he would need, and made it out to the law firm.

Michael Johnson, accepted the check and then said, "Now I am representing both you and Candidate Collette." John looked at Jeremy Levy, and asked, "Are you also covered by Attorney Client Privilege at this meeting?"

John's question caught everyone by surprise. I guess they didn't think John would ask. But when he did, they realized they were dealing with an overly cautious and astute man, and whatever he was carrying on him must be really explosive information.

Jeremy said, "No, I'm not. I have my own attorney."

John then said, "I'm sorry to say, but I must insist that you'll need to leave this meeting."

Candidate Collette turned to Jeremy and said, "Jeremy, please comply with John's request. Michael and I can handle this. We can make other arrangements for you later."

Jeremy got up and left the office. Once Jeremy stepped out, John said, "I'm sorry for that, but I must protect all of us. Michael, do you have a laptop that you can bring in that will take a disk and thumb drive?"

Michael replied, "Yes, I do, as a matter of fact. Let me get it off my desk."

As Michael went to get his computer, John said, "Candidate Collette, you'll understand my extreme caution."

Collette said, "John, please call me Jeanne. We are past that formality."

"Thank you, Jeanne." John replied.

Michael came back into the office with his laptop and sat it on the conference table.

John hesitated, and asked, "Michael we are both covered under a confidentiality agreement with you, but are Collette and I covered against each other? You'll have to forgive me, but I've not done this before, and I keep thinking about loopholes."

Michael responded, "John, it could be a debatable issue if really pushed. I could draw up a non-disclosure agreement between the two of you. It would close the circle. But I can't do it now."

John said, "Maybe I'm being overly cautious. Screw it. Draw one up that we can sign later. It won't hurt." Then looked at Jeanne and asked, "Is that okay with you?"

Jeanne replied," I have no objection. You can never be careful enough."

John reached into his jacket pocket and took out both the disk and thumb drive. He handed them to Michael who immediately inserted the thumb drive, "What you're about to see is an illegal operation that is run by people who work for Senator Roberts to guarantee him a win in the election you are running against him. That operation will be wrapping up in a few days. They'll be inserting 250,000 fraudulent votes against you."

Jeanne, Michael, and John moved their chairs together as Michael played the video. John explained what was going on, and who the participants were. He told them that he filmed it all with a special spy cam he bought just for the occasion. He made it clear that they were unaware of his activity and because he didn't have their consent in the State of Florida, he was taking the video illegally. He mentioned that he had an audio taken the same way.

After John played the video, Jeanne said, "That Son of a Bitch! He's going to pay for this."

John said, "The video with audio clearly proves that the ballots being produced were intended to steal an election and the people being shown in it are guilty of committing more than federal crimes. The recordings should be sufficient evidence to nail these socialists. This other thumb drive is a recording of conversations at the campaign office. You can say, it speaks for itself. You can hear the Senator incriminate himself. I suggest that you get the FBI in on this and have them catch them in the act. Once they finish with their printing of the ballots the place will be wiped clean."

"The woman Annette, that I pointed out, is a really sharp woman. Admittedly I've been intimate with her. It wasn't because I intended to cheat on my wife. I used her for information. I know how ugly it sounds, but I decided to do whatever was necessary to take these people down. If it was using her, so be it. I did my job a little too well because she began expressing feelings for me. My wife Katherine knows nothing about what I've been up to. I don't want her to find out if I can help it. I'm sure you understand my dilemma. I lied to her about where I was going for three days a week for six months. She thinks I've been going to computer school when I've been working as a spy at the campaign office of Senator Roberts. She'd never have agreed with me doing it. I hate the Senator that much that I've put my marriage on the line, not only because of the lie about what I was doing, but because of the unexpected but necessary relationship I've had with Annette."

John paused for a moment, then said, "I couldn't help myself. I saw a chance to help David Tripp for being brutalized by that fuck over and over with his investigations and getting away with it. He needs to pay for the damage he's done to that man and his family and this country. I think about how much more President Tripp could do for us if he were not always battling that man and his phony ass committees. You can see the stress in the President's face when he's forced to talk about it."

Collette said, "John I feel the same way about President Tripp. I've met him. He's a gracious man. He genuinely cares about America and its people. John, I promise that we will not mention your involvement with Annette. I can assure you of that. You've been acting like a regular James Bond. If Katherine finds out, it will only be from you or Annette. That's a possibility if she should want revenge against you. It might even come out in an investigation. How you play it out is up to you. She'll understand your passion for the country and the President and that your affair was meaningless in the sense that you had no feelings for Annette."

John said, "I'll have to deal with it sooner or later. But not now. Knowing Katherine, she'll ask me for a divorce."

John then continued and said, "One more thing. A guy named Brad wrote their sophisticated program that produced the ballots printed. It guarantees Senator Roberts a vote on every one of them, but he slickly varied the down ballots so that it would be difficult to pick up in an audit when they are not all glaringly the same. How he got the information on the individual voters is with the help of paid postal employees that have been feeding info on people recently moving out of state and providing their names and addresses. Annette has also been getting copies of recent deaths within the State and illegals, etcetera. I don't know exactly how they have gotten all of it, but an election audit would be hard pressed to pick up the fraud. They have been working on the steal for months. Actually Annette mentioned that she did the same fraud for some Senator or Congressman in another State on their last election. I can't remember who that was. I don't know Brad's full name or where he does his work. Annette would not disclose that to me because she gave her word to him to protect his identity. She said she convinced him to at least talk to me over the phone. I don't think she realized that his number could be tracked back to him in the right hand. I believe Brad dropped his caution because of her and her guarantees that I was someone he could trust. I didn't push her for his last name and address. She would've wondered why it was so important to me. I was hoping that you'd have the law enforcement connections to get it done. Please write this number down. Just don't call it. I'll call him myself."

Michael Johnson, said, "I have a special ops security and investigation firm that are my clients. They do a lot of D.C. work. They can do the trace if you call from their office. We might want to do that first before asking the FBI. I personally don't trust them to not bury everything. They are left leaning, and the deep state part of the agency is in tune with Senator Roberts."

Jeanne said, "I agree with Michael, John."

John said, "I have a meeting this afternoon at two o'clock at the airport. I can't miss being there, I'm picking up Sarah Foster. She's a Nobel nominated reporter with the Wall Street Daily. The same reporter stood up to a Federal judge and refused to release her anonymous privileged source. I'm going to fill her in. She'll be picking up the investigation today. I'll be stepping away. Between you and her, and the information I gave you, you should be able to take it all down. As far as anyone else is concerned I wasn't involved. Her employers legal team is giving me a letter guaranteeing my anonymity. If you want to meet with her and coordinate the investigation, she would be instrumental. I consider her a safeguard against the FBI. They will not be able to bury anything once she publishes everything and you have copies of whatever you give them. I believe you will need them for warrants and arrests. I see no way to avoid it."

Jeanne said, "Yes, I would like to meet her. I do recall her and her heroic stance against the left-wing establishment. Meeting her today is tough, my schedule is full for the rest of the day, but I can tomorrow. My schedule is light."

John replied, "I'll give her your number. You work that out with her."

Michael asked John, "When do you want to call this Brad guy?"

"Set it up. I'll be there. You have my cell number," John replied.

Michael said, "Why don't we have some lunch. It's just twelve o'clock. You'll still have plenty of time to go to the airport. I have to admit that I've never run across anyone that has taken on such a risky investigation and risking his marriage to do it. I don't know if I would have taken it that far, but I do admire your patriotism and I think you've done Jeanne and the country a great service."

"Michael, my actions have not been easy, and I don't have MI6 training," John said smiling.

Michael laughed and replied, "No I guess not, but you've done amazing work."

Michael, John, Jeanne, and Jeremy all went to lunch and idly chatted about different things and were careful not to mention anything that shouldn't be discussed in public. John got up and left at one o'clock to go meet Sarah. He shook everyone's hands and said, "I'd love to stay longer, but I need to go. I'll wait for your call, Michael. We need to locate the computer guy fast. We don't want his computer erased if he learns about anything. Once we do that you and Jeanne can call in the Feds or the State's Special Task Force. I leave that choice up to you."

John left the restaurant and headed to the airport to meet Sarah. It would take him a half hour to get there. He would need another ten minutes to park his car and another ten to walk to her gate. He grabbed the Sarah sign he made from the front passenger seat and then waited for her to show up.

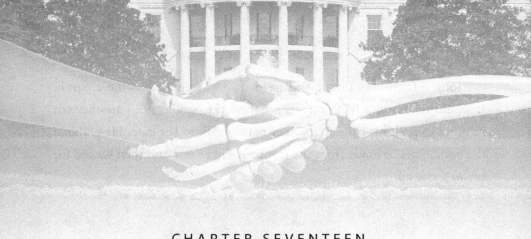

CHAPTER SEVENTEEN

ANOTHER WOMAN IN JOHN'S LIFE

Sarah's plane landed on time and her departure was quick. It was a domestic flight and most passengers had carried on luggage. John only waited fifteen minutes before he saw her walking toward him, pulling a small suitcase on wheels. He knew it was her from what she said she'd be wearing, jeans, a white top, and sneakers. As he watched her walk toward him, he thought, "What an attractive woman." She looked exactly as she described herself. About five feet five inches tall, with Auburn hair and light hazel-colored eyes which had conjured up an attractive vision in John's mind. But what he was seeing was more than attractive, she was stunning. The way she walked and carried her curvaceous athletic figure kept his eyes fixated. He said to himself, "You can only dream this shit up in Hollywood. Only James Bond meets one beautiful woman after another. I'm feeling like him."

Sarah saw John, holding the sign with her name on it. She smiled, and gave a quick wave. He smiled and rocked the sign back and forth acknowledging he was the guy she was meeting. As she walked up to him, she said, "John I presume."

John replied, "I'm him." He then extended his hand and said, "It's nice meeting you."

Sarah shook his hand and said, "It's nice meeting you as well."

John then offered to carry her suitcase, but Sarah refused his offer by saying,

"No, thank you John, it's on wheels and light. I can pull it."

John then said, "My car is not far. It's parked in the garage." He then asked, "How was your flight?"

"It was good. It's only a two-and-a-half-hour flight. It seemed like less. The time passed by quickly because I authored an article for the paper and sent it. I brought the laptop with disk capacity as you asked," Sarah replied.

John said, "Great! As soon as we're in my car, I'll give you the video to watch as I drive. The disk will be yours to keep. You'll need to safeguard it. You'll know why once you've viewed it. It's part of the evidence I have to take down a sitting Senator. An immensely powerful one at that. You'll also be able to listen to the audios. They're as incriminating as you can get. You'll hear the Senator incriminate himself when he's talking to me at his campaign office. I planted a bug in it. I also planted a bug in his Campaign Manager's office. I'll need to yank them out of there soon."

John and Sarah reached his car. He said, "This is it."

Sarah said, "Nice car, I love Audi's."

John replied, "It drives beautifully and can move out when you need it to. I wanted an Audi after I saw Jason Statham driving one in the movie Transporter."

Sarah said, "I saw that film. Jason is a great actor."

John said, "Let's get your laptop out. You'll need it in the car."

Sarah opened her suitcase and took out the laptop and also a voice recorder.

She said to John, "I assume you'll let me record you as you explain the videos."

"No, not at all. I'm glad you brought one," John replied.

As soon as they were in the car, John told Sarah to reach into his glove compartment and take out the disks. He told her they were numbered in order. As they were driving Sarah inserted the first video. It showed what was going on in the warehouse. As Sarah watched, John explained to her what was happening and who was doing it. He left out no details. Sarah recorded everything John was telling her.

She said, "John, you're right. This is explosive, It'll not only shake up Washington, but it'll raise the hackles on the APP. They will all start demanding that vote recounts be taken in all the races that they felt were stolen. The Socialists will scream that what we have is an isolated incidence. The war will begin on the Hill, and President Tripp will want to set up a Special Counsel Investigation to begin looking into everything."

John said, "I'm sure of that. I hope he does. I hate the Socialists, especially Senator Roberts. He has single-handedly investigated Tripp with every committee that he influences as well as getting some of the District Attorney's to open separate investigations against him as well. And without cause. They have no crime. They're trying to make one up."

Sarah said, "I have the same sentiments. I think he'll want to keep it away from deep state control and the FBI. David Key, the head of the agency has stonewalled Tripp and a few of the APP led investigations. He's dragged his ass on releasing documents. It's obvious by his actions that he's biased."

After driving for a half hour, John approached the warehouse. He made sure that he kept his car out of sight. He parked for a moment and pointed to the operation. He said to Sarah, "That's where the action is, where the stealing is taking place. You can bet that Annette is in there getting it done along with Jim, Lizzie, and her little comrades."

Sarah said, "John let me get my camera out of my suitcase. I have a telephoto lens. I want to take a few shots, then we can leave."

It took only a few minutes for Sarah to get her camera and take the pictures she needed. As she was doing that, John pointed out two white vans parked outside of the bay door near the entrance and told her to photograph them and if she could zoom in on the license plates. He said, "I'm not sure if that'll help because they may be stolen plates. I don't know that. I'm just thinking aloud."

Sarah replied, "If they are, we'll find out and that will only bode against them."

John began getting a little concerned about being there too long. He didn't want to be spotted. He said, "Sarah. Let's go. You have the photos and know the place. We'll need to get you a rental car as soon as possible. We have just two hours to do that. You'll need time to come back here and wait for them to leave. They'll be loading the vans with the ballots and heading off at six this evening. I can't go with you this time. I can't tell you which one to follow. They may be heading to the same drop off or two different ones. I know that one will be delivering to one or two of the southern counties, and the other to the northern counties, so I don't expect that you'll need to drive more than one to four hours tops in any direction. You can photograph the drop off point and whomever is taking the delivery of the fraudulent ballots."

Sarah said, "Let's get the car. I wouldn't miss this chance. John, thank you for the opportunity to be involved. This story is unbelievable. I have a confidentiality agreement for you. I and the editor have signed it. I promised to call him and fill him in on what you've shown me and that you are for real."

John replied, "Great. I'll get it from you at the Avis office. We can go to the one that's eight miles from here. You can return it at the airport. Avis has a rental office there."

After getting the rental car, Sarah, and John drove to a nearby Starbucks for a quick cup of coffee and to let John look over the Anonymity Agreement. After John reviewed it, he said, "Sarah, thank you. It seems complete."

"John, after what I've seen, and heard, I can certainly understand your insistence on having anonymity. You'll be stepping on some powerful toes. He has many deep state allies. You need to be careful about repercussions if your name ever leaks out. You may want to get a carry permit. I'm quite serious about it. I have one. My exposes have gotten me death threats. But I'm not deterred by them. I personally can't stand the Socialist ass holes, and anytime I can uncover dirt on them, I author scathing articles," Sarah said.

As John listened to Sarah and heard her words, he became emotionally attracted to her. He thought to himself, "This is my kind of woman. She thinks like I do. She's ballsy and is extremely attractive." He couldn't help himself when he said, "Sarah, I'm so pleased to meet you. I love your attitude and your personal politics, and I must say, you are extremely attractive."

Sarah, being very forward, reached over and placed her hand on the back of John's hand as it laid on the table above the agreement and gently closed over it as she said, "I find you the same. I'm also pleased to meet you."

As soon as he heard Sarah say those things, and felt her hand on his, he knew that she was letting him know that she was attracted to him. Even though he said what he did to her, she carried the attraction beyond what he expected of her. It actually surprised him, but he was openly willing to take it further. In that moment, Katherine was no longer in his thoughts.

And as for Annette, she no longer meant anything to him. Besides, he had already dismissed her in his life, the minute he showed her on tapes committing a federal crime. As he looked into Sarah's eyes, he felt nothing but an uncontrollable lust. They were beautiful and captivating. She was like a siren to his psyche. Her light hazel glistening eyes lured him right in.

. He lost all sense of reality and justified cheating on Katherine again. He excused his action, by thinking, "I've already cheated on her once, so why will my doing it again make any difference. She'll never forgive me for the first time so fuck it."

Sarah looked at John, and said, "I've been taken in by you too John. Yes, I'd like to see you again."

"I wish that I could go with you, but I can't. Just be careful following the van. You don't want them to pick up your tail," John said.

Sarah replied, "John, I've been tailing people since I was an investigative cub reporter. I'll be okay."

John said, "I suppose you will. But I'm already worrying about you, and we just met."

"You're sweet John. It's nice to know that, but just relax. This dame is pretty tough," Sarah said.

John laughed as he held her hand and said, "I believe you. Look, please stay connected with me. Let me know the location of the drop off."

Sarah said, "I will. I promise. But I think I should go. I want to be waiting a little ahead of six o'clock. We can't afford to let them go before I get there."

"You're right. Okay. Let's go," John replied.

Sarah drove off to the warehouse. John headed home. He thought about the events of the day and was elated at his successes and what he had done. He thought about Sarah and felt an uncontrollable rush come over him. He paused for a moment in his thoughts, taking a mental break. He needed to step back and look at what he had done. He then said to himself aloud in the car, "John, John, what the fuck is the matter with you? You need to forget Sarah. You got involved with Annette for a reason and not because you fell in love. She was no more than a means to an end, but Sarah would be something else. If Katherine finds out about Annette, regardless of my reasons for being with her, she'll want to divorce me. It just wouldn't matter how I justified it. She would not accept the affair as a necessity to take down the Senator and stop an election steal as an excuse. To her cheating would be the ultimate sin. If I get involved with Sarah, I might as well pack my bags."

John was no longer the same man he was five months ago. He was doing things that even he couldn't believe. He murdered an innocent man, justifying his death as a steppingstone to assure his success at killing Senator Roberts. He crippled one Senator and murdered a Congresswoman and now was planning on assassinating Senator Roberts even though he might not have to. He didn't care about the outcome of an investigation. He wanted the man dead. He owed that to the innocent man that died as a toxin test subject. He also had a deeply imbedded hate for the Senator which he could not shake. John constantly was talking to himself, and arguing with his Hyde alter ego.

He told himself that he loved Katherine, yet he didn't hesitate to have an affair with Annette. He argued with himself about the justification, yet worried that she'd leave him if she found out. When it came to Sarah, he abandoned all reality by willingly fanning a flame between them. The moment he felt Sarah's hand touch his, he thought nothing of Katherine. His feelings for her became make believe.

John was confused mentally. Did he really know what love was? Certainly that part of his psyche could be questioned. He was full of hate and in a very dark place because of it. His impulsive behavior began to control him.

He evidenced schizophrenia at times, because of his disordered thinking and behavior. His Dr. Jekyll was becoming the more dominant part and enabled him to plan his assassinations, and successfully create another more exciting life through his lies to Katherine and anyone he needed to manipulate.

John did not hear from Sarah that night. He worried about her. He also was anxious to know if she was able to successfully tail the van and find the drop off point. It wasn't until the next day that Sarah called him. When his cell phone rang. John answered, and could hear Sarah say, "Hello, John. It's Sarah."

John said, "I was worried about you. Did everything go well?"

Sarah replied, "You were right. One van headed north, and the one I luckily picked to follow stayed south. I followed the van to Miami. I was able to photo the hand off of the ballots and got good clear shots of the address and the man accepting the boxes. It was to someone's home. They loaded the boxes in their garage. I then followed the van again all the way across to Naples where it dropped off more boxes at another home. I already got the names of the residents at those addresses. I'm having my office find out if they can produce employers."

John said, "That's terrific. I'm wondering if they're postal employees. It would be a good cover for walking the boxes into the polling places. I knew you were the right person to get involved."

Sarah replied, "I thought the same thing about them being postal employees. I'll bet they drive their postal vehicles to their homes and load them up with the ballots. That way no one at the Post Office gets the wiser, nor would the polling place."

John asked, "What's your next move?"

"I'm heading back to Ft. Lauderdale. I should be there between noon and one. I'm going to get a room at a hotel. I'll call you again when I get there. I'd like to meet with Candidate Collette. Can you set up a 2 o'clock meet?" Sarah replied.

John responded, "I'm sure I can. She said that she'd be available for you whenever you could see her today. I'm going to text her number to you. Let me know what time you'll be there."

"I'll do that. I'm heading out now. My odometer showed that I traveled 154 miles one way yesterday. It took me about two and a half hours, so I'm anticipating the same time back," Sarah said.

John wanted to be at the meeting, not just to stay deeply involved, but to see Sarah again. She already had a hold on him and dismissed how wrong it was for him to start another affair. He couldn't resist. She was too beautiful, too intelligent, and too much like him. He started to justify his infidelity by starting to find fault with Katherine. Something he had never done before. He started telling himself, "Katherine is a sweet lady, but that's all she is. She has absolutely no interest in doing anything but watching TV all day and that isn't me. Christ! She gets off on watching anal TV shows like, 'The 90-day Fiancé.' or some other mindless tripe. I can't stand doing that. The only thing I'll watch is Vox News, and their conservative commentators discussing politics. What's happening with President Tripp is my only interest."

John was mentally laying the groundwork to leave Katherine although he wouldn't admit it to himself. He knew that he was not going to stop committing murders, it had become a part of his psyche, like some serial killer. Senator Roberts was next on his list, if he didn't murder somebody else before him, although it appeared unlikely with the election date drawing near.

As he continued to do work on his property, John's mind never stopped thinking about everything over and over. He, in a fit of uncontrolled emotion, said, "That's what I'll do. I'll kill Lizzie. What a perfect thing to do. I'll kill her while she's in the warehouse. I can imagine the dilemma Annette would be in. I'll get the little piece of shit to die on the floor of the warehouse while they're in the midst of committing a federal crime printing thousands of fraudulent ballots. Annette would be in a 911 dilemma. If she calls for an ambulance, they'll automatically notify the police, because they'll find Lizzie's corpse with no determined cause of death. She couldn't afford to take a chance that the police might see the phony ballots. She'll have to have Lizzie's body moved outside the warehouse. If she does that, she'll be exposing her clandestine operation to the police if they investigate Lizzie's death. and see her taking Lizzie's body from inside the warehouse on nearby surveillance cameras. What reason could she use? She'd be hard pressed to find a legitimate reason even if. she thought Lizzie died of a stroke. That's settled. Lizzie is next. Then the Senator."

John's cell phone rang. It was Jeanne Collette calling. When John answered Jeanne, said, "John, I spoke to Sarah. She'll be meeting me at three o'clock this afternoon. We had a brief talk over the phone, and I'm excited about our meeting. She was a smart move for the both of us John. Thank you."

John replied, "I think so, for sure. Everything from here on out will be a matter of carefully planned timing. If she comes out with an article too soon, the fraudulent ballots will disappear, and everyone will skirt prosecution. We need to nail them in the act."

Collette replied, "John, I agree. But if she does come out with an explosive story against the Senator, just ahead of the election, it'll ruin him, and guarantee he'll lose the election. With the videos and the audio recordings and the additional proof gathered by Sarah, all of the people involved in the fraud will all be arrested."

John replied, "That may be the case, but I obtained the evidence illegally. You know what their lawyers will do in front of a favorable left leaning judge. Get the evidence suppressed because it was gathered without a warrant. The prosecution will more than likely drop the case. They need to be caught red handed."

Jeanne said, "John, that's valid, but honestly, I'd let the little rat conspirators go, knowing we got Roberts out of DC. Think about how much that would help the President's agenda. He'd gain a greater majority in the Senate. I don't know if you've heard, but American Patriot Party Governor Richard Blair has elected an American Patriot to replace Socialist Senator Pelovski in the Senate. It's all over the mainstream media today. They're all demanding that he replace a National Socialist with a National Socialist. He already made his speech and announced his choice. It's his absolute prerogative when replacing a Senator. President Tripp is one happy camper. Her leaving reduces one vote on their side and adds another vote on our side. That increases the Senate margin by two. And when we take Senator Roberts out of the race the same margin change will happen effectively giving President Tripp an even greater cushion in the Senate to block anything the NSP tries to push through and to pass whatever laws and bills he needs."

John replied, "No I didn't hear the wonderful news. I'm excited for the President. I love that guy. He's the best."

"I do too," Jeanne replied. Then asked, "Will you be able to be here by three o'clock?"

John replied, "I have every intention to, but I can't promise anything. I'll call you later and let you know. Michael Johnson was supposed to set up a tracing call to Brad, their computer accomplice at his black ops investigation and security company client. We need to find out who he is and take possession of his computer and hard drives. I wanted to get that done as soon as possible."

Collette responded, "John, as a matter of fact, I spoke to him this morning and he said that he was going to call you today about it. I know he had to go to court today for some client. He may have gotten tied up. Call him. John, I have to let you go. I have someone waiting outside my office."

John immediately dialed Michael's number and reached him while he was driving to his office. "Michael. This is John Meade. What's happening with my call to Brad," John asked.

Michael replied, "John, I did not forget, I had an emergency at the courthouse today which sidetracked me. I already spoke to my contacts, and they'll do it with no problem. I'll text their number to you. When you call, speak to Peter Miller. He knows what you need and will do it for you on a minutes notice. I told him it was a critical matter. You won't need me there."

"Send it, we don't have too many days left to pull this off," John said.

As soon as John received the text, he called Peter Miller and arranged to place his call to Brad. Peter availed himself to assist John at any time he could get there. John set it up with Peter to be at his office by 5 pm. That would give him the time he needed to go to Jeanne's office and see Sarah again. He could take her with him when he traced Brad's call.

John didn't hesitate to leave his house without giving a thought to Katherine. He just quit making excuses and said to himself, "Fuck it." He'd worry about her questioning later.

When John arrived at Collette's office, Sarah had already arrived and was in with Jeanne. When he walked into her office, he saw them sitting together. Sarah looked at John and gave him a really warm smile. He ate it up and said, "Sarah. I'm so glad that you're meeting our next American Patriot Party Senator. She's going to be a force for the good guys."

Sarah responded, "I'm sure she will. I've been telling Jeanne what I did yesterday and have shown her my telephotos. Take a look at them. I had the license plates blown up so that we could see the numbers clearly. My office has tracked down who owns the vehicles. The only thing is the plates were stolen. So they won't help in identifying the drivers, but we now know who owns the homes the ballots were dropped off at. It's just as we thought, both of the homeowners are postal employees. I imagine there are more postal employees involved at the other counties."

"Sarah excellent," John said.

Jeanne said, "We were just trying to decide the best way to break the news. We need to stop Aaron Roberts before the election is run. You can never tell whether he'll win anyway without cheating. We are dead even in our internal polls. I don't want him to pull out a win, and he wangles his way out of everything. John, you may be right about suppression of the evidence."

Sarah added, "I can hit front page on the story, but we need to remember that mainstream media will suppress the story as long as possible."

Collette added, "They'll want to keep the story away from the voters. I recommend that Sarah breaks the story today. We have only five days before election day."

John added, "Look. There's one particularly important piece of evidence that we need. That's Brad's hard drive. It actually has the names of every fraudulent vote. At least under an audit we can prove the attempted steal. Let me ask you. Can't you call the Governor's office and let him get a swat team to break in on Brad's location and grab those hard drives. Once we have them and him, we win. Forget the FBI. Governor Santos is a true Patriot and honorable guy. He can call in his Attorney General to pull this off. I'm sure that they have the pull to get an immediate warrant to do the raid. I'll be calling Brad this afternoon at 5 pm at the investigative firm Michael Johnson set me up with. Sarah can present the evidence and protect me with anonymity."

Collette replied, "John, I'll put a call into the Governor right away. I like your thinking. See if you can track down this Brad character. Once we have his information, we should be able to have Sarah run her story. Hopefully, the Governor will have his Attorney General Whitman stop everything he's doing and handle all of this."

John asked Sarah, "Do you want to go with me to Peter Miller's office? He's the guy who's going to trace my call to Brad?"

Sarah said, "Yes. If he's able to trace the call, we'll be able to locate where he is, and I'd love to know that information."

John got up and said, "Jeanne, do your thing. Get the Governor on the phone and let's get this thing going."

John and Sarah headed out of the office to see Peter Miller. As they were walking toward John's car, he said to Sarah, "I haven't been able to stop thinking about you."

Sarah looked at John, paused for a moment in her stride, and said, "John, I haven't been in a relationship for some time, because I was hurt once, but I admit I am attracted to you. And yes, I've thought about you. Just don't say or do anything you don't mean. Please."

John took Sarah's hand and pulled her gently toward him, leaned over and kissed her. She moved her body slightly away from him, looked into his eyes, and then put her hand around his neck and kissed him. John felt total elation and a rush of passion. It was not the I want to have sex with this woman feeling. It was I want to be with this woman feeling. I want her to share in my life.

John said to Sarah, "I have no intention of hurting you. I can't believe my feelings. I really know so little about you. We've really only just met.

But I swear to you, you have pulled me in, like the sirens did to Jason and the Argonauts. You're irresistible."

Sarah replied, "You've affected me in the same way. Fate has brought us together. But we need to slow everything down. Let's just concentrate on what we're doing."

John said, "You're right."

John and Sarah walked into Peter Miller's office, which was full of computer screens and other equipment, including drones. Peter greeted them. He said, "I understand from Michael Johnson that you want to trace where a phone number comes from?"

John replied, "Yes. I need to get the name and address of a person we know only as Brad."

Peter said, "We can do that, but let's try the uncomplicated way first. We'll do a reverse phone look up. It will display his name and address. If we can't get the information that way, we'll use your cell phone and synchronize it up to our call tracing equipment. We plug this cord into your iPhone. and then into the machine. The second Brad picks up, it kicks in instantly. It will pinpoint his location and display it on the monitor within seconds. As soon as it has identified his location, you'll see a red dot blink on the monitor and display an address. We'll pull up the owner from the tax records. If he's renting, I suggest you drive by and check his mailbox. Either way, it'll only take a few minutes to give you everything you want."

John said, "Terrific. Let's do it. Here's his phone number. I'm assuming it's a cell phone."

Peter went into the company's reverse phone look-up system first and within seconds it displayed the name and address of its owner. It indicated William Newman with the address of 2623 Hawthorn Road, Hollywood, Florida, 33020.

John saw the information and said, "It's not Brad unless he's been using an alias. If he is, I don't blame him with the illegal shit he's doing."

Peter said, "Ok. Now we'll call him directly, and use our system to pinpoint his location. If it's the same address, we'll know for sure that's where he is. If it comes up at a different location, then we'll know he's operating out of a different address than the one the phone is registered at. Let me have your phone for a second, I need to connect it to our tracing system."

Peter hooked up the phone and handed it back to John and said, "Ok, make your call. The only number he'll notice on his caller ID is yours."

John asked Peter, "Can you record our conversation?"

Peter replied, "I can, but it's illegal for us to do that. I'll help you with some things, but I can't risk our company licenses for what amounts to a wiretap."

John said, "I understand." Then he called Brad. After a few rings, Brad picked up and said, "Hello."

John replied, "Brad. This is John, Annette's friend. She said it was okay to call you. Is that correct?"

Brad said, "I did say it was okay. You know what I'm into, so I am very guarded."

John replied, "That makes the two of us. I've been working with Annette at the warehouse. My ass is out there, also my friend. But not as far as yours. I prefer not to talk about anything surrounding that issue over the phone."

Brad responded, "I agree, so what did you want to discuss with me?"

John replied, "I need to know if you can hack a computer school and pull up their final exam that will need to be taken next Tuesday, complete it for me, and then send it to me, so I can take the test myself on that date?"

Brad replied, "Annette didn't mention that."

"What did she mention?" John asked.

"She just said you wanted to discuss something about what you were learning and needed some clarification," Brad replied.

"Brad, honestly, I don't understand it enough to discuss what I know and don't know. I just need to take that test and pass it," John said.

"I want two grand in cash to do it. I'll call you back with a meeting place when I'm done," Brad replied.

John said, "No problem. I can do that. It's worth it to me. Please don't ask me why. It's personal."

Brad said, "It's something to do with your wife. Annette told me. What's the name of the school?"

John replied, "The Academy of Computer Programming. They offer single course completion certificates. They're located in Cypress Creek."

Brad asked, "What's your last name and address?"

John answered, "My last name is Meade. My address is 1126 South Island Road, Fort Lauderdale, Florida, 33311."

Brad said, "I'll find you in their files. These schools usually have the same tests. They rarely change them."

John said, "I assume you work from home."

Brad responded, "No I don't. I'm not stupid. I have a small rental. But that's enough about me. Let me go and take care of this now. I can use the cash."

"Brad, I appreciate your help. I'll get the cash tomorrow and wait for your call," John said.

John hung up, turned to Peter, and asked, "Did you trace him?"

Peter responded, "Got him. The address he's at is not all that far from the residence we picked up before."

John looked at Sarah, who had already written down the information and asked, "Well are you ready to go look at the place?"

Sarah replied, "Let's do it."

John said, "Peter thank you. We really appreciate it." John then said to Sarah, "Let's go girl."

John and Sarah headed straight out to Brad's address. As they were driving, John's car phone rang. He didn't bother answering because he knew it was Katherine.

Sarah asked, "Aren't you going to answer?"

"Nope. I'll call them later. It can wait," John answered.

Sarah said, "John, after we see where he is, we can let Jeanne know. Like you said, we need to get his hard drive."

"The minute we lay eyes on the building we'll do that," John replied.

John was already beginning his lies with Sarah. He was living so many, that they became blurred with the real truth. His life was now so entangled he didn't care what he told anyone, so long as it kept him on the path, he had taken for himself. As he looked over at Sarah sitting next to him, he thought to himself, "I'm so into this woman. I wish I had met her at a different time and under better circumstances. If I didn't have to account to Katherine, I could be honest with her. My lazy ass wife is getting in my way. I have to figure a way to get away from her."

John was now lost mentally. His mind swirled in and out of reality. He started wondering who he really was. Was he in love with his wife, or wasn't he. She no longer excited him. He was starting to feel that Katherine was like an old slipper. Worn out and becoming uncomfortable. He didn't like her always telling him to calm down whenever he would curse at the asshole Socialists on TV. She should be shouting with him, he thought.

Sarah said, "John, that's the address right there. Let me take a photo of it."

John stopped the car, waited for a minute as Sarah snapped away and then drove past the small house. It looked like it was about 1200 square feet or even a shade less.

John said, "Well now we know where he is."

Sarah said, "I would love to look in his mailbox and see if there's anything in it. It would be nice to know his name."

John said, "We shouldn't take a chance right now. If he should see us doing that, he would be out the door and gone with everything. It would be better to look in his trash. I see a trash can just on the side of his house. Hopefully, we'll find some discarded mail."

Sarah said, "Okay. We can come back later tonight."

"Sorry sweetness, you'll have to do it yourself. I need to head out. Just be careful. I'll take you back to your car," John replied.

Just as John finished speaking his cell phone rang. He looked at the number and sighed a sigh of relief as he saw it was Jeanne Collette calling and not Katherine.

"Jeanne, please tell me that you spoke to the Governor," John said immediately when he answered.

Jeanne replied, "Yes, I did. He called Barbara Whitman, the States Attorney General. She's meeting with me this afternoon to look at our evidence. This matter is going to move fast. The Governor was really upset with what I told him. Between you and me, he has no love for Senator Roberts and always felt he was a very underhanded Senator. He promised immediate action. Whitman will get the Search Warrants by tomorrow if she determines the evidence supports that action. How did you do in locating this Brad guy?"

John answered, "We located him and where we believe his computer and hard drives are located. Michael's contact Peter Miller traced his phone to his location. We were just in front of his place minutes ago. We're not sure of what his last name is yet. Peter did a phone reverse look up and produced the name of William Miller at the address. Is his last name Miller? We don't know for sure. Is his real name William, or is he using Brad as an alias? We don't know that either. Sarah is going to come back later in the evening and look in his trash to see if she can find some mail. I can't be with her."

"John, that's too risky. Not by herself. Let me make a phone call to Michael Johnson and see if he can have one of his Black Ops men go along with her just in case. We don't know this guy or what he's capable of doing if he catches her going through his trash," Jeanne said.

"That would be great. Call us back as soon as you can," John replied.

John turned to Sarah and said, "This thing is starting to roll. Jeanne spoke to Governor Santos, who has already contacted Florida's Attorney General. She'll be seeing Jeanne tomorrow to look at the evidence to determine if she can get search warrants issued. She's going to call us back after she asks Michael to have one of his Black Ops clients meet you somewhere before you go onto the property looking through Brad's trash. We don't know what he's capable of."

Sarah replied, "Actually, even though I would've risked it, it would be more comforting with back up."

John and Sarah reached Jeanne's office where she still had her car parked. John said, "You should go up and wait in Jeanne's office. She can arrange to have the bodyguard meet you here. I have to go, but I'll call you later to see how things went." As Sarah was releasing her seatbelt and preparing to get out of the car, John reached over and held her hand, his heart pounded for a moment, as he was so conflicted emotionally, and said, "I can't resist my feelings. It's so hard to do it with you. I know what you said, about stepping back and taking it slow, but I need to kiss you, if you'll let me. before you get out of this car. I want to savor a moment like that with you."

Sarah looked at John, then moved toward him, without saying a word, and kissed him passionately. She then asked, "Is that savory enough for you?"

John smiled and replied, "It was not savory enough. Can I have just one more?"

They kissed again. This time John said to her, "I believe I'm falling in love with you. Before you say anything, I know Sarah, I know. How can somebody say that after just being with someone for two days? It's just the way I feel."

Sarah replied, "John, I can't deny that I'm attracted to you. I am. I also know that you're married. I did some research on you before leaving New York. I had to after what you told me. I lost control of myself when I touched your hand, and I know that you took it as a come on and I would have felt the same way if the situation were reversed. When I told you to let's step back and go slow, it was not because I didn't have a strong attraction to you, it was because I did. I don't want to be responsible for your wife being hurt. I wouldn't want that myself. Even knowing that, I kissed you again and enjoyed every fleeting moment. But John, I don't want to lead you astray, and I don't want you to do something you may regret with Katherine. Yes, John, I know her name. It's easy today to learn so much about someone so quickly. I'm not upset about the fact that you said nothing. I would be upset if you wanted more from me, then did nothing after I willingly gave myself to you."

John sat back with his shoulder against the driver's side window, looking at Sarah, in silence. For the first time in a long while he was left speechless. An unexpected, and uncontrolled emotion swelled up in him, and his eyes watered. He then, said, "Sarah. You are so right. I'm much more the man, than what I've been. I never expected to feel the way I do about you. It just happened. You are not wrong about anything and I'm sorry I lived a lie around you."

Sarah saw John's eyes, and knew he was truly sincere, and believed that he had fallen for her. She said, "I won't fault you, because I know what strong feelings can do to someone's sensibilities. It happened to me. I let myself get hurt very emotionally. I don't want that to happen to either one of us. If we are meant to be, it will happen. In the meantime, I'm going up to Jeanne's office and waiting to see what happens. I'll call you later. I promise."

Just as Sarah stepped out of the car, John's phone rang. He saw it was Jeanne. The minute he answered, he said, "Jeanne, we're in your parking lot right now."

Jeanne said, "That's great. I was in contact with Peter, and he said he was sending someone over to my office to accompany Sarah tonight. He has a carry permit."

John said, "That's fantastic. I feel better already. Let me tell Sarah. She'll be up in a minute."

John hung up with Jeanine and told Sarah what was said. Sarah responded, "Well everything's a go."

John replied and said, "Yes, it is." He then said, "There is one more thing I'll need you to help me with. The bug I planted in Senator Roberts' office and in Betty's needs to come out. I have to remove them quickly. I don't want them found either by him or the swat team or whomever raids the place."

Sarah said, "Let's talk about that tomorrow. We'll figure something out. If you can get me in to see Roberts and Betty for interviews, I'll try and create distractions long enough for you to get them."

John replied, "I'll try. If Roberts even gets a hint of what's going to go down, he'll do a sweep of his office looking for a bug. I honestly believe the Secret Service will protect him. Okay, Jeanne is waiting for you. We'll talk about it again later. I'm going to the warehouse tomorrow to find out from Annette where she is in the operation. We have less than a week to pull all of this off. If she's changed anything we'll need to know."

CHAPTER EIGHTEEN

ONE WOMAN IN, ONE WOMAN OUT

Sarah headed to Jeanne's office, while John drove off. As usual, John began having his one-way conversation with himself. So much was happening so fast. He started a shit storm, that was going to have huge political ramifications. He was excited about so many things. Sarah's expose would take a hammer to the National Socialist Party and put a hatchet to their expanding voting rights bill. It would be killed on the hill, even by members of their own party. He hoped that she would be nominated for a Pulitzer Prize in Journalism. Her investigative reporting story would be that powerful. He just couldn't shake his feelings for her. He was smitten and he knew it. He just dismissed Annette as collateral damage. His relationship with her was no more than a means to an end. He knew that when he got home, he was going to be confronted by Katherine. He ignored her call and never called with any excuse, or even to find out what she wanted.

He said, "Fuck it. I'll face the music and tell her the truth about everything, except the murders. I'd be insane to do that shit. She'd have me arrested instantly. I'll just tell her about working at Senator Roberts campaign, and what I had uncovered while I was there. I know how to spin it, to fit my narrative. I'll admit to the affair I had with Annette to get the info I needed. I'll tell her exactly like it was, Annette was no more than a means to an end. If I know Katherine, she'll tell me to leave. I'll grab some stuff, get a hotel room, and call Sarah. God, I want to be with her. I want to get in the fast lane with her."

His thoughts paused a minute as he gathered in his emotions. He stared straight ahead at the road, when he uncontrollably began speaking to himself again, "Sarah pumps me up. If everything goes as I hope over the next few days, I'll either knock off Lizzie tomorrow, or leave her imprisoned in a vegetative state. Annette will be stuck with her one way or the other. I'll swirl the toxin in the coffee they all drink, and fuck all of them up. They deserve it. I'll have to think about that a little more. I don't want to screw up any chance I'll have being with Sarah. I'll just put Lizzy in a Pelovski state of mind. Speaking of that Socialist bitch, I wonder how the special election in her state to replace her will go. It's going to be held the same day that Senator Roberts has his. Only I know how that's going to turn out."

"My next step is to get the frogs off my property. I'll need to decide what to do with them. I don't want to lose the toxin source. There has to be someplace safe. Somewhere where I can care for them. I know they won't be able to link me to the frogs. I bought them with cash and never gave my correct name to the proprietor and as he said, he's sold thousands of them, and he does not sell them poisonous. Fuck. Another dilemma."

John pulled up to his home. This time Katherine was sitting outside, smoking her horrible cigarettes. The first thing John thought was, "I'll finally be rid of those smelly things and her smelly clothes. Good riddance to that."

In his mind he was already out of the house and Katherine's life. He thought, she's young enough, still extremely attractive, she'll have no problem meeting someone. Hell he already had. He became instantly cold toward her. It was a defensive mechanism. He had to be as matter of fact as he could be. An 'It is what it is,' attitude.

As he got within feet of Katherine, he could see the look of anger on her face. The first thing she said, is "Where have you been? I damn sure know it hasn't been at the Academy. I called them and asked if you were in class. I told them I was your wife and needed to talk to you. The person told me you were not there. He said the instructor told him you were rarely there. What have you been doing? Are you seeing someone else? Tell me John. I want to know now."

"Getting into this in front of the house is not what we want Katherine. Let's go inside. I prefer to be civil. I'll explain everything if you let me. Not everything is always as it seems," John replied.

John opened the door to their home and Katherine followed right behind. No sooner did the door close behind them that Katherine began to assail John. She said, "This better be good. Because if you cheated on me, you would need to leave."

John looked at her and just let her speak. He said nothing at first. Katherine took his momentary silence as an admission of infidelity. She said, "You did, didn't you? Then she angrily asked, "Who is she? How long has this been going on?" Katherine for the first-time struck John in his chest a few times and shouted, "You son of a bitch, you mother fucker."

John just stood there and took whatever she did or said to him, and then just said, without any emotion, "Are you finished? If you want me to explain my actions, I will. But I won't bother to explain shit to you with you carrying on so insanely."

Katherine looked at him with tears in her eyes, and stayed quiet, giving John a moment to hear him out. "You're right. I haven't been going to the Academy, except for a few classes over the last six months. I was volunteering at Senator Aaron Roberts campaign office."

Katherine, before John could say another word, said, "Do you expect me to believe that? You hate the man with a passion. You hate all Socialists. You better produce something better than that."

John with a raised tone replied, "If you won't let me explain, I'll go pack my bags and walk out of your life forever."

John's words struck a hard chord with Katherine. She emotionally responded, "Okay. finish what you were saying."

John snapped back, "I do hate the motherfucker. The only reason I did was because I wanted to derail his election. I didn't know how, but I figured that if I worked among all those sleezy scumbags I could get some dirt on him. As a matter of fact, I did. I planted a bug in his office and recorded him admitting to campaign fraud. I went to Candidate Jeanne Collette's office and passed the information on to her. I got involved in their intent to steal the election by helping them print fraudulent ballots. I even video recorded them in action with a belt buckle spy camera. I gave that evidence to Jeanne Collette as well. She's been in contact with Governor Santos, and he's moving to get a search warrant through the States AG. It will all be in the news within the next two or three days. You'll see it I'm sure on VOX News. The other left-wing media may suppress the story hoping Roberts wins."

Katherine said, "Why didn't you just tell me?"

John replied, "Because you would've said, "Don't get involved. Don't take a chance like that. Don't do this or don't do that, like you always do when I want to do something you may not like. So I kept what I was doing secret from you."

Katherine said, "Do you know what I've been going through? I haven't said anything, but I've been wondering why you're always late or disappearing for hours on the days you don't go to school. I could only take your Home Depot or Lowe's excuses for so long without beginning to wonder."

"Why didn't you just ask? That's all you had to do. I would've told you sooner. I should have. But it's too late for that," John replied.

John could see that Katherine was softening and not pushing for more answers. He wanted her to be more confrontational because he genuinely wanted to leave her for Sarah. He was willing to throw his marriage out the window for her. That's when John, knowing he didn't have to say anything more, decided to own up about Annette. He figured that it would be the straw that broke the camel's back as the old saying goes, and send Katherine off the deep end.

Katherine replied, "I thought that you would tell me on your own. I don't know. I was afraid you were seeing another woman, and I couldn't face hearing it. That's the one thing I could never forgive you for. I would want you to leave. There could be no reason good enough for that with me."

As soon as Katherine finished saying that, John saw his chance to get away from her and be with Sarah. He knew that they only knew each other for such a brief time, but he felt that Sarah truly had feelings for him and from the things she said and how she acted towards him, he felt the same thing. It was now or never as far as he was concerned to make his move. Besides, he knew that he had murdered two people and because of his luck, his third victim lived. He didn't want her dragged into that. She wouldn't be strong enough to handle it if he got arrested.

John's thinking was erratic. How ridiculous a thought. What if he were arrested when he was with Sarah? Wouldn't she be in the same predicament. He didn't factor that into his thinking because that would kill one of the reasons, he was using to leave Katherine.

John said, "I need to tell you the one thing that you don't want to hear. But if I don't tell you now, It will more than likely come up later. I did have sex with another woman. But not for love. It was just to break her down emotionally and to get her to trust me so that she'd tell me the things I needed to know about the election fraud. She meant nothing to me Katherine. You can believe that or not. I took pictures of her committing a federal crime and recorded her telling me incriminating evidence."

Katherine, without speaking, slapped John across the face and said, in a low but stern voice, "Get out of my house!"

John said, in an almost mocking way, "Spies use women all the time. It's just business as usual with them. The women they screw are considered collateral damage."

"Get the fuck away from me!" Katherine shouted. "Who do you think you are, Jason Bourne?" That crap happens just in the movies and you're no actor. Leave, please leave! Find a hotel and stay out. When you're ready to get your clothes and things let me know so that I won't be here when you are. Get a lawyer and get a divorce, I want half of everything and the house. I deserve that you mother fucker."

John looked at her, and said, "Okay. It's yours. But let me go peacefully. I don't want us to start saying things we don't mean and then regret later."

John turned and went into their bedroom, and started putting his clothes on the bed. He went into a closet and pulled out two suitcases and proceeded to pack his clothes. As he was doing that, he thought about Sarah, and with any luck, he could be with her that night. He wanted that very badly. It would make it all okay. He also thought about his frogs. He needed to get them out of his workshop. He wasn't worried about their survival. They were being fed, the temperature was controlled, and he had rigged up a water bottle that kept water in their pond. He wasn't finished with his murder weapons, at least not yet.

John said to Katherine, as he was walking out of the house, "I know you hate me, and I understand that. But I did what I did for the good of this country and my President. Having meaningless sex with another woman to accomplish that was necessary. But you wouldn't understand my patriotism. It's a shame. I just hope that we can remain friends at least. I'll call you when I need to come over."

With that said, John loaded his car, and drove off. Katherine watched him leave and closed the door behind him.

As John was driving, he said to himself, "That was easier than I thought." He picked up his phone and said, "Siri, call Sarah."

Sarah answered the phone and said, "John. I didn't expect you to call me tonight."

John excitedly said, "I had to. I can't stop thinking about you. I know that it sounds crazy, but I've fallen in love with you. So much so, that I left my wife. My suitcases are in my car and I'm heading to the hotel where you're staying. Please don't tell me that I made a mistake or that I misread your feelings. That savoring kiss you gave me is still on my lips. I can still feel and taste it. I feel like a smitten boy whose experiencing his first puppy love. I'm head over heels."

There was a moment of silence on the phone, as Sarah listened to John. She had feelings for him, but never expected him to leave his wife.

Sarah replied, "John, I can't believe you did that. I'm so sorry for Katherine. It can't be easy on her. Are you absolutely sure that this is what you want? I don't want to be hurt by any impetuous moves you might regret later."

John replied, "Impetuous! No not at all. Sarah, Katherine, and I were just sharing a home. There was always civility and friendship. But love? Not really. I would marry you tomorrow as crazy as it seems, but legally it couldn't happen anyway. I'll be hiring a divorce attorney as soon as we get past this week."

Sarah replied, "John you certainly are a determined man. Don't bother getting a room. I'll call the hotel and ask them to give you the key to mine. Call me after you get there. I think we're a little crazy, but a good crazy. I'm happy that you want to be with me. Whatever happens we'll make it an adventure."

John said, "Sarah, yes, we will. You've made me an incredibly happy man. I'll call you after I get to the hotel."

Sarah, waited outside Brad's home with her bodyguard waiting for the right moment to dig in his trash hoping to produce some discarded mail, that would disclose his name. Sarah watched his home through a telephoto lens. She moved her sight across his windows looking for movement. There was light coming through only one of them. They had been sitting in her rented car for over two hours when the light went out and the front door opened. She could see a man about five feet eleven and looked to be in his early thirties, get in a car and drive off. As soon as his car turned the corner, she started hers up and drove quickly to his house. She went to get out of her car to rush to his trash can when her bodyguard Tony stopped her. He said, "I'll get what you need. If he comes back unexpectedly, I don't want you there." Sarah sat back, and said, "Okay. Please hurry."

Tony moved quickly up the driveway and over to the side of Brad's house to the trash can. As soon as he reached it, he took off its lid, reached in, and pulled out the entire black plastic trash bag, and brought it back to the car. He yelled at Sarah as he got near the car, "Pop the trunk."

When she did, he threw the bag in and hopped back into the car. He said, "Let's go to the shopping mall parking lot we passed about a block back. We'll look through the bag there. Once we finish, I'll put the bag back into his trash can. If he should notice it missing, he could get spooked. I don't believe he'll look into it tonight."

They opened the trash bag and began digging into it looking for that one piece of mail that would give them Brad's identity. They got down halfway in his garbage when they pulled up a computer science magazine. It had a mail label on it. It told them that it was a subscription and the likelihood it was his. It tied in with his work. Sarah laid the magazine flat and photographed the label with her iPhone. She read the name clearly. It said Bradley Newman, and had the same address as the one Peter had pulled up using the reverse phone look up.

While she was doing that, Tony pulled another envelope out of the trash. It had Senator Roberts Campaign Office address in the upper left corner. He looked in it, but it was empty. He said to Sarah, "I think you'll want this."

Sarah took it from Tony and when she read the return address, she said, "Bingo. This definitely ties Brad to the Senator."

Tony replied, "Yes, it does at that. Keep it. We might be able to pull a print and cross match it to our database. Our company has access to the National Security Admin's search engine."

Sarah replied, "Wow, you must be doing some serious work for the government."

Tony smiled and replied, "You can say that."

Sarah and Tony drove back to Brad's trash can. They could see that the light was still out. Tony grabbed the garbage bag, moved swiftly, and put the bag back and returned to the car.

As he sat back in, he said, "Mission accomplished."

As they were driving down the street, Brad's car passed them on the way back to his house. Tony said, "That was close."

Sarah drove back to Jeanne's office and dropped Tony off. As he was leaving, he said, "We'll try lifting the prints and matching any that we find on it. Peter will call you tomorrow with whatever we find out. If we identify his, we'll check to see if he has any priors. If you ever need me again, call the office."

Sarah said, "Thank you Tony. I appreciate your help."

As soon as Tony walked away, Sarah called John.

John, answered, "Hi sweetheart. I was waiting for your call. I didn't call you because I didn't want to take a chance I'd call while you were digging in Brad's garbage alerting him to someone being outside his house. You see that happening in the movies all of the time."

"That's Ok. We found a computer magazine subscription with his name on it. His last name is Newman. The other man's name we tied to the first house we think belongs to his father."

"My bodyguard Tony found an envelope in the trash, with Senator Roberts return Campaign Office address on it. It was empty. I think it was a cash payment for what he does on the ballots."

"You may be right. Speaking of cash, I need to withdraw $2,000 cash tomorrow morning from my bank. I need to pay Brad for hacking into a computer school. I'll tell you all about it later. He called me a little while ago telling me he did what I wanted and wants the money tomorrow. We can meet him together. He doesn't know either one of us. That'll be a goof."

Sarah asked, "When are you supposed to meet him?"

John replied, "I told him at one in the afternoon. He said he would wait for me in the Publix parking lot on A1A."

Sarah responded, "Yes, I'd like to go. I can get a photo of him from some vantage point. I don't think we should meet him together. I'll get out of the car just before the parking lot and walk into it. He seems overly cautious and may be apprehensive with me there."

John replied, "You're right. Okay. We'll do it your way. I can't wait to see you. I want to hold you in my arms and just feel you against me. I was worried, but felt you would be all right with a professional black ops mercenary."

'I'm headed to you now. I should be there in twenty-five minutes," Sarah replied.

Sarah arrived at the hotel and went up to her room. When she entered, she saw John, standing in front of her with flowers in one hand and a bottle of champagne in the other. She smiled and said, "John, how sweet. I see you are a romantic."

John walked up to her, handed her the flowers, and then kissed her. He said, come let's sip some champagne and toast a new beginning and a future together. One full of adventure. We'll climb the Himalayas, cross the Sahara Desert, paddle the Amazon River, and go on a Safari."

Sarah said, "How about forgetting all of that. Let's go to Venice and take a gondola down the Grand Canal, walk along the Champs Elysees in Paris, or eat at an outdoor café on the Las Ramblas in Barcelona Spain. I'd like that better."

John laughed and said, "That sounds terrific. Let's go to all three places and wherever else you want once we get past what we've gotten ourselves into with taking down Senator Roberts and his gang. I can't wait to see that man in handcuffs. What a momentous day that will be for the President and the country. I'm so looking forward to the headlines in the Wall Street Daily and your name at the top of the column. I hope you get nominated for the Pulitzer Price."

Sarah looked at John, and she saw him genuinely happy. She was herself at that moment. She envisioned herself with John in all of the European places she mentioned. Touring Europe together and enjoying each other.

John looked at Sarah looking at him, for that moment and was thinking like thoughts. He took her by her hand and pulled her up to him and kissed her. At first softly on her lips and then on her face until he reached her lips again, and then they both kissed passionately, until they found themselves across the room and on the bed. It took only moments for them to undress and make love. John said, to himself, "I cannot rush this moment. I need to make it last. I need to satisfy Sarah all night. I want her to wake up next to me in the morning and want me again. I've found my soul mate." John held back more than once, during their love making session. Sarah could not, more than once.

When they finished, they just lay together, with Sarah having her arm across John's chest and her knee over his leg. She said, "Wow. What did I get myself into?"

John laughed and asked, "Did you like?"

Sarah replied, "Couldn't you tell?"

"Yes, I could. I just hope I can keep that up with you until I'm eighty."

Sarah laughed and said, "Eighty! I don't think so."

John said, "My mother told me my Dad was bothering her when he was eighty."

Sarah said, with a laugh, "She told you that?"

"She did. She told me after he passed away from a heart attack and we were reminiscing about him," John replied.

"I'm so sorry to hear that," Sarah said.

"It's okay. It was some years ago. Let's have a glass of champagne."

Sarah said, "That sounds good." Then asked John, "how is it that your dad was in his eighty's, and you are only, what? In your late thirties? I'm guessing."

John replied, "I am thirty-nine. I am the youngest of seven. Or as my Mom said, 'the baby of the family.'

John poured the champagne, handed Sarah her glass and then said to her, "I pledge myself to you for the rest of my life. I promise to adore you and to be with you in sickness and in health until the day I die. Now I'm married to you in heart and mind. You're stuck with me."

Sarah sipped the champagne with John and said, "That was the most wonderful thing anyone has ever said to me. I just hope you mean it. Please don't ever hurt me. I've given myself to you like some love-struck schoolgirl."

"I have every intention of marrying you as soon as you'll say yes, after I'm divorced. I already said yes to Katherine about what she wanted in a settlement. She wants the house and half of our assets. That's okay. Sarah, I'll still have enough money for us to travel the world for the rest of our lives and never work. I'm worth in liquid assets well over one hundred million dollars."

Sarah asked, "How did you get so wealthy?"

John was proud to answer Sarah's question. He told her, "I was a visionary. I believed in tech stocks when they all came out and bought them when they were priced right. Many people missed the boat back then. I didn't. I also have many millions in Bitcoin. I was buying it when it was only a few dollars a coin. Now it's over $40,000.00 apiece. I have a bundle of them. That should tell you something. Every so often I cash out when I need to replenish my liquidity."

"I plan to liquidate a little at a time. I want enough money in hand so that we can just enjoy our lives and if you don't want to work again, you won't have to. That's up to you. I'll support you in anything you want. I want a villa in Spain, in Italy and in France and I want to go to Italy and buy a Lamborghini and drive through Europe together."

"Are you serious?" Sarah asked.

"Absolutely," John replied and then, although he didn't need to tell Sarah about his marriage, he said, "You know Katherine had no interest in anything, except television. Everyone watches TV, but she made it her lifestyle. She'd get up in the morning, and before doing anything else, get a cup of coffee and go smoke a nasty cigarette on the patio. Then she would come back in, sit on the couch, and watch TV all day, except when she went shopping for food. She had no hobbies and no interests whatsoever. It always bothered me. There were times I thought of leaving, but didn't. I don't know why. I'm telling you, because I want you to understand why it really was not difficult for me to leave her. I fell in love with you at first sight."

Sarah in a sympathetic voice said, "John, I went through a lot in a previous relationship, and it hurt. I've always been hesitant with the men I've met since then. None of them filled the void in my life. But you, you've made me feel something none of them could. Just like in that Tom Cruise movie, where his wife said to him, 'You got me when you said hello.'"

John replied, "Sarah, that's exactly how I felt, only it was the minute I saw you walking towards me at the airport. You had this captivating look about you. It was va-va-voom and angelic all rolled into one? You lit me up all at once. You possess all the traits I've always wanted in a woman and as a bonus, are extremely beautiful. I was serious about the divorce. I want it to be a no contest. Give her what she wants and be gone. She'll never have to worry about anything. She'll get over it."

Sarah started to laugh and said, "I looked va-va-voom and angelic all rolled into one? John you are too funny. That's a new one for sure."

With that last, "She'll get over it," comment he made about Katherine, it became obvious how callous he had become. One minute he could be caring, and feel for others, and in another minute be cold and heartless. He could love you one minute and kill you the next. Annette is a prime example of that. Even though he first thought of her as a pawn in his scheme to uncover dirt on the Senator, he admired her and began to have feelings for her. He even compared her to Katherine and found Annette more desirable and even lusted for her. Then like flipping a light switch off, didn't care what happened to her. She became, as he thought in the end, collateral damage.

From the beginning of his escapade, he lied to Katherine and justified it as a necessity to stop what he considered a scourge by the Socialists. It was a sign that he was willing to risk his relationship because he simply lost interest in her. His Political Stress Disorder was very real in his overzealous approach about setting things right for President Tripp. He did murder two people, and cripple another with paralysis and now was planning to increase his body count.

CHAPTER NINETEEN

THE INVESTIGATION OF THE BAD BALLOTS

John received a call from Peter at the security firm about Brad, while he was with Sarah at the Hotel. When John answered the phone, Peter said, "Good morning, John. Got some news on your boy Brad. His prints were on the envelope along with another we were also able to identify. Brad does have a prior record. It shows him spending six months in County Jail for hacking county records three years ago. Nothing more. His name is confirmed as Bradley Newman. It has him as thirty-two years old."

John replied, "Thanks Peter. The name confirmation helps." He then asked, "Does it show his father's name by chance?"

"Yes, it does, under his bio info. It's William. His mother Joan is deceased," Peter replied.

John asked, "Thanks Peter. Who is the other party you uncovered from the fingerprints?"

Peter replied, "We identified, a Betty Ryan. We were able to get her info because she has a prior, for protesting and was arrested for tussling with a police officer. She was given a suspended sentence and three months of probation. Other than that she's clean That charge goes back ten years ago. It indicated she went to Miami University back then."

John said, "I can see her protesting. She's a resolute left winger. She's Senator Roberts' Campaign Advisor."

Peter said, "Anyone that supports him has to be whacked. I don't want to talk politics, but I really dislike that man for his unfounded and relentless attacks and investigations against President Tripp."

John said, "Peter, you're a man after my own heart. I feel the same about him. The names I have for him all end in fuck. Peter, thanks for the help. I'll tell Sarah and Jeanne Collette about what you've found. Did you have a photo of Brad in the report?"

Peter replied, "Yes, I do. I'll e-mail it to you, Will that work?"

John replied, "Perfect. Thanks my friend. We appreciate your efforts."

After the call, John related what Peter told him to Sarah. Sarah after hearing the news, said, "Let's get this info to Jeanne right away. She'll need it to pass on to whomever the AG assigned to handle the probe. Several warrants will need to be issued. They'll need two for Brad. one for his father's home, one for his rental, one for the warehouse, the Senator's campaign office, his home and warrants for everyone else involved. This is going to be one hell of a wide sweep and one hell of a story."

John replied, "Yes it will. Send her a text with the info and ask her if you can meet later today to get up to date. I'm going to go over to the warehouse to find out exactly what's going on and get a last-minute update from Annette. I also need to run home and pick up a few more things. It won't take me more than ten minutes. I need to get some account info. I'm going to move some money around. "I'll call you and let you know where I am and when I'll meet up with you later." John then looking at Sarah, and admiring her beauty said, "Oooh, give me a kiss you sexy thing."

Sarah laughed and said, "Just a kiss. We need to get a lot done today."

John said, "Even though it's tempting, I hear you. We're going to have a long and wonderful life together, so just a kiss it'll be."

Sarah asked, "Didn't you want to get the bugs out of the Senator's office? Let's try to do it today. There's little opportunity left. Set up a meeting for me with him today. Tell him I want to do an interview with him on his campaign. We can play getting the bug out of his office by ear."

John replied, "I'll call Betty, his campaign manager and arrange it. I'll let you know if and when he's interested in talking to you. Remember you work for a conservative newspaper and are not partial to his left-wing policies."

Sarah said, "Just make it clear that I promise to do a fair and impartial story on his re-election campaign and to find out where he stands on a few of the politicized issues."

As John left Sarah, he said, "I'll do that. Have a good day my love. See you later. Oh! We need to meet Brad at one pm to give him his money. Peter said he was sending me a photo of Brad. It's a three-year-old mug shot, but should suffice."

John decided that when he went to the warehouse, he was going to carry out some more carnage. This would be his last chance. But first he had to go back home and get his frog terrarium. He wanted them out of his workshop. On the way home he saw a climate-controlled storage facility and immediately decided to rent a small unit so that he could place his frogs in it. It would give him the time he needed to decide what to do with them later. Right now he had to move quickly on a lot of things.

John called ahead to Katherine and told her he needed to get just a few things, could she give him just ten minutes to get what he wanted. She told him that she was heading out to an attorney's office anyway at that moment and would be gone at least an hour or more.

She said to John, "Please don't hurt me anymore. You've hurt me enough. Just take what is yours and nothing more."

John replied, "I promise you I won't. Everything in the house is yours. I just want some more clothes and my sundries. That's it." He then asked, "Is the lock still the same?"

"Yes, it is. I have changed nothing," Katherine replied.

"Okay thanks. I'll be there in another twenty minutes," John said.

"I'm walking out the door now. You agreed to half of everything plus giving me the house. Are you still in agreement?" Katherine asked.

John replied, "You've got my word on that. I will not change what I said."

John arrived at the house, rushed to the workshop, and carried the terrarium to his car. He wanted that out of the way first. He then went into the house, grabbed some more of his things, opened his safe, and removed paperwork and some jewelry he wanted. He made his foray short. He still had a lot to do. He made sure to call Brad and set up a meet with him, and get his bullshit diploma. He could care less about it now, especially since he didn't need to con Katherine anymore. He needed to pay Brad for the job he did for him, just to keep everything status quo.

As he headed out, he went back to the storage facility, put his frogs in his seven-by-five-foot storage room. He was happy about the temperature that was maintained in it. They kept it at a constant seventy-five degrees. Exactly what his frogs needed. What made it ideal is that there was an electrical outlet in the room. He decided to get a special plant light and timer when he got the chance so that the frogs would not be in the dark all day. In the meantime, he went to the bank and withdrew the cash he needed for Brad and to have carry money on himself. He decided to use as much cash as possible. He wanted to eliminate any paper trails of his whereabouts as he moved from place to place.

He called Brad and confirmed to him he had his money and would meet him in the Publix parking lot on route A1A at one pm as agreed.

John described himself and told Brad what car he would be driving, and that he would be wearing blue jeans with a striped, blue T-shirt and that he'd be waiting for him at the Publix entrance. He then called Sarah, to tell her that he was going to meet Brad, and asked her if she still wanted to go with him. She told him to pick her up at Jeanne's office and that she would fill me in on her conversation with Jeanne.

John knew that he still had to call Betty for Sarah's interview with the Senator, so he called her from his car while heading to Sarah.

When Betty answered, she said, "Betty Ryan speaking."

John said, "Betty. There's a well-known reporter who works for the Wall Street Daily that wants to interview the Senator and ask him about his stance on the hot political topics today and his views regarding his campaign chances etcetera. Her name is Sarah Foster. She'd like to meet him today, later this afternoon if that's possible."

Betty replied, "I'm not sure if the Senator would want to talk to her. She works for a right leaning paper that does not have a love relationship with the Senator." She then asked, "How do you know her?"

John thinking fast, not expecting Betty's query, said, "She's a friend of my wife Katherine. They've known each other since their university days. She called Katherine when she was heading down to Miami, and wanted to get together for old times. I asked her if she would like to interview Senator Roberts. Even though I suggested the meeting, I prefaced it upon his approval first. She said she would love the opportunity. I did ask her if she could be fair and impartial knowing the right leaning political views of her employer. She told me that she promised she would be and was a non-biased reporter. She made it clear that she was a fact-based reporter and not some TV commentator that twisted the truth. She will only be down here a few more days. I'd appreciate it if he could. She'd also like to interview you about how the campaign is going and where he stands in the polls. I told her you were his campaign Manager. She actually knew who you were."

Betty replied, "Hold on for a minute. Let me talk to him."

After a few minutes, Betty came back and said, "He agreed to the interview. He's available today at five pm. Will that work?"

"I'll call her and get back to you," John replied, then asked, "What about you? Will you do an interview also?"

Betty replied, "Yes, after she finishes with Senator Roberts. She'll need to make both interviews as short as possible. John, you know what this place is like right now. There's too much left to do in too short a period of time with the election being only days off."

After he hung up, he issued a sigh of relief and felt he just skirted disaster. He thought, "I'm glad she bought that bullshit. I didn't anticipate her asking me about how I knew Sarah. I should've anticipated that before I called."

John then got on the phone and called Sarah. When she answered he immediately told her about what Betty said and made sure to mention his lie about Katherine knowing her from university days. Sarah replied, "That's okay with me. Five o'clock works. I'm glad you mentioned the Katherine thing. Sarah then laughing said, "Don't worry, Mr. Pinocchio, I'll cover for you."

John laughed in response, "Mr. Pinocchio? Okay. I get the humor."

After John picked up Sarah, they headed to meet Brad. When they approached the Publix parking lot, John let Sarah out. She walked to adjacent shops looking for a vantage point to get a good close up with her telephoto lens without being noticed by Brad. John parked near the Publix entrance and proceeded to wait by it until Brad showed up. John didn't know that Brad was already parked and watching for John to show up from his car. Although Brad was cautious, he had no idea that Sarah was lying in wait to take current photos of him. When Brad spotted John, he left his car and went to him.

Sarah was watching and although she did not know if it was Brad or not walking toward the Publix entrance, she zoomed in on his face and took several clear shots just in case it was him. If it weren't, she'd delete the photos.

Brad walked up to John, and said, "John I presume?"

John said, "If you're Brad I am."

Brad said, "Here's your diploma, copies of your transcript, and final exam. I know you didn't ask for these, but I thought while I'm at it, I'd make them for you. If anybody ever inquired, you went there, your records would support it. I even filled in your attendance record. I put in a few missed classes over the six months so that it would be more in line with someone's memory of you missing classes. The diploma is a copy of someone else's that finished the course when you were supposed to. I just changed names on it."

John said, "Brad, you're terrific. Thanks." John then reached into his pocket and pulled out an envelope with $2,000 dollars in cash in it and said to Brad, "Here's your two grand as agreed. You can count it if you like."

"I believe that it's all there. If not, I'll simply erase all your records at the school," Brad responded with a self-assured smile.

John responded, "I believe it." He then continued and said, "You did a fantastic job on the campaign. Very sophisticated programming. You made Annette's job much easier. I hope the Senator is paying you some hefty bucks. I'm not sure he will win without the 250,000 ballots. The poll that was taken just two days ago showed Collette one point up on him."

Brad said, "Believe me I'm satisfied. John, look I don't want to seem rude, but I just came to swap what you wanted for my money. I'm not looking to make friends and the less I know about you and vice versa, the better off we are. If you need me to do anything else. Call me."

"Hey, you're right. It's best for the both of us and thanks you saved my ass with my wife," John replied.

All the time they were talking, Sarah snapped away and even nonchalantly walked past them while they were talking, and then went into the Publix supermarket. Brad who was facing in her direction looked her over, only because she's a stunning looking woman. When John saw Brad looking behind him, he turned for a moment and saw Sarah walking past, not looking at them.

Brad, looked back at John, and said, "Sorry for that, but I couldn't help but look at that woman. Beautiful face and figure."

John simply replied, "She was fine for sure."

Brad said, as he started to turn away from John, "Nice meeting you. Say hello to Annette for me. My job is finished and I'm taking off."

John hearing that, said, "Going on a vacation?"

Brad replied, "You can say that."

John then quickly asked, "Where are you going?"

As Brad was walking backward and away from John replied, "Not sure."

John then started walking toward his car just in case Brad watched to see if he would leave. As he was walking, he called Sarah and told her to walk along the stores and wait for him at the AT&T store. John smartly watched Brad get into his car and drive off as he had gotten into his and also started to drive, making sure Brad turned into traffic and left. He then turned and headed to Sarah.

Once she got into the car, she said, "I got several close shots of his face," and then asked," How did it go?"

John replied, "It went great. It was short and sweet. He seemed content that we did legitimate business. He got me a whole bunch of stuff from school. Here take a look."

As Sarah opened the envelope and was glancing over the papers, John said, "Sarah, my love, you are a ballsy lady. Brad looked at you walking by and commented how beautiful you were. I told him, 'She's okay. I've seen better.'"

Sarah, looked at John, and said, "I know you didn't say that."

John laughed, and said, "No my beautiful lady. I'm playing with you. All kidding aside, we have to move quickly to nail Brad. He hinted he was leaving on a trip someplace. I tried to get him to say where, but he wouldn't. It sounded like it was going to be soon. I probed him a little about the money he received from the Senator. He didn't give me an amount, but he seemed quite satisfied. I'm sure from the way it sounded he has enough to run."

Sarah replied, and said, "Let me call Jeanne and let her know what's going on. Things are moving really fast. I'm not sure what the next move is. It will be up to her and the State Attorney General."

Sarah began speaking to Jeanne and related what happened and told her that from what Brad told John, he was going to take off on a trip somewhere and would need to be grabbed before he took off without Annette, Betty and the Senator finding out. That grabbing of his computers was critical.

Jeanne then told Sarah that she was already in conversation with the State Attorney General about what was currently happening, and that he was assigning a Special Task Force to start an immediate investigation.

She said she was expecting someone to show up at her office to look over the evidence. She asked Sarah to be there and to add whatever she knew about Brad and the urgency to strike while the iron was hot.

She also told Sarah that the Attorney General was concerned about the admissibility of the recordings in court, and getting Search Warrants from a judge, being that the party obtaining them did so illegally, regardless if they remained anonymous. Jeanne told Sarah that if the alleged recordings gave the AG sufficient probable cause that a crime was in the process of being committed would seek them, regardless of how the evidence was obtained. He said that the severity of the crime, and its national implications, would leave the judge with no other recourse but to grant one. He opined that, if he were the judge, he would grant the warrants, because he would not want to be held accountable for allowing a crime of that magnitude to be committed when there was ample evidence of probable cause.

Jeanne also told Sarah that under any circumstances, that the AG would do whatever was necessary to stop the illegal ballot dump and to catch the perpetrators in the act. She said that the Governor was outraged at what she told him and would stop at nothing to have all parties involved arrested.

Sarah, then related her conversation with Jeanne to John and that she was going to Jeanne's office to meet with the investigator's.

After hearing what Sarah told him, John replied, "That's terrific. So far everything is a go. I'll drop you off there, then I'll head over to the warehouse, and get any last-minute update that I can from Annette. I'll call you later. It looks like we'll be having a late dinner."

John dropped Sarah off at Jeanne's office while he headed to the warehouse. His heart was pounding at his excitement. He thought, "Now for the coup de gras. I'm going to knock off a few of those little Communist fucks. Yep. I sure am. God! I need to see them drop like fly's clutching their chests in agony. Ooh what a lovely sight that'll be."

John, out of nowhere, became Mr. Hyde. He lost all sense of reality again. He didn't need to kill Lizzie and her cohorts, or Jim. He was even going to risk losing Sarah and for what? For some sick pleasure. They would all be going to jail. He started to sing his little melody, "Zip-a-dee doo dah, zip-a-dee yay, my oh my what a wonderful day, oh you little commie fucks, my deadly toxin is coming your way, Zip-a-dee doo dah zip-a-dee yay."

When John arrived at the warehouse, he saw a delivery van sitting outside. He could see ballots being loaded. As he walked passed the van, he recognized the driver as someone he met earlier when he was helping load them. John, smiled, acted jovial and asked, "Gary, how's it going?"

Gary replied, "Good so far. I believe I have one more run after this and we're done."

John asked, "Where's this dump going?"

"I'm going to drop them off in Congressional Districts, six, seven, ten and eleven.

They're all up in North Florida. It'll take me two days. Someone else will be doing the rest of the State tomorrow. One through five are left. Then we're done. That'll be the longest run. We'll make it with three days to spare," Gary responded.

John said, "That's great news. We need to keep that NSP seat in the Senate. I love it when Tripp squirms. Roberts knows how to turn his screws."

Gary replied, "Fuck Tripp and the horse he road in on."

John looked at Gary, as he kept walking toward the open warehouse door with an evil look. He thought to himself, "You can keep repeating that bullshit from jail."

As John entered the warehouse, he thought about what he was about to do, and decided to hold off until he knew exactly when they would be folding up the operation. Based upon what Gary said, they wouldn't be finished until tomorrow. If he killed them all now, Gary would be a witness to him being there, and knowing everyone was alive when he arrived.

John looked across the floor and saw Annette looking at him. He smiled and waved at her. She just stood there looking at him as he came closer to her. When he reached her, he asked, "How's it going? Is everything done?"

Annette replied, "We're finishing the last ballots now. They'll be boxed and leaving here tonight."

John replied, "Gary told me he's running North today to do his thing and that the remainder of the Congressional districts will be done by tomorrow. It looks like you did what you said you'd do; finish with about three days to spare. Congratulations. That's cause for celebration."

Annette replied, "I'm glad it's done and over. I'm worn out. The Senator owes me big time, for this. We'll be having drinks tomorrow night at the campaign office. I assume you'll be there. You have been part of this."

John said, "Now that you tell me, I will, but my part here has been little. All I've done is load some boxes and sign ballots, although I got writer's cramp. I signed thousands that day."

Annette replied, "That's true, but your contributions at the campaign office are equally important. Pulling in a few million dollars for the Senator is no easy task. He's incredibly grateful to you, believe me. You could have a great political future being on his staff."

"I can't make up my mind about it. He offered already but I've never given him a definitive answer. I'm not sure if I want that kind of life. Who knows. I might change my mind later. I'll see how things play out," John responded.

Annette said, "Betty told me that you set up an interview with Senator Roberts and her with some big shot reporter with the Wall Street Dailey."

"Yes. I did. She'll be there at five o'clock this afternoon. I promised to be there for the introduction. I assume Betty told you everything. She's Katherine's sorority sister from college days, or she knew her from that time. I've never discussed her with Katherine. They've only spoken a few times over the years. I only met her once several years ago. I thought that while she was here in Florida it might be good publicity for the Senator. If he doesn't like the interview, he can always cut it short. I figured nothing ventured nothing gained."

"It was nice of you to think of the Senator and Betty," Annette replied.

John said, "It was no big deal really," then laughing said, "Just getting in a few brownie points. So when will you be cleaning up here? I'll give you a hand."

Annette replied, "Early, around 10 a.m. The place will be swept clean. There will be no trace of us here after that."

John asked, "Will Lizzie and her helpers be here?"

"Just Lizzie, Jim, and I and now you." Annette replied.

John responded, "Sounds good. I just stopped in to say hello. We haven't spoken for the past few days; I was thinking about you."

"I thought about you too John. Thanks for stopping by. We can have a drink after we finish here. Brad told me you paid him for the college papers. So I guess after this you won't have to lie to Katherine anymore."

John smiled, and said, "Yeah. Thank God for that."

Annette had no idea about John and Katherine and what had happened to their marriage and John was not going to tell her either. Especially because he moved on to Sarah. It was none of her business and he now had the time and place to knock her off along with Jim and Lizzy.

John then said, "I'll see you in the morning. When we finish, we can have lunch. Excuse me for a minute, I need to use the men's room before I head out."

John did not need to relieve himself. He wanted to undo the frosted window in there. He needed to be able to get into the warehouse without coming through the front door on his next trip to avoid the security camera out front. John had sized up the window previously and was sure he could climb through. Once he lifted the window just enough to unlatch its two lower catches, he left. He felt certain no one would notice it. He only needed to lift it a quarter of an inch.

As John walked away from the men's room he walked back to Annette, squeezed her hand gently, and gave her a goodbye kiss on her cheek and said, I need to head over to the campaign office. I'll see you in the morning.

Annette just stood for a moment and watched John walk away. She couldn't help herself. She still loved the man, There was something so charismatic about him, that she couldn't let go.

Annette had been sucked in, by one evil devious crazy man, with a hidden personality and sick agenda. Unfortunately, she was unknowingly playing a leading role that would not get her an Oscar.

As soon as John got in his car, he called Sarah. When Sarah answered John said, "I'm finished here and am on my way to you. Annette said they are wrapping up early in the morning. That's when they're planning their exit. She asked me to help her hide all traces of what they were doing. I told her I would just in case there were any last-minute things we should know about. It shouldn't take more than an hour. After that, the operation to steal the election will come to an end, other than dumping all the ballots across the State on election day. How's it going with Jeanne?"

Sarah said, "Everything is moving. We met with Tom Talbert, a Detective with the States Special Crimes Task Force. The Attorney General assigned him to move on the operation. He said what we showed him, and what he heard on your recordings, was more than sufficient evidence to justify Search Warrants. Jeanne's attorney Michael Johnson was the one who presented everything and made it clear that his source was protected under Attorney Client Privilege. I also presented him with my investigative work on Brad. I gave him the close-up photos and told him that he had a record of computer hacking. I also gave him my video's on the ballot deliveries and the addresses, as well as the license plate numbers on the vans. He said they would be getting the Search Warrants tomorrow. According to him they would be raiding the warehouse by early afternoon, and the drop off addresses that I gave them as well as the Senator's homes and offices here in Florida and a Federal Warrant for his D.C office."

John replied, "That's fantastic news. This is going to be huge. A major political blow to the National Socialist Party. and you'll have the cover story. Baby, Pulitzer Prize for you. God, I can't wait to see Roberts on TV with his hands cuffed behind his back along with Betty, being led away. What a coup this is going to be for President Tripp. He can play this to the hilt. This will destroy the Socialists efforts for expanded mail in ballots and ballot boxes and ensure passage of voter identification. They won't be able to scream racism on this shit."

John became so elated he began to sing, "I'm so excited, I just can't hide it, I'm about to lose control, and I think I like it, and I know, I know, I know, I want you."

Sarah laughed and said, "I want you too. You're so funny. All of what is happening is because of you, not me."

John replied, "You and me forever."

Sarah said, "Hurry over here. John we'll need to be at the Senator's office by Five o'clock,"

"I'm leaving now. Don't worry we'll make it," John replied.

After John picked up Sarah, they rushed straight over to Senator Roberts office to conduct the interviews and to hopefully get the bugs he planted removed from both offices.

When John took Sarah into the Campaign Headquarters, he told her where the bugs were planted, in the event that she was able to remove one. They had no plan specifically. They would play it by ear. John saw Betty coming out of her office toward them. As she came up to them John introduced Sarah to Betty.

"Betty, this is Sarah Foster, with the Wall Street Dailey," John said.

"Sarah, it's nice to meet you. Your notoriety precedes you. I've read a lot of your columns," Betty said.

Sarah said, "It's nice meeting you. I've heard about you as well. You're quite the Campaign Advisor. I was impressed with how you took Senator Roberts over the top in his last election with that pulverizing ad blitz you ran. They totally excoriated his APP opponent, Barbara Reynolds."

Betty replied, "She ran a hard-fought campaign herself. But she had a lot of baggage. We had a lot to pick apart. Please, let me bring you to meet the Senator."

As they walked into the Senator's office, Betty introduced Sarah to Senator Roberts, who in turn graciously greeted Sarah. He then said, "Ms. Foster, please, sit. John, please join us." Sarah replied, "Please call me Sarah."

Senator Roberts said, "I will. It's much more cordial with first names. Call me Aaron."

Betty said, "Senator, I'll leave you to the interview. I need to make several calls. Sarah, when you're finished with the Senator, I'll be in my office. John will bring you over."

That moment gave John relief, because he didn't think he'd be able to retrieve the bug with her in the Senator's office.

When John sat down in front of the Senator's desk, he made sure to sit on the side where he had planted the bug. He just needed to wait for that one moment he could reach under to where he placed it and quickly pull it off. It was held there by a stick-on base. His heart was beating a little bit as he anticipated that one opportune moment. Sarah, while conducting her interview, was seeking that opportunity.

Sarah began asking the Senator a little about his background, and as he related his life story, Sarah being very astute said, "Aaron, do you mind if I look at the photo gallery you have displayed on the wall behind your desk?"

Senator Roberts said, "No not at all. Let me go through some of them for you. Some of them reflect priceless moments for me."

John immediately noticed what Sarah was doing and readied himself.

The Senator got up from his chair, and turned toward the photo display. Sarah got up from her seat and walked toward him until they were both facing the back wall. John, saw his opportunity, slid off his chair onto one knee and ran his fingers quickly under the bottom rim of the desk. As soon as he felt the listening device, he pulled it off and put it into his pants pocket.

He quickly sat back into his chair, fully relieved that he had it back. Now he'd have to get the other one from Betty's office. He smiled and said to himself, "God, I love that woman. That was a smooth move using that photo display."

Sarah looked back at John for an okay signal. He nodded with a grinning approval. She then said, as she turned back toward her seat, "Senator you've led a colorful life here in politics. I'm quite impressed. But let's get past the bio part of my interview and get into the hard knocks politics of your campaign. Jeanne Collette, your opponent, is in a dead heat with you with some polls showing her with a slight one or two-point lead. Why do you think that is?"

Aaron replied, "There's a two-to-three-point margin of error in the polls and my own internal polls show we are actually ahead by two. Jeanne has had a strong campaign, but remember no APP candidate has won in the district for several decades. I'm quite confident that there are sufficient votes that will swing my way when the election starts. I'm not concerned."

"Senator, I appreciate your typical politicians response, but you have danced around my question. Why do you think Collette is showing a lead in all the major polls? She is a pro-gun; second amendment advocate and stands for strong borders. You aren't on either issue. You also said, on National Television when asked about the rising crime rate that you supported defunding the police and that the rise in crime had to do with too many guns in the hands of the people." "Would you clarify those issues? It seems contradictory to me. If there are too many guns in the hands of the people, why would you want to reduce police protection for the citizens?"

Aaron replied, "You take the guns away from the people and gun violence goes down."

Sarah responded and queried, "Senator, you strongly believe what you just said? Do you think that criminals will still not be able to get guns, illegally? Wouldn't disarming citizens increase crime?"

"We are not disarming them now, and crime, in your own words is on the rise." Aaron replied.

"Wouldn't you attribute the rise in national crime to laws like the 'No Bail Law' in New York City, or laws in California, that consider any theft of $900.00 or less a misdemeanor, without arrest. They are emptying the store shelves out there. That "No Bail Law" let a serial bank robber out, after being caught robbing his seventh bank, to immediately go rob his eighth. In California, it was reported that they let an illegal alien off after being accused of rape, to go and rape and murder a teenage girl three days later. Do you agree with those laws in light of what has happened?" Sarah asked.

Aaron replied, "There are many laws that have been written that need to be changed because very few of them are perfect. That's why we write amendments to them. I don't agree with the California Law, and I don't agree with the very liberal "No Bail Law" in New York. You know that I'm a moderate. Those are very liberal State laws and the last I heard we live in a Republic. My position as Senator in Washington does not allow me to change State laws. I can only join in the approving of new Federal laws."

Sarah asked, "What about immigration Senator? We are being flooded with illegal aliens and they are now being released right here in Florida and are being put up in hotels, with free medical and many other social benefits at the cost of the taxpayers while we see hundreds of thousands of homeless veterans living on the streets across the country. Wouldn't these brave men and women deserve our help first?"

Just before the Senator had a chance to respond, Betty paged his phone and told him that there was an important matter happening in Washington and he needed to take the call. It was the Speaker of the House calling. The Senator said to Sarah, "I'm sorry for this, but I will need to cut this interview short. I'm sure you understand, Please go and interview Betty. We can do this again at another time."

Sarah got up, reached across his desk, shook the Senator's hand, and said, "Nice meeting you Senator."

Both John and Sarah got up and left his office, and headed to Betty's office. Sarah asked John, "I assume you were able to get the bug?"

John said, "That was really smooth, Sarah my love. I got it. Now I need to get the other one out of Betty's office. Sarah, I swear, I almost told the Senator that he's full of shit. Those answers were completely ridiculous. What makes it a joke, is he believes his own crap."

Sarah said, "That's typical of all politicians, but his responses were idiotic. He just wasn't prepared for the questions, like Hillary was with Bernie."

John and Sarah walked into Betty's office. John asked Betty, "Can you sit with Sarah for the interview, now, being the one with Senator Roberts was cut short?"

"Yes, come in, I'm glad we can do this a little earlier. I need to meet some people afterwards," Betty replied.

Sarah said, "I promise to keep it short."

John, just like in the Senator's office sat in the chair right where he had planted the listening device. Sarah laid her recorder on the desk and said, "Betty, I would like you to tell me about the Senator's chances of winning the election with the polls showing his opponent ahead. We have only days left."

As Betty began explaining what she thought, John was trying to figure out how to get the listening device. It was not going to be easy. He needed only a few seconds to get it, but getting down on one knee to reach under the desk would be impossible the way things were.

Betty and Sarah were having a really friendly dialogue; nothing like the one Sarah was starting to have with the Senator. John in desperation said, "Would anyone like some coffee. I can get us a cup."

Sarah replied, "Yes, I would. Light with two sugars."

Betty said, "I guess I'll join you. Make mine like Sarah's."

With Betty's response John left to go to the Break Room. He poured the coffees in the paper cups they had and added the milk and sugar, but smartly grabbed a few extra packs of sugar, napkins, and stirrers, placed them in his pocket, then headed back into Betty's office clutching all three coffees. When he went in, Sarah reached up and took a coffee from John. John then put Betty's down on the desk in front of her and his next to where he was sitting. He handed napkins to both women, and then proceeded to reach into his pocket to pull out several more bags of sugar, but purposefully let some slip out of the palm of his hand onto the floor, and conveniently where he needed them to land. He smiled, and said," Oops!" He pulled his chair out a little bit and immediately knelt down to retrieve them and the audio device he planted. Sarah just kept talking to Betty to keep her eyes off John for those few moments. After quickly completing his task, he sat down and said, with a smile, "Thank God, I dropped only the sugar packets, and not a cup of coffee."

Sarah just smiled, and then continued to interview Betty. They sat in her office for about a half hour, when Sarah said, "Thank you so much Betty. I think I have enough to run a column."

Just before leaving Sarah asked one last question. "Betty what do you think the final margin of victory will be?"

Betty replied, "We believe he will win by at least 100,000 votes. We are quite confident, on the mail in ballots. They usually favor us Socialists."

With that John and Sarah said their goodbyes and left the Campaign Office. All the time they were there they acted just like acquaintances, and nothing more. Once they were on the elevator leaving the building, John said, "We make a wonderful team."

Sarah said, "Yes we do at that."

John replied, "Now and for life. I'm crazy about you."

Sarah said, "I'm crazy about you too."

CHAPTER TWENTY

THE DEATH TOLL RISES

It was the morning that John was going to go to the warehouse and help Annette clean out the place and remove any evidence of a printing operation. Especially the computerized high-speed printer. It was also the morning that John would start his carnage again. When he left the hotel, he gave Sarah a kiss goodbye and told her where he was going. Sarah was going back to Jeanne Collette's office. She was going to be in on the investigation that John started and wanted to start preparing for her headlining story that she would release at the right moment. She needed to record all the events as they happened.

John, before going to the warehouse, stopped, and picked up some latex gloves. He didn't want to leave any fingerprints climbing in and out of the unlocked window. All he knew is that he wanted them to die before they moved the printer so the police forensics unit could extract the information from its hard drive and use it as evidence of the attempted election steal. He knew that it would have national implications and make the need for voter identification no longer a point of contention. It would allow President Tripp to push through his signature "Fair Voter Act," which the Socialists were fighting hard to stall. They felt if they allowed it to pass, they would no longer have the same wide-open opportunity to cheat on elections in the future.

He had pre-planned his entrance and exit into and from the warehouse to avoid the front entrance surveillance camera.

John parked his car two blocks away along a residential tree lined street and walked to the alley way between back-to-back warehouse buildings until he got to the bathroom window.

He stood in front of the window and listened carefully to be sure no one was inside as he opened it. After feeling sure the room was empty, he slowly pushed the window all the way up. and then climbed through it. He carefully lowered himself face down onto the floor. Once he was in, he shut the window. He removed his latex gloves temporarily, then applied the liquid bandage onto his fingertips. He waited a few minutes until he felt that it had dried sufficiently enough for him to wipe his fingertips into his small toxin filled pill box.

Once he was ready to assassinate Annette, Lizzie, and Jim, he opened the bathroom door slowly and looked inside to see where everyone was. He did not see anyone at first, until he noticed all three of them were in the coffee break area, and not looking his way. He couldn't believe his luck. He immediately took advantage of it, and moved quickly toward the entrance door, constantly looking to see if they would spot him. Once he got slightly past them, he turned and started walking toward them as if he had come through the front. As he got closer to them, he said, "Hey, don't drink all of that coffee." They turned and saw him. Annette said, "I didn't even know you came in."

John laughing replied, "That's because I have superpowers. I can become invisible."

Lizzie laughed and replied, "Prove it."

As John got close enough to her, he said, "Okay, close your eyes and count to three, then open your eyes."

Lizzie, being a little gullible, did as he asked. John, tip toed quickly behind her holding back a laugh."

Jim and Annette started laughing as Lizzie looked to the left and right then quickly turned around to see if John were behind her. John quickly moved in the opposite direction each time staying out of Lizzie's sight. As she turned completely around to face John, he said, "Lizzie you're too funny. You actually went along with my insanity."

Lizzie laughed and replied, "John, I knew what you were going to do. You're an idiot."

John had deftly changed their bewilderment from not seeing him come into the warehouse to one of laughter and quickly to a past thought. He was now ready to make his move. He needed to get the toxin onto them, and all within seconds of each other. He needed them to all collapse within a minute or two of each other. He knew the effects of the toxin varied slightly from person to person. His first target was Jim. He stepped toward Jim and stuck out his hand in a shaking gesture, and said, "Jim, I just wanted to say, it's been nice knowing you."

Jim reached out and shook John's toxin laden finger tipped hand. John gripped it tight and made sure to press and pull his fingertips along Jim's skin as he pulled his hand away. He did the same with Lizzie, after he said to her. "It's been truly nice knowing you also Lizzie."

It took less than a minute to put a heavy coat of the legal toxin onto them. Now it was Annette's turn. He turned toward her and took her left hand into his left and said "I truly have enjoyed getting to spend part of my life knowing you. It's a memory I will not forget so easily."

Annette looked at John, and replied, "It has been a time worth remembering. I've enjoyed it." She smiled, then kissed him on his cheek and when doing so took his other toxin coated hand into hers, getting the deadly poison onto both of her hands. She had just double dosed herself.

All the while John was holding Annette's hands, he moved his fingertips continuously over them as if massaging them gently, letting Annette think he was being affectionate. While John was murdering her, he had absolutely no remorse. Annette had already become an afterthought.

John knew from his previous murders that the toxin took about five to six minutes to work.

He needed to try and kill that time with them. He needed to be sure that none of them walked outside the warehouse while the toxin was taking affect. He wanted to watch them all collapse in agony and savor their demise. He said, "Well folks, what can I help you do to clean up in here?"

Jim said, "You can help me get the printer onto the van out front."

John replied, "Okay let's do it."

As John and Jim were walking toward the printer, he heard Annette yell out, "John, Jim, somethings wrong with Lizzie." They both turned to see Lizzie writhing on the floor clutching at her chest. They ran toward her to see what they could do. John of course was just going through the motions. He thought, "Shit Lizzie bought it quick. Probably because she was a skinny petite woman." As Jim was bending down to help Lizzie, Annette collapsed right in front of John and landed near Lizzie. John just stood there and watched her die. He didn't move a step to do anything. He thought, "Good riddance." Jim who still didn't show any signs of being poisoned looked across Lizzie's body at Annette, then up at John and said, "What the fuck is happening? I think Lizzie's dead."

John replied, "I have no idea what the hell is going on."

Jim then moved over Lizzie's body to get to Annette. John could see her eyes wide open and staring at him, as she died in front of him. Jim yelled to John, "Help me give her artificial resuscitation. Pump her chest."

John looked down at Jim as he was breathing into Annette's mouth thinking that shit is not going to help. It was at that moment that Jim raised up on his knees clutching at his chest making a loud moaning sound. Jim's eyes looked at John, as if saying what did you do? John just smiled as Jim fell over Annette's body. After a moment of standing there gloating at his work and seeing all three bodies lying together, John said aloud, "What a pile of shit." He then knelt down and felt for pulses. After being satisfied that they were all dead he rushed to wash his hands thoroughly of the toxin, then put his latex gloves back on before locking the front door from the interior. As John was walking back past the bodies, he realized that he was leaving out an important detail. The method of suicide. He stood for a moment thinking about what to do and said aloud, "Why didn't I think of it before.? Damn it!" After pondering a few minutes, he realized the idea of filling a paper coffee cup with laced water using the frog toxin. It was the same method that he used on Senator Pelovski. After quickly preparing the toxified water, he went to the bodies, lifted their heads, and poured a small amount down each one of their throats making sure not to get any onto their clothes. He then closed each one of their hands around the cup being sure to get their fingerprints on it. He smartly remembered to use Lizzie's left-hand, remembering she was a southpaw. A mistake using her wrong hand could screw everything up. He deftly made it to look like they all drank from the same cup. John stood up, looked down at the bodies, and said, "Perfect," before carefully laying the cup near Jim's outstretched hand, noting he was the last one to die.

John then got a cleaning rag and began wiping every area he could ever remember touching previously. All he could think of besides lifting boxes and loading them was using the bathroom and being at the break area table containing the coffee maker. After satisfying himself that he wiped off any print evidence, he went to the storage room and found the front surveillance camera recorder. He played the tape that was in it, and could not find any evidence of himself on it. He searched through the room, and found a small box containing older recordings. He didn't want to waste time looking at them, so he decided to take them with him.

He then went to the bathroom window and climbed out after dropping the tapes to the ground. Just before walking away he looked at the ground and made sure that he left no footprint evidence. He then closed the window hard, being sure the latches clicked tight. He tried lifting the window and was satisfied it was locked. He knew that once the police entered by breaking down the front door, they would soon theorize that they committed suicide and would not look for an assailant.

John made his way down the alley way to his car. When he got to the end of the buildings, he looked in all directions to see if there was anyone that would see him emerge from between the buildings. Being satisfied he would not be noticed, went to his car, made a U-turn, and meandered back through the same residential area he came through before coming out onto a main avenue. He simply merged into traffic and then headed back toward the warehouse.

John knew that he might be required to account for his whereabouts after he left Sarah. So he did what he considered the perfect alibi. He drove back to the warehouse, parked in front knowing the surveillance camera would record him. He walked up to the entrance door, and rang the entrance bell, obviously knowing no one would answer. He repeated those actions a few times over several minutes. He then used his phone to call Annette knowing she would not answer. He was just making his alibi stronger. It was all a planned act to show his innocence. He realized that when they caught Brad, that he'd mention John as part of the election steal, but he knew that he had a perfect reason, which would be more than amply supported by Jeanne Collette, Sarah, Michael Johnson and Peter Miller, the security guy. How could they even consider him. He was trying to get them all arrested, and risked a lot getting the evidence, he had no motive to murder them. He knew he could account for the time when he left Sarah. It was making the trip to the warehouse which would be corroborated by the surveillance camera and the time record on the tape. Sarah could confirm the time he left her. It took him less than fifteen minutes to murder all three people, and wipe the place down. He felt certain that that amount of time would not be questioned in how long it actually took him to drive between the hotel where he and Sarah were staying and the warehouse. It would be impossible to prove. Not everyone drives at the same speed, traffic varies, and routes may differ. Fifteen minutes more or less shouldn't be questioned.

John even made sure to call Sarah from outside the warehouse. When she answered her phone, John said, "Sarah! Something seems crazy. I came to the warehouse to help clean the place out, but when I got here, I found the front door locked, but all three of their cars are parked out front. I rang the front bell, knocked, and even yelled, but still no one answered. I've been waiting here for a while. I'm coming back. Screw them. Annette knew I was coming to help. If they had to go somewhere she should have left a note on the front door or called me. Are you still at Jeanne's office?"

Sarah replied, "Yes. I'm sure that Annette must have some explanation. Don't worry, we have enough to get them arrested. I'll see you here."

John played it to the hilt. Sarah had no idea about John's maniacal plot, and he had no plan to let her know. What had become apparent is that life meant nothing to him. He was relishing what he was doing. He didn't trust the Socialist run courts, and partisan judges. All he knew was that every scheming one got away with crime after crime. None of them were ever held accountable. John had one more assassination to do, and that was the Senator. He was the reason his murderous journey began, and he was going to finish the job, one way or another.

John arrived at Jeanne Collette's office and as soon as he saw Sarah, Jeanne and her Campaign Advisor Jeremy Long, he said, "How's everything going?"

Jeanne responded, "It's moving along quickly. The search warrants will be issued today for all the locations we can identify. They'll be served sometime tomorrow on election eve. I discussed the matter again with Governor Santos and Barbara Whitman, the Attorney General, and they agreed. The only warrants executed today will be against Bradley Newman. We all feel that his computer and anything else he has will be important pieces of evidence in securing convictions. Barbara Whitman stressed concern about the evidence we gave her. She's questioning its permissibility because she does not know how it was originally obtained by you, Sarah's anonymous source. But once they secure the phony ballots, and Brad's computer, and make arrests, they should be able to put them all in jail. They secured wiretap orders and have placed wire taps on the Senator's and Betty's phones and Annette's. They placed them sometime this morning."

John replied, "I hope so. They cannot get away with what they're doing. When will they raid the warehouse? I went there today in the guise of helping them clear out, but when I got there, the door was locked even though their cars were parked outside. I rang the bell, knocked, and yelled loudly but I got no response. I stayed for a while assuming that they walked somewhere together, but they never showed up and Annette didn't answer her cell phone when I called. Now we'll have no idea where they'll hide their computerized printer."

Michael responded, "I wouldn't worry about that. The Fed's will get one of them to talk."

John said, "I suppose you're right. I can't wait to see them all in handcuffs. Especially Senator Roberts and Betty. What a sleazy pair."

Sarah said, "I'll be releasing the story sometime tomorrow, after I get word that all the warrants were executed. It will be a major headline and will be all over television minutes after, I can assure you."

John thought about what Jeanne said about Annette's phone being tapped and smiled to himself. He hoped they were able to pick up the communications he left on her phone. His first message said he was outside the warehouse waiting and to give him a call back. His second call said he was leaving and that he was disappointed that she left him standing there. If the Feds were able to record his messages, it would solidify his already solid alibi should he ever need one. John believed that he had sufficiently eliminated himself as a suspect. He knew one thing; they'd have extreme difficulty identifying the toxin that caused their deaths. As far as he knew, nothing had ever come out about a toxin causing the death of Congresswoman Waterman, or the permanent paralysis of Senator Pelovski.

John listened intently to the conversation that was going on in Jeanne's office and while doing so was playing out the assassination of his main target in his mind. He was not sure if he would be able to ever get to do it after his planning and murders. He did not know if the Senator would be served with the Search Warrant and be arrested with Betty the next day on election eve or early on election day or even be served until after the election. He knew Sarah had to time her breaking story so that she would affect the outcome. Defeating Senator Roberts was absolutely imperative. She could just report that they stopped the steal by securing the ballots before they were inserted into the count and that an investigation was underway to determine if the Senator had any part in it. Any doubt of his innocence should sway the voters away from someone that might not serve in office. He actually fretted over his dilemma until he thought, "What am I worrying about? Fuck it. It makes no difference. He's a dead man walking. I've got to kill that mother fucker. He just might squirm out of it. He's the type that has a lot of shit on a lot of powerful people in D.C."

He became insane for a moment. His lips were moving but not vocalizing his thoughts. He worried after what Jeanne told him, that the evidence he had amassed might not be admissible. Senator Roberts and Betty might just get away by denying any involvement and claiming complete ignorance of what Annette, Jim, and Lizzie had done. He thought that Betty and Aaron would say that their staff took it upon their fanatical selves, and with them all being dead would not be able to refute the Senator's and Betty's claims. Even the envelope with Betty's fingerprints on it in Brad's trash, tying them together, might ever be allowed as irrefutable evidence.

He had to discuss it with Sarah and see what she thought. He wanted her to publish her story, but he wanted the Senator around on election eve so that he could attend his planned Campaign Office party for his staff. That would give him the opportunity he needed. He just wanted that one glorious moment to plant his deadly handshake on the Senator and the night before the election was run. It would be mission accomplished and provide a reason for the Senator's demise. Everyone would think that the stress of the breaking story gave him the usual heart attack. After that he would just enjoy his life with Sarah. Even with how much he claimed to love Sarah he was still willing to murder the Senator. The problem was John was feeling untouchable. He had successfully murdered five people and immobilized another permanently, with every likelihood of getting away with it. He actually couldn't help himself. He enjoyed doing it. He was so insane that he had mental orgasms whenever he murdered one of his politically motivated targets and deep down, he would be equally as excited about his next victim. It was apparent that he could easily slip in and out of his dual personality. He was a charming, intelligent, and romantic man one minute, and seamlessly became a sly cunning murderer the next.

After staying fairly late at Jeanne's office, John and Sarah left to have dinner at the hotel where they would wait for any further updates on what was progressing from Candidate Collette. Sarah steadily continued to write her groundbreaking story, covering everything that had transpired. She was brilliant at her job. She conferred with John on the facts, and he enjoyed her including him in on her expose. John was excited, as he sat back on a comfortable chair and watched Sarah. He looked at her with self-satisfaction. He knew that he had now found the woman that completed his life. He did not stop to think that his feelings were the same when he first met Katherine. He no longer cared about then, he only cared about now. In Sarah he saw an extremely attractive woman with ambition. His last memories of Katherine was of a chain-smoking woman with no ambition, that spent the day watching ridiculous reality TV shows.

The one admirable thing that John voluntarily did was make sure that she would not need for anything. He gave her fifty percent of all of his disclosed assets and home, and that was in the millions. He felt comfortable that she could sit in front of the TV for the rest of her idle life and smoke herself to death.

It was 10.30 pm when Jeanne Collette called. Sarah answered the phone and replied to Jeanne, "No it's not too late. I was working on my expose. John's been conferring with me." After a moment, Sarah, listening to Jeanne said, "Hold on a minute, let me tell John. John, Jeanne told me they arrested Bradley, and have his computer and files."

John immediately responded and said, "Fantastic."

Sarah, then told Jeanne, "We're both excited. What's the next step?"

Jeanne replied, "They'll be raiding the warehouse in a little while. I've been told that they are now watching the place and that, strangely enough, their three cars are still parked out front."

Sarah said, "Hold on a minute, let me tell John. John, Jeanne said that they'll be raiding the warehouse tonight and that Annette's, Lizzie's and Jim's cars are still out front."

John responded, "It's possible they left and came back. But it seems strange that they would be there so late after finishing the ballot run. I hope they nail them in the act."

Sarah then started to talk to Jeanne again. "Please let me know the minute they arrest Annette, Lizzie, and Jim. I want my story to be in the morning's addition. We need to have it shown as breaking news on all the networks, especially the local channels. The voters need to know what's going on. We have one more day, until the ballots begin to drop."

Jeanne responded, and said, "I'll let you know as soon as it happens. The Governor made it clear to his investigators that I was to be kept abreast as it happened."

Sarah ended the call with, "We'll be here waiting for your call."

After Sarah hung up, John went and kissed her and said, "Pulitzer Price baby, Pulitzer Prize. Your story will change the political climate, and swing more favoritism to David Tripp. The Socialists will be running and hiding. Now there's concrete proof of elections being stolen, and you'll be coming out with a breaking story that will expose all of their lies."

John and Sarah sat back and enjoyed the unfolding events and patiently waited for Jeanne's next call. Sarah gave John her laptop and said, "Read what I've written. Tell me what you think."

John read every word carefully and when he finished, he said, "This is excellent. You have an incredible way with words. I love it. Wow! It's powerful." Another hour passed, and still no word from Jeanne. John knew that when they broke into the warehouse, which he fully expected, they would find the bodies all piled on the floor and there would be crime scene tape and forensics called onto the site. It would not be just an in and out police raid. A lot would transpire before the call came to Jeanne and she called Sarah. John was more anxious to learn what forensics would conclude after examining the scene. He expected suicide to be their decision the way he laid out the scene. It went well past twelve o'clock and still no word. John and Sarah decided to call it a night and get some sleep, but not before they made love.

Sarah's cell phone rang at two am. It was Jeanne calling. Sarah said, "Hello, Jeanne?" Jeanne replied, "Yes. Sorry for calling so late, but I knew you would want to know that they entered the warehouse and found Annette, Lizzie, and Jim dead at the scene from apparent suicides. The coroner said that they've been dead for a few days. That's why John could not get in when he went there. Special Investigator Marc Scarponi from the States Special Crimes Unit called me and told me that they confiscated the printer, and that it will be brought to the local police impound as evidence until they could move it to another location where their computer forensics experts would go into its hard drive. He also said that they looked at the surveillance tapes and saw John trying to get in without response, and waiting out front for a while before he left. The tape did not show anyone else come to the entrance from the estimated time of death until they entered. He told me that John was not a suspect. The video ruled him out immediately. They just want to speak to him as soon as possible. I gave them John's cell phone number. I hope that he won't mind."

Sarah asked, "No I'm sure he won't. Did investigator Scarponi state the cause of death?"

Jeanne replied, "I asked him that, but he could not officially say until after the autopsy. He did indicate that on the surface it looked like suicide because there were no signs of violence or a struggle of any kind, nor were there any signs of forced entry. He said the door was locked from the inside and the only other means of entry was a bathroom window which was also latched from the inside. There was also a paper coffee cup lying next to Jim's body which they felt had contained some kind of poison they mutually ingested. He said when putting all the facts together, his initial report will indicate Death by Suicide."

Jeanne then went on to say, "Scarponi curiously asked me how would they know about our raid beforehand, or that they were being watched? He felt it was possible they caught wind of what was going to happen and decided that they could not face long term incarceration or be forced to testify against the Senator. He made it clear that that was speculation on his part, but something he would not readily dismiss. Right now his report would also indicate cause of death as, 'Undetermined, pending autopsy.' He did state the Coroner indicated that whatever was ingested mimicked heart failure in all three bodies, but ruled out any possibility of simultaneous natural causes because the odds of such an event would be impossible to calculate."

While Jeanne and Sarah were talking, Sarah put her hand over the phone and whispered to John, "The State's Special Crimes Unit, wants to talk to you. They viewed the surveillance tape at the scene and saw you trying to get in."

John replied, "That's fine with me. I don't think I can add to what they already know."

Sarah then said to Jeanne, "I'm sorry to hear about their deaths. I guess they won't be witnesses against the Senator or Betty," and then asked, "Do you think I can speak to Special Investigator Scarponi at this hour?"

Jeanne said, "I'm sure he's not sleeping yet. I just got off the phone with him. I'll text his number to you. We'll get together tomorrow. Call me."

Sarah replied, "I will, but one more thing. Did they raid the addresses of the people who were delivered the ballots?"

Jeanne responded, "I did not ask him that. I don't know why. I was so in shock about the deaths that I forgot to ask. When you speak to him, find out."

Sarah ended the call with Jeanne and immediately retrieved Scarponi's phone number and called him.

As soon as he answered, Sarah introduced herself to him and said that she got his number from candidate Collette and wanted to know how quickly she could speak to him. She told him who she was and that she was with John Meade, the man he saw waiting outside the warehouse, and was willing to meet with him tonight, if that would help."

Scarponi said, "Yes, I do want to talk to him. Candidate Collette and her attorney Michael Johnson told me everything about what has transpired, as well as Attorney General Barbara Whitman. I was told that Governor Santos and State Attorney Whitman would make a joint statement. They would be making a public announcement about the sting operation sometime around 11am. I was told that I could provide you with any information you needed that would not impede our investigation. I've been made aware of your investigative efforts that set our operation in motion. I'm available in the morning. We can meet you at your hotel at 8 am. Does that work?"

Actually, I need to have my story to my editor by 5 am to make the morning press. I know it's asking a lot, but can we meet now? John will be with me. We can come to you, or you can come to us," Sarah said.

Scarponi replied, "Wait there. We'll be over to you. We're just getting ready to leave the scene. We can be there within thirty minutes."

Sarah said, "Thank you. I really appreciate it. I'll see if we can get a pot of coffee sent up. It's late so I don't know if the hotel still has room service at this hour."

Scarponi replied, "That's appreciated. If not, thanks anyway."

Sarah turned to John and told him what Investigator Scarponi told her and that they would be at the hotel within a half hour. John said, "We better freshen up quickly. I'll call the lobby and see what we can get at this hour. I'll straighten out the bed."

Just as coffee and pastries were being delivered to the room, Investigator Scarponi and Investigator Peter Richardson showed up. Sarah invited them into the room. They all introduced themselves to each other. Sarah said to Marc Scarponi," I can't thank you enough for coming at this hour. I have a five am deadline to get my story out in the mornings edition. I just need you to fill me in on what you're able to disclose. Do you mind if I record our conversation? I will stop recording anytime you think it necessary. I certainly don't want to compromise your investigation."

Marc replied, "I have no objection and we'll proceed as suggested. I would like to talk to John first if you don't mind?"

John replied for Sarah, and said, "Ask your questions. I'm not sure how much I can help you. Candidate Collette called us and told Sarah what happened and also that you wanted to talk to me because you saw me on the warehouse surveillance video. She also told us that you found Annette, Lizzie, and Jim deceased inside. T was floored when I heard that. I still can't believe it."

"I don't know anything about what happened. All I can say is that I went there to help Annette. She told me a few days back that she was going to be moving things from the warehouse, and I told her I would be happy to help. We worked together at Senator Roberts re-election Campaign Headquarters. I went there to do as I promised, but the place was locked. I saw their cars parked outside so I assumed that they should be inside. I rang the bell, but no one answered. I waited a minute or so then banged on the door and even yelled, but still didn't get a response. I tried calling Annette's cell phone and sent her a text that I was waiting outside, but still no answer. I finally gave up waiting, and called Sarah to tell her I was coming back to meet her at Candidate Collette's office. I left after that."

Marc replied, "We assumed all of that from the videos and what we extracted from her phone. We did find that you had several calls to Annette over a period of time."

John said, "Yes. That's correct. I worked with her for six months. I was a new volunteer at the Senator's office, and she helped me a lot. She was a super nice person and always willing to give me pointers and even helped me solicit campaign funds by giving me some referrals in the beginning."

Marc then asked, "Did you have an intimate relationship with her?"

John answered, "Intimate? No. I went to her apartment on a few occasions, but we never had any intimacy. I went there once when we went to lunch together and she asked if I minded taking a ride with her to her apartment because she had to take care of something. I was there for about ten minutes. She went into her bedroom while I sat and waited for her in her living room. I did not ask her what she needed to take care of. It was none of my business. On another occasion after having lunch she again drove me to her apartment. When we got there, she came onto me, but I wasn't interested. I told her that I didn't mix business with pleasure in so many words, but I was honored that she found me attractive. I don't think she liked my refusal, but we remained friends. She really was a nice person and quite funny at times. Other than that, nothing."

Marc continued his questioning. "Did you notice anyone or anything that seemed unusual while you were at the warehouse?"

John replied, "No. I didn't see anyone, or nothing struck me as unusual outside the warehouse. The only thing that was unusual was that Annette did not answer the attempts I made to get into the warehouse. I thought they left to go somewhere else and would be back. That's why I waited for a while. But when she wasn't taking a minute to text me back, I thought screw it. I came to help her, and she ignores me. I left. It still made no sense because I thought we had a good friendship. I never in a million years would have thought that something had happened to all three people in the warehouse."

"How did you and Sarah meet?" Investigator Richardson asked.

"Why do you ask? How we met has no relevancy to your investigation. I'll tell you that answering your question will put me in a compromising situation and in violation of certain non-disclosure agreements. All I can say is that I've assisted Sarah in her investigation," John replied.

Peter than asked, "Before going to the warehouse, where were you?"

John replied, "I was here with Sarah. I left her to go directly to the warehouse and you know when I was there and when I left, I went directly back to Candidate Collette's office. If you know my arrival time, you can go back about thirty-five minutes to know the approximate time I left Sarah. You have all of the times and know that I have a solid alibi, although I shouldn't even be considered a suspect, if I am at all. Your questioning seems to allude to that. I'll be happy to tell you how I met Sarah, but it'll be with Attorney General Whitman. My involvement in the entire sting operation and my answers will need to be protected under an immunity agreement."

Marc then immediately asked, "Why would you need an "Immunity Agreement?"

John answered, "Because there's another investigation separate and apart from the one, you're now starting. I suggest you contact Attorney General Whitman and ask her to fill you in on those precedents. Please don't ask me anything that does not pertain to your investigation into the deaths of those three souls."

Marc Scarponi was a very astute investigator and began to realize why John would not answer the questions and insisted on only doing so with some assurances from Attorney General Whitman and with an Immunity Agreement. He knew that there was a confidential source that opened the investigation and caused the issuance of the Search Warrants. He quickly put two and two together and realized that John must be that source. He was aware that John worked at the Senator's Campaign Office and realized that he must have made the video's and recordings of the conversations he heard. He knew that those recordings may have been acquired illegally and why John refused to talk about those details. It was with that epiphany that had him back off their inquiry into anything other than the deaths of the three people.

Marc said, "Sorry John. You and Sarah are by no means suspects in our current investigation. I believe I understand why you want immunity and will respect your wishes. I'll talk to AG Whitman and arrange for that agreement so that we can talk further."

John replied and said, "I by no means meant to seem confrontational. But the agreement is my only protection."

Marc then began to tell Sarah whatever she needed to know to finish her groundbreaking article for the morning's edition. After about an hour the Investigators left. Sarah then sat at her computer and added all the remaining details and e-mailed it to her Morning Editor for final approval. Sarah waited for another hour and got a go ahead on her article and congratulations on her next Pulitzer Price expose. Headlines would read, "NSP Caught Trying to Steal Senate Election."

After getting her e-mail response, she got a phone call from the paper's owner Jonathon Turnbull, who was informed of what would be hitting the streets and the airwaves that morning. All he said to Sarah was congratulations. "You're a super star. I hope that this not only gets you nominated for a Pulitzer Prize, but a winner of it. Excellent job as usual. See you when you get back to New York."

After she hung up with Jonathon, they both went to bed. The next morning they were still sleeping when they got a call from Candidate Collette. She told Sarah her phones were ringing like crazy since the story hit. There were reporters already outside her headquarters clamoring to speak to her. She said that Senator Roberts and Betty were whisked away by the States Special Crimes Unit for interrogation and that President Tripp's Press Secretary called her and said that President Tripp wanted to talk to her after he finished with his Security Briefing. She said that they were going to wait until noon before they took a poll to get a reading on how she stood against Roberts since the story hit. She also said that multiple raids were made around the state to secure the 250,000 ballots.

They would be counted to determine if they had gotten them all and she would let us know about that by tomorrow sometime.

Sarah wished her good luck and to let us know what the polls showed, then hung up with Jeanne. They decided to go back to bed for a while longer and get a few more hours sleep. There was nothing more they could do. At least not at that moment.

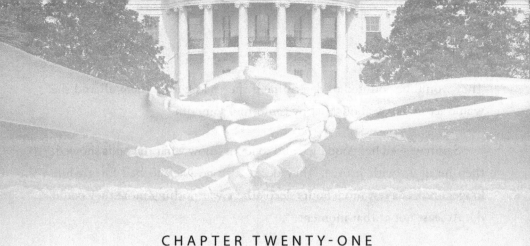

CHAPTER TWENTY-ONE

THE SENATOR BITES THE DUST

Sarah spent that morning writing the continuation of her expose and would for as long as she kept compiling information on which she had the inside track. Sarah would go back to Candidate Collette's office and continue getting up to date inside information that was being given to Jeanne from AG Whitman's office and the Governor. Her continuing investigative reporting would be front page each time the paper was published.

John was ecstatic about how things were working out. He felt that he was going to continue to get away with murder. But would he get away with taking out the Senator and Betty? Was he pushing it too far? John remained resolute in his determination, no matter the outcome. He had already changed the political landscape in Washington D.C. with the death of Congresswoman Waterman and Senator Pelovski's permanent incapacitation. Both of their replacements in the House and Senate were American Patriots effectively adding two additional votes to their margin in both Congress and the Senate. John knew that if he took out Senator Roberts, President Tripp would have the sixty votes he needed without having to use an unfavorable 'Nuclear Option' when passing bills in the

Senate. John would affectively give President Tripp carte blanche in the Senate with the demise of Roberts.

The day moved at a steady pace. Both he and Sarah went to Jeanne's office monitoring the ongoing events. Sarah and Jeanne hit it off extremely well and seemed to form a friendship. Jeanne and John were in the same mode. While John was at Jeanne's office, he got a call from Katherine. She asked him if he could meet her at her attorney's office to sign the uncontested divorce decree? John said that he would go, but would like his attorney to look it over. John called Michael Johnson, Jeanne's attorney, and asked him if he would look it over and tell him if it was okay. Michael Johnson told him he would be happy to provide that service through his law firm, because he did not practice divorce law, but would ask Lucas Levy an associate to do it.

John explained that it was a simple "No Contest" divorce because Katherine agreed to his terms. Michael set up an appointment for him at five o'clock that day.

John went to Sarah and told her where he was going and why. When he did, he asked her without hesitation if she would marry him. She joyfully accepted.

When John went to Katherine's attorney's office, he saw her sitting there and waiting for him. He smiled and said hello to her, then walked over to her and to her surprise he kissed her on the cheek. He said to both Katherine and her attorney, "I have an appointment with my attorney at five pm to look over the agreement. If he raises no objections, I will sign it at that time. I'm sure they will be able to notarize my signature there. Katherine, if you want to sign it, I will have him record it after I've done so. Katherine, I promise I will not go against my word. I assume this decree states what we agreed to?"

Katherine replied, "Yes, it's as we agreed." She then said to her attorney, "I want to sign it now so that you can notarize my signature. I want this over with today."

After she signed the document and handed it to John, she said, "Please see that I get my copy."

John replied, "You'll have it this evening if no changes need to be made. I can drop it off at your house."

Katherine then said to John, "I hope you're happy with Annette."

John said, "Annette passed away. They found her body yesterday. I don't know the cause of death."

Katherine said, "I'm sorry to hear that."

"Don't be. I told you that I didn't have romantic feelings for her. I'm sorry she died. But I'm not grieving over it," John replied.

"I'll see you this evening with the divorce decree. I'm sure that it'll be all right. I don't want to leave you hating me. I'll always remember our years together. I have no regrets, but I need to move on with my life."

John turned and walked away from Katherine and headed off to Michael Johnson's office to meet with the divorce attorney to get the agreement signed. As he was driving, he called Sarah. "Hi, Mrs. future Meade. Guess what I've got?"

Sarah replied, "I like your name, but I want to keep mine for professional reasons. Do you mind?"

John replied, "What's in a name. All I care about is making you, my wife."

"Will you marry me? I'm so in love with you. I'm crazy already," John said.

"John, are you sure about what you're asking me? It's a commitment for life. If I say yes, I want it to be without regrets. I do love you and yes,

I'll marry you. Please don't ever hurt me like you've done to Katherine," Sarah replied.

"Ooh sweetheart, I will love you with every part of me and for the rest of my life. I have the divorce agreement with me already signed by Katherine, and I'm heading over to Michael Johnson's office to have the attorney give it a quick look and let me know if there are any snags. I don't expect any. I'll sign it and have it recorded post haste. Once that's done, we'll buy rings and get married wherever you want. Let's just elope and fly to Europe after we finish with what's going on," John said.

"That sounds wonderful. I want to see Paris and Rome and drive that Italian race car through Europe," Sarah replied.

"I'd love that too. It's going to be the best time of our lives. I've always wanted to get a gondola and meander through the waterways of Venice. I'll call you when I leave the attorney's office," John replied.

Sarah said, "I'll still be at Jeanne's office. She gave me some workspace so I can continue with my story. I'd love to be able to interview Senator Roberts to get his side of the story. Do you think he would speak with me?"

John replied, "I'm not sure, but there's only one way to find out. He was expected to have a get together with all of his campaign staff the evening before election day, which is tonight. He has no idea about my part in all of this, so I assume he'll expect me to attend. I can call him and find out if things will be as normal after all that's happened. When I do, I'll ask him if he would want to give you his side of the story. You never prejudged him in your expose, which was extremely kind, although you left enough doubt about his innocence to affect a voter's confidence. See you later as a free man."

John made a call into Senator Roberts office to find out whether or not he was still going to have a staff get together. He had to call in twice to get to speak to him. When he was put through to the Senator, he said, "Senator, I'm so sorry about what I saw on the news this morning. I was in shock. I can't believe what happened to Annette, Jim, and Lizzie. I hope that the news does not affect your favorability with the voters. I know that I'm just one person, but you still have my vote. I don't believe you had anything to do with the phony ballots. I never heard Annette, Jim or Lizzie ever mention your involvement while I was helping them. I actually saw no reason for it. You would have won without them anyway. Why would you risk everything?"

Aaron replied, "Thanks for that John. I had nothing to do with it. Annette took it upon herself to steal an election for me. I'm still going to fight this. I'm going to hold a press conference in about an hour. I'll be telling them the truth. Complete deniability."

John said, "Speaking of the press, are you willing to speak to Sarah Foster? I know that she authored the breaking story. It's apparent that she was doing investigative reporting while she was here, and it seems the real reason she was in Florida. She did visit her old friend, my wife Katherine. Senator, I had absolutely no idea about any of this. If I did, I would have brushed her off. She contacted me a little while ago and wanted me to find out if you would give her another interview. She would give your rebuttal front page in this evening's addition. That would give voters your side of the story before casting ballots. I read her story, and I did not see where she made direct accusations at you. When I spoke to her, I told her a few things in no uncertain terms, but if what she is offering will in any way help you, I told her I would ask. If you are willing it will have to be now, because she'll need to get it to press on time for tonight's special edition."

The Senator paused for a moment, and said, "Okay John. Tell her I'll do it. It's possible I can trip her up and get her to tell me who set me up. I'll be talking to the staff tonight. I expect that you'll be there."

John responded, "Yes Senator, I will consider it an honor to shake your hand in front of the cameras. I'm not afraid to show my solidarity with you. I will contact Sarah as soon as we hang up and tell her to head over to your office."

John called Sarah as he was pulling up to the attorney's office. "Sarah, get over to the Senator's office. I'll head over there as soon as I have the divorce agreement looked at. It's only three or four pages long so it should be quick. Be careful, he told me he was going to try and get you to say how you produced your information. He may well suspect me although he acted very friendly toward me. He knew I was helping at the warehouse and coincidently know you. If I were him, I'd suspect me, although I gave him six months of no reason to think so."

Sarah replied, "I'll go there now. Don't worry. He won't trip me up. Get the divorce decree and get us married. I'll see you at the campaign office."

John said, "I will my love. There's nothing I want more."

John arrived at the law office and had Lucas Levy review the divorce agreement.

After taking twenty minutes to read and review it, Lucas told John that it was straight forward. He discussed the terms of settlement with John which he found to be as agreed. After John signed the agreement, Lucas Levy called Katherine's attorney to ask if he had any objections for his office to record it. He confirmed that it was signed as presented and if he had no preference his office would record the agreement and deliver Katherine's recorded copy back to his office. After the attorney's spoke, Lucas said, "I'll handle the recording. I'll have it taken over to the courthouse tomorrow. You'll be legally divorced after that. You were very generous to your wife. She certainly won't need to work for the rest of her life, if she doesn't squander it."

John replied, "She deserves it. She was a good wife in many respects, but I fell out of love with her. She became a different woman and not the one I fell in love with. Thank you for handling this for me at such a short notice. Please record the agreement post haste. I want my relationship with Katherine to be a thing of the past."

Lucas said, "It will be done tomorrow. Call me in the afternoon. You can pick it up."

John turned and headed out to Senator Roberts campaign office to meet up with Sarah, and to assassinate the Senator later in the evening when he would be holding his private staff meeting along with some other politicians. John wondered if any of them would be showing solidarity with the Senator regardless of the news story or separate themselves from him until the smoke cleared. He knew loyalties were political conveniences.

He thought about Betty, but really didn't care whether or not he knocked her off. Both of them dying would raise too many eyebrows unless he could transfer the blame to her. John just had to be sure that no fingers would be pointed at him. As he drove to the campaign office, he considered every idea. The one that stuck with him was implicating Betty in the deaths of everyone. He thought about planting the small toxin laced pillbox on her. He didn't care if she was blamed for their deaths or was accused of providing the means. Murder, suicide, suicide murder. Who gives a shit he thought so long as a finger was pointed at her. He didn't care what motive might be conjured up. It would all be conjecture. They wouldn't be able to ask her if she was dead.

He had to separate Betty from everyone long enough to knock her off, clean off the toxin from his fingers so as not to risk getting any on himself while he set up his crime scene. He would make sure to wipe his fingerprints off of the pillbox and put Betty's onto it. Once he did that, he would then put the liquid skin and toxin onto her fingertips and smartly leave the open pillbox lying next to her body near her outstretched hand just like he did with Jim at the warehouse.

He needed to figure a way to get her into an empty office away from everyone without being noticed. John figured he would need ten minutes to pull it off. He was confident that he would make it work and was determined to do it. He figured that he could entice Betty away from the crowd by telling her that he had some extremely important inside information that involved her and the Senator and that he was only willing to tell her because he trusted her. She just had to meet him in a place that was private and where no one, especially Sarah, would see him talking to her. John would suggest one of the empty offices on the upper floor where he could pull off his scheme, feeling certain that no one would be up there. He expected that everyone would be down with the Senator wanting to know what he had to say about the breaking news story.

Once he knocked Betty off, he would slip back in with the crowd and wait for his moment with the Senator. As soon as John arrived at the campaign office, he saw Sarah was already in with the Senator. He decided to execute his plan immediately. He went to Betty's office and saw her on the phone. She saw him and waved at him to come over to her. When he stepped into her office, he said, "Betty I need to talk to you privately, but not here. It's extremely important. It needs to be private and away from prying eyes. I'll meet you on the third floor. It should be empty with everyone down here. Please go now, we need to talk."

She asked, "What's it about?"

John said with an urgency in his voice, "Betty, not here."

Betty replied, "Okay, I'll meet you there."

John said, "You go first. Take the elevator. I'll take the stairs."

John then stealthily headed for the staircase located just outside the entrance to the office. He did a quick look around to be certain no one would see him enter the stairway. Once inside, he immediately applied the liquid skin to two fingertips. He blew on them trying to speed up the drying time. When he reached the next floor, he started walking down the hallway at a quick pace to meet Betty. He stopped for a brief moment to coat two of his fingertips with the toxin, which he needed to rub onto Betty the second he reached her. Time was of the essence. Every second counted.

He saw Betty step out of the office located just across from the elevator. He rushed to her by speeding up his steps. As soon as he reached her, he took her hand with his heavily toxin coated fingers and pulled her into the office with him. He shut the door and said, "Betty sit down. You'll need to. What I have to tell you is not going to be good. It will affect both you and the Senator. I know who informed the Feds about the election steal. You won't like it or even believe it. It was Annette. I believe that she committed suicide and killed Jim and Lizzie." What John was telling Betty was immediately adlibbed. He just needed to get her into a conversation long enough for the toxin to kick in.

Betty said, "John, I don't believe you. Annette wouldn't do that. She was loyal and dedicated to the Senator. She had no reason to do it. If anyone did it, it was you. It seems too coincidental that you not only know the same investigative reporter that broke the story, but also about our ballot operation. It's simple math."

John laughed to himself and said, "Betty, yes it does seem like it when put it that way, but what you see is not always what you get. It's coincidental and just that. I didn't know her personally. My wife Katherine knew her from college. It's now apparent Sarah's real reason to come down here was to investigate our attempt at election fraud. Remember, I was there committing a federal crime along with everyone. How she found out, I really don't know. I would be insane to put myself in harm's way. I worked hard for Senator Roberts. Didn't I?"

Betty replied, "Yes you did work hard for the Senator, and yes, you would be crazy to tell anyone about what was going on, but I'm sorry John,

I still think you are the rat. No one else I can think of fits the bill. To me it was a process of elimination."

John, knowing he wasted the five minutes he needed and that she was going to die any moment, said, "Okay you got me you socialist bitch. You're right about me. But what you don't know is I murdered Waterman, vegetated Pelovski, knocked off Annette, Jim, Lizzie and now you."

Betty looked at John, with a horrified look on her face, and said, "You Bastard."

John laughed as he watched Betty starting to show signs that the chest pain was kicking in and said, "That I am and loving it. Make it quick. I don't have all day." With those last words,

Betty grabbed at her chest in the usual heart attack ritual while slumping down. John moved quickly behind her placing his arms under her armpits as she died. It made it easier for him to place her body onto a nearby office chair. Once he set her body the way he wanted it, he made sure her right arm hung down on one side of her body laying the poison pill box on the floor just under her dangling fingertips. He decided to open her mouth and wipe the toxin inside it with his toxin coated fingertips. He needed to make it seem she had ingested the poison. He had removed his fingerprints and applied hers to the small pillbox. After being satisfied with how everything looked, he left quickly, making his way down the staircase, wiping off the door handles on both floors with his uncoated hand.

Before exiting the staircase, he opened the door just enough to scan around. When he saw no one anywhere nearby, he made his way back into the campaign office. He timed himself and saw that it took him only ten minutes to pull off his scheme. Now he was ready for the Senator. He eased among the staff making sure to not touch anyone or anything with his still heavily toxin coated fingertips. He only needed to touch the Senator and to do it quickly. He wanted both Betty and the Senator's times of death to be within fifteen to twenty minutes of each other. He figured that guessing the time of death was not that accurate and in all the confusion and excitement no one would be checking their watches.

Just as he reached the Senator's office, he saw Sarah stand up and shake the Senator's hand and as he stepped into the Senator's office, heard her thank him for the interview and promised him she would fairly relate his side of what happened and what he knew.

John then moved quickly toward the Senator and asked, "Is your interview over Senator?"

Senator Roberts replied, "I believe so." John then reached over toward the Senator with his toxin coated fingers while saying, "Senator, let me thank you for everything and for meeting with Sarah." The Senator reached out and shook John's hand saying, "It was my pleasure. I just hope Sarah writes my rebuttal as well as she wrote her expose' about my campaign."

John, while still firmly pressing his grip said, "I'm sure she will. I'll be walking Sarah down to her car and then I'll be back to listen to what you will tell everyone. I believe she'll need to contact her paper to get your story told by this evening's edition."

. John then turned and walked Sarah out of the Senator's office. He said, "Honey wait a minute, I need to use the men's room. I'll only be a minute."

John moved with some haste and as soon as he went in, he went straight to a sink and applied plenty of soap and water and used paper towels to wipe his hand clean of the toxin. He thought, "Wow, Deja Vue. I've played this same scene out in this bathroom twice."

He left the bathroom quickly and went back to Sarah who was waiting for him at the exit door. He took her by the hand and said, "Well honey, everything I've wanted to do is now done. The divorce papers are being recorded tomorrow. We can get married whenever you want after that. I love you more than anything. I know it seems impossible to meet someone and be in love so deeply so quickly. But it has happened to me with you."

Sarah replied, "I love you too. It must be fate that we met the way we did. I knew I was attracted to you from the moment I saw you at the airport and impulsively touched your hand when we were having coffee. I've never flirted like that before. I just couldn't resist."

John responded, "I'm glad you did and when you did my heart leaped. I wanted to kiss you the moment I saw you walking up to me at the airport. We were meant for each other. If our first weeks together have been a heck of an adventure, imagine the rest of our lives together."

Sarah replied, "Yes they have."

John said, "Honey, I don't want to abruptly cut off our love talk, but I need to go back inside and listen to what Roberts has to say. I'll leave as soon as he finishes with his bullshit speech. I'll see you back at the hotel. I assume that you'll be authoring your story and sending it to your editor."

Sarah said, "Yes, I intend to do it as soon as I get back to the room. I might have to ask him to hold the presses for a while. I want my story to hit tonight." Sarah kissed John and said, "Don't be too late."

With those final words from Sarah, John turned and walked back inside the campaign office. He knew the Senator would be falling over at any moment, and John didn't want to miss the show. He was about to experience his most joyous moment. John was actually surprised that the Senator was still alive. He could see the Senator standing just outside his office talking to what he assumed was a Federal Agent. He had that look. The Senator looked over at John, then beckoned him over. John took a deep breath and made sure he maintained his composure, because he did not know what to expect.

As John reached the Senator, he was immediately asked if he had seen Betty. John calmly replied, "I saw her in her office for just a minute and said hello, just before going to the men's room then into your office. I didn't pay attention to her whereabouts after that. Why do you ask?"

Roberts replied, "I cannot locate her. I need to confer with her right now."

John said, "I assume you called and texted her? Didn't she respond?"

Roberts replied, "I did call her, but she left her phone in her office. I was told her car is in the parking lot so she didn't leave, and she wouldn't have without letting me know."

"She may have left with one of the other staff to get a bite to eat and forgot her phone. We all do that once in a while," John said.

Roberts said, "That's a possibility. But it's not her modus operandi. She always informs me of her whereabouts."

John replied, "Senator, I'm sure she'll show up any minute now. This is your big night. I don't think she'd just disappear. She must have gone to the ladies room."

Roberts replied, "That was the first place I had checked. Ooh, my God, my chest! I have a pain in my chest! Somethings wrong! I think I'm having a heart attack!"

John thought, "About fucking time. That took longer than I expected." John reacting quickly grabbed the Senator along with the agent as they tried holding him up, but failed. As he was collapsing, they decided to lay him gently on the floor. John dialed 911 immediately, and when emergency answered, John said, "Please send an ambulance to Senator Roberts campaign office, it looks like he has had a heart attack." While John was getting medical help, the agent was applying artificial resuscitation. John said, "Let me pump his chest while you give him mouth to mouth."

John was just going through the motions. He knew the Senator was a goner and certainly wanted him to die.

As he was pumping the Senator's chest, he said to the Agent, "Check his pulse."

The agent pressed two fingers to the Carotid Artery in the Senator's neck but couldn't feel one.

John playing the scene to the hilt, said to the agent, "Let's keep going. Not feeling a pulse doesn't mean he doesn't have one. We can't let this man die."

John then clenched his hands and pounded the Senator's chest like you see in the movies. As he pumped away, he said aloud, "God damn it Senator, don't die. Fight for your life."

The Agent grabbed John's arm and said, "That's enough John, he's gone. It's no use."

John said, "I can't believe it. He seemed so healthy. The horrible news about the election must have put too much stress on him. What else could it be. God! What a tragedy. His whole campaign has suffered one tragedy after another. I think he would have won no matter what."

After John put on his act, he got up and stood there looking down at the Senator and faked sorrow. He slowly walked away from the Senator's body with his head down, thinking, "I got you, you mother fucker."

The EMT's showed up carrying their emergency equipment and began working on the Senator, hitting him immediately with Defibrillator Paddles, after detecting an irregular heart rhythm. They gave him an injection of Epinephrine while placing an oxygen mask over his face. One of the medics checked the Senator's pulse again and when he did, he said to the Agent, "I can't feel one. I think we lost him." The four men, John, the FBI agent and the two EMT's picked up the Senator's body, put him on a gurney and rushed him to the ambulance. The Agent got on the phone and began telling someone what had just happened. After he got off the phone, John walked over to him and asked, "What's your name?"

The Agent replied, "I'm FBI Agent, Raymond Gonzalez. Thanks for your help with the Senator. We gave it one hell of a try."

John replied, "I thought we had him there for a minute. Do you think that they'll bring him around?"

Agent Gonzalez said, "I hope so, but I have a feeling he isn't going to make it. It didn't look good."

John responded, "All we can do is hope. If you need me to make a statement with you about what happened. Please call me. I'll give you, my number."

Agent Gonzalez said, "John, here's my card. I must leave and follow the ambulance to the hospital. If you call me later tonight, I'll be able to tell you if the Senator was revived. I'm not hopeful, but miracles do happen."

John replied, "We can only hope so," while thinking, "I hope the fuck not."

FBI Agent Gonzalez rushed out of the building while John just stood there gloating about the success of his assassination. He started to mentally hum his favorite tune, "Zip-a-dee doo dah, zip-a-dee yay, my oh my what a wonderful day, Senator Roberts, shit did come your way, Zip-a-dee doo dah zip-a-dee yay."

John walked through the horror-struck campaign office staff and guests to outside the campaign office to head over to Sarah. He called her and told her what had just happened. She was in shock. She couldn't believe what John was telling her. She asked if she thought he would survive. John, still needing to cover up his insanity, said, "I hope so, but it doesn't look good. I have FBI Agent Gonzalez' business card. He said it was all right to call him later so I could get an update on the Senator. I'm heading to the hotel now. I'll see you soon."

John thought, "I can't wait until someone finds Betty. I'm sure that they will speculate as to her exact role in everything that happened. There won't be anyone left at the campaign office after they find that bitch's body. People will keep their distance from that place. They'll think it's cursed. Thanks to me."

John reached the hotel and went straight up to Sarah. When he opened the room door, he saw Sarah on the phone talking to her Editor. She was relating the most current events and getting her morning column dictated. He could hear her speaking of the Senator's death and what was expected on election day. John walked over and gave her a kiss on her cheek as she was speaking. He heard her asking her editor, "Will Candidate Collette run unopposed? What about all the mail in ballots that have taken place already? I haven't run into this before. So you think that Governor Santos will make an appointment until the next General Election. If you're right, then Collette will surely be going to the Senate. Santos is a solid Patriot and party loyalist. There shouldn't be much noise from the left, especially after they were caught trying to steal the election. That's great. You're going to print a Special Edition. When was the last time that happened? Okay, I'll speak to you again tomorrow."

When Sarah ended the call she turned to John, got up and kissed him and then said, "Honey, I'm so sorry that you had to deal with the Senator's death. I'm sure that that wasn't pleasant for you. Do you want a drink?" she asked.

John replied, "Actually, I do. Let's go down to the Bar and get one. I need to unwind. I can tell you all about it over a drink." He then pulled Sarah to him and kissed her again. When their lips parted, John asked Sarah, "Are you ready to become my partner for life? My divorce is done. All I need to do is get a copy of the recorded agreement. I want to make us legal."

Sarah said, "Yes, let's do it."

John asked, "Is next week too soon?"

Sarah replied, "Next week is good. We can get married in New York City."

John took Sarah up in his arms and twirled about in total joy. Sarah laughed. John said, "You've made me the happiest man on the face of the Earth. Today is the most fulfilling day of my life."

Little did Sarah know that John was including his assassination of the Senator and Betty, in his euphoric comments. His convoluted mind was, to say the least, one of a kind.

Sarah got an e-mail notification on her laptop. She opened it up and found that her Special Edition article was sent by her Editor for final approval. As she was reading it, John sat back in an easy chair and just admired her. He started laughing to himself as he thought about all of the people he murdered. He realized that they were all ad libs. He recklessly played them all by ear. He never knew whether or not he would be able to pull them off, he just winged his way through one assassination after another. John sat smiling like the Cheshire Cat, chuckling to himself, thinking they should dub him, "The Ad Lib Murderer."

It amazed him, that as awkward as he was, he murdered everyone successfully and without any suspicion that he knew of. After gloating to himself, he thought, whose next on the hit list. With that last thought, his mind shifted to his frogs. He needed to slip away from Sarah under some pretext, and check on them. After planting his only toxin filled pillbox at his murder scene with Betty, he needed to start harvesting some more. He felt that his work was still not finished. That there were many more scumbags like Senator Roberts walking the halls of the Capitol.

Later that night, Sarah called Agent Gonzalez and confirmed that Senator Roberts was pronounced dead, with the hospital declaring the cause of death as heart failure. He said to her, "It's like John said, the stress of what happened to him being implicated in the attempted election steal and his staff all seeming to have committed suicide was too much on him. His long political career was over."

Sarah replied, "I imagine it destroyed his life. But his dishonesty brought it upon himself. Regardless, I'm sorry it happened? Thank you for the update."

After the Senate race was over, Jeanne Collette won. Her margin of victory was the largest ever recorded, because those who would have voted for Senator Roberts saw no need to go to the ballot box. The news of his death, as it was being announced on all of the TV stations, kept everyone from voting. There were some die hard left wingers who voted for him symbolically.

Governor Santos immediately appointed Jeanne Collette to the Senate until the next General Election to quell those on the left who wanted to have a new election with another NSP candidate, even though the law was clear. There was no doubt, that this one insane man had affected the balance of power in both the Senate and Congress.

John met with the Attorney General's Office, using Michael Johnson as his legal counsel.

John received immunity from his crime of falsifying the computer schools records. Although Sarah never disclosed her confidential source, Michael Johnson felt that John should receive protection for his illegal recordings while he had the opportunity and a willing Attorney General. He wanted John covered for unseen events as an abundance of caution, regardless of the fact that those affected by his illegal actions were dead or immobilized for life. Only Brad remained alive but was still touched by John's hand.

The FBI concluded that Betty had orchestrated everything while trying to portray the Senator as an unknowing bystander in Betty's clandestine operation to steal an election that she thought would be lost. The left leaning Mainstream Media, put out articles that attempted to support the innocence of the Senator and said that Betty's actions were not needed. They claimed using registered voter information and historical facts that Senator Roberts would have won his election by at least a five-point margin. The conservative TV stations debunked their claims as nonsense. John could not be happier because nothing pointed to him.

It was a campaign staff member that discovered Betty's body slumped in the office chair when they returned to the third floor of the campaign office. The FBI also concluded it was Betty's actions that led to the suicides of Annette, Lizzie, and Jim, and declared her death a suicide as well. They put out a statement that they found an empty pillbox next to her body that they believed contained some form of undetermined lethal substance which she ingested to commit suicide. They stated they would know more about the substance after they received a Coroner's report. Several weeks had passed when John learned from Sarah, who got the updated information from FBI Agent Gonzalez that the lethal substance ingested by Betty, Annette, Lizzie, and Jim was the same deadly alkaloid poison, but their data bases on toxins had no exact match. They could not as of yet. identify its origin.

Senator Roberts' death, and the death of Congresswoman Waterman remained as coincidental natural causes except to FBI agent Jamison. He didn't buy the coincidence, although he couldn't prove otherwise. He had a gut feeling that John was somehow involved even though his alibi's seemed airtight, and he had no apparent motive.

John happily moved to New York City with his loving fiancé Sarah. He remained his insane toxic self and had every intention of planning his next moves on members of the left leaning Mainstream Media and any ranking National Socialist Party member he could shake hands with.

The End

Printed in the United States
by Baker & Taylor Publisher Services